Omniscient Obsession

A novel
by

Murphy Grey

www.mgbp.us
or
www.omniscientobsession.com

OMNISCIENT OBSESSION

a novel
by Murphy Grey

This book is a work of fiction that occurs in a parallel universe. Any similarity to your world is both coincidental and intentional. Elements of truth weave throughout the book.

Published by Gray Bull Publishing
PO Box 61
Hudson, IN 46747

ISBN 0-9754706-1-2

Manufactured in the United States of America

Chapter 1--ENIGMENT

Cycles go round and round.

I was in my third year of college when an impulsive streak changed my life.
Hope, dreams, and enthusiasm ignite my rocket launch from the space race sixties.
I became a fountain of ideals, a magnate of principle, and a purveyor of prosperity.

The candles on my twenty-fifth birthday cake were still smoking when my downhill run began. I passed the quarter century pinnacle and plunged through twists, turns, and the tunnel of my darkest days before emerging to an omniscient flash and a hitchhiking obsession that sank roots into my subconscious and permeated my being.

It was the darkest hour in the low point of my life. I could sink no further.
Luke and I were heading south from St. Ignace, Michigan when heaven's portal flashed.
It was Martin Luther King Jr's birthday; the secret of the universe imprinted in my brain.

I thought my ship came in, nirvana was at hand. That was eons from truth.
I had no idea of the enchanting goddess that stood between me and my dream.
My downhill run would continue.

I found a roller coaster to hell and a conspiracy that threatened to erase the fabric of existence. Hi, I'm Dan Murphy and I lived to tell. The answer to my twin enigma flashed twenty-three years ago, ten years after Neil Armstrong's step on the moon.

The first enigma sprouted with an astrological report seven years before the answer.
The forecast focused on the certainty I would gain great notoriety in the arts.
Everything else made sense.

I had no interest in arts. English was my worst subject.
Math, science, nuts, bolts; I was a craftsman not an artist.

Two years after the first, Grandpa Murphy introduced the second enigma.
An article in 'SCIENCE OF MIND' magazine about polygraph experiments
concluded 'a life force flows through everything'. Science didn't know.
I pondered the mystery til it submerged with the first.

Heaven exists in the mind; spirit exists in nirvana.

I guard the secret with my life as I cruise the interstate and listen to Elvin Bishop's CD, "Sure Feels Good". It's the dawn of a new millennium. We're approaching a Freightliner with a huge American flag waving from its trailer doors. Pride wells.

I toot my horn and thrust my thumb through the sunroof as
I pass the patriot on the slingshot expressway to fantasyland.
"Fooled Around and Fell in Love", strikes a major chord as
the Las Vegas skyline thrusts into view.
The gold crescent of Mandalay Bay beckons.
We check in.
An alluring rhythm issues a siren call
and draws me to the Rum Jungle where
scantily clad maidens on chrome railed skywalks,
jump, bounce, quiver, and shimmy to the beat.
My mind goes with the flow.

Chapter 2--ENVIRONMENT

Red men roam green land. They create a village where two rivers form a third. They live there for countless generations, hunting game, gathering sustenance, trading along the three prong liquid highway.

Then white men invade the pristine land and build a fort. Settlers follow. Trees are cleared, crops planted. The fort at the foot of the Elkhart Valley becomes a town. The City of East Bend sprouts at the confluence of the three rivers.

The Joseph River sinks roots into the flat land of western Ohio and cradles the birthplace of the man who uttered, 'a small step for man, a giant leap for mankind'. From that magnetic point, the Joseph River cuts a lazy swath across fertile farmland as it transports agricultural chemicals, debris, and topsoil to the Elkhart Valley.

The Mary River anchors a taproot in Michigan forests and grows, creeks gorging her sides as she flows south into the swale of the gentle divide. At the low point in the tabletop ridgeline, the clear and pure Mary dashes into the muddy Joseph and forms the Abram River. The Abram slowly winds its way west to Lake Michigan.

Some passengers drop and bury as the Abram mixes and mingles with the gravitational sump of Michigan. Most hang as the Great Lake divides and swirls molecules in opposite directions. Flow slows, the sump deepens. Joseph and Mary continue their split course to the sea.

East Bend is a city of churches where honest people live by the fruit of their labors and give their neighbor a helping hand when they need it. It's a city where friends are close yet independent. Where people live their lives and practice the Golden Rule.

Dan Murphy spends his growing years in the serenity of the gentle plateau, watching corn grow and seasons change. Nothing prepares him for the journey to the center of his soul and the edge of insanity.

Not his aunt Ev who knows all the psychic numbers

or the Reverend Thorn who keeps him on the straight and narrow.

No one could foresee the consequence of their actions.

Shock takes a new meaning as the fabric of existence

swirls to nothingness.

Chapter 3--ENCHANTMENT

Joseph and Mary molecules unite in the Pacific.

My eyes draw to the statuesque goddess with the bronze trench coat. The morning sun creates a golden halo around her cascading locks. My spellbinding magnetic spiel stops. Her spell takes command.

"Raphael. That girl is beautiful,"
I never make comments like that, and I don't ogle.

A pin drops as she enters the door. My eyes follow as she walks to the counter. Raphael listens intently. I turn back and continue my animated spiel.

Raphael Rafensbarger has been a tool and die maker at GM for twenty-five years. We met six years ago, during my second tour at GM, and became steadfast friends. He's a wheeler dealer who would give the shirt off his back if I ask. I don't.

My black hat is planted on my head. Brown straw pokes my ears.
"Magnetism is the key to the future. It's the basis of life and all that is," I say.
I glance back. The goddess is gone.

We finish our breakfast and drive up Springdale Road to see a school of dreams cohort I haven't seen in seven years. Ty Quiznick greets us when we walk in.

Joseph and Mary molecules sail east on the Westerlies.

"You can see and taste the difference," Ty says.
"Chemical analysis shows it. Impurities vanish with a ground rod."

"Why a ground rod," I ask.

"So electrons can flow. You have to put the magnet on the house side of the pump," he adds. "Nobody knows exactly how it works. We just know that it does."

I see the picture in motion, thanks to the revelation and college chemistry.
"I know how," I say. Ty casts a skeptical glance.

"'The inventor, Bob Farnsworth, doesn't even know how," Ty counters.
"What's important is that it works. Only God knows how."

Rain falls on the tributaries of the Joseph and Mary rivers.

Raphael and I head south on Springdale Road. We pass the Coney King where we ate breakfast. Now that Raphael has seen the magic magnet, I tell him how and why. If he knew about the vision he would know it blazed on Martin Luther King's birthday but Grandpa Evan is going to be the first to hear about it. I haven't seen him yet.

I needed confirmation that I had been blessed with the secret of the universe so I went to the library after we returned from the Upper Peninsula, three weeks ago. THE HEART OF THE ATOM told me all I needed to know. Science and Religion were definitely opposite faces of the same coin; simple yet complex, obvious yet hidden.

The Joseph River embraces the Mary.

Raphael pulls up to a car dealership on Springdale Road. We go in.

He goes out back to talk to the mechanics. I meander around the showroom.

I'm standing right front center, facing a line of office cubicles in the back, looking through the side double doors to a spectacle in progress. I'm pulled out the doors and towards a man of five-feet-eight with a snow-blower strapped to his back.
A pretty lady pulls fruitlessly on the starter rope.

I walk up and say, "Let me help you." The elegant female steps aside.

I look at the contraption, never looked at one close, and reach up.
My hand pulls to a hidden lever. I push it and pull the rope. The snow-blower roars.
I smile at the girl as I spin on my heels and head back inside. My green checked bell bottoms float in the arctic breeze.

Raphael, who I haven't seen in twenty minutes, is facing me from the spot I was standing before the spectacle pulled me out the showroom doors. I walk over to him and spin to face the doors I just came through. We stand in silence. The girl walks in.

She's halfway across the line of offices when my jaw drops. It hits me.
"Raphael, that's the same girl I saw this morning," I utter, jaw agape.
Raphael starts on an intercept course. I follow.

She goes into a cubicle. Raphael's fifteen feet behind. He stops at the door.
I come up behind him. She's seated behind a grey steel desk, mouth open, doughnut poised to enter.

Raphael says, "Mind if I have a seat?"

She looks up, startled, crumbs falling to the desk, and nods at the chairs across from her. Raphael walks in and has a seat. I stand in the doorway. She looks at me.

I slide along the wall to her left, Raphael's right. Like Science and Religion,
I see both faces at the same time; a double viewpoint. I stand there.

"You get many older New Yorkers in," Raphael asks, "The seventy-two to seventy-four models." His seventy-four Chrysler New Yorker sits out front.

I'm going with the flow. But the flow isn't talking so I stand, watch, and listen.
Her glances give cause to pause.

"Do you like horses," Raphael asks.

"Oh yes," she perks, "I used to have one."

"You don't have one anymore."

"No," she replies wistfully.

Raphael's eyes light, wheels turn.
"How'd you like to go partners on a racehorse," he asks.

He's on a roll; it's his turf. In addition to his tool and die job, the multi-talented Raphael farms a hundred-sixty-acres, raises horses, and deals in cheap commodities. Racehorses are his passion, gambling his thrill.

The wheels spin. His eyes turn inward. Her eyes dance to me.
"Mind if I smoke," he asks.

"No," she says as she pulls an ashtray from her desk and hands it to him.

I sense an opening and take a seat beside Raphael. "What's your name," I ask.

Instead of answering she hands me a card. I look at it and read it out loud.

"I'm Dan Murphy and this is Raphael Rafensbarger."

She confirms my pronunciation as she extends her angelic hand. "Audra Diamante." Her face radiates a self assured quality. Her eyes captivate mine.

I talk about the world's greatest car salesman. She read the book. It gives us common ground and carries us five minutes. I need to find more about her. The next thought comes out. "How old are you?"

"Twenty-four," she responds.

My heart strings tug. I take a chance at disappointment before she entwines me. "Are you married?"

"No."

My heart rate increases. I want to ask if she has a boyfriend but can't. Gates clank in my mind. I ask, "Are you from this area?"

"I graduated from North Side."

I'm stuck on the boyfriend question but afraid to ask. More gates clank shut. Attraction swells my tongue. Just thirty minutes ago I didn't have a care in the world. My confidence was supreme and my mind serene. Now I don't know what to say.

Joseph and Mary merge to form the Abram River

Raphael jumps back on the racehorse theme. Relieved and disappointed, I light a cigarette. And then another. Raphael has a plan and he's looking for a player.

They banter. I watch. Her eyes flash to mine.

I try to think of something to say. Anxiety grows. I need to know if she has a boyfriend before my heart becomes entranced. I can't handle another disappointment.

Raphael pitches his best; progress is elusive. His silver tongue slips to beggar's mode. "We wouldn't have to buy an expensive one." He's down to a thousand apiece.

"It's a luxury I can't afford," is her final stand.

He looks at me and asks, "You ready to go."

I want to say something to captivate this enchanting maiden but I'm spellbound; my brain's locked. "I don't think she wants to buy a racehorse," comes out.

Raphael stands to go. I linger, disappointed that I can't muster the courage. The words won't come. Raphael waits. "Nice meeting you Audra," is all I can say.

Enchantment carries me across the showroom floor. "She's a nice girl," Raphael says. "Too bad she doesn't have any money."

I jump out of character for the second time that day, "I'm going to see that girl again."

Chapter 4--ENSLAVEMENT

Joseph and Mary molecules mix and mingle in the Abram.

"Hello Audra, this is Dan Murphy. I was with Raphael Rafensbarger when he talked to you about buying a racehorse a couple weeks ago."

"Yes," her voice rises softly, "How are you?"

"Good." His fingers tremble. He's using Don Cartier's phone at Concord Carpets. His head jerks to see if Don is still with the customer. He doesn't see him. "I've been thinking about you and looking for an excuse to call."

"Oh," she says.

In addition to being shy, he's secretive about romantic interests. He hasn't mentioned Audra to anyone including Raphael since they left the dealership. His stomach twists.

"There's a presentation of a revolutionary water conditioner this Friday night." His throat tightens. "I've been wondering if you'd like to go," he says and quickly adds, "We could go out for a drink afterwards." A dozen rehearsals and he still flubs it!

"I'm sorry but I can't. Maybe some other time."

"UH. OK. Well, uh, I'll call you later." Perspiration pops from his forehead.

"Okay," she says. "Bye-bye."

The Abram winds its way west to Lake Michigan.

He can't afford to upset the delicate nature of an attraction this powerful. The cliff of his emotions is steep, disappointment deep. His courage must strengthen. Attraction must be equal. He has to have her but not before she has to have him.

'She left the door open.' His heart does back flips. His bones tingle. His muscles quiver. A subdued "Yeah," escapes as his arm thrusts into the air. His head jerks. He puts on a stone face and walks out to see Don.

Dan knew Don Cartier from a school of dreams venture, five years earlier. Ty Quiznick and the magnetic water conditioner drew them back together within days of meeting Audra. Concord Carpets rings a silver bell on the synchronicity scale.

Dan spends his spare time at the store, brainstorming about the miraculous magnet and helping with the occasional customer overload. Uncle Bob taught Dan how to measure and sell carpet. Occasionally Don throws Dan some scraps. Wade Yangster uses them for decorating schemes in his fort, by the Lutheran Hospital.

The spring thaw is still a month away. Temperatures hover around freezing. Piles of dirty snow linger in parking lots, accumulating dust and carbon, compressing to ice, slowly melting. Every now and then they get a fresh white coat.

The southern branch of the Abram flows south with the Illinois River down the mighty Mississippi.

Dan's coming back from an evening carpet call a week later when he decides to swing by the dealership to see if Audra is working. He doesn't know what he'll say. He has to see her. She invaded his mind. He can't get her out.

Her eyes sparkle when he walks through the door. She's talking to some people. 'What do I do now,' he asks himself. He paces, pauses, and gazes at the showroom cars.

A man comes over. "Can I help you," he asks.

"No thanks, I'm waiting for Audra."

"She's busy with some customers and asked me to help you."

Dan scans for Audra. She's thirty feet away, by the office cubicles. He turns to the man. "You can tell me about the TC3 Horizon."

"Why don't we go for a test drive," is his reply.

"UH." Dan glances over; he doesn't see Audra. "OK," he hesitantly says.

Dan follows to a four-door Horizon. Not exactly his style but he doesn't care; he's not here to buy a car. The man drives up Springdale Road. Dan drives back.

When they return, no one's in the showroom. The salesman vanishes. Dan stands in the middle of the floor facing back. His eyes are drawn to the open double doors on his left, opposite the magnetic snow-blower doors to his right.

A cool breeze blows in. Behind the breeze is a black TC3 Horizon hatchback. That's his style. He saunters through the breeze and wonders if she set this up.

As he walks around and admires the car, he notices keys in the ignition. A cable slips through the cells of his mind. He goes back around, opens the door, slides in, and starts the engine. He's hooked.

It's not the car he's hooked on. He turns the ignition off, gets out, goes inside.

Audra's like a bee returning from the mother lode as she floats across the floor. "Tell me about the TC3," Dan says.

She mesmerizes him with a list of superlatives. The cable in his mind tightens. Her brilliance enslaves him. She finishes. He's spellbound, on auto pilot. "Let's talk price," he says. With no money or means to get any, his enslavement is complete.

She leads him to her cubicle and sits behind her desk. He sits on a chair and faces her. She writes on a notepad, hands it to him, and waits.

Dan looks at the number on the pad and starts to squirm. How can he tell her he didn't come here to buy a car; he has no job, no money. He doesn't want to barter on price and drag this charade any further. He searches silently for the words.

"Where do you work," she asks. Her hand flashes to her mouth, eyebrows rise.

"I don't," he answers. His mind jogs. "Can I use your phone?"

"Sure. Dial nine for an outside line."

"Hi Don, this is Dan. Sorry about not calling you right away."

"Did they buy?"

"No."

"I thought the delay was because you had to work to close the sale."

"I did but they still didn't buy."

"What happened?"

"I measured the area and gave them a price. They waffled and wouldn't commit."

"Did you drop the price?"

"Yes, and I went over your reasons for putting plywood down but I could tell they didn't agree. I decided to quote just carpet."

"Did you knock out all their objections and push to close?"

"Yes, it was a long drive out there so I pushed hard. Their objections were weak. I had a feeling they were holding something back."

"And?"

"After they set the appointment and left the store this morning, they bought elsewhere. It's being installed tomorrow-without plywood."

"They let you drive all the way out there, measure everything up, barter with them, and they had already bought somewhere else?"

"Yeh."

"They could have called and saved a sixty mile goose chase."

"Yeh, I know. I'll see you in the morning." With that out of the way, Dan returns to the more important issue of dealing with the present situation.

He searches for something to say. A half baked idea comes out. "I'm planning to write a book and have given some thought to setting up a foundation. A high school friend is now a lawyer at a local bank. He may be able to help me."

The vanished salesman enters. "Here are the keys to the TC3," he says as he hands them to Audra. He leaves.

"They're giving me a loaner while they do some work on my car," she says.

"Is it the black one?"

"Yes."

Dan's foot taps the floor. Audra's eyes flicker. Her head cocks ever so slightly.

Dan notices the tapping and stops. The words won't surface. He hopes hers do. He can't muster the courage. It's too soon. Cora's crushing blow, losing his truck and Sheba had shriveled his heart to ceramic fragility. His vision fired it but the flame of love tilts the scale and raises the stakes.

He throttles his heart. He can't afford to get his hopes up. Another blow could kill him.

"I don't know if it will do any good but if I get some money I'll be back to buy the car," he says as he stands to go. His black hat is firmly planted on his head.

"Call me as soon as you find out," is her quick reply.

"I will," he says as he walks out the door.

'Damn. Maybe things will still work out,' he thinks as he drives off in his Nova.

The northern branch flows thru the Great Lakes toward St. Lawrence.

Niagara Falls first.

The next day is Thursday. Dan calls his former classmate at the bank. "Tuesday is the soonest I can see you," Dale tells him.

Dan calls Audra to tell her about the delay. "Call me as soon as you find out," is her anxious response. He reads her tone as more than desire to sell a car.

Hope pulses as his tunnel vision focuses on sweeping Audra off her feet. His heart pounds, blood courses to his brain. His mind explores the possibilities.

Hope builds as her magnetism binds him. The time table alters. Before Audra he could take his time and let the book develop without pressure. Now he has to push the schedule.

The love bug chomps his heart and leaves no choice but to pursue the half baked idea. He's convinced that success at the bank is his only option. His course of action is set, the chance slim.

His infatuation is deep. His mind pushes all else aside. He's never been attracted so powerfully. He needs her more than anything.

Thoughts bump the O-ZONE as his search engine makes a right-turn into the fantasy compartment. He imagines driving his Nova to the dealership, walking in, signing the papers, plopping cash on the table in a no trade deal, then asking, "Why don't you follow me in the Horizon?"

His mind floats on a sea of bliss. It could be Romeo and Juliet. It could be heaven. She'll sell cars and I'll write my book. 'When I'm published we'll ride into the sunset and live happily ever after.' His heart jumps with anticipation.

Emotion takes charge. His heart takes control. Love's in command. He has a concept of what the book introduction should contain and spends most of the weekend hunting and pecking on an old portable typewriter; draft after draft.

Starting with a chronology of great discoveries, Dan weaves a tapestry of interest for the secret of the universe, the one he's been blessed with. It's a secret that will go to the grave if he doesn't get what he wants. That something is Audra Diamante.

But Murphy's Law has bitten him too many times. The euphoria of his vision won't float him past this heartbreak. It's too powerful. He's had too many in too short of a time. He needs a back-up to keep his heart alive, time to stabilize if it's crushed again.

Joseph and Mary molecules flow through the Gulf of Mexico.

Dan harbors the spark of another hope to keep him afloat if his plan fails. Further from reality and a longer shot than money at the bank, it's his life preserver. He can't count on another revelation to save him. He can count on nothing but hope and it can drown him. Audra is liquid oxygen.

Everything hinges on Dale at the bank.

Chapter 5—ENMESHMENT

Niagara rumbles.

The sun is bright, the sky a magnificent blue. It's Tuesday morning. Hope charges my heart as I walk into the bank. My stomach twists as butterflies float in rumpled rhythm.

Dale has his hand out and a grin from ear to ear. Butterflies synchronize. We walk into Dale's office and chat about years past and the football team that took us to state. I was the center. Luke was right guard. Batman and Robin were on the left. Spike was throwing. Tiny Tim was catching. Ba-Lou was buttressing. Big T was bulldozing. Dale was scat backing. We reminisce.

I talk about my plan and hand Dale the book introduction that I spent the weekend writing and revising. I made some last minute changes but didn't have time to retype it. Scribbled notes and corrections pepper the one page intro. Dale twists and turns the paper, smile on his face, as he reads the penciled additions.

The phone rings. Dale answers.

I want to believe that I'll be successful in my quest but Murphy's Law has bitten too many times to believe that smooth sailing is ahead. In my school of dream days I was brazen enough to believe it but age and experience have tempered idealism. The chance is too slim, there's too much at stake to be confident.

I know myself. I know how ferocious failure can be. I know the weight of the anchor on my heart. The past year has stripped its strength. It won't take much to sink it.

That's why I prepared a flame of hope this morning; a skyhook to grab. Hope is the only fuel I have left. The secret won't save me. The book is too far off.

Bonnie Franklin shot a dagger into my heart on the night of my vision. She was spilling her guts on the Johnny Carson Show when Luke and I walked into Luke's country house on that fateful night. That's when my empathic signals started.

The Saint Lawrence heads for the Atlantic.

Dale cocks the phone receiver. I hear Concord Foundation waft out. Dale cocks the receiver back to cover his ear. I bristle at the thought. 'Too small; they're thinking too small.'

Dale hangs up, picks up the book intro, gives it a final glance, looks at me, smiles and says, "Dan, I wish I could but I can't help you. I just handle the legal end."

An iron hand grasps my heart and squeezes. Squeamish butterflies squash in my twisted gut and squish into a torrent of raging ruckus that permeates my body and oozes from my eyes. I knew the plan was weak but I blurted it to Audra and had no choice but to follow through. Reality sticks its staunch starkness into my melting face.

I put on my game face when I leave, make it to my car without spillage, and buoy myself with the thought that it may still work out. Audra dominates my mind. I wonder about her reaction and what I'm going to say as I meander toward the dealership.

I can't call her. I have to tell her in person. I take a lap around the mall, across Springdale Road from the dealership, to build courage. It's time for action.

I pull my Nova to the front door, get out, and go in. My confidence is low. The anchor drags on my heart. The setback at the bank pierces it.

Audra scurries into her cubicle. I go to her door. She's crying. I don't want to embarrass her so I step aside. My mind is blank; in limbo between fantasy and reality. 'Maybe she got fired, lost a car deal,' I think.

I sneak a peek. She's composing herself. Still stunned by my shattering, my mind shears between paranoia and need to embrace her. Emotions block logic.

I prepare to enter. I don't know what I'm going to say but I can't stand out here. My mind swirls in a fog. I muster the courage and walk in.

"Do you still have the car," I blurt.

"No," she says weakly.

I take a deep breath. My voice softens. "I didn't get the money anyway." I think about rejection at the bank and my voice scrapes a bitter edge, "Nobody understands."

"I understand," she says.

Her compassionate tone encourages me to mount my moral high horse. Frustration flops priorities and alters reality. I snap, "Why'd you sell the car?"

She cries, "I didn't. Her understanding smile evaporates as her empathic eyes mist. Her voice wavers, "Do you hear that man on the radio," she points up and pauses as her face tightens. "He's my boyfriend."

My ceramic composure crumbles as I plunge into despair. My mind squishes like the squeamish butterflies. My vision vaporizes, dream disintegrates. Daggers puncture my chest. Defeat pummels me. 'I have to get out of here.' Hope loses charge, desperation commands, Hollywood controls.

"If I get the money maybe I'll be back," I say as I make for the door.

I hop in my rust-pocked Nova and drive away. Emotional control hangs by a silver strand. I have to keep hope alive or my heart will die. Destiny swings from a star. I stop at the Post Office and mail the flame of hope to make it one more day.

The Gulf Stream steams north with equatorial warmth.

Nobody's at the homestead. I think about Audra's reactions and realize the boyfriend statement was a defensive measure. It's only been fifteen minutes since I sent the flame to Tinsel town and I'm already falling apart. I'm hopelessly hooked on Audra. Anxiety oozes from my pores. I call Raphael.

"Don't call her unless you want a screaming woman on your hands," is his advice. My mind slices a twinkle of hope. I don't question him and let the twinkle enlarge. Wish takes charge. Screams of joy, is my thought.

My mind swirls with possibilities and the need to know. I pace and debate. Bias tilts to Audra. My heart pumps. She wants me as much as I want her, is my conclusion. Blood surges. My fingers tremble as I dial the phone. Anticipation clogs my throat.

"This is Audra," the serene voice answers.

"Hello Audra, this is Dan Murphy." I choke, "Want to go for a ride in my limo?"

"Limo," she retorts. "I thought you had a Nova."

My composure melts. Hope sinks. Tears build. They hold. Voice verges on breakdown. "That is my limo," gushes out.

An abrupt "No," is all I hear before the phone slam.

I blew it; should've listened to Raphael. Damn this impulsive streak. Suddenly, nothing matters. My face relaxes into a frustrated calm.

'That's that. No use crying over spilled milk.'

The flame streaks to the West Coast. 'Have to wait to see what turns up.'

THE DRUM STARTS TAPPING, THE RHYTHM IS ROLLING.
THE BEAT UNMISTAKABLE AS THE SONG STARTS GROWING.
THE OLD BEAT IS SOFT BUT EVER PRESENT.
THE PAST IS DEAD, THE FUTURE'S DAWNING.
OVER THIS WOMAN
THERE'S NO USE FAWNING.

Chapter 6—ENRICHMENT

The comet stretches its magnetic tether from the sun and slingshots back.

Doug and Leroy Lucker were underclassman when Dan captained the Concord High wrestling team. They share a two bedroom bachelor pad they call the clubhouse. It's the perfect place to regroup and forget emotional frustrations.

The brothers shuck and jive. Dan enjoys the ride. Audra submerges with excited banter about going to Florida to see Regis, one of Doug's collegiate wrestling mates.

"Why don't you go with us?" Doug chides.

"Yeah," Leroy chimes. "We'd have a great time."

The wrestling triage is between jobs; the brothers are looking for a cheap holiday.

"I can't afford it," Dan says

"Wouldn't cost anything to sleep and Regis has plenty of food," Doug offers.

"It'd cost next to nothing for gas," Leroy adds.

Dan sidesteps. Outwardly, he's at ease. Inside, a battle rages. Uncertainty controls his mind. Audra commands it. He can't commit and can't afford to let the opportunity pass. He'll need the trip if his hopes are false. "When are you leaving," he asks.

"Day after tomorrow, early." Leroy pipes.

"With three of us driving we can be there by midnight," Doug adds.

"I can't go that soon," is Dan's answer.

"We can leave this weekend then."

"I can't say I'd be ready then."

The brothers press and won't take a maybe. Dan's forced to make a choice. It's been less than eight hours since Audra slammed the phone.

"I can't go," is his answer.

"You have to go."

"I can't."

"Why not?"

"I can't say."

"Why can't you tell us?" They badger.

He relents with the hope they'll lighten up. They listen intently as he talks about the beautiful maiden and the coincidences surrounding her and how he can't push it. The talk is futile, it goes over their heads; the badgering continues. "How soon will you know?"

"I don't know," Dan says.

"Why not?"

"Why don't you guys just go? I can't afford it anyway."

"No, we want you to go with us?"

"I can't go til I know and I don't know when that will be." Dan wishes he never mentioned Audra. "I need to give it a couple days rest before I even think about it."

They won't accept it. They push. It's two to one. They win. Dan parts with, "I'll try to get the matter resolved as soon as possible."

The comet streaks past Pluto and into Neptune's realm.

Urgency pushes him. He begins to believe he can resolve it sooner.
The next day he writes a letter expressing his feelings and polishes the book intro.
He calls the dealership that evening. The harmonic voice of a goddess answers.

"Hello. This is Audra."

Enchantment blossoms. "Hello Audra, this is Dan Murphy. I'm sorry about the way things went yesterday. It wasn't good and I apologize for my rash behavior. I'm really nervous and shy about talking to you. I wrote a letter expressing my feelings."

"Uh," her voice trails into "I'll talk to you later," and slides to a soft landing.

Dan's feet leave the ground and hover when he hangs the phone up. His mind tilts and swirls. There's a chance blooms and grows to a raging river that overflows its banks.

He's alone and paces in circles, in and out of the house. He wants to see her more than anything he's ever wanted in his life. He knows that he can't go rushing in but it's difficult to keep himself convinced of it. Anxiety tears him apart.

Audra pulls him to his Nova. Butterflies assemble. His heart does somersaults as he starts the car. His mind heads for the K-ZONE. He has to know.

Neptune's gravity pulls at the passing comet.

As Dan walks into the showroom he sees Audra scurry out back. 'Uh-oh; did I blow it again,' he wonders. 'What do I do now?'

He's like a high-strung racehorse on a bed of blazing coals as he walks haltingly to Audra's office, lays the two letters in the middle of her desk, jots a note to meet him, places it on top of the stack and under a paperweight, and walks out. Instead of leaving his Nova parked in front of the dealership, he drives it to the pizza parlor next door.
He orders a beer and waits.

His fractured composure can barely contain the torment. Squeamish butterflies flutter hither and thither in disarray, bounce off the walls, crash into the ceiling, and dive bomb the floor of his stomach. He wants to rush back, put an end to the raging ruckus.

It tears him apart but he has to wait. He's rushed it too many times.
This love brings him closer to hell than he's ever been.
Uncertainty eats his heart and divides his mind.

He wants her; needs her; has to have her. She's part of him. Fear that her love isn't as real as his, shreds him. The next beer doesn't settle him. His stomach knots.

Thirty agonizing minutes pass. Self doubt sets in, never a good sign for Dan: 'What's wrong with me? I need to get a handle before this woman drives me crazy. Damn this impulsive streak!' His head twirls

Six weeks ago he was a picture of supreme serenity. Now he's a time bomb ticking toward oblivion. He can't stand the suspense. He leaves the pizza parlor.

He drives through the country like he always does when he needs to think. He doesn't want to be bothered by anybody or anything. He puts it on auto-pilot and cruises, wandering with a purpose and a multi-faceted question biased to his needs.

He cracks the door to the fantasy compartment and coils in a cover of comfort, insulating himself with the thought that their love is forever. Positive and negative energy, climbing and growing on the double helix to heaven; minds meshing and melding, locking, twisting, spiraling to nirvana, in a dance through all eternity.

The comet grazes one of Uranus' moons. The course alters.

Adam's at work the next morning. Patty and Emily are still asleep. Dan looks in the phone book. She's listed. He calls her at home.

His tongue does a pretzel twist. She hangs up. He calls Leroy. It's the day they wanted to leave for Florida but held off to wait for Dan. "I don't have an answer and I'm really nervous. I need more time."

"Call us as soon as you find out," is the anxious response. "We're ready to go."

Need and fear collide. Dan's been in love before but nothing like this. The love bug chomps relentlessly at his mind. He can't go to Florida with uncertainty hanging over him. He has to back off. He's pushed it too often. He spends the weekend in solitude.

The magnetic Abram circles the globe.

Monday morning Dan goes to see Wade Yangster. The sky is dotted with silver pillow clouds, floating along like wayward ships on an azure sea. Spring saturates the air as Wade works on the evolving fortress in the central city. He calls it the fort.

The fort is a collage of themes. Like the clubhouse, it's a place where Dan can go to relax and forget what ails him. A variety of plants and paintings adorn the unconventional house and soothe his mind. Unique oil paintings, created by Wade and strategically placed around the fort, open the eye to the fantasy of existence and the vastness of the human mind.

A theater of ideas reinforces the structural integrity of the house. When Wade runs out of decorating materials: carpet samples, beam cutoffs, boards from a packing crate, etc., he cordons off an area and starts another theme, creating something from nothing. Talent and creativity more than make up for his lack of money.

Layers of asphalt roll around the fascia and eaves and give the house an Alpine flair. The rounded roof edge and steep pitch shed snow and water. Durable stucco walls shield wood from earth, wind, and fire. It's one of the few stucco houses in East Bend.

Wade doesn't think, talk, or act like an ordinary person; nothing average about him. His unique personality has a generous attitude, an undying spirit, and a rustic sense of humor. He's New Age in some respects, old fashioned in others.

While Wade finishes his current project, Dan bangs drums in the living room. He never played drums before and starts to get the hang of it after tinkering with the different sounds. His first rhythm session ends with a trip to the lumber yard.

Planet Earth circles the sun.

Dan sits in his Nova and thinks about Audra while Wade goes into the lumber store. Clear blue skies surround Dan except to the southeast where orange flashes punctuate the black clouds hanging over the city center. His developing empathic sense and theory of how the mind of man can influence the atmosphere tell him that something is about to unfold. He feels a piercing pull on his groin and a cold grip on his heart.

Wade comes out of the store with a couple bags of stucco premix. "I need to stop at the courthouse," he says.

Black twisting balls of torment hover over the courthouse when they arrive. Lightning knots them together. Wade goes inside. The zipper rips, buckets pour. Dan looks at the large clock on the bank across from the City-County Building. Thunder bellows at three o'clock.

Wade dashes out between deluges. A fantasy, too real to dismiss, plays in Dan's head. The feeling is strong. Familiar cars drive his imagination. He silently ponders the premonitions as he drives from the thunder center.

Interference and involvement hang in Dan's mind. The thought that Audra is there with the Lucker brothers and others, weighs heavy. Barry, Dan's older brother, is there from Santa Fe. Gene flew in from Houston. The strange premonitions are strong.

Our solar system circles the galactic center.

At Wade's house, a thought flashes. Dan calls his uncle Bob. "Hello Betty, this is Dan. Is Bob there?"

"No Dan, he went to the carpet store a couple hours ago." Dan introduced his uncle Bob to Don recently and they became good friends.

"I get the feeling that everyone's waiting for me?"

"Yehh..." her voice drops and drags as if his question is the answer.

Dan's thoughts sail beyond the O-ZONE to the P-ZONE, the land of endless possibilities, as he ponders the premonitions. Can they be real, he wonders.

He dials Concord Carpets. Don answers with remnants of tears in his voice. Dan checks his gut feeling. "Wish I knew where Audra was?"

Don perks. "Did you say Audra?" his voice rising, betraying a hopeful tone.

Dan steps back. 'What's going on? How many people are involved?' Shackles rise. "No," is his answer; "Is Bob there," his question.

Now Don steps back. "Haven't seen him," is his off handed reply.

The Milky Way circles the universe.

Chapter 7—ENGAGEMENT

Joseph and Mary molecules ride the St Lawrence to the sea.

I bang on Wade's set of seven drums and five cymbals and ponder the day-thunder bursts downtown, courthouse premonitions, Betty's response, Don's response. Was Audra really there? Are my premonitions real? I wonder.

The power of love flows though my arms. With two hours total time on the drums I watch in amazement as my arms rotate back and forth, round and round as if they were someone else's. My ears listen to the rhythm unfold as my arms drum to an inner beat. My mind is occupied with Audra.

I come to the conclusion that there's nothing I can do about the present situation, wind down the percussion, talk to Wade, and head to my parents. Twilight creeps, darkness dawns. The house is empty when I arrive. The nightlight comes on.

There's a note on the refrigerator. 'Call Detective Holman at three o'clock.' I was downtown at three o'clock! I don't know a Detective Holman?

I turn the note over and make the three-minute drive to my sister Candy's house. Lights are on but no one's home? I turn around and head back to the homestead.

The door's ajar. I search upstairs and downstairs. No one is there.

I look at the refrigerator. The note is facing me.
I look through the house again and do a lap around the outside.

I dial the detective's number, four hours late. A honey voice answers the phone. "This is Dan Murphy. I just found a note to call Detective Holman."

"He's gone and won't be back til eight tomorrow morning," is the sweet reply.

'Sure sounds like Audra.' "Is this Audra," I ask in a voice that starts out with wonder and descends to a question with a tone that could be considered irritated.

"No," is her quick response.
"Would you like to call back tomorrow," she anxiously asks.

Her denial digs deep. My "No," is just as abrupt.

The quick change of events sends me dashing back to Wade's house. As I pass the City-County Building, across from the courthouse, I wonder if that really was Audra and if she's still there. It's too surreal to believe but the question still nags. I keep driving. A couple blocks later I do a U-turn, return, and U-turn again.

The Gulf Stream and St. Lawrence flow side by side.

My eyes watch with strange detachment as energy flows through my arms and drumsticks to the drums and back to my ears. My arms beat freely, back and forth, cadence flowing to the sea of love and back again. The rhythm is jungle.

My mind sifts through the events of the previous week and weighs the possibilities against probability. My senses are keen as my search engine starts at the beginning of the Audra file and moves forward, isolating and combining factual and imaginary data, turning and churning plausibility's. I match and cross-match conclusions. My arms chart their own course. An hour later, when my conclusions reach the present, a disturbing thought enters.

'If that really was Audra on the other end of the phone, she could be in serious distress.' My heart leaps to my throat as concern floods my mind. Panic pokes needles into my brain. My arms stop beating. My legs start moving. I jump into the Nova.

My left brain takes command as I race downtown. My right brain controls the pedal. My body charges with anticipation.

Traffic is light. The light turns red. Red flashes from the right.

An ambulance crosses in front of me and turns toward the direction I came from. The driver looks at me then jerks right to continue straight. No other vehicles are at the intersection to impede the hasty maneuver.

Seems strange for an ambulance to change course and alter its momentum so abruptly. I think of Audra and wonder if she was in it. The light turns green.

I proceed to the courthouse while my left and right brain engage in battle. Panic commands. Thoughts jumble. Logic controls. Thoughts peak and pulse. Love charges. Resolution is imperative. A reverse jiffy turn at the City-County Building and I'm on a cross-town run to East Bend Catholic, direction ambulance was last headed.

Instincts key. There's no activity at the emergency room. I leave. My brain jogs. I remember that Grandma Murphy is at Lutheran Hospital; direction ambulance was turning before it veered right. I head there.

The driver in the car next to me looks over, abruptly turns away, and speeds off. The white Mustang looks identical to Candy's and even though my look was brief, I could swear it was George, my cousin from out of town. George is three days younger than me. Grandpa Evan's birthday falls between ours. Aunt Ev is his mother. Synchronism chimes.

It's almost midnight when I pull up to the emergency entrance. I ask the guard, "Have any EMS vehicles arrived in the last twenty minutes with a young female?"

"Can't say," is his reply.

"My grandmother, Dorothy Murphy had surgery today and I forgot. I'd like to see her." The guard writes on a pad and walks away

Three minutes later he comes back and says, "Someone will be out to escort you." I'm surprised my request is honored. It's well past visiting hours.

A man in a uniform comes out. I look at the flag on his shoulder and badge on his chest. He's an East Bend police officer. Amazement intensifies. Positive ions swirl under my black hat to reinforce my thoughts and open the K-ZONE.

During the long, silent walk through the hospital to the wing on the far side, I think about Audra and ponder the significance of my vision on Martin Luther King Jr's birthday. Martin Luther's actions, hundreds of years ago, led to the Lutheran church and this hospital, the hospital I was born in twenty-nine years earlier. My first sight of Audra happened at Coney King and adds a trivial synchronistic tie.

Granny glows when I walk in. "Gramma, you look twenty years younger," I say.

"Oh, thank you," she says as her hand reaches past the smile on her face to pat her head. "I had my hair done after surgery." Her youthful radiance extends beyond her hair-do.

"How'd your knee surgery go?"

"The doctors are amazed at my progress," she beams. "They say I should be able to go home soon."

I sense Audra's presence. A white curtain blocks the other half of the room. "Where's Audra," I ask.

"Who's Audra," she asks in a tone that suggests implication more than innocence.

"That's the girl I'm going to marry." The thought spurs me through the L-ZONE to heavens door. "She's brilliant and wonderful. If only I could find her," I hint.

Granny giggles then straightens and says, "I don't know Audra."

I'm reluctant to look behind the curtain or in the bathroom so I pace, prowl, hint, contemplate, and wait for Audra to show herself. She doesn't.

On my third trip out of the room to check exits and entry's the policeman standing at the nurses station breaks his self imposed silence. "It's time to go," he commands.

Pluto enters Neptune's realm.

Thoughts coalesce as I drive to my parent's house. It's still vacant. The air is charged. I call Candy.

"Audra. I don't know any Audra," she replies in an inflamed tone. Another denial! I hop in my Nova and head to Candy's for a face to face.

My blood pulses. The Mustang is missing. There's a car sitting at the end of Candy's sub-division street. Tail lights flash. Instead of pulling into her driveway, I go to investigate.

I get to within fifty feet and the car takes off. The dark haired driver looks vaguely familiar. I can see no other passengers in the big four-door or any reason for the car to be stopped where it was.

I follow the car out of the sub-division, down the county road, and up the state road toward town, watching for a head to pop up. When I get close, the four-door speeds up. My pace is unhurried and constant. The mouse like actions reinforces my thoughts.

I catch the mouse at a stoplight. There's no cross traffic. The four-door takes off. I wait for the light and question whether to continue this cat and mouse game.

It's a mile to the next traffic signal. The mouse, with a big lead, slows to a stop on the other side of that intersection. I'm closing in and make it through the yellow light.

The four-door is stopped across the road divider from another car. I slow to a stop. The mouse takes off.

The other car appears to be stalled in the left turn lane. Four men occupy the car. My eyes draw to the back seat where a man jerks back and forth, anxious to get the car moving. The man looks at me and freezes. I can't believe my eyes.

His face melts and transforms to that of someone else. The melting impression of Barry, my brother from Santa Fe, imprints on the video in my head.
The day and night of the chase becomes unforgettable.

My mind tilts with the moment as my courthouse premonition is confirmed.
It launches on an intercept with the O-ZONE. The mouse scampers away.

I see him slip around the corner as I crest the hill. I round the corner and follow at the speed limit, gap closing as a stoplight on the six-lane bypass momentarily holds him.
I catch him at the next light.

He turns left at the back street to the mall as I pull up. Sidetracked by the face melt and hanging in the O-ZONE, my mind goes straight to their destination.
I follow my thought.

At the dealership, I park the Nova, and walk around the car lot. A silver TC3 Horizon sits in the middle of the showroom. Across Springdale Road, the clock in the mall parking lot points to one o'clock. Headlights flash from the inside corner of the mall. My right brain charges. I go to investigate.

My eyes focus on the dark inside niche of the mall as I hop in my car.
Springdale Road is divided, lot entrances are offset, roadway is lower, and piles of dirty ice block the view for part of my journey around and over to the dark inside corner.

When I arrive at the inside corner, there's nothing there. Street exits radiate like a dual compass from the huge mall. The mouse slipped away.

Joseph and Mary molecules from the Mississippi branch meet, mingle,
and separate from St. Lawrence molecules as they circle the globe.

Back at Candy's house, I pull up and park on the street. My parents come out the front door and intercept me as I walk across the lawn. Candy ducks back inside.
Bill's nowhere in sight. The white Mustang sits in the driveway.

"We need to take you to the hospital," Patty says.

"Why," I ask.

"You've been acting strange," she says.
"Candy said you made a big deal about some girl named Audra."

"I didn't make a big deal. I just asked her where Audra was."

"She doesn't know anyone named Audra," Patty persists.

"So what's the problem?"

"We need to get you to the hospital."

"For what?"

"We need to find out why you're obsessed with this girl."

"Obsessed? Who said I was obsessed?" My temperature starts to rise.
I stay calm.

"Grandma said you were at the hospital making a big commotion."

"I was there but I wasn't making a commotion. I even had a police escort.
He waited outside the room while I visited with Gramma."

"She said you were pacing in and out of her room and talking about marrying this girl who we've never met or even heard about."

"I don't see where that's anybody's business unless I choose to tell them." Things start to look mighty peculiar. 'How and why would grandma even contact them? They haven't been home as far as I can tell. It was after midnight when I left the hospital. She was happy and smiling when I left, maybe even delighted and definitely not concerned. There's only one answer and I don't like the smell of it.'

"You don't even know her," Patty responds.

"How do you know?"

"You never mentioned her."

"That doesn't mean anything. How do you know so much about her?"

"We need to take you to the hospital, don't we Adam."

"You mean the nut ward?"

"There are people there that can help you."

"This is crazy,"

A red meteor skims the heavens.

Knowledge and fear collide. I can't believe this is happening. I have to take the blame for their blunder. My left brain is acutely aware of what's happening; my right, aware of the consequences of resistance. My instincts are keyed.

Mom's actions betray her. Her reaction is unjustified. She's avoiding my questions and making an issue about something she should know nothing about. I haven't told anybody what I've seen and thought today. Conspiracy makes sense. I better play this out.

A bright green meteor flashes across the sky.

"I don't need any help. There's nothing wrong with me but something is definitely wrong here. I just need everyone to keep their nose out of my business and leave me alone."

"Adam," Patty pleads.

"Come on Dan. Let's go," Dad says.

It's crazy and I know it but it's two to one. They're in control. I live in their house. What choice do I have? They're my parents. It's a commandment.

Chapter 8—ENLIGHTENMENT

Angular momentum propels the planets through the cold, black vacuum.

Dan's philosophical brain leans toward religion which needs continual cultivation to keep from being scattered by the winds of change or choked by seeds of discord. As he irrigated the fields of his mind, he caught glimpses of neighboring farmland: Catholic, Unitarian, Baptist, Pentecostal, Presbyterian, Episcopalian, Christian Science, Reformed, Nazarene, Mormon, Church of Christ, Jehovah's Witness, Amish, Quakers, etc., etc. The list of farms under the Christian banner is endless.

Most follow a basic farming manual known as the Bible. Some create variations according to their individual beliefs. Dan notices that most of the differences between farms seem to be from different interpretations of the Bible - superficial discrepancies of minor importance in the grand scheme yet jealously guarded by the different branches.

The seeds of mysticism and metaphysics, planted by Aunt Ev and Grandpa Evan, remained dormant in the fertile fields of his mind. An occasional sprinkling of enlightenment sent roots deep into his subconscious, safe from the surface clatter of traditional thinking. Subtle differences tugged at his maturing mind.

The pull became undeniable with the cognizance that Christianity is only one of the major religions of the world. Reincarnation, while intriguing, is one area he had trouble accepting because of its contradiction to his faith. Then he discovered that reincarnation was part of the Christian doctrine prior to the seventh century; it was arbitrarily discarded because it allowed another chance at life and gave the church less control in this one.

Continents split and drift with the elastic crust, floating on the molten sea.

Dan Murphy was born after the miniature solar system surrounding the nucleus of the atom was discovered and before Watson and Crick unlocked the mystery of DNA. Adam Murphy was born at the same time Hubble discovered that the Milky Way wasn't the only galaxy in the universe. Evan Murphy was born after Gregor Mendel's genetic discovery but before it was recognized and he was proclaimed the Father of Genetics.

Dan was drawn to science with no final truths - a continuous quest and exploration. College knowledge, geology and biology, gave reason to reflect on his religious reality. His vision revealed the foundation of existence, the basis of matter.
It illuminated the common denominator of Science and Religion and revealed that they are indeed, dual opposites of the same substance - two sides of the same coin.

The need to know and survival are his driving forces. He's an all or nothing guy; settling for nothing rather than compromise. It's habitual and many setbacks in his adult life are a direct result of this obstinate stance. He was born under the sign of Taurus.

Self doubt is not part of his mind set. Decisions are normally slow and methodical. Questions and answers are placed into the stew of his Cosmo Bank, subconscious mind, and allowed to brew to postulate possibilities. He assesses probabilities and doesn't

conclude anything until he's ninety percent positive.
The only thing he's a hundred percent certain of, is death. When, is the question!

His aggressive posture and no nonsense attitude come out when he's in command. He's John Wayne with a black Stetson, sitting on a blazing white stallion, perched on the pinnacle of positivity. He doesn't barter to get more or give less. Except rare occasions when he's joking or being satirical, he says what he means and means what he says.

On the other side of his reality he's a frightened boy, malleable as a chameleon, stripped of negative positivity at a young age. He didn't know what anger was after it was psychologically taken from him. Emotional doors in his right brain were locked.

Dan grew up with the stability of a family rooted in religion. He knows the Ten Commandments and follows them. His knowledge of Emerson's Law of Compensation gives him a sense of serenity. Always hard working and willing to go the extra mile, he knows it's only a matter of time before the breaks start coming his way.

The vision is the break he was awaiting; Audra an intriguing and enigmatic bonus.

THE SEEDS OF SWEET SUCCESS AND SUCCULENT SATISFACTION
ARE STREWN AMONG BOUNTIFUL BOULDERS OF BELIGERANT
BIAS THAT REVOLVE AROUND AND SURROUND HER.

Dan has the inner strength and security to know that being fallible is human. If he makes a mistake he admits it. He understands that crossing the line between right and wrong to cover a mistake causes a loss of self worth and often means crossing that line again and again til it no longer exists. He has no interest in the dark side except to avoid it.

He knows that many sweep mistakes under the proverbial rug and hope they vanish. Then they find the need to cover them again and again.

He sees the delusion and wonders if that's what's happening now
and when it will end.
He wonders who's weaving this web of deceit?

Chapter 9—ENTHRALLMENT

Joseph and Mary molecules flow into and out of the Antarctic Wave.

Oval saucers, like a jackrabbit staring into the headlights of a big rig, dominate Mom's face. Her brows arch like exclamation points. Low light in Dad's truck highlight the ridges and valleys surrounding her eyes. She's past ridiculous; on the verge of hysterical. "We love you and would never do anything to hurt you," she pleads.

"Is something wrong," I ask.

"No. We're just concerned with you and your obsession with this girl." The horror in her eyes belies something much deeper. How bad is it, I wonder.

The comet breaks and imprints on Jupiter's face.

Like Barry's melting face, it's a sight that is forever blazed on the video in my head. What the hell am I going to do now, I wonder as we roll down the road to the nut ward. I'm sandwiched between Mom and Dad. There's no escape.

I'm calm and serene with the knowledge that Audra loves me. I'm unsure of the details about the courthouse debacle or what happened afterward just that it was botched. Now they're taking me out of commission til they can decide how to correct it.

The spider strings a dragline and radiates spokes from the hub.

Dad's silent as he drives toward town. Mom finally stops begging. I wonder if Audra will be there. Judging by Mom's face, it's doubtful.

We pull up to East Bend General and go in. Mom and Dad flank me. Dad talks to the lady at the counter while Mom relapses to hysterics.

Her pronounced pleadings keep my mind wondering what really happened. I start to panic with the thought that something may have happened to Audra. It passes with Mom's continuous "We love you," pleadings.

She's like a baby that can't be reassured after the trauma of an earthquake. Keeping Mom calm controls my anxiety. The thought of being locked up doesn't bother me nearly as much as being separated from Audra! I long for her.

"It's only overnight," Mom says as I walk to the counter to sign some papers. I have no choice. I'm forced to go along with the insanity. The life sentence begins.

Two big, black men in white coats and pants come walking down the hall. They escort me to an elevator. We go up. The elevator door opens to a glass cage. Concern grows as I wonder what I got myself into.

A buzzer sounds. The orderlies open the solid, half-inch thick, glass door. I notice a disheveled girl sitting in the lounge area. She doesn't seem to be all there.

We walk to an elbow high, wrap around counter at the intersection of two right angle hallways that extend in four directions from that point. Three nurses are behind the counter. Two nurses come around. The orderlies leave through the glass door.

The two females escort me to the far end of a hall. A short, skinny guy in plain pajamas gawks as we approach. "Go to bed Gerry," one of the nurses says as we pass.

They take me into what they call the presidential suite, at the end of the hall. It's spacious, with a large bed in the middle of the room. It lends credence to my belief.

A chunk of the comet breaks from Jupiter's pull and heads for the sun.

The next day I pace up and down the hallways and wait for Patty to pick me up. Morning turns to afternoon. Patients try to engage me in conversation but I'm not interested in talking. Audra consumes my mind. Love consumes my soul.

I throb and pulse with the expectancy of being united with Audra. Adrenaline flows. Anxiety churns my stomach. Solitary pacing becomes more anxious. I regret signing the papers and wonder how much longer it will be. Mom said she'd pick me up in the morning. It's after two o'clock.

Finally; Patty arrives. I'm ready to go. She wants to talk to the nurse.

I call Audra at work and close with, "I'll be there when I get there." Just need to get my car, I think.

Patty and the nurse talk and I walk, anxiety growing with each step. Finally, they call me over. The nurse is the nicest I've met. She seems to be in charge.

"Before we release you, you have to promise to go by the Mental Health Center."

"What. They said I'd have to spend one night here and that was it."

"You need to stop by the Mental Health Center," the blonde nurse says.

"What for?" Anxiety starts to stretch the scale.

"You're not going there to stay. You just need to talk to them."

"This is ridiculous," I reply. My mind spins; I can't believe this is happening. "I want out of here."

"You can't go until you agree to talk to Mike at the Mental Health Center."

I pace some more and think about how crazy this whole charade is. What choice do I have? "Okay," I say. "Let me out of here."

Patty and Nurse Bonnie conspire, I pace. I said Okay. What's the problem now?

Finally; we leave. On the way to the MHC I ask, "How long will this take? I talked to Audra while you talked to Bonnie. I told her I was coming to see her.

"There's something I have to tell you," is Patty's answer. "Before I came to the hospital, I went to see Audra. She has a boyfriend. She's getting married in two weeks and asked me to give you this letter."

I look at the photocopy of the typewritten introduction to my book and say nothing. That Audra, she's a clever one, I muse. She saw how these meddlers botched everything with their self effacing roles. She's taking them out of the loop. I sigh.

The note I put on top of the two letters clearly stated that I wanted the original, typed intro, back; not a photocopy! The handwritten personal letter was hers to keep.

We pull into the MHC parking lot. A larger building looms on the left and a smaller one on the right. The two hundred spot lot jogs around and between the two buildings. A hundred acres of grass and trees surrounds the complex.

We walk up to the smaller building. It's all brick on this side except for two reinforced glass doors. Patty pushes the buzzer button. I clasp the book intro.

Minutes pass. A smiling face opens the door. The door locks behind us. We wait by a wrap around counter in a large room with a half-cathedral ceiling. A dozen or more people walk or lounge around a TV and radio.

Mike Mires comes out to greet and usher us down a short hall and into a large room with a table and three chairs. Seeing Mike puts me more at ease. Mike and I played on the same little league team almost twenty years ago.

"She doesn't want to see you," Mike says.

"How do you know?"

"She has a restraining order on you."

"I talked to her just before I came here. She didn't mention a restraining order." I look at the intro letter clutched in my lap and wonder how much more I have to endure. "I haven't harmed anyone. This should be nobody else's business," I retort.

The spider spins sticky silk in a spiral over the frame and radii.

Patty and Mike jabber. I pace. Don't know what they're talking about, don't care. I'm charged, enthralled, no longer tongue tied about talking to Audra. I pace like a caged animal. I don't like the locked doors and want out. Claustrophobia increases urgency.

Finally; Mike unlocks the door. Patty lingers to talk while I walk out into fresh air. Relief turns to wonder when I see Adam driving up in his pick-up. Trailing behind is Bill in Candy's white Mustang. What the hell is going on? I wonder.

Conditions ready the Siberian Express for a polar run.

I go from one imprisonment to another. I'm sandwiched between Adam and Bill. "You have to forget about that girl," Adam says. "She has a boyfriend."

"If that's true then she can tell me." Their actions solidify my belief. "Why is everyone sticking their nose where it doesn't belong?" Steam spews from right brain to left brain. My blood boils.

"There's a restraining order on you. They'll take you to jail"

Steam spouts. I pound on the dashboard. "Then take me to jail right now." I'm sick of this interference and mad as hell. Anger like I've never known bubbles.

It's the first time in my life that I remember being more than mildly upset. My formula is simple. I never let anything bother me til now and this really bothers me.

They're making an issue about something they should know nothing about. They didn't even know Audra existed before yesterday and now they're convinced she has a boyfriend, and a restraining order. What is really going on, I wonder.

Silence punctuates the trip downtown. Adam and Bill talk to the desk sergeant while I pace up and down the concrete corridor, muttering and becoming more agitated.

My blood pumps intermittent bursts of arterial rage. "This is ridiculous," I say to the walls. I even pound them a couple times when I'm around the corner; once in plain view.

A big, black policeman, I know from college days, walks past singing "Only the Strong Survive." It leads me to wonder how big this conspiracy really is.

I've never been behind bars. Adam and Bill can't persuade the desk sergeant to lock me up. 'Somebody has some sense around here.' A small smile surfaces.

The ride back to the MHC is silent. I have no desire to escalate the charade. I'm squished like a sardine in the middle of the steel on rubber.

We drop Bill at the Mustang. Adam proceeds toward home, stopping at a pharmacy on the way. I passed the pharmacy on the mouse chase last night.

I wait in the truck while Adam goes inside. My Nova is a half mile away. In high school I could run a half mile in two minutes. I have a stack of blue ribbons. It'd probably kill me to break three minutes now.

Adam stops at Bill and Candy's. The white Mustang's in the driveway. My Nova is still sitting on the street. My heart pumps.

"You have to come into the house to take one of these pills," Adam says.

"What kind of pill?"

"They'll help calm you down."

Calm down? I haven't said a word in a half hour. How much calmer can you get?

I hesitantly follow Adam into the house where he pulls a horse tranquilizer out and hands it to me. I gulp it with some water. "Give me your keys," he says. Bill and Candy flank me.

Arguing does no good. They're adamant in their demand. I relent and hand them over. There'll be no seeing Audra tonight!

They huddle in the dining room, I pace in the kitchen. My heart pumps harder than it's ever pumped, pounding like a bass drum. The sound is deafening. I expect it to pop out any minute.

Why is everyone trying so hard to control me, keep me from Audra? The pounding continues. What gives them the right to stick their nose in this?

The trio continues to conspire as I pace. I could care less what they're talking about. There's only one thing I'm interested in and they're not going to let me have it.

I don't even care what happened as long as Audra's all right. Sooner or later they're going to have to give my keys back. I can't believe how hard my heart is pounding, like a piston about ready to blow its top.

The chunk of comet crashes into a hunk of iron in the asteroid belt and displaces it from its orbit.

Chapter 10—ENTRUSTMENT

The Antarctic Wave is circumpolar with exits and entries.

Adam shakes him. "Dan, wake up." Dan rubs his eyes and looks at the clock. Five A.M. Adam has a pill and a glass of water. Dan gulps it and falls back asleep.

An hour later he's up with the sun, willing it higher, waiting, pacing, wondering if this will be the day. Hoping it is.

It's a game he's going to have to pick his way through. Not that he wants to participate; he doesn't see much choice. He wonders who has his keys. Adam's at work. Emily's gone to school.

Polar cycles and currents alter with temperature change.

Bad luck's been following him ever since he left Perdiddle Tech to join the school of dreams and chase down the road to riches. He met Ty Quiznick and Don Cartier at two different schools on the golden highway. Ralph McCoy came from yet another school of dreams on the road that so far has yielded a golden goose egg and five years worth of life changing experiences.

Ralph is partially responsible for Dan's presence back in the Rust Belt. Cora was the main draw. She was his first love. They met after the astrological enigma bloomed. He was a machinist at GM. She was an engineer at AT&T. Their love blossomed.

She slammed the door without warning. "I can't see or talk to you anymore." She wouldn't tell him why. He didn't push, demand, beg, plead, stalk, or chase after her. His heart was crushed but he respected her wishes and lived with the pain in silence.

Years later, after he moved to Texas, she called. His tumultuous life turned upside down. A roller coaster to hell brought him back to Indiana to live with her. She pulled a second vanishing act and left him towing a U-Haul in circles, his mind spinning.

He was dumped at his parent's door with no money. Then his new truck was repossessed and Sheba, his faithful companion, was struck and killed by a car.

Ralph followed through on his promise for employment as a framing contractor but the Midwest winter had frozen that to a dribble. Logging expeditions with Luke Johnson were the only light in an otherwise bleak existence. It was his darkest hour.
Then heavens portal opened. Then he met Audra. Now this.

Glaciers grow from the Arctic Cap.

Patty gets up later than usual and ambles around. She has her usual sit down, wake up cup of coffee and then another. Time crawls like molasses. Dan paces.

He doesn't mention Audra for fear of perpetuating the game. He can only wait. Patty doesn't offer any information. His questions about his car are brushed off.
Hope sinks and waits.

He wonders how it got to this point. What they hope to accomplish? Where will it lead? Who's pulling the strings? And why?

Patty gets out the milk and eggs and pancake mix and bowls. She has to refill her coffee cup. If she moves any slower he's going to have to call the coroner. It's driving him crazy. He tries to sit. He's so charged with the power of love, he can't sit.

Patty measures the mix. The phone rings. It's her friend Shasta.
They talk about who knows what, for ten agonizing minutes.

El Nino hibernates in the Pacific.

Patty cracks the eggs and adds milk. She mixes the batter. She gets out the pan and then the Crisco. The phone rings. Dan's ready to pull his hair out.

Another five minutes passes. She turns the electric burner on.
Dan watches it heat up and then watches the shortening melt.

Patty's not giving any clues. She slowly pours the thick batter into the hot pan. She adds more milk and brushes off more questions. Then it occurs to Dan that they might still be working on the surprise aspect.

His mind soars to la-la land. His heart pounds. He eats flat pancakes.

Bill arrives and talks to Patty. Dan keeps his distance and allows hope to charge. Audra bursts like a bouquet of yellow roses, in his thoughts.

Patty leaves. Thoughts flip, 'They're not going to let me go anywhere!'

And flop, 'Mom went to get her!'

Bill goes to the TV room in the basement. Dan follows. Bill's mouth is tighter than Patty's was. The fact that his car is still sitting in front of Bill's house is all he's able to get out of him. Dan doesn't mention Audra. He doesn't want to force more lies.

Time and again, Dan thinks he hears a car coming into the driveway and races up the stairs while Bill sits and watches TV. The false alarms force Dan back to his seat.

He walks up the stairs at the next sound. Suspense kills him. Another false alarm. Minutes turn to hours. No answer at the Lucker brothers all morning.

He forces himself to sit instead of jumping at every noise. Nothing on TV holds his attention. He goes up to his room and comes back down.

It's real this time! Dan tries to remain seated while the car pulls up the limestone driveway. It's impossible. He takes the steps two at a time. His heart races when he sees Patty's car and stops abruptly when he sees she's alone.

She takes her time coming in. Dan's ready to swoop for a clue. He opens the door but holds back. Patty moves slightly slower than the thick batter.
Finally she asks, "How would you like to take a vacation?"

Dan's heart jumps to the O-ZONE - 'They're going to send us on a honeymoon!'
"Where to," he asks.

"They said you could rest and relax at the Mental Health Center."

Dan's heart falls to the H-ZONE. "They? Mental Health Center?"

"The people at the Mental Health Center, they're so friendly."

"I don't need that kind of vacation." 'They're not going to let me see her,' sinks in. His heart sinks to the sub C-ZONE.

"It's really nice."

"I've seen it and it's not that nice. Besides, I need to start writing."

"You can write there."

"I need my books."

"You can take them with you."

'I sure as hell don't need to be confined', he thinks as he tries to side step. "I agreed to go to the hospital for a night, then the MHC. Now you want me to take a vacation there?" The turn of events sends him pacing back and forth.

"Audra might come to see you."

Niagara roars

The magic carrot dangles like a siren luring a sailor to the rocks. The winds of caution wail. Hope charges. His lovelorn brain ponders askew. His mind jumps to the T-ZONE, where fantasy's become reality. "OK," he says.

The hunk of iron moves toward Earth with remnants of the comet.

The staff member who shows Dan to his room and orients him to the routine of the glass cage was a freshman on the wrestling team, like Doug Lucker. It calms Dan's fears about being in a locked facility. The walls close in when Stan leaves the room.

Dan glides down to the K-ZONE and wonders why he allowed this to happen. He paces up and down the long hallway and out into the great room where most of the twenty or so inmates hang out. An attractive black girl named Linda hands him a book.

It's the Koran, the Islamic holy book. He takes it, flips through the pages like he's rifling a deck of cards, and hands it back. "What did it say," she asks.

"All growth comes from within," he answers without hesitation.

"That's right. How did you know? Have you read it?"

"No," Dan says. He's impressed that she would know and wonders about her cosmic awareness and connection. He continues, "Positive grows and negative controls. That's the number one Universal Law. Positive energy, Truth, is the invisible force that knows and grows. It's the Supreme Soul that is and always will be. It's the innate instinct of the homing pigeon, the bee, and the ant. It weaves through matter creating growth and understanding, cohesion and change. It can be seen in inspirational flashes. Truth is life and resides in every atom and cell of our body. It's God within and connects to Allah."

"How do you know all that," Linda asks.

"By reading, observing, and learning. But mostly by opening myself to what is within and understanding it. It's something everyone can see if they look beyond the superficial, cloaking effects of anti-Truth. Computers can display and compare volumes of data but only Life can create a thought."

Dan goes back to pacing the fifty foot hallway and stops every fifteen minutes to look out the locked glass door at the far end. He gazes at the equal numbers of black and silver vehicles in the parking lot. No other color is present among the thirty or so cars.

He wonders about the cosmic connection:

The TC3 Horizon that hooked him was black.

The mouse chase led him to a silver Horizon.

Hours pass. Dan sees fewer cars with each gaze but rarely sees any leave. The color balance remains equal as the number of cars in the lot dwindles.

He asks the patient who joins him, "How many cars are in that lot and what color are they?" The inmate points his finger as he counts.

"Five silver and five black," is the patient's final answer.
Dan eliminates the possibility that he's hallucinating. His feet have always been on the ground even if his head gets stuck in the clouds now and then. He's never hallucinated or heard voices, even in a drunken stupor. His physical senses have always been trustworthy. But with something this strange he had to check to make sure.

The sky fills with dark clouds and turns somber. Lightning knifes through the air followed by long and loud rumbles of thunder. Linda tells him, "God's angry."
Dan doesn't disagree. Ear splitting thunder is the reply.

The cars continue to magically disappear until one black, one silver, and a white car remain. It's the first white vehicle Dan sees. It's the last to leave that night.

Joseph and Mary molecules round the Arctic bend, some go under.

He calls Audra from the pay phone in the lobby when no one is around. Wouldn't matter since most are entrenched in their own worlds but that's the way Dan is. It takes all his attention to talk to her. When it comes to love he's as shy as a hermit crab. If he was telemarketing, he could talk to strangers non-stop in a room full of people.

The second time he calls, she asks, "Why are you calling me?"

"To make sure you're okay," he replies.

"Well believe you me," she blasts in stormy defiance, "I'll always be okay."
The phone slams. Medication clouds; thoughts swirl into despair.
He decides to wait til he's free of his glass caged existence.

Water plunges over Niagara.

The rest of his vacation becomes a dull existence punctuated with a few interesting moments. The patients or inmates as he prefers to call them are lively as wet spaghetti. Once in awhile, one gets into a tiff with staff about medication. Most gulp like guppies. Many flop in the great room and watch TV or listen to the stereo. Some play table tennis or cards. A few walk the hallway. Dan is often one of them.

Patient rooms and the great room are framed with steel and glass and look out to grass and trees. Patients with privileges can roam the grass and trees when they want. Dan is relegated to the staff escorted walks. "We need to know you better."

He brought his books but can't think about writing. Not in the glass cage. Not with Audra out there and the future looking so cloudy.

Everyday a counselor takes the patients into a conference room for group therapy. They round chairs into a circle, like a wagon train, and sit facing the center. The counselor tries to open their shells with specific questions. Sometimes inmates offer insights. Most, silently hope they won't be called upon.

Dan listens and observes. When called upon, he assesses the plain and simple and is promptly berated for seeing black and white when all is grey. Dan gets the impression, 'What can a nut know? Trees,' he thinks. He learns to keep his mouth shut, sit, and wait.

Depression seems to be the most common affliction. Medications, determined by a psychiatrist who Dan only catches glimpses of, vary according to a patient's label. There are schizophrenics and manic-depressives. Some inmates hear voices.

Most seem normal and seem to like and depend upon the regular schedule. Many entered the mental health system as a safe haven, like a zoo where they feed you, house you, and separate you from predators and stress. Dan would rather be elsewhere.

His fantasy and reality cells play tug of war. The more he thinks about what he believes has happened, the more improbable it seems as medication buries memories and connections. Then he thinks about the things that are too real to dismiss.

The pendulum swings

Back

and forth.

Tick.

Tock.

Nineteen days pass.

Dan is escorted to the psychiatrist's office. Dan's seen him come and go in his platinum Mercedes with Maryland license plates. He thinks about D.C.

Chapter 11—ENAMORMENT

The sun goes east to west across the globe.

The victory of release is hollow. I amble listlessly around the house, depressed and despondent, at the point most go in. I don't complain. I'd rather be depressed outside the cage than depressed and inside. Freedom is my most coveted possession.

Each day despair increases. I've been out three days. The psycho allotropic drug bathes my brain in an intoxicating stupor and submerges memories. I quit taking it.

"I can't believe Audra was never interested," I tell Patty.

"Maybe you could call Detective Holman. Shasta says he's Audra's father."

"Shasta!" I step back. "How would she know?"

"Oh...She heard it from someone that works downtown."

If nothing happened like everyone claims then why is it the talk of town?

My heart sparks. Doors unlock. Gates crack. My Cosmo Bank opens.

Patty goes to her bedroom and emerges with a piece of paper. "Audra wanted me to give this to you." It's the handwritten personal letter I left with the book intro.

Fuel pours on the spark. Flames erupt. Hope takes charge.

Enamorment takes command. Mystery controls. I dial the phone number.

"Detective Holman please."

"He's gone for the day," the unfamiliar voice responds. "He'll be back at 8 A.M."

The solar wind flares around the meteor and burns comet fragments.

"So you're the guy that's been harassing my daughter."

"I'm not harassing her!"

"That's not what she says."

"I haven't seen her in a month."

"You called her."

"That was over two weeks ago."

"Look, I have to go out now," the sergeant says.

"I'll be back after three o'clock if you want to call back.

My heart jumps a notch and sings softly. Flames glow to embers.

I hop in my Nova for a meditation cruise.

Radio station WXTC hypes 'Paradise Rising". It's a three day event that culminates in a battle of the bands at the Sports Arena. The O-ZONE opens.

I think about the synchronistic links: Joseph and Mary, secret of the universe, Martin Luther King, 2000 in twenty years. Do they think something is going to happen, I wonder.

TICK

Can't be. TOCK.

The Battle for Reality begins. My brain starts to unfold. The L-ZONE charges. Clues resurface from the night of the chase. Hope and confidence grow.
Concern controls. Only one way to settle this, I think.

Is detective Holman in?

"What's your name," the lady asks.

"Dan Murphy."

She makes a call.

"If you'd like to have a seat, the sergeant will be with you shortly."

My palms are clammy, cells vibrate with nervous chatter.

The sergeant stands in the doorway. He's a half head taller than me at six-foot-six and ruggedly handsome with a white shirt and grey slacks. Punctuating his chest is a burgundy tie with royal blue rings fading into themselves, like starships jetting to the future. A leather harness grips his body and cradles a cannon above his left hip.

I wonder if he's really Audra's dad or part of a clandestine plan. Thoughts of the cannon in action, myself in cuffs, or on the floor with blood oozing, are blocked.
I follow him down the hall and into a room. I don't like the closed in feeling.

The detective closes the door, sits behind the desk, faces me, and leans forward.
"I want you to quit harassing my daughter," he says with force and fervor.

I'm undeterred and unafraid. "I'm not," is my response.

The sergeant's face erupts in a scowl. "She's not interested in you," he says, his determined black eyes piercing my steel blue. I stand fast.

"I don't believe it," I say with conviction. "She has to tell me."

Sergeant Holman's face turns to a quizzical question. "What makes you so sure?"

"I left a typewritten and a handwritten letter on her desk with a note on top of the letters and under a paperweight that said the handwritten was hers to keep but I wanted the typewritten original back. My mother gave me a copy of the typewritten letter and then, three weeks later she gave me this." I pass the handwritten personal letter to him.

He reads it and passes it back. The light goes on. He leans back to ponder.
He looks at me, tone changing to open, and says, "Friends call me Satch." He pauses, tone changing to friendly, and says, "You know there's a restraining order on you."

"That's why I came to see you."

"Audra is very intelligent."

"I could tell."

"Likes attract each other." I don't disagree. We hit it off and talk about nothing.

Ten minutes later we walk out to the reception area.
"I'll tell Audra you said hi," he says. "Call me if you need anything."

I float to the Nova. Whoopity doo dah sails through my mind.
I didn't ask the obvious question. Satch is black. Audra's white.

The comment about the restraining order was more caution than warning. I meander along analyzing the situation. My mind jumps back and forth. My body gets closer and closer.

I view the video on the kaleidoscope in my mind: Coney King, snow blower, defensive comment about man on radio being her boyfriend, phone slams, the chase. Thoughts lock in the L-ZONE. I meander closer to the dealership. It takes two hours to make the fifteen minute drive.

My subjective analysis and conclusion pushes. Love pulls. I make a few laps around the mall to muster courage, drive across to the dealership, park in front, and walk in. The snow blower door is on my right, the black Horizon door on my left. A white TC3 Horizon sits in the center of the showroom!

A familiar man comes toward me from the right. Smaller in stature and height than me, he whispers, "She's behind the counter," as he passes. Behind him is a portable two foot by five foot counter that stands four feet tall and sits right smack on the spot I was standing when the snow blower spectacle pulled me out the door and Raphael drew me to Audra, seven weeks ago. Satch called her, I imagine.

I move around the silver Dodge that blocks the backside of the counter and advance on the front side. The two men standing at the front of the counter look apprehensive as I approach. One man steps forward and raises his hand like a traffic cop. "Stop or we'll call the police."

I pause. "They already know," I say. I've spent too much time building my courage to back down now. They step aside as I continue toward the counter.

I lean over the counter and gaze into Audra's nervous eyes. A potato chip dangles between her hand and mouth. The bag's in her other hand.

"I love you," I say. She stays in her crouched position. I'm uncertain what the look in her eyes is saying.

I look around. One of the men is talking on the phone. I did what I came to do and can't believe I did it! My script is done so I go to my car to await the next move.

I stare through my windshield and dealership glass at an academy performance. Audra flails her arms and stomps her feet. Men jerk and dance around the showroom. Tranquility erupts. 'She's solidifying her undercover position.' Whisper man is missing.

Then it hits me. He's the guy that was wearing the snow blower that enchanting February day and the mouse driver on the night of the chase. Enamorment embeds as my love takes a quantum leap to the P-ZONE.

Ten minutes later, two officers pull up in a squad car. They talk to Audra and the others then come out to my car. "What are you doing," one asks.

"Just sitting here," I say, an amazing calm enveloping me.

"Well you just can't sit here. You're going to have to move along."

"No problem," I say as I fire the Nova. I drive off in the rust bucket. Now that I've removed all doubt of my love for her, I can leave. Enamorment blossoms.

Constant radio hype of 'Paradise Rising' fuels my belief that something larger than life is about to happen. My journey to the fantasyland of the Q-ZONE is boosted by the knowledge that prophecies tend to be self fulfilling. I don't want to believe it but the possibility is overwhelming. Ingredients of an intoxicating rocket propellant seep into my mind. I know better but I'm being swept by the wave of synchronicity.

Confident that Audra will soon be in my arms, I sleep well. She's the only thing that matters. Once we're together, I can write my book and dreams can become reality.

A new day dawns. 'Paradise Rising' enters its second day. Confidence changes to concern as I think about the number of people involved. She may have the naysayers fooled but it appears there's a portion of East Bend that thinks different.

I battle with the reality of that thought. Concern mounts with growing awareness. The situation is out of control. I don't want to spend another minute without her.

But there's a problem. There's a restraining order. They've run me off once. Except for her whisper man accomplice, she doesn't want her co-workers involved. My mind levitates between the P and Q-ZONES.

I question my assumptions. Opposing views battle throughout the day. I should call Satch.

On one hand, it's the wrong way to go. TICK

TOCK On the other, it's the only way I can.

The inner battle rages. The battle of the bands is tomorrow night!

It's four-thirty. It's been a day of fantasy, worry, and careful deliberation of what to do. I decide to make the phone call.

The sun bubbles with magnetic disturbance.

"Hello Dan. I heard you stopped by to see Audra after I talked to you yesterday." Satch smiles though the phone as he adds, "You can't be doing that."

"Yes I know. That's why I called. I need to see you."

"Well, come on down," Satch says sounding like "The Price is Right".

I curse myself for waiting so long and hope I can make it in time. Normally, it's a twenty minute drive but with rush hour, I need to move it if I'm going to make it. Three rivers and four bridges separate me from downtown. I have to choose the quickest.

I look at the options as choices narrow. I'm halfway when I'm forced to choose between the shorter, narrow route and the fast paced longer run. I catch yellow at the by-pass as I squeal around the corner. Then I notice the gas gauge.

Too late; the gas station was back at the corner. With the lights and this traffic it'd take ten minutes to get back to it, I think as I look ahead. My brain strains to think of a station that I don't have to backtrack or sidetrack to.

Anxiety swirls in my mind as my eyes bounce between road, clock, and gas. The needle hasn't budged from the peg and I still have miles to go. I'm running on hope and fumes as I sail the bridge at sixty and squeal the tight swoop to Washington at thirty. Flash, that's my Nova, hasn't gulped yet.

The tone in Satch's voice sucks me through the H and L-ZONES to the O-ZONE. My hope and belief is that Audra will be there. It becomes a fact and adds to the urgency. Her love pulls me downtown as I race time against fumes.

The sprint crawls to a stop as I catch the pack and two consecutive red lights. I'm in the right lane with the option to cut across to the gas station, two blocks over if it looks like I'll catch the next red. Flash makes the choice!

He chokes. I push him off the side and look at the traffic. I run and jump onto a crawling semi-rig; grabbing the door handle firmly and thrusting my arm and head though the open window. The driver's eyes freeze in my direction.

"You have a radio in this truck," I yell.

"Yeh."

"I need to get a message to Detective Holman at the City-County Building."

"This radio is only inter-company."

"Ohh." Desperation oozes from my face.

The nose of the truck starts lifting, jerking, and jumping as it moves forward. "I can call dispatch. They can call him on a land line," the driver offers.

"Good." The truck rumbles and lurches with the green light. "Tell him Dan Murphy ran out of gas at this location," I yell as I pull away and jump.

My brain spins in turmoil. I wonder if the message will get through as I walk to the gas station. My black hat keeps the confusion covered.

The phone at the station has been vandalized. They won't let me behind the glass to use theirs. Mulligan's Tavern is across the street. I dart through traffic.

It's five minutes to five o'clock.

The bartender's slow making change. My cells chatter with anxiety.

Chapter 12—ENCHANCEMENT

The iron chunk hurtles through Earth's wake.

"Sergeant Holman is gone for the day. You can try back at 8 A.M. tomorrow."

Dan's mind swirls in a whirlpool of indecision and worry. The choice is simple. He has to get gas in Flash. The Nova's been empty plenty but never dry.

Now he's walking, worrying, and wondering. Its five-thirty before he gets his can deposit back, parks in Mulligan's lot, and orders a beer. He's harried, like the Indonesian male mouse that forgets to eat or sleep in its frenetic mating frenzy. His brain sizzles.

He's sitting at a table in the empty bar. Three barstools are occupied. Audra consumes his mind. Worry squeezes his composure. He feels his face sagging into a lump of despair.

He's still reeling from Cora's blow, nine months earlier. Emotional ping-pong is driving him batty. His mind is tilting, his gyro has gone askew. Each dashed hope bounces the balance toward the edge of sanity.

South America sucks Africa and enlarges the Red Sea.

After worrying beyond reason Dan decides there's nothing he can do about it. If the message got through then maybe Audra will show. He has to wait and see.

He moves to the bar and orders another beer. Two phone calls come in. Dan strains for a clue. The bartender gives nothing away til he looks up at the parking lot monitor and announces, "There he is."

Dan looks too late to see so he watches the door. A grinning face comes through and walks over to him. The friendly stranger sits down beside Dan and orders a beer.

Dan's face droops like a Bassett that lost his lollipop treats. The man breaks into a bigger smile and says, "Girl problems?"

Dan surprises himself. "Yes, and I don't know what to do about it."

The friendly stranger turns to Dan with a big grin. "Housewares, luggage?"

What kind of answer is that, Dan wonders. 'Who is this guy? Where do I know him from? He looks so familiar!'

Beer and anxiety send Dan to the men's room. He eyes the pine woodwork of the small room as he relieves himself. He hears banging against the pine door.

The one-by-six pine slat door won't open. "It'll just take a minute to get these beer cases moved," floats through.

Funny time to be moving beer cases and blocking the door, Dan thinks. He stands in the confinement, grades the craftsmanship of the tongue and groove design, and wonders why it's taking so long. Claustrophobia is light.

The door opens, a patron waits. Dan walks back to the bar and orders another beer. He'll nurse it and hope Audra shows before it's gone. It's six thirty.

The familiar face spouts a pirate's grin and says, "Gotta go."

The Earth spins from west to east.

Dan's gut kicks him. The air is quiet. Audra flashes.

"Do you know Audra Diamante," he asks the bartender. "She sells cars at East Bend Chrysler and went to North Side."

"Naw. Can't say that I do." A pause later and an octave higher he cements the act with, "What's she look like," as his face turns to a quizzical knowing.

"She's tall and slender with brown, wavy locks bouncing off her shoulders. She's beautiful," Dan sighs as his face sags to futility.

"Yes she is," floats down the bar.

Dan perks and turns to the patron on the other side of the pirate's stool. "Do you know her?"

The patron turns forward and stares as the bartender frowns and scurries away.

Dan's instincts key and his eyes focus internally while he searches for external clues. His mind and body charge. He spins on his stool and stands up. He adjusts his black hat and looks around. Tables are still empty. Four tables over is a dance floor.

To the right is an elevated bandstand. The lights are off. There's a small portable bar, similar to the one at the dealership, by the wall on the far side of the dance floor. A bigger group of tables are spread on the left side of the floor.

Dan looks around, letting his instincts focus and moves towards the dance floor, surveying his surroundings as he goes. He walks across the floor to the darkness hovering around the portable bar. He stops three feet short and listens before moving closer. He steps forward, puts his hands on the bar, leans over, and peers into the darkened void.

"Audra," he asks in a quizzical hush.

"Yes," wafts out of the darkness in a whisper.

Dan's heart spikes. 'Oh my God' hits him. He reels back a step. Thoughts rush. To think she's here is one thing; reality, quite different. He catches his breath.

Before he can move, the bartender yells, "Hey. Get away from there."

Dan freezes. He's one step from heaven. The bartender glares.

Dan second guesses. 'Did I really hear yes?' Thoughts jumble. He side steps to a table and sits to survey the spot. His heart beats like a drum. His stomach turns. He was so close.

'Why did the barkeep wait five minutes before he said something?'

Dan ponders reality and plays back the video in his mind. The step back altered the pathway. Then the bartender's yell distorted it and splintered the filing sequence. He hears yes but he's not positive. He concentrates harder. Too much interference!

For now, he's stuck on the sideline, wishing he'd followed through on his instinct. He walks to the bar for another beer while keeping an eye on the dark portable. Back at a table, his stomach twists.

The band comes in and sets up. People start filtering in. He can see that he blew it again. She wanted to walk up behind him and tap his shoulder. Now he has to wait. Something he hates almost as much as surprises, especially when his heart is fluttering.

Authority held him off. He can't barge up there now. It's doubtful she'll move. She probably feels like she did when she clasped her mouth. She's afraid.

The bartender killed Dan's initiative. His stomach twists tighter. His wallet's too thin and stomach too tormented for any more liquid courage. He's out of smokes.

He has to get out of there. He can't leave Audra. He can't go to her. He can't sit. He hates the predicament.

He goes outside for fresh air and curses himself for cowardice.

A car pulls up to the stoplight.

"Linda," Dan shouts.

"Hey Dan. What are you doing here?"

"Waiting for Audra."

"Still waiting for that girl?" Linda says as she shakes her pretty head and tsks her tongue. "You should forget about her."

"Got an extra cigarette," he asks.

She hands him her freshly lit smoke. They talk. "The patients miss you," she says as the light turns green. She's back to work but staying at the MHC.

Hope drags him back inside. He sits there for awhile and realizes the futility of it. He knows the bartender whisked her to a less cramped spot the minute he walked out. Who knows what his intentions are. She'd be in his arms if it wasn't for him.

Rays from the golden god glance off the Northern Hemisphere.

Dan chastises himself as he drives away. If only he would've followed his instincts and not let the bartender thwart him. More torture is his penalty.

He picks himself up by dreaming how it can be:

'The harmony of their bonding and the infinity of their love.
Paradise rising on a golden sunset.'

The L-ZONE opens a side door to the P-ZONE. He bathes in the V-ZONE. Reality pokes its head around the corner. Lights flash. UH—OH.

Chapter 13—ENTRANCEMENT

Rays from the golden god strike the Southern Hemisphere.

The friendly stranger with the pirate grin! Five years of sliding to a corner cell in my mind and thirty pounds of weight blurred my recognition. Now it slaps me.

I know that if Ron is still married it won't stop him from forming ulterior motives. He'll use our former friendship as a launch pad for his ambitions which certainly aren't pure. His extra pounds took some good looks but he still has his friendly smile and suave manner. The manipulating SOB probably left instructions to call if anything went wrong. I can only hope that Audra can resist his wily charms.

Glaciers scrape across the Canadian Shield.

The gold sun peeks through silver threads in a scarlet sky. Disappointment shorts me. Linda sparks me. I fire Flash, my Nova, and head for the Mental Health Center.

Don't know why I didn't recognize that sorry SOB when I saw him last night. He talked about wanting to work for the police department when we worked at GM. A mutual friend recently told me that Ron was trying to get his foot in the door by doing some undercover work. It's the undercover work that bothers me.

Daggers poke into my right brain. I know his blackmail tactics and guileless charm. I hope Audra's disappointment didn't allow this reptile access to her heart.

WXTC is harping about the final day of 'Paradise Rising' and hyping the battle of the bands at the Sports Arena tonight. The Audra file opens. The MHC submerges.

Joseph and Mary molecules sweep by England on their way to Antarctica.

My arms steer a circular, zigzag route toward East Bend Chrysler. Audra takes control. Satch's command goes underground. Fantasy takes charge. 'Paradise Rising' pulls me toward the O-ZONE. Positive grows.

I assume Satch knows about last night's debacle. I don't give it another thought. Audra rivets my attention. I float between she loves me– she loves me not.

The bartender's interference sends me on a collision course with the R-ZONE. Ron resurfaces. 'Paradise Rising' continues to antagonize me and ignites the rocket brew.

I think about cosmic synchronicity: North, positive. South, negative. My vision. The essence of life. My book. Audra. Audra. Audra.

My mind shifts polarity; brain magnetically rerouting microscopic chemicals on alternate pathways to mirror charge change. My right brain grabs command. The left grapples for control. 'Paradise Rising' charges right.

WXTC puts the pressure on. Fantasy blocks objectivity. Satch is a submerged option. Subjectivity rules my thoughts. Audra's in command. I'm losing control.

Hope builds on the questioning belief that she was at Mulligan's last night and Satch knows about it. He set it up with Ron Snider as the escort. The undercover team that waited down the street solidifies my queasy belief. Gates to the Q-ZONE unlock.

Hope hovers on a charging heart that burns with tortuous longing and need to embrace Audra. Urgency controls. Caution commands. Audra's my ground. Tunnel vision locks my focus and sends my mind soaring.

Several hours have passed since I diverted from the MHC and started the meandering route to Audra. I slip into the opposite side of the mall parking lot, circle the mall, and pass in front of East Bend Chrysler on the other side of Springdale Road. Masking tape X'es the showroom windows. I see it as a sign that she wants me to stay back; away from her nay saying co-workers.

I do a U-turn, head back past the dealership, around the mall and back again, finishing with a flurry of ovals around the inside corner of the mall, where the light flashed on the night of the chase. Then I back Flash against the street side curb, nose facing the inside corner, with East Bend Chrysler in my rear view mirror. 'Paradise Rising' holds me hostage. I shut the engine off with the radio on, sit and wait.

The yellow bulb in the blue sky peeks through gray tufts of wispy pillows and creates an impenetrable glare on the dealership glass. Trying to distinguish figures through the glaring showroom windows is impossible. My rear view mirror doubles the distance. I assume she contacts Satch.

Thirty minutes pass. I pull forward to the inside corner of the mall, where the light flashed, and against the red curb. 'Paradise Rising' is counting down. I see the dealership in my rear view mirror at double the distance from my former position.

The sizzle of rocket fuel ignites a spark and sends me higher into the stratosphere, knocking on the door of the S and T-ZONES. I stare into my rear view mirror, peripheral vision aimed forward. My focus shifts too late as I watch a statuesque figure come from my left, turn, and walk briskly into the mall, wavy brown locks cascading off the shoulders of the dark bronze raincoat, like the one Audra wears.

I'm taken back for the second day in a row. The bartender's interference robbed me of the courage I had on opening night when I brushed aside all odds and walked up to Audra, crouched behind the counter, and said "I love you." I get out of my Nova, smoke a cancer stick til the cherry licks my finger, and wait for her to come out the door.

It doesn't happen. Fifteen minutes later I go inside. Instincts hone.

Driven by hope I meander with a purpose, letting my instincts guide me through the first floor and up to the second, charge heating, trail becoming vivid, as I'm pulled through stacks of luggage to a corner of Housewares where a smiling twenty-two year old stands guard to the entrance of a small photo studio.

My right brain is in command. My left is partially blocked by the open gate to the fantasy cell. Endless possibilities control my heart.

I walk up to the kid with the suspicious grin and ask him a few questions. He doesn't volunteer any information. The back lighted grin remains.

I hesitate then walk inside. There are six chairs on my left, three to a side. To my right is a gray hallway that goes eight feet to a red brick wall and turns right. My eyes turn inward. I ponder the air.

I creep right, down the gray hall, and turn right again. Minutes pass. My black hat keeps positive ions swirling.

It's a twelve foot hall with red brick on the left. Three closed curtains punctuate silence on the right. The walls are eight foot high partitions.

My gut tells me she's in one of the dressing rooms. Which one?

Glaciers melt and recede, dragging their toe and footholds.

I turn, stand, and listen then slowly step to the left and inch my way to a decision. My hand reaches. I hear a whisper to my right. I look at the other two curtains. I don't want to scare her by ripping them open. Which one? Time stands still as I look within.

Emotions charge to capacity as my mind nears overload. It could short if she's not there. The left fights for control. I think. I ponder. I look for divine guidance to point the way, give me a clue. Some noise would help.

My heart's on red alert. The cells of my body tingle with frightful anticipation. My main spring is tightly coiled. I step on the hot coals to my right. I'm ready. I reach.

The voice sounds. "You can't be back here."

I jump and turn around. What the hell?

The kid's not smiling. He's in charge. I look back at the curtain.

Interference derails me again, seconds from knowing. If I was a lesser man, I'd sit down and cry or if bolder, I'd rip the curtains open. I do neither.

I bite my tongue, put my chin up, and walk out of the photo area. I case the joint. There's only one way out of there; I can visualize any type of construction that would allow for a hidden exit. All the walls and dimensions dovetail perfectly.

Unless there's a hole cut in the floor, I know there's none through the outside walls which I can see over the partitions, she has to come through that doorway or over the top. I need a cigarette so bad I can taste it. It's been over an hour since the sidewalk blow. But I've come this far and I'm not leaving til she accompanies me.

I meander around Housewares. A lady smiles as she passes. I do a double take.

It's my mother, twenty five years younger. She vanishes around the corner. Can this Paradise thing be real, I wonder. Rockets fire and propel me to the T-ZONE.

My body heads back to the photo booth. The nicotine devil claws me. Her pull is stronger. I'm not leaving without her!

The kid's smile smirks as he stands guard. He watches me pass. I sit on the far side of the lounge area where I can watch the door and escape routes.

A man and a boy walk in.

The boy looks to be fifteen or sixteen. The man could be his father but it doesn't look that way. They block the door and hesitantly ask some questions. I'm open.

"Mind if we have a seat," the boy asks.

"Help yourself," I say, gesturing to the three empty chairs.

They sit down. "How long have you been in love," the boy asks.

I blink and duck at the phantom surprise. Love? Where'd he get that from? "Since the first time I saw her," I reply.

The boy grins. A shrieking laugh wafts over the partition. I back peddle. "Well not exactly the first time."

Muffled tears waft in. I'm uncomfortable. I should rush to her but I can't. My love and respect are too strong and my nature too shy to charge in at this embarrassing moment—like the morning after my failed bank bid. I have to give her time to compose.

The man and boy get up and go. Anxiety builds. I pace Housewares department to ponder the next move while keeping an eye on the photo booth area.

I stand on the border of the T and U-ZONES, entranced by the reality that this is actually happening and afraid that it isn't. My fingers tremble. My mind battles with the growing uncertainty.

I'm like a high-strung race horse walking on a bed of coals. So close I can feel it. My brain balance tilts to far right. The left keeps a tenuous grip on reality.

The disappointing turn of events have me rattled for the second day in a row. Belief and facts clash. The slightest bit of tampering can push me over the edge.

Two policemen walk up. I have nothing to hide but her. I'm nervous but not afraid. I wonder if Satch has anything to do with this. I keep calm when they ask, "Do you have any ID?"

A slight fear compounds my entrancement when they continue to question me. My mind takes the back door to the P-ZONE and snakes through the R-ZONE. "Do you know Sergeant Holman," I ask.

"Yes. He's a detective downtown."

Entrancement builds as my mind ponders whether the officers are part of the plan; the whole affair has been cloaked in mystery. My mind slides toward the U-ZONE, the point of no return. I want Audra to be in my arms on a deserted island. Authority stands between me and paradise.

It's the last day, the final hours of 'Paradise Rising.' The battle of the bands is about to begin. It's the perfect ruse while Audra and I vanish in a fantasy land of bliss.

My mind slides to the edge. Thoughts charge emotional control. Cops command. Circuits are overheating. The main spring is tightening, getting ready to blow.

Surrealism surrounds me and bathes my mind in a stupor. I see a lady leave the photo area. Our eyes meet. She's the right age and has the knowing look of Audra's mother. She smiles as she passes.

Red lights flash as I add the latest to the weeks mind boggling file. Assimilation is slow, rushed, confusing. The spring unhooks. A lifeline loops from the left. Reason holds control. My right retains command. My heart charges to the edge.

"Do you want to go anywhere," the officer asks.
Authoritive intimidation opens the interference gate and blocks the left. Overload!

I can't think to say no. I can't think about anything but Audra and she's buried in the turmoil. The fact that I've honed in two days in a row, heard her, stopped both times feet from knowing, adds to the seriousness of this derailment and snaps my lifeline.

My mind boggles as I float in an ether of uncertainty. Battles between the hemispheres of my brain continue. Thoughts ripple through my rice paper house of cards, mortared with mystery. My brain reboots and dredges the day's first objective.

The summer solstice arrives in the Southern Hemispheres.

The police car sits behind my car which has been parked in red for over an hour.
No handcuffs chafe my wrists as I slide into the back seat of the cruiser.
No door handles on the inside. A screen separates me from freedom,
trapped in the man's car for the first time in my life.

My left brain regains control. I can't believe I allowed this to happen.
Disappointment grips my composure.

I think of Audra sitting alone in the booth. Tears are ready to spill. Despair rules.
My left cements control. My right has to take charge. My heart will die without hope.

Fantasy takes command. I have to believe that Satch and Audra will rescue me.
My only desire is to be grounded in her arms. Circuits jam on red overload.

Mental survival is my only option and Audra, a pleading hope.

I need her more than I've ever needed anything in my life.

And I need her now.

I cling to the hope that she'll come.
I watch my car and the mall shrink from view.

I pray in silence.

Glaciers recede in the Southern Hemisphere.

Chapter 14—ENCAGEMENT

Polar caps melt.

At the MHC, Dan talks to Mike in the same room they talked a month earlier. Dan stretches his arms in am imaginary embrace and talks about being grounded. Audra consumes his mind. He's unsure if Mike is part of the Audra-Satch plan if or it exists.

The sea rises. Rivers merge.

Fantasy and reality blur as Dan watches the scenery pass Mike's car. Silence deafens. They cross the river and pass through downtown. Hope charges.

At Lutheran Hospital, the engagement site, hope surges. Dan and Mike walk through a back entrance and around to the elevator. Thoughts of Audra's waiting embrace calm Dan in the confining space as they go up.

The door opens to a wall of disappointment; no Audra. To the right a counter wraps around some nurses and stretches fifteen feet. A hundred foot hallway parallels the nurse's station and ends in a large room at the far end. Dan wonders if Audra is there.

Mike introduces him to Fran at the counter. Across from them is a cubicle of couches and chairs occupied by half dozen people. Behind the elevator, two of the three pay phones are in use. Between the cubicle and phones a hallway perpendicular to the counter stretches eighty feet to an opaque glass cross. People wander both halls.

Fran introduces Dan to another nurse. Mike leaves. The two nurses escort Dan down the hall to the glass cross. Three-quarters of the way they go into a room on the right. On the left is a small bathroom with commode and sink. On the far side of the empty room is a four by six foot window covered by a thick mesh screen. Dull yellow coats the walls. A two-inch thick mat and a thin blanket grace the gray tile floor.

"Take your clothes off and put these pajamas on," the nurse says. Dan wonders what kind of party they're planning. He thinks they're being presumptuous.

They take his clothes and say, "Don't leave the room." They leave. He waits.

The Louisiana Delta vanishes and grows underwater.

He's been patient for over an hour, lying down, pacing around, wondering what's taking so long. 'Maybe Mike went to get her.' Hope dwindles.

He needs to find out what's going on. Out of the room and up the hall he marches. Fran is coming toward him. "Who's in charge here," he asks.

"I am," she says. "Get back in your room."

Dan does an about face and marches back with Fran on his tail. He wonders if he ruined their surprise. The door slams behind him; deadbolt thudding as he turns around. He watches through the square foot of reinforced glass as Fran walks away.

Lake Michigan washes Illinois to the Gulf of Mexico.

Concern grows as darkness dawns. The battle of the bands has begun. He has to believe she'll come. Anxiety climbs past H-LEVEL to P and beyond.

A childhood memory of being locked in a toy chest surfaces. It was terror when his left brain lost control and right took command. Panic grew, time became exponential.

Now he's in a bigger box and can't afford panic. The door's too solid. The heavy mesh screen is anchored over the window with thick lag bolts. He's at their mercy.

Dan keeps sane by believing Audra will come. Sleep's elusive. Night turns to day. Three nurses bring breakfast. They lock the door behind them and watch him eat.
Dan picks at his food and hopes for Audra. Hope fades with the thud of the deadbolt.

The Abram flows straight to the Mississippi.

Sunshine laces his face as he looks down Fairfax Street and across to a small park with a baseball diamond, swings, slides, and lots of grass and trees. Across from the park is a large supermarket. The view is a distraction that works for awhile.
Dan paces and wonders when they're going to let him out.

His wish comes true at mid morning with the slap of the deadbolt.
He waits beside the four foot door as it swings open. They tell him to stand back.

Bonnie, the blonde nurse from East Bend General, the nurse that insisted he talk to the MHC a month ago, walks in. He can't believe his eyes. Hope charges as Dan wonders how and why Bonnie switched to a completely different hospital system.
Another nurse unlocks and opens his tiny bathroom.

Bonnie takes him up the hall and around the corner. Hope sinks.
He doesn't see Audra. The thought that she may show starts to fade. It's hard to accept a concept he doesn't totally believe; can't believe! Bonnie takes him back to his room.

Dan sinks to the mat as the deadbolt thuds. 'What have I done to deserve this,' he wonders. Their silence stirs his imagination. Bonnie adds mystique.

The New Madrid fault fractures.

A hollow clunk spills from the locked bathroom. Dan holds his breath as he edges closer to the door. He hears a light clop then another, the rustling of fabric, and water tinkling. He hears a garbled throat and a forced whisper, "Yes."

His mind flashes to Mulligan's Tavern and the wafting whisper from the darkness. He tilts his ear to the hole where an eye peep used to be. The sound of four digits tapping in split unison comes through. Tap, tap, tap, tap...Tap, tap, tap, tap...Tap, tap, tap, tap.

The Mississippi flows backward as the Gulf of Mexico floods Missouri.

Dan paces in circles, anxiety rising as he thinks about Audra being locked in his bathroom. His heart throbs, mind steams, and ears whistle. Fear and excitement collide. He starts to hyperventilate as the reality crowds his thoughts. Excitement overwhelms him.
"Keep calm. Don't get excited, don't talk," he says to the door.

If she were to say anything he might faint. He takes deep breaths.
The source of the sounds was unmistakable especially the Tap, tap, tap, tap.
He wonders if it could be some sort of spirit. The garbled sounds were like an old lady til the forced whisper reminded him of the wafting whisper at Mulligan's.
The battle between his mental hemispheres jumps to a new level.

An hour passes. He calms enough to accept her presence. She doesn't answer. No sounds come from the bathroom. Two nurses bring lunch.

Dan motions for one to open the bathroom. She silently agrees. Dan watches as keys jingle and the door swings open. He slowly walks over and looks; nothing there. He's stunned and wonders if the spirits are playing with him.

He ponders the situation as he slowly eats lunch. He wonders how she can be there and not be there. 'Did she flash away when they opened the door? Is she a spirit?'

The gates to a surreal insanity are opened and seeds are planted. Later that day a female voice wafts from the hall, "Doctor, it was wonderful. I was free like a bird." Seeds are fertilized; thoughts turn ethereal.

Audra's spirit transfers to a pigeon on the ledge of the five story wing to his right, and below him. Big males strut and whirl around the small female. She cowers.

Dan focuses 'Stay away' at the males. They leave. More come. Sometimes she appears willing to accept their advances. He concentrates harder. She cowers. They fly.

He watches the little pigeon for hours. Sometimes she flies away but comes back. Dan's left brain wonders, 'How can this be?' Here comes two more. She's caving.

Concentration intensifies. Heart commands. Charge transfers to his right brain. Shade on his left increases and alerts systems to tighten control and hold command. Reason floats to charge. The heavy mesh screen starts humming like an electric fence.

Dan looks at the bolts lagged into the wall and is careful not to touch the screen. There aren't any wires that he can see. It's possible the bolts anchor in steel. It doesn't make any sense to electrify it; he's eight stories above the ground. The hum is steady.

He slowly and carefully touches the screen. The sound stops. No vibration. He takes his hand off. The buzzing resumes then stops when he touches it again.

His thoughts focus more on the screen than the pigeons and it still hums. 'Is it some kind of magnetic field created by my thoughts?' His forehead touches the mesh; the humming stops. The more he concentrates on the pigeons, the louder the buzz.

His mind opens to unknown realizations. He can't overlook the phenomenon; his steel trap mind won't let it go. It becomes a building block in his imagination. The compartment behind the surreal gate takes on a permanent expansion.

Yelling, crying, and wailing penetrate from the adjacent cell. Dan loses count of how many times the tormented soul cries out, "Mr. Wellworth." He gets the sense that this soul is imprisoned in the wrong body. Freddy, his younger brother, permeates his thoughts.

The tormented soul is moved out and replaced by a hyperactive male who screams and slaps out a continuous drumbeat on the door and walls. Dan wonders what kind of nuts he's imprisoned with and how the tormented soul got out of lock-up so soon. The drummer is moved out and Dan remains in his isolation cell.

A female takes the drummers place. Her yells and screams seem like a game. Dan is petrified by the confinement. The female seems to relish it.

Like Columbo, the TV detective, Dan notices things that are unusual or out of place and often doesn't say anything. He mulls thoughts over and stores them in his Cosmo Bank for the analytical Spock-side to piece together. Memories may get cloudy or submerged but not forgotten. Theories incubate and propagate.

He wonders why they're keeping him locked up when others who are obviously off their rockers are released around him. He hasn't beat on the walls, kicked or hit anyone or done anything except be a model patient. Every day he asks when they'll let him out.
It's always the same answer. "You're doing better. It'll be soon."

Chapter 15—ENTHRONEMENT

Dust swirls over the Sahara and gets caught in a global current.

The deadbolt slaps open. My head buzzes with anxious uncertainty. Fear permeates my bones; claustrophobia embeds in my marrow. Emotions barricade behind logic. I'm lucky my mind isn't locked up. The encagement has drawn my psyche to the sub-basement.

Bonnie guides me up the hall. It's my first trip since Audra was locked in my bathroom. If I had a choice, I'd never set foot in that padded room again. Traumatized like an orphaned puppy, I shake, fearful of what's around the corner.

Patty and Shasta are sitting in the lounge cubicle. Mom brought clean clothes. I'm wearing the same pajamas they gave me when they took my shoes, socks, and clothes. My feet are frozen. Black wool socks warm them like a magic heater.

We talk about nothing. The pair leaves. I'm free from the dreaded room. I need a shower. I haven't had one since the last morning of 'Paradise Rising', cruel joke that turned out to be!

Memories linger. Everything I heard and thought while locked behind the cell door is alive and haunting. Bonnie shows me to the shower. It's small and scares me but not as much as my own bathroom. I avoid that hall and my room for the rest of the day.

That night the Lynyrd Skynyrd song, "Free Bird," draws me to the dayroom at the end of the other hall. Memories of Audra on the ledge haunt me. I quiver with hope and uncertainty as I look for her. Fear and loss are my reality.

A blazing fireplug of jumbled energy, jaws on fire, marches in. She just thumbed a twenty mile ride when her husband's truck broke down. The stranger was probably afraid to drop her off anywhere but here and relieved when she got out at the front door. "I wasn't going to sit there any longer. I needed to be here," is her defense.

That's my introduction to Daisy. She's the life of the party. Her motor never stops. Her philosophy diametrically opposes mine. She loves the security and serenity of the psyche ward. When life becomes too tough to deal with, she checks in for a vacation.

I say, give me all you got. If I go bonkers, leave me alone; I'll sort it out. Captivity drives me crazy.

I'm talked into a card game with Daisy and the guy that was locked next to me, the one who was drumming and beating on the door, cursing and yelling obscenities at all hours. I wonder how he got out so soon. He arrived two days after I did.

His name is Bill Compton. It's the same as my brother-in-law, Candy's husband. The inmate in the room before Bill was Freddy, same name as my brother. His cries were so vivid I could see his anguish. I lost count of the number of times he cried, "Mr. Wellworth." I'm shocked when I learn that Freddy's last name is Wellworth. It validates my premonition.

The female that said she was free as a bird was referring to hypnosis. It led to Audra on the ledge. I'm angered to think doctors are playing God with peoples minds.
It all synchronizes in the conspiracy file.

The Himalayas thrust up.

Daisy, Bill, Sam, and I play euchre at a corner table in the dayroom. Magic floats up and surrounds us. My back is to the hall. Thoughts of Audra permeate my mind. My head buzzes with anticipation. I expect her tap on my shoulder at any moment.

The thought scares me but I have to go back to my cell.
The mat has been replaced with a bed but the horror remains.
The thought of them locking the door keeps me awake.

I can't even think about using my small bathroom. I only glance for Audra as I pass. I'm leary of the confining, common bath-shower but no horror haunts it.

The Smoky's grind down.

Dr. Bowser and Dr. Koolthorpe are the reigning gods of the eighth floor.
They make their appearance for the ten o'clock therapy session. Patients lap, slurp, and jump like puppies searching for a bone. I trail the pack as they trek to the day room.

Bowser holds court, smiling and sitting on his throne, stomping on his heels and slipping into and out of his Gucci loafers, thoroughly enjoying his role as a deity to be revered. Koolthorpe is an equal god. He exudes an air of serene confidence with a Sherlock Holmes briar dangling from his lips.

Together, the twin gods dispense their wisdom to the adoring multitudes;
fifty plus patients. I sit by the door where I can see everything. Audra's appearance is a fading hope but not dead. I can't stop thinking about or looking for her.

The third ring of the circus is Dr. Waybright. A deity in the making,
he strives for ruler stratus. If he shines too bright Bowser will nonchalantly disrobe him. His Haughtiness has put in many years to reach the exalted position and wants to make sure he keeps in the proper pecking order. I see Waybright's cavalier attitude forming.

The afternoon session, is convened by lesser gods. Dr. Waybright is king of this court. Psychologists, whose stratus is below the clouds, assist him. The odds of a patient nodding off are greater in the afternoon; patients have been bouncing off walls for eight hours, less respect is commanded.

I'm told that I'm bi-polar and need to take lithium carbonate; different prognosis and medicine from the MHC. Every morning they stick a horse needle in my arm and draw vials of blood. They give me handfuls of pills to build the lithium in my blood
to clinical levels; a level normal people don't have or even come close to.
The gods rule my need for it.

Life in the nut ward becomes a dull routine. Breakfast, medication, blood draw, group therapy, lunch, medication, group therapy, crafts, dinner, medication, snack, bedtime; day after day. There are interesting moments and interesting patients.
Nurses frown when I call them inmates. Some are voluntary. Many are not.

After two weeks of polishing the halls they give me the privilege of leaving the floor and going outside for short periods and then longer. Sometimes a sweet and lovely candy-striper named Britney accompanies me. Audra pushes her away.

When I'm alone, I like to go to the park and sit on a picnic table, listen to the breeze rustle through the trees, birds chirping, and squirrels barking. Leaves are sprouting, grass is growing green. The weather is pleasant, it's peaceful and relaxing. If I have time I'll walk the five blocks to Wade Yangster's fort. As long as I don't miss a meal or therapy session I'm free to come and go. God forbid I miss medication. That's the ultimate sin.

Everyone drills me with the importance of taking my medication when I leave!
I hate the way it makes me feel and zaps my motivation. I have no choice while imprisoned.
Summer is ready to start and my captivity is about to end.
I can't wait to see Audra!

Chapter 16—ENCOURAGEMENT

A meteorite blazes though the atmosphere and punches the planet.

The yellow god pierces aqueous blue and pours bountiful rays over green corn and beans. Gray concrete cuts through brown fields and forms a network of cul-de-sacs and dead ends. A rural sub-division starts to emerge. It's been years in planning and approval and is Joe Matlock's newest project.

I drive my black van into the emerging development. I cashed Flash, my Nova, for an Econoline in decent condition. Straight ahead the concrete turns to stone, dirt, and then a hole in the woods. On my left six concrete slabs on raised pads are scattered in the maze of gray and brown. Truck sized stacks of lumber sit by two of them.

I hear Pop-Pop-pop on the main road. Wade and Tom drive up in my old Nova. Tom cleaned her up, jacked the rear, and put a pair of cherry bomb mufflers on.
He's Flashes proud owner and the first of this year's crop of helpers.

It's been seven months since Wade and I finished the last house and four months since I met Audra. Over two years since I was scalped in Texas and narrowly escaped death. Sheba died nine months ago. They hooked my brand new truck shortly before that. Cora hooked me to Indiana and submerged me a month before the truck hook.
The last couple years have been a slice of hell but I'm still standing, barely.

Lithium saturates my body with languor and saps my motivation. Seven weeks of popping pills have turned me to a zombie. I don't feel like working but know I have to.

Everything and everyone tells me I have to forget about Audra. I can't but as far as everyone knows, I have. She's submerged in a corner of the K-ZONE.

A huge comet enters the solar system.

I read the blueprints and call numbers to Wade and Tom. They measure and mark the slab and stretch chalk line between the marks. I snap red lines on the gray concrete; square, perpendicular, and parallel. We snap some forty-five degree lines.

I give Wade a list of corners, headers, and channels to build and then start spreading, cutting, drilling, and detailing green plates and white plates for wall construction. Tom sorts, spreads, and restacks the lumber pile and helps Wade.
We take a break.

So far I'm doing Okay; sluggish but the discipline and energy of starting a new house make it easier to keep Audra submerged. I cringe when Tom talks about being locked in a basement when he was growing up. Haunting memories surface.

Wade and Tom start spreading studs and framing walls. My mind is lethargic and dull but I manage to plate, detail, and cut cripples faster than they can get the walls up.
By the end of the day we have a good start on the two-thousand-foot single story.

The grind starts. The next day we finish framing walls and plumb, line, and brace the emerging ranch style house. The medicine drags and disappointment creeps.
I have trouble keeping focused. I push Audra back and push on.

Wade and Tom cover the house with plywood and building board. I mark joist and rafter lay out. Motivation becomes harder to find. The exceptionally warm and humid weather adds to my lethargy and prompts more breaks.

Tom goes for soda pop. Wade gives me pep talks. Audra stays hidden.

An Amish crew of seven led by two brothers, starts framing the house next to us. They're Joe Matlock's number one crew. The number two crew spends most of their time on Joe's duplex project on the other side of town. My crew is first in line for layoff.

The Amish way of life is nineteenth century on the farm but on the job they're twenty-first century equipped. Their religion prohibits them from owning or driving motor vehicles but they can ride in them. They hire non-Amish drivers with modern vehicles to transport them and their tools to destinations where horse and buggy travel is impractical. The driver is an essential part of this Amish crew; he works with them.

Wade and Tom spread and nail ceiling joists. I cut and spread rafters.
Time drags. We stack the rafters to form the roof.

I hate the way the lithium affects my motivation and performance. Disappointment over the near misses with Audra adds to the zombie effect.
I'm ready to give up. Tom keeps popping and Wade keeps pepping.
I don't feel like going on.

I ask the Sam, the elder Amish, if he wants to finish my house. He's too busy.
I clank the gate on Audra and concentrate on the task at hand.

I stop taking the medicine. We sheet the roof, nail on composition shingles, install the metal fireplace and triple walled flue in the chimney chase, and set windows and doors.
I'm losing the zombie effect.

We trim the recessed entry with cedar and finish the front of the house with vertical siding and brick mold. When it's clean, inside and out, drops done and
holes filled, we lock the doors and head to the duplex project.
I start feeling like myself as my blood normalizes.

Joe Matlock invites me to his church. I'm introduced to the pastor, Ben Jones.
Ben was a farmer before the Lord called him to become an ordained minister.
Reverend Benjamin Jones anoints me that Sunday.

A month later, Wade and Tom take-off to do a job they promised to do while I was listening to the birds chirp and squirrels bark. The third house is not quite finished.
I can finish the odds and ends but I'll need at least one man to start another house.

Reverend Jones answered the call to serve as pastor of Joe's church when the founding minister went on a mission to Guatemala. In the three years Ben was pastor, he built his own house and shepherded construction of the new church for the growing congregation. Now the original shepherd is coming back and Ben is stepping down. He's unemployed. Our needs mesh.

My younger brother, Freddy, gets laid off from GM as gears of the Rust Belt economy grind down. Eight years seniority at GM isn't enough to hold a job. I framed his house two years ago and got hooked back by Cora. Freddy joins the crew.

By the end of the summer I'm back in stride but not enough to think about my own place with the winter slowdown looming. Adam and Patty notice my reserved attitude and lack of joy. Joy is totally tucked but not dormant. Hidden roots are wedging through cracks looking for nourishment, waiting for opportunity.

Then everything changes. We run out of slabs to frame on. Freddy gets called back to GM. Ben steps into an opening left by Ralph McCoy as Joe's partner.
I'm unemployed.

Antarctic water clashes with the Australian current.

Ben calls me to clean some loose ends on Joe's nearly completed duplex project. Wade, Tom, and I framed a double unit in early summer. I work two weeks.
Clean-up is caught up. I'm unemployed again!

Cold and warm water swirl over volcanoes in the Tasman Sea.

The Amish crew is framing the final duplex. Their driver takes a leave of absence to harvest crops on his farm in Hicksville. Sam asks, "Do you want to fill in for him?"

In the mornings, I drive to Andy's farm to pick him and his son up, then over to pick up Enos, Andy's brother-in-law, and finally to Sam's farm where we load the tools and Sam and his two teenagers hop aboard. Sam and Andy alternate in the passenger seat. The rest of the crew piles in back with the tools.

Everyone has been up before dawn doing chores on their respective farms. The rest of the family smiles as they go about their chores. They wave as the smiling crew drives out. Even three-year-old Sammy is scurrying about, busy with tasks.

The Amish way of life isn't like the rest of America. Modern conveniences are shunned as they hold back the hands of time. In their homes and on their farms they don't have electricity or phones. Water is drawn with a hand pump and cows are milked the old fashioned way. Horse and buggy is the rule.

If it's fancy, it ain't allowed. Dress is plain black, grey, brown, or blue. Buttons and zippers are too new fangled. They have a hook and loop system that serves fine. A few Amish own steam-powered, steel-wheeled tractors. Most farm implements are small and pulled by teams of horses. Change in the clan is resisted with a vengeance.

The exception is when they're away from the farm. Community-standards vary between the different pockets of Amish across the country. This crew is outfitted with compressor, nail guns, and saws that are the envy of non-Amish.

The three boys, Jake, Jonas, and David take a liking to me and call me Grizzly. A week after I start, Enos takes off to harvest crops. Sam and Andy start trading off days to tend their harvest. Another week and they both take off. Sam sends his third oldest to help the dwindling crew. Peter's thirteen, eager to learn and help out. Jake is the oldest at sixteen. Jonas and David are fifteen. I'm in charge of the teenage crew.

We're in the middle of framing a twenty-five-hundred square foot, story and a half when I'm left with four boys to finish it. The first floor is framed and second floor sheeted. We erect scaffolding to reach the ridge, fourteen feet above the floor, build walls and dormers, stack the rafters, and sheet the roof. We're ready for roof shingles.

Ben shows up as the scissor-truck is maneuvering into position.
The flat bed raises five tons of felt, stone, and tar composition shingles,
packed in ninety pound bundles. It clears the redwood fascia by three inches,
and stops parallel and level with the roof edge.

I've already carried a dozen bundles up the incline when Jake and Peter chide me to carry three bundles; two-hundred-seventy pounds. I'm six feet tall; two-hundred pounds of bone, muscle, and hair and two bundles is hard enough. The cheering begins.
They're a great bunch to work with so I agree. The chorus erupts.

I place the first bundle on my shoulder and Ben helps the boys put the other two on top. So far, so good. I think about almost five hundred pounds of weight punching a hole in the half-inch plywood. I thank God for my size thirteen's and hope I don't step on a soft spot. Its thirty feet to the top of the half pitch roof, almost a thirty degree incline.

With the center of gravity above my head I have to watch my balance or everything goes down. I take the first step off the truck. The plywood sags.

I keep going, feeling for solid ground. Black felt covers the nail pattern. I feel the two by six rafters bow as I trudge, step after creaking step. Half way up I misjudge rafter placement on my crosswalk to the top. The plywood buckles and splinters.

Two-hundred-seventy pounds becomes a thousand. I keep going, spurred by the cheering section's growing chants, "Come on Grizzly. You can do it."

Ben jumps in and adds to the excitement. My legs are burning, starting to vulcanize. Can't stop now, only five feet to go. "Come on Grizzly."

Encouragement is unabated. My legs are ready to buckle as I take the last couple steps become rubbery. The cheering section holds them up. I make it to the top.

They unload the top two bundles. I set the third down and collapse on top of the pile amidst howls of victory. I rest for a minute then help unload the rest of the truck.
On the way home, we sing along with the country songs on the radio.

Tasman Sea volcanoes harbor life thought to have died with dinosaurs.

The harvest is over and the crew is back to full strength with their regular driver.
"We don't need you to pick us up anymore but we'd like for you to stay on," Sam offers.

"You don't need me and work will be slow for you soon enough," I say.

Idle time spreads fertilizer.

Audra's roots start reaching for the surface.

Growth becomes harder to control.

Chapter 17—ENCLANMENT

Polar ice creaks and cracks.

In the weeks preceding Thanksgiving and Christmas Dan helps with the annual turkey harvest at Luke's homestead. In between he does odd jobs and visit friends around town. Wade's fort and Leroy's clubhouse are common destinations.

The black hole explodes with compressed energy.

Six months of submerged growth; roots multiplying, spreading, shooting, sprouting, creeping, crawling, forming an internal web of triangles with binary connections like the one Dan imagines in the external world. The tap root wedges into his Cosmo Bank, shoots deep, and entwines in a garden of mystique and mystery. The obsession consumes him.

Free time allows him to fertilize the L-ZONE. Audra fills it with a bouquet of possibilities; an exotic bloom showered with anticipation and nourished by a tap root to the OZ-ZONE. The Rust Belt grinds to a halt.

He sold his Ohio property on land contract and set up an automatic payment account for his mortgage. The difference between the land contract and mortgage accumulates as emergency cash. No worry as long as the buyer makes payments.

The Abram splits for Niagara Falls and the Gulf of Mexico.

Dan's alter thoughts shoot to California. He's had a month to think about and prepare for it. If this attempt to connect with Audra fails, he's gone.

It's Christmas Eve. He's been thinking about it and it's time to connect. When he gets the nerve to dial the number, someone walks in. Time runs out.

The next day he keeps to himself as much as possible to concentrate his focus, build courage, and wait for a quiet opportunity. The new decade and anniversary of his vision are around the corner. It's dark when opportunity knocks.

His fingers tremble and his voice is weak. Constant mental rehearsals aren't enough. He tries not to think about the last time he tried this. "Hello, Audra?"

"No. This is Rebecca."

The voice is pleasant enough and has a familiar ring but it isn't Audra.
Dan thinks about Leroy's friend, Rachel. His Cosmo Bank rings bells.

Friendly familiarity draws Dan into conversation. His suspicions solidify when Rebecca says she's married. He wonders where her husband is while she chats with this stranger on Christmas night. She denies knowing Audra but seems eager to talk.

"I work at Control Data Systems on Springdale Road. Do you know where that is?"

Dan looks into his cryptic cell. East Bend Chrysler is on Springdale Road.
"Why don't we meet at Acme Restaurant on Saturday morning," he asks, hoping for Audra.

"I have to work," Rebecca responds. "How about the following Saturday?"

"OK, Saturday," Dan flips the calendar, "the fifth of January, at ten A.M."

"That works for me," she says.

"I'll be wearing a black felt hat and burgundy leather jacket."

"I'll see you on Saturday, the fifth," she confirms.

Dan wonders if that was Rachel, if Audra will be at Acme Restaurant in eleven days or if all of this is a pipe dream. He had planned to take off for California before then but he'll wait to see what develops. He's not going to let it drag out like last time.

The Mississippi roils and churns on its journey to the delta.

Grandpa Evan was at the Murphy Christmas get together, two days earlier. Dan showed him the letter from California, on the sly. If nobody else believed in him, Grandpa Evan did. Evan was in rare form that day, the orneriest he'd been in years.

Joseph and Mary molecules head south through Lake Huron.

Two nights later Ben calls. When they worked together Dan opened the Audra file. Besides Luke, Ben's the only person to hear Audra from Dan's lips since his release at the end of May. Neither was involved in the spring weave and botched debacle.

"Can you come out to Sam's Saturday morning to help cut some firewood?"

"Sure. What time do you want me to be there," Dan asks.

"Eight o'clock."

Glaciers grow in the Northern Hemisphere.

The snow's as polarized as his thoughts Saturday morning. Quarter-inch-long rods of crystalline water dust the driveway and cars. Dan inspects the frozen rods on the vehicles and ground. They're identical and easily seen, highlighted on old snow and shiny hoods.

They reflect yin and yang like a bar magnet and look like tiny white electrons. If no two snowflakes are alike then this is their polar opposite; identical structures.

Glaciers recede in the Southern Hemisphere.

Dan notices the girls gazing out the second story windows as he drives up the long lane to Sam's farmhouse. Four girls, four years to Jake's sixteen year old twin, girls who rarely gave him a more than a side glance in the past, fill the windows facing him.

Peter and his grinning younger brother come out to greet Dan
It's five til eight. "Ben's out in the woods," Peter says.

Dan notices the girls' window hopping as the trio goes around the house and down the quarter-mile lane to the woods. They do a complete three-sixty of the second floor. The tiny rods on the ground are identical to the snow fifteen miles away.

Audra charges his brain. Like the cycles of the magnetic Abram,
his thoughts return to her. He controls the growing possibility that she's here.

"Rnn rnn rnnnnnnnnnnn," blasts from the woodlot.
Jake's smile stretches from one end of the woods to the other. "Hey Grizzly," he yells.

Ben chain-saws logs into twelve and twenty-inch lengths. Jake and Jonas toss twelve-inch chunks into the steel wheeled wagon hitched to Sam's steam powered tractor. Little Sammy sits in the driver's seat. Sam sluices hand felled logs with horses.

Three hours later, wood fills the back of Ben's pick-up and Sam's wagon.
Sam, Sammy, and Ben drive up the lane while Dan and the boys walk and sing their country

favorites. "All the gold, in California, is in the middle of a bank in Beverly Hills, in somebody else's name. So if you're dreaming ...., California's a brand new game." The lone look out at the second-story window is the youngest girl.

Ben and Dan are invited to join the family for a home cooked Amish meal. They wash at the hand pump in the summer kitchen, boys grinning from ear to ear as they show Dan the ropes. The group then goes through the regular kitchen to the drawing room. Tantalizing aromas waft from the side by side, wood burning stoves.

The drawing room is plain; three straight-back chairs punctuate the sparkling space. Dan hangs his coat on one of them. The wood floor and wainscoting gleam with polished perfection. Wood doors, five of them, transfer the wainscoting luster toward the ceiling.

Aroma beckons. Mouths water. The girls open the door to fetch the men.

The long table is set with two platters of meat and two large bowls of each of the rest of the culinary delights. Two steaming loaves of fresh baked bread sit on platters. The door to the drawing room is closed and everyone seated prior to Ben saying grace.

Steak patties from a cow, processed on the farm, are baked to a golden brown. Corn, roasted and sliced from the cob, basks in butter-laced water. Green beans simmer in succulent broth. Fresh cole slaw is grated and tossed to creamy perfection. Potatoes from the fall harvest are boiled tender and whipped with fresh milk and homemade butter.

In front of each of the thirteen place settings is a large glass of ice cold milk. Not sterile and homogenized but rich, creamy, and delicious; straight from the morning milking and chilled by the frigid air to the perfect temperature. Home cooked doesn't get any better!

Sam sits at the head of the table, Ben to his left. Dan's at the opposite end with four girls and their mother on his left and the five boys on his right. A disjointed symphony erupts as silverware strokes china plates.

The girls whisper on the drawing room side and erupt into giggles, eyes averted. Dan doesn't catch them looking his way once, not even sideways. Most of the talk is between Sam and Ben at the other end. Occasionally the boys will say something. In between bites they grin at Grizzly.

The door to the drawing room floats open. Ten seconds of silence punctuate the air as everyone freezes. The four-year-old gets up to shut the wide open door. The symphony resumes.

Silent thoughts take charge. Excitement builds. Dan keeps control.

Desert is rhubarb pie, pulled from the oven and allowed to cool with the heavenly aroma titillating olfactory anticipation. Ben thanks the Almighty for the food. Straight-back wood chairs clatter amen.

"Let's go play a game of basketball," Jake says.

Dan goes to the drawing room, puts his coat on, sticks his hand in the pocket, and feels something other than keys. He pulls his hand out and stares at the matchbook from Acme Restaurant. His mind explodes with suppressed realization.

The polarized snow, Ben's early arrival, the girls, the door;
all contribute fuel to the blazing belief he couldn't accept til now.

There were no matches in his pocket when he put his coat on the chair. He can't go looking through the house. He wonders if she'll walk through the door.

It's been over nine months since he last saw her. She's been a phantom since the day his Nova ran out of gas by Mulligan's Tavern. Petals blossom, his mind sprouts bouquets.

The Atlantic and Pacific join.

Any thoughts about playing basketball are dashed. The new evidence calls for increased vigilance. He keeps the view between the house and Ben's truck in shifting focus as he nonchalantly walks around the game. They close the sliding door. He cracks it open.

He wonders what she's so afraid of, what power exists that would compel her to pledge his friends to silence and hide behind them. Dan's eighty percent certain she's there. Not enough to be bold but more than enough to be alert.

Game ends. The boys jaw and stall. Ben's eyes turn inward. "I have to go," he says.

Dan watches him drive out. After an investigatory smoke pass, he's kept a razor focus on Ben's truck when he realized she might try to slip away after the failure to connect. Trying to think of all the possibilities consumes Dan's concentration as he balances real and imagined with a bias towards Audra. Why, is his biggest question!

He can't leave. If she's in the house, she's probably still there. He chats with the boys for a clue. "Can you give us a ride to K-Mart later today," Jonas asks as if on cue.

Dan hears a baby cry, cocks his head to it and back to Jake.

"We have kittens and calves," Jake says, smiles rippling under his straight face.

Sounded more like a lamb!

Chapter 18—ENSHROUDMENT

The monster comet heads toward Pluto.

Black asphalt fades to grey limestone as I drive into Amish country. Red creeps toward yellow in the ropy blue sky. Green free trees in brown woods cast streaky black shadows onto snow white farmland.

As I drive the fence lined lane to the rendezvous point, I notice three horse and buggy rigs hitched to the wood rail that wraps around two sides of the lone farmhouse and separates it from the barren farmyard and new barn to my right. The odds of Audra being there escalate with buggy population. My heart flutters.

An Amish boy answers the door and invites me into the plain, wood house. I follow him toward an opening on the far right and observe light dancing off the polished surfaces with my two-hundred-degree peripheral vision as we clack across the wood floor. I smell the aroma and feel the heat of hickory baking on a glowing flame. My sensors feel the heat blast as we near a four-foot opening.

My eyes bounce and then pull to the figure in the dark room on my left. Three feet short of the opening my forward momentum reverses to a flash of brilliant white encased in a cherry oval that stretches to a flattened heart. My heart does a flip-flop and head a double take to the prettiest smile I've ever seen. The dark bar, nine months earlier, flashes to central command and opens an H-Level cell of the Cosmo Bank.

The darkness illuminates with her glowing smile. Radiance flows from the straight-back wood chair. My jaw drops and hits me.

It's Mary, Jake's sixteen-year-old twin. Shocked and too stunned to say anything, I follow the vanished boy into the kitchen where Jake and Jonas are gathered with three boys around a polished oak table and a bottle of Jack Daniels. "Grizzly," Jake yells.

Smiles stretch around the table. The oldest looks to be in his early twenties. The other two are Jake and Jonas' ages. I decline a swig of the bottle as instincts key.

Hope surges as the probability of her presence charges my brain. I joke and banter with the boys as I wonder whether she'll show herself or chicken out again. Anticipation surged when the drawing room door floated open five hours earlier.

"You ready to go," Jake asks.

I'm waiting for Audra to pop out but I can't say that. Three boys grab folding chairs and head out. I sneak a peak to see if I can spot Audra in the darkness as we pass through the living room. Mary smiles again.

The boys situate their chairs in the back of the van. Jakes grabs the navigator's seat. I'm silent while the boys chat excitedly about the forbidden journey.

I see the mouse chase sequence starting all over again. I'm powerless to stop it. The other choice scares me. What if I'm wrong?

The rendezvous at the Acme Restaurant in seven days submerges. My thoughts are on the here and now. I can feel the charge building. The timetable moves forward.

At K-Mart, I go in with the boys but my mind is still peering beyond the flash of white in the darkened room. I wished I'd done or said something when I had the chance. She probably won't be there when we get back.

I fret. I think about the conspiracy surrounding her and how she just added an inner layer to the cobweb of deceit; three way partnerships woven with binary connections into a web of illusive proportions. Concern takes charge. My mind creeps to the O-ZONE.

A horse and buggy is missing when we return an hour later, just as I suspected. As I drive home, I feel my mind float into eternal bliss. Audra and I fade into the sunset.

Trapped in an obsession that won't let me go and passionate for it's fulfillment, my mind tightens and focuses on the illusive dream. Nervousness teams with paranoia to create urgency. Enshroudment cloaks reason.

I see the progression of her game from the courthouse to here and can understand her reluctance to follow her first or second thoughts. That's always the way it is on the dark side which is why I avoid it. I'm not interested in covering tracks or second guessing.

The uncertain knowledge that I may be wrong exerts a powerful block to calling or seeing her. Even if I'm right she can always play coy and the dragnet of friends will back her. When you have a love this great and a web this tight it's easy to misstep and get caught in the tangle. Look what happened after the failed bank bid! She even had Satch fooled. The longer this charade continues the more dangerous it becomes.

If I didn't understand her dilemma, although I certainly don't understand it all, I would walk away from it. I think about leaving her in the photo booth and how I have to hang in there for her. I don't like it but it's her game and I have to trust that she's doing what she has to do to avoid a repeat of her earlier disappointments.

The next day, I visit Ben in search of clues. Direct questions aren't allowed. I don't want to force him to lie.

The visit produces no answers. Hope grows that this will be resolved soon. The suspense is grinding on my psyche. I go the homestead.

"Luke called," Patty says when I walk in the door. "He's at his Dad's farm. He wants you to call him," she adds.

Cycles of heaven go to infinity and back.

"Heh-lo," Walt answers.

"Hello Mr. Johnson," I say. "Is Luke there?"

"Hoa-ld the phone."

Silence lingers.

"Murph," Luke says. Then silence. "Say it," Luke says. More silence. Luke chides again, "Say it." Twenty more seconds of silence.

Finally I hear Brandy, Luke's girlfriend, speaking in an unprepared voice. "Hi Dan, how are you?" After a few minutes of meaningless chatter, the call concludes leaving me to wonder what that was all about. Then it hits.

I see Audra, unable to speak, passing the extension to Brandy.

I jump into my van. It's dark. It's two miles and three minutes to Walt's farm.

I'm a half-mile away when I can see the long driveway stretching to my right.
I scan up the road for tail lights. A car passes but it's not them.
If what I suspect, is true, they wouldn't hang around.

The huge comet streaks into Neptune's realm narrowly missing Pluto.

"They left right after you called," Walt says.

They must've had the motor running to skedaddle that fast.
I'm patient but these new developments tear at me. I know she's not trying
to torment me but she's sure doing a good job of it. Suspense grinds my heart.
The tantalizing tid bits of her presence rip and shred my mind.

She loves me.

She loves me not?

I don't know how much more of this I can take. If this charade doesn't end soon I'm going to have no choice but to split for California to preserve my sanity.
This all could be a dangerous illusion! No need to go crazy over it.

Chapter 19—ENGULFMENT

Pluto follows the comet into Neptune's realm.

Dan is past the gravitational pull of the planet in the P-ZONE where a plethora of plurality produces pandemonium and potential possibilities that are positively Pandoric. It's New Years Eve, the last day of the seventies. In twelve hours the eighties begin.

The K-Compartment is locked. Alter and counter corridors are closed.
The Acme rendezvous in five days is out of sight, behind a filing cabinet in D-Level.
He has to find Audra or leave the madness behind and he needs her right now!

His purpose is tightly focused. His tunnel vision sees only her.
She's the girl of his dreams. Destiny brought them together.
Fear and something dark keeps them apart.

His right brain shades left producing dark spots and loosing finger holds on reality.
Dan cracks the fantasy gate a little wider. Audra's love pulls him in.

Like the Indonesian mouse that goes for days without eating or sleeping in its frantic and frenzied search for a female in estrus, Dan is harried. The obsession consumes him.
Propagate or not, the male mouse often doesn't survive.

Hope spirals down a black void. Desperation grows, brain chemistry alters, perspective tilts, hope stirs his impulsive streak and unlocks buried emotions.
An unavoidable urgency rips and gouges his harried soul and shreds his frenzied mind.
His heart screams for Audra.

He was ready to go to California. The Christmas call changed everything.
Now, he can't go. But he can't stay here and be tormented any longer.

His mind splits.

His heart is heavy. His head hangs low. He's looking for a clue.
He calls a crisis hotline to talk to a neutral party for an answer to his dilemma.
He doesn't know what he's going to say but doing nothing is driving him crazy.

"This sounds like someone I went to school with," says the voice on the other end.

Dan's memory jogs. He remembers that his high school buddy works there.
He switches to his right covered left-brain cells and talks clandestinely.
He hints for clues, something to hold onto, a match.

"The Stars are playing tonight," Denny suggests.
"Their phone number is 539-1257 if you want to check on starting time."

Dan wonders if this is their grand plan; unveil the union before a cast of thousands.
He doesn't like the idea but it's his only clue. He's desperate; he calls.

"Stars Arena, Moose Cadieux speaking."

Moose Cadieux is the coach of the East Bend Stars, a professional hockey team.
The arena is well staffed. 'Why would Moose answer the phone?'
Dan steps back. Fertilizer pours on his theory.

His imagination implodes with 'Paradise Rising' and the conspiracy surrounding it. Hopes dash and clash. The radio promotion ended ten months earlier but the video circuit in his mind replays it in the present, like it was yesterday.

Obsession's in charge. Necessity commands. Caution controls.
Passageways to the myriad cells of his fantasy compartment are open wide.

The clear Mary dashes into the muddy Joseph to form the magnetic Abram.

Dan's skewed brain digests and analyses the mountain of sensory and imagined data. He ponders. He paces. Audra's phone number is behind the filing cabinet in D-Level with Rebecca or Rachel. Deception selectively shades his left brain.

He focuses on the present. Luke was the last person he knows to have contact with Audra. Dan jumps into his van and drives to the Johnson homestead.

"Luke's at Brandy's house," Walt tells him. That's thirty miles, cross country.

Dan relaxes and settles into friendly conversation at the large dining table.
Walt is the last person that Dan would expect to be involved in a clandestine operation.
Luke, on the other hand, likes excitement. The conversation yields no clues.

A half hour later he's headed south, calm and serene. As he drives the back road shortcut he reflects on the days since the phone call. Anxiety creeps, his mind harries.

He's on the edge. His mind floats and dangles. 'I can't stand it any longer!'
'I have to get away from here!' 'I can't leave!'

By the time he arrives at Brandy's, his mind hangs at the edge of oblivion.
His composure is torched with futility when he walks in and confronts Luke.
"Where's Audra?"

A blank expression hovers over Luke's face. His retinas expose innocence.
"I don't know," is his reply.

Dan paces in a sea of despair. Hope drains from his face.
Brandy's eyes curl with compassion and concern but her mouth says nothing.

Pacing produces the answer. He tells Luke and Brandy, "I'm going to stop at my grandparents on the way to Raphael's. If I don't see Audra by the time I get to Raphael's, I'm headed for California."

Its twenty miles across flat farmland dotted with patches of wood to Patty's parents. Most of the roads are chip and seal. Some are stone. The sky is grey, his mood black.

He doesn't want to leave Audra but he can't stand the torment any longer.
He has to put her behind him like he did Cora. A new life and new focus await him.
"California Here I Come," drowns the road noise. His mind is made up, almost.

The Abram winds west.

At the Becker homestead Dan tells his grandparents, "I'm going to Raphael's house then California. I can't find Audra and," his brows furrow, "I'm tired of her game of hide and seek. If she wants me, she can come find me."
It's the first time he mentions Audra to them.

His thoughts turn to the weather and his theory of how the minds of people affect it. He thinks about the web. "East Bend's going to be engulfed in a blizzard."

Their faces are long. Worry circles their eyes as the futility of trying to stop him permeates their faces. Like Luke, they don't deny Audra's existence. It fuels his belief. "I really wish you'd reconsider," Grandpa Tom says. Granny holds his hand.

Hope flickers. "If Audra shows, I'll stay," Dan says as he walks out the door.

The sky grows dark as he drives the thirty miles across table top farmland. V-shaped ditches, ten feet deep with drainage culverts poking every hundred feet, run precariously close to the asphalt roadway. He has a quarter-tank of gas in the Econoline and twenty dollars in his pocket. Determination and disappointment clash.

Joseph and Mary molecules dump into Michigan's sump.

"He's at the horse races in Toledo," Shari, Raphael's wife tells him. "Luke called," she adds.

"When?"

"About fifteen minutes ago. They want you to go to the Moose with them."

Bells ring. Bingo! His heart leaps. "Where's the closest gas station?"

"I don't know if the pump in Eden is still open," Shari says. "Other than that, Oakdale's the closest"

It's eight miles in the wrong direction - no time to be wasting time. Backtracking is contrary to his nature. He'll take a chance and go forward into the unknown before he'll knowingly go backward. It's a habitual trait.

His heart pumps. "The Letter," plays in his head. He decides to go for it. He calls Luke, "I'll be there in an hour and a half if I don't run out of gas. I need to run home to shower and change"

"Call me if you run into any trouble," is Luke's response.

The sky is black as he heads west.

No stars shine through.

No gas stations are open.

Chapter 20—ENVELOPMENT

Light and matter spiral into the black hole.

The van coughs and sputters. I plead. "Come on Betsy." She goes another half mile before choking in the westbound lane of lightly traveled State Road One-Nineteen. The nearest gas station is at least eight miles away.

I grind the engine, refusing to believe it won't run. She fires. I go thirty feet; then ten feet. Futility forces me to give up while there's still power in the battery

I swear to holy hell for a couple minutes. I'm so mad I hit the steering wheel once or twice. Here I am; worrying about a phantom, chasing after her, acting like a love-sick lunatic while she lolligags behind my family and friends. I've had it with her games. If she wants me she can come right here because I'm not budging.

I pace the corridors of my brain as I sit behind the wheel. A half hour passes. Three cars have passed from the east; one stopped. I sent him on.

I wonder if I should forget the whole affair. Then I think about Audra. How I can't let her down? Well she's going to have to prove she's worthy because I'm still not budging.

Ten minutes later another car stops. I tell him to get word to Luke through the Johnson Turkey Farm. Traffic from the east starts picking up. Most go around me. The few that stop, I flag on. Those that don't swerve soon enough get a flash of tail light. I lean back and brace for a rear ender if they're on a kamikaze mission. Headlights from the rear become solid.

I've never seen so much traffic on this bee-line to Tabletop USA!

Time passes. My vision clears. I see fear turn to panic in the web of love.

I'm leaving town. Audra's slipped away. 'Paradise Rising' is gone. Paranoia gains charge. Schizophrenia commands.

People spin out and lose control.

They come unglued.

POOF!

POOF—POOF.

POOF----------POOF-------------POOF.

Opposite of popcorn on a fire. POOF---POOF-POOF, POOF---POOF,POOF.

From somewhere -- To nowhere.

Black fingers start to grow in the night sky.

Then,

slowly,

people reappear.

They see other people vanishing and poof again,

adding

to
the
chain
reaction.
People poofing
in and out of existence
and creating a polarity vortex.
Intensity increases. The web of life buckles
and sucks into a hole of nothingness.

Two cars have passed from the west. The line from the east is growing. Headlights stretch to the state-line. No need to tap the brakes anymore. The steady stream swerves behind the car it's following.

Occasionally there's a break but they're fewer. We're talking New Years Eve and more farmers coming from Ohio than I knew existed. Eight o'clock at night. Headed to the vortex to nowhere! No headlights dance off my windshield only tail lights.

I see black fingers flickering across the charcoal sky as the funnel to nowhere takes shape. I see panic pumping the vortex, the cumulative sweep of mind and matter. People that form the cause become the effect. Web conspirators, proportional to their paranoia and involvement, become the first wave of mind erasure.

I think about Audra and plead for her to hurry.

I imagine how big it can be when I think about my black college chum singing, "Only the Strong Survive," as he passed me in the halls of City lock-up ten months ago while Adam and Bill tried to convince the desk sergeant to put me in a cell.

I see the paranoia of the masses, concerned citizens wanting to know why people are being sucked up, cars and all vanishing to nowhere. I see local media getting involved and adding fuel, propagating the paranoiac flow of people to the tidal wave of non-existence, fear and apprehension growing, blazing like a fire out of control.

Experts try to make sense of it.
Nobody understands it except me and I'm sitting dead in the road, waiting.

Those that don't know about or see the vortex are unaffected at first, unless they're close to a suction center - swirling fingers of nothingness that suck matter and leave truth behind. Those that can't deal with the truth, forget it. Most don't even know it happened unless someone tells them; someone away from them since anyone close would have the same recollection of nothing. That could start a new round of poofing.

They might have been puzzled when the show they were watching skips a scene or two. Many that knew a little probably had the knowledge stripped. Those at the apex of the vortex would be more resilient to erasure; embedded memory.

People flick like flashing lights on the City wide Christmas tree, polarity sucking as people poof and return. The vortex twinkles back and forth and extends its dark fingers outward. Cycles reverse and repeat til paranoia ceases to be and memory is gone.

But memory lives on. The seed exists. Not everyone was affected; fuel for the next flare up. I wonder where it will end.

My emotions freeze as I witness the terror. My fantasy cells expand, exposing more doors. My Cosmo Bank gathers seeds.

Trillions of bits blast from the galactic hole.

THE COLLAPSE OF THE WEB OF LOVE
WILL HAVE UNIMAGINABLE CONSEQUENCES
AND PROPEL DAN TO THE DEPTH OF HIS SOUL.

Two hours of watching the steady stream of inbound traffic is all I can ponder. I come to the conclusion that she isn't going to show so I get out of the Econoline and stick my thumb out. The first car pulls over.

"Can you help me push my van off the road and give me a ride to town?"

The motorist puts his flashers on and helps push the van onto the grass berm.

When I hop into the Samaritan's car I notice the campaign hat on his seat, like the one Smoky Bear wears. It doesn't register. His face does. "Nice hat," I say.

"Thanks," he says as he picks it up and puts it on the back seat. Shortly after the hat goes in back, the conversation ends. My black hat is on my head with ions swirling like the vortex to nowhere. I hover at the gate to the paranormal.

My mind is stunned, focused on my inner screen. It's too bizarre, too incredible, too unbelievable, yet too real to dismiss. The mind boggling thoughts become a swinging gate at the edge of reality; a gate to a world so immense and awesome, it scares me. It's a side gate to the rarely used ninety percent of my brain where nothing is impossible and the implausible is common.

The secret of the universe is the key to the main gate that opens to cathedrals, passageways, and cells of Immaculate Conception. It connects to all corridors and entries, providing answers and making mysteries simple. It's a universal gate of galactic proportions. It's a door to the heaven within and a universe beyond the imagination.

Audra and the conspiracy of fear opens an alter passage to an alien and mystifying world. It's a world so frightening that I have to eliminate emotions to endure it. There's nothing I can do about other peoples paranoia, only my own.

The Samaritan drops me off at a tavern at the outskirts of town. He's late for the Stars game at the Sports Arena. I order a beer. Joe Matlock's number flashes. I call it.

Joe says, "Why don't you call Ben? He's the one who anointed you."

What does anointing have to do with anything, I wonder. More fodder for Cosmo Bank files. Ben isn't home. I'm stuck in the builder's corridor. I call Ralph McCoy.

The gas ignites, polarizing and capturing heavy matter in its magnetic tether.

Ralph says, "I don't understand it. Experts can't explain it, and I don't put much faith in the doctors."

I don't ask Ralph what he's talking about. I know.
It pushes me further down the alter passage and expands my envelopment.

The passage opens to a large fantasy cell with many gates, one leading to the vortex gateway via a different route. I begin to discover that the maze of corridors and passages are interconnected; light years apart and seconds from reality.

I nurse another beer. I need to integrate the input. I call Leroy.

Leroy arrives in shell shocked silence. His face is glazed, like he's been through the vortex a few times. I feel like my shock is over and I'm stuck in an alien world.

"Can you take me downtown," I ask. I need to check something.
I can't believe what my brain is telling me. It's radically different from believing or knowing. So far reality is being confirmed.

That's the way it was ten months ago. I had the premonitions and then confirmation. Arguable confirmations that found no arguments except within myself. Like now.

Leroy's daze remains. He drives along in zombie mode.

It's ten o'clock at night on the last day of the decade and the streets are barren.
"Take me to Lutheran," I say.

Pompeii uncovers.

Leroy stands there listening to me talk to the guard although I'm not sure he's listening. He hasn't said a word. His face is void of expression.

It's the same way it is on the drive to Adam and Patty's. Leroy's driven me all over town and hasn't said more than a handful of words. Neither have I but I remember everything. He looks like he doesn't remember anything except shock.
I register it in my Cosmo Bank.

CONSPIRACY is the headline on the newspaper clipping at the homestead.
I look at it and think about it. Dad never cuts stories out of the newspaper! The conspiracy in the story is different from the one I'm thinking about but that's not the point. He never cuts stories out of the newspaper! I've lived with him over twenty years! I know the guy!

There it is. Next to the phone. In big black letters. CONSPIRACY.

I sit down and punch numbers. "Lutheran Hospital."

"Eighth floor please."

I recognize Fran's voice and ask, "Are Luke and Ben there?"

"Dan, are you OK?"

Bingo! I didn't say who I was, she hasn't heard my voice in nine months, I was already in the H-Cell of L-Block, I knew the voices that could be answering, she had to search her whole brain to match my voice and name. But most importantly, she answered a question with a question which has been happening ever since this ordeal began.

I hang up the phone to ponder.

The dual opposites of the Hemispheres go on and on and on.

"This is my last smoke," I tell Adam as I flash the smoke and crush the pack. That's a conclusion I came to while sitting on Highway One-Nineteen. When the pack's empty I was done. I'd start the eighties without the nicotine devil.

I didn't want any part of anything negative and cigarettes are as negative as it gets. They're so negative you can't get away from them. Negative feeds the vortex.

POSITIVE GROWS, NEGATIVE CONTROLS

I call the hospital a half hour later. The eighties have begun. There's rustling, hooting, and hollering, in the background. The person I'm talking to sounds like a patient. Certainly not a staff member! It all comes together.

Luke called Ben. Audra was with Ben. They arrange a transfer. Dark fingers whisk the city. Luke and Ben take her to Lutheran Hospital. She's the key to 'Paradise Rising.'

Luke and Ben vanish in amazement. Audra's put in a cell like I was, for her own protection; over her strenuous objections. I can see and feel it all happen. I'm not going near that place. She got herself in, she can get herself out.

When the staff started poofing, the nuts went wild and took over the floor. Some hid. Most were in bed. The crazies were left. Pandemonium's in charge. The staff returns to chaos.

Meanwhile, Audra's safe in her cell. She glimpses flying bodies through the glass. Order returns. I repeat my vow. I'm not going near there. She has to get herself out. She'll have fun trying to explain it to staff when they come back with amnesia.

Is Audra the queen of the exponential web?

Is Patty the alter weaver?

Is it all my imagination?

Are memories blocked? Or erased?

My Cosmo Bank fills

My mind spins.

Questions and answers,

questions and answers,

questions, questions, questions.

It can't possibly be! It has to be.

Chapter 21—ENTWINEMENT

Pluto advances deeper into Neptune's realm.

Ashen skies and silence greet Dan on the dawn of the new decade; exactly what he would expect after a night of reigning confusion. If it was bright yellow and blue he might question his thoughts more. Pewter gray meshes perfectly with his reality.

Adam's truck is gone. Patty and Emily are still sleeping. Hot coffee is in the pot.

Dan sits at the round, oak dining table, sipping a cup of beige java, thinking about the dark fingered night, wondering if his thoughts are real. He can see how it started with Grandma Becker sounding the alarm from the far side of the web, the twin fingers of panic creeping, crawling, and spreading across the triangle mesh of controlled fear til the linked web collapsed into nothingness. He understands; it makes sense.

Adam returns with bacon, eggs, and a bottle of grapefruit juice. His eyes are gray screens instead of their normal clear blue. An opaque glaze leaves them dark and depthless.

Dan wonders about a dark power, how the vortex affected minds, what else went wrong? As always he gives it quiet deliberation until he can decipher exactly what happened and how it could have. He has to be careful to find the answers.

After breakfast Adam takes Dan over to see Ben. Adam has never been to Ben's house. Dan has his dad drop him up the street. He's not giving any secrets to the dark side.

Ben doesn't have the glaze in his eyes, just sleep. They go to the partially finished basement, away from the sleeping family and talk. Dan asks no questions and Ben offers no answers.

A long distance phone number to the next county flashes on the screen in Dan's head. With Ben's permission, he calls the number. It's been six years since he last dialed it.

Nan answers. Her brother Bart is Dan's buddy from GM. Bart's been serving Uncle Sam around the globe for over ten years. He's in the Philippines now.

Dan can tell that Nan and her family, visiting her parents for the holidays, weren't caught up in the vortex and is doubly convinced when Nan states, "East Bend is a mess."

Dan's shocked response is, "I know." Reality stuns him. The call concludes. Any thoughts about the vortex being an illusion are shattered.

Ben is no help. His entreaties to the Holy Ghost send daggers of pain into Dan's scull. Dan calls Adam and waits for pick up at the drop off point.

Dan decides to distance himself and let things gel. Adam takes him to his van and puts five gallons of gas in the tank. Dan heads back to Raphael's farm in the Ohio tabletop.

The atom reveals reality.

On the way to the racetrack Dan is pensive. He wonders how Audra is handling the confinement. With the staff's amnesia he doubts they've let her out. He imagines her anger. They probably sedated her.

Attendance at the raceway is light on the first night of the eighties. Dan thinks about Audra and decides to call the hospital. There are no public phones at the track. He reasons there's nothing he can do about it anyway; he can't rescue her from a locked facility.

The universe surrounds it.

Gray clouds block the morning sun when Dan decides to head back to the city, a day and a half later. Rest on the farm gave him time to reflect. California recedes to the back of his mind. He detects no trace of the vortex.

Dan races over dry powder on the arrow straight road with a confidence that escaped him a couple days ago. His mind is open when the light flashes in his head. Understanding floods the K-Compartment of his right M-ZONE.

Serene with the mini revelation his mind jumps to the Y-ZONE. The clouds start to break up. Wisps of powder blue grow to bright sunshine.

The suns invisible tethers hold it.

Patty is sitting at the oak dining table when Dan walks in the door. For the past year Dan's been spouting about Science and Religion being the same coin with two faces. His mini revelation gives confidence to further that understanding.

Religion, on one side of the coin, knows but doesn't understand as evidenced by the huge number of beliefs and religions in the world. Science, on the other side of the coin, understands but doesn't know; undeniable proof after years of testing and experimenting is necessary for acceptance. Theories are built upon solid data and not assumptive speculation, subject to peer reviews and scrutiny from all sides - not ecumenical dogma based on faith and loose evidence imposed by a few like minded individuals or entities. Dan doesn't believe either way is right or wrong but that truth exists in everything, literally and figuratively; understanding that can only be found within.

So far, the message has fallen on deaf ears. His new insight gives hope to illumination. Dan sits down at the table.

"A man is facing an audience, his left is their right; his right their left. Their right his left and their left his right. Visualize it."

Patty's face crinkles into a puzzle. Dan can see her thinking, 'yeah so what'. His mind clicks like a computer, faster than his mouth can spit the words out.

He jumps back and forth from constantly changing viewpoints, hoping the scales will drop for her like it did for him. She listens as he gyrates between extremes, her face screwing tighter as her eye's get wider.

Dan tries to jump Patty to the experience, to force the K-ZONE gate open. She's capable of going beyond the average person's C-ZONE limit. A core polarity has to switch inside her head. The light has to come on.

"Down is up, up is down. North is positive, south negative."

Confusion reigns on her face. Bafflement crawls. She's close but the switch doesn't budge. Understandable since it took years of post-education learning and observation for Dan to be ready to grasp the concept. But that doesn't stop him from trying.

"Every thought carries with it the seed of an equal and opposite thought."

Dan looks at the big picture, details as needed. He marvels at the clarity and freedom of thought; if he could just get Patty to see it.

Comparisons become wilder; desperate.

Fear creeps into Patty's face. "Let's go see Reverend Thorn," she says.

He continues spouting. She's adamant. Dan sees nothing to gain by dragging the pastor into a conversation when he's unsure of how to convey the understanding and certainly not ready or in the right frame of mind to explain it to a man of the cloth.

They walk across the road to the clergyman's home. Dan went to school with his kids; they created a workout area in the garage. Dan's weights sit in the corner.

He's on a roll.

Audra's in a cage.

The reverend's in focus.

The huge comet named Hudson enters the realm of Uranus.

Chapter 22—ENGRAVEMENT

Galaxies spread and float through the endless vacuum.

I feel like a fool for agreeing to this insanity but as usual I was outnumbered and given no choice. Pounding my fists on Dad's dash is the most violent I've ever been. Their actions solidify my belief. Now they have both of us under lock!

I'm sitting in the great room of the glass cage in the MHC when three men in suits escort a straight-jacketed girl through the front door and stop at the wrap around counter. The suits take the straight jacket off the twenty-something woman and leave.

Barney takes the nice looking lady down apparition hall, where the black and silver cosmic car event turned white after the night of the mouse chase, ten month's earlier. My curiosity is aroused. I walk to the counter and slide across from Will who stands at the favored observation post at the head of the hallway.

"Where'd they bring her from," I ask.

"Lutheran." Will pauses then asks in a knowing tone, "Do you know Janet?"

"No." My mind triggers as I look at the deeper meaning behind Will's question. Bells of synchronicity ring as I think of Audra being detained against her will at Lutheran. My mind enters the N-ZONE as I skirt the border of reality with flashbacks to my encagement at the engagement site and the impossible soul switching I believed was happening then. The free bird on the ledge exerts a powerful draw.

Galaxies move toward the Milky Way.

I see Barney leaving a room at the end of the hall without Janet. I wait til the way is clear then sneak down the hallway to the room. I enter.

Janet is lying on a two inch mat on the floor of the room. She looks at me. Her eyes invite. Her magnetism draws me to her, on my knees, hovering over her, looking into her eyes, wondering if it happened again. Her eyes say yes.

Grabbing her pants and panties and jerking them below her knees in a swift maneuver, she commands, "Make love to me."

I freeze in my kneeling position, hovering over her. I don't doubt the possibility that soul switching happened again but I have to be certain. "Audra. Is that you?"

She looks at me, pants down, eyes pleading, her inviting body beckoning. I'm unnerved as I ponder. How can this be? How do we make it right? Why won't you answer?

She waits. I consider. Will it be cheating? Will it make the transformation permanent? My confused mind won't allow blood to flow to my lower anatomy. My heart says yes. My mind says no. My body says wait.

I remain frozen. Audra wouldn't be that blatant. It's not her body! The clock is ticking and there's too much to consider. "I can't," I say.

She pulls her pants up and runs out of the room.
I sit there stunned, unable to move.

Galaxies move away from the Milky Way.

Janet comes back with Barney. He looks at me, still sitting on my haunches, and says, "Dan, you have to leave."

I go back to the great room without saying a word. Confusion reigns. My right brain charges. My left controls. Thoughts lose command in the N-ZONE.

Janet comes down the hall and sits on the sofa. I sit next to her, shoulder to shoulder. The warmth and attraction are undeniable. Words are slow. I don't know where to start.

She hasn't answered and probably won't. Somehow the switch had to be her choice. Both parties would have to agree. What would make her do something like that?

Embarrassment from our initial encounter pushes us apart. My belief loses strength. She spends a lot of time with the doctor and drifts away.

I see an advertisement in the paper. STEAKOUT AT THE ACME. That's where I'm supposed to meet Rachel tomorrow. I can't make it.

The weak force holds mass apart.

Six days after my incarceration Adam comes in with my suit. It's the first I've seen him since he dropped me at my van on New Years Day. "Grandpa Evan died," he says.

My emotions are frozen from all that has happened in the past two weeks. Emotional neutrality is the only way to stop sensory overload from seizing my brain. I attend the wake and funeral without a tear. Surprising considering the affection I felt for Grandpa Murphy. He planted the seed and was the first to know of the revelation.

He died of a massive coronary nine days short of the first anniversary of my vision. Grandma Murphy and Uncle Max were at church when it happened. I know why he stayed home that Sunday. I was watching the same show.

The strong force holds mass together.

Five days after the funeral, two policemen in blue uniforms and silver badges come to the MHC, handcuff me, put me into the back of a paddy wagon, and transport me downtown. The van drives down a ramp. I see we're at the City-County Building through the small window in the rear door.

The van stops. The door opens.
I step out and look up at the honeycombed concrete.

They take me through a door and down a series of windowless corridors. I keep mental notes of the steps, turns, and direction changes as we walk the fluorescent halls. I'm still handcuffed. When we reach a long tunnel I determine the direction to be south which means we're going under the street to the old courthouse, where the insanity started while I waited in the pouring rain and watched black, twisted balls of torment turn orange. It's the spot that anchors the conspiracy.

New concrete gives way to old as we go through a door at the other end and up a concrete stairway. The two policemen escort me to a service elevator and up and through a section of the old courthouse that the public never sees to a small iron-bar cell. They lock the cell and leave me sitting there with handcuffs on.

I have no idea why I'm here. Anxiety is building. I managed when we were moving but sitting here by myself and no idea of what to expect is killing me. I don't know how much more I can endure. With all the security measures they're taking, they're probably going to try to pin the vortex on me and sentence me to life.

Electromagnetism surrounds mass.

Minutes become hours. My teeth grind. The walls close in. Hold it together another minute I silently repeat. The mantra manages to keep anxiety out of the X-ZONE.

Finally, a pair of brown uniforms opens the gate and takes me down the hall. They take off my handcuffs and take me through a back entrance into a courtroom. I'm placed in the witness seat next to the judge's bench. Besides the sheriffs and court staff only three other people are present in the room.

Gravity attracts mass.

My mother, Reverend Thorn, and the doctor with Maryland license plates sit on the other side of the wood railing in the grand old courtroom. They won't let me get railroaded, I think. I don't know what I'm going to say if they bring up the vortex.

The judge enters and raps the gavel.

"Reverend Alvin Thorn."

Reverend Thorn stands and gives his background and degrees. He continues, "I've been the pastor of Holy Cross Lutheran Church for twenty years and have known Dan since he was ten years old. My oldest son and he were classmates."

The judge asks, "Is he a danger to himself or others?"

"I've never known Dan to be violent but," the corners of his mouth turn up, "with his physical stature he can be intimidating."

The doctor from Maryland is next. Patty watches.

"Why should he remain in your custody," the judge asks.

"He's mentally ill and will require an extended hospital stay."

I sit on needles and wonder if the judge will throw the book at me or throw away the key. Nobody's brought up the vortex and I'm not going to. I wonder if the judge will. It doesn't matter what I say. I'm cooked before they put me on the grill.

The weak force repels contact.

"I'm ordering confinement in the Mental Health Center for a period not to exceed ninety days," the judge rules.

Not a life sentence but now that it's official, I'm a certified lunatic. Saying OK on the night of the chase got my foot in the door. Now they have a noose around my neck!

They return me to the MHC as uncivilly as they took me. Janet's gone, whisked off while I was out. Seems strange for a straitjacket case to leave that soon! I wonder.

The strong force attracts cohesion.

Intrigue follows the next day in the form of a lady named Sue. I'm immediately drawn to her mystique. My gut tells me Audra jumped from Janet to Sue. It opens a new can of worms to probe and wonder about.

I talk to Sue about Audra. She has an active interest in what I have to say. As always, I avoid asking direct questions and probe the perimeter. Her talk is cryptic.

I can almost swear that Audra is hiding in Sue's body. The fact that it could happen is not only unbelievable but impossible. Yet my conviction is strong. I think back to the day of the chase and wonder what really happened to create this kind of fear and subterfuge.

"You're going to have to go back the way you came," I say.

"You scare me," she says. "How could you know?"

Chapter 23—ENFEEBLEMENT

Cycles expand to infinity and back again.

Dan watches as skin on Sue's face constricts around pinpoint eyes. Her mouth tenses to a flat pucker. Mystery cloaks her guarded thoughts.

He follows her gaze to the frightful sight that is escorted in by three suits. The entourage stops at the wraparound counter to remove cuffs from the skinny man whose uncoordinated body bends his face to ugly. Dan observes Sue's intensity and ponders why.

During the two days Sue's been in the glass cage Dan's spent a lot of time with her. Her magnetic draw is alluring; her intrigue, captivating. She's ten years older than Dan. Her gold hair clips to a page boy and curls around her straight face. Her thin lips reveal occasional flashes of white.

Her blue eyes are deeper than they appear and have cleared since her arrival. The veil drops as she watches the sight at the counter. A cloud covers her penetrating gaze. Dan takes the clue and sits across the room to observe the forces at work.

Earth cycles around the sun in a magnetic tether.

The concept of soul switching is still hard to believe; his Cosmo Bank says it's possible. He looks at how the soul separates from the body at death as evidenced by the immediate loss of weight and energy. He's read about people who died and came back to life; how they saw their bodies lying on the table as the doctors tried to bring them back, how they traveled down a tunnel toward the light and saw people who preceded them in death. He believes that the soul never dies; it merely shifts dimensions as it cycles between life and death. Dan's never heard of it but he understands how soul switching can occur.

He thinks about the ominous song he heard in the cage ten months earlier. He hasn't heard it since. "I was walking through the halls of karma. Just the devil and me. Lord have mercy on my soul," are the lyrics he remembers.

He thinks about Mulligan's Tavern and the whisper wafting out from the darkened bar and Ron, the serpent, as her escort. Dan wonders if Ron visited her at Lutheran and used her soul switching tactic to follow her here. He thinks about the ugly uncoordinated body across the room, probably the only one Ron could trick into switching.

It's all too crazy to believe but Dan can't help wondering. He knows Ron and sees how the series of events could happen. Sue's reaction to the sight is too intense, too fearful.

The moon cycles around the Earth in a magnetic tether.

Rip and Barney, who Janet said was evil, spend a lot of time talking. Dan eavesdrops on a conversation where they're discussing weapons of mass destruction while Rip points to one of his drawings. Dan files it in the Cosmo Bank for cross-reference. Dan's assumptions firm as he listens to Sue and watches her reactions when Rip's around. Dan spends more time away from her and watches Rip move in. There's a connection but it's private and Dan isn't privy to it.

As the days go by, Sue's psyche seems to strengthen. She assumes quiet confidence. Rip's coordination takes a serious lean; he appears ready to topple over at any moment. Sue seems to glow with an inner assurance.

Dan starts to develop a lean like Rip as a weight presses down on his shoulder. It's heaviest when he sits down. The push builds for three days; power pulses.

Weight takes a geometric jump when Dan tries to stand. It hunches him when he sits and crumples him when he walks. In bed is the only place it doesn't seem to matter.

A humming sound rises in Dan's head. Sue sits in sober stillness. Rip hobbles around; Dan isn't doing much better.

Luke and friends come to visit. The weight is pressing heavy. Ants eat his pants. It's a strain to sit but he can't go bouncing up and pacing every other minute with visitors sitting at the table.

He takes a momentary leave to pace. Pressure seems to ease with movement. He has to focus to stand and walk without leaning. His legs tire. The weight presses hardest on his right shoulder. His head buzzes with an eerie hangover.

Rip's body almost contorts to the floor as he hobbles around in a comical gait. He tilts more than Dan has ever seen. Rip says, "I'll get you Dan," as he passes.

Dan wonders what made him say that. Sue sits in her spot aglow. The weight on Dan's shoulder is almost unbearable.

By the time Dan gets back to Luke and friends, it feels like he's carrying three bundles of shingles up the roof. Dan tells his three friends some of his thoughts. They shake their heads with mouths agape.

Summer solstice and winter solstice happen at the same time.

It's been cold, teens and below. None of the inmates want to go out for a walk; the staff won't let Dan go out alone however they let him out to start and warm-up his van every morning. He gave up his freedom with the condition he drive his van to the MHC. That was before his freedom was officially taken from him!

So he freezes for ten to fifteen minutes every morning while his van warms up and his fingers numb. He could easily drive off but the thought never crosses his mind. With the noose on his neck it would just prolong his incarceration when they caught him. He has no interest in extending his stay.

Ralph McCoy calls to see if Dan can go to Dayton, Ohio for a one day job. He's been in the glass cage three weeks and doesn't question the request. Surprisingly, the MHC approves it.

Dan leaves after supper to pick up materials and directions from Ralph and then to his parents house for tools and sleep. Before hitting the sack he calls Sue at the MHC. "You might want to talk to Norm in Kansas City," she says with a twinkle in her voice.

Dan reels as he looks at the implications. No one, other than Luke, knows Norm. His mind skyrockets. It's the most tangible piece of evidence since the vortex that confirms what he believes. Sue could only know about Norm through Audra and Luke. The power press was strongest when Luke was at the MHC a week ago.

Realization overwhelms him. Self defense layers melt.

"What do I do," he asks in a child's voice.

"Oh brother," she chides, "you men are all alike. Things happen and you fall apart."

Dan wonders if she's referring to Ben and Luke at the hospital. He strengthens. Realization weighs heavy on his mind and alters pathways, opening corridors and cross-connecting passages, unlocking selected cells, locking others.

The dual opposites of the hemispheres go on and on and on.

Four A.M. comes early. The temperature is ten degrees. Old Betsy fires up.

Snow blows. There are times he can barely see as he drives south on the interstate. Not much traffic to worry about in the pre-dawn just slippery concrete and steep ditches.

The trek through blinding snow is driven with Audra in command of Dan's mind and Sue's body. By the time he arrives in Dayton the wind has stopped and only occasional snowflakes float to the ground. Fresh snow gives everything a pure appearance.

Thoughts of Audra-Sue dominate his mind. He can't wait to get back. He returns to the MHC by supper.

Sue and Rip are both gone, vanished.

Dan wonders about Audra's connection to Ralph McCoy.

The job in Dayton was for a Moses Abraham.

Dan wonders how all the pieces fit.

Chapter 24--ENCLAVEMENT

The Westerlies carry Joseph and Mary molecules east.

Odd that Sue and Rip are both gone, vanished like Janet, while I was gone.
I wonder if Audra wanted to get back to her own body and Rip followed?
I wonder why they would allow a court restricted inmate to drive out of the state alone?

I'm still in the glass cage, still not able to go out alone except to warm my van.
It's been almost a month since my last cigarette; over a year since my vision.
I wonder how many survived the vortex with an intact memory of it?
As usual I have more questions than answers!

The nicotine demon has been in full arrest since Vortex Eve.
I have no cravings and no desire. People light up and it doesn't bother me.

Then a fellow patient hands me a cigarette. Cigarettes are a privileged ration in the cage and I didn't want to offend the inmate's gracious offer. I look at it and think, 'What can one smoke hurt?'

I find out with the first drag. It's like the devil reaches down my throat and says, "I got you now boy!" One drag and thousands of tiny barbs and two huge gaffs find their way to my brain, jamming the circuits, and making way for their buddies on the death squad. I can see the prince of darkness howling with insane delight.

I lose my freedom from cancer sticks. Within a week I'm back to two packs a day.
Two weeks later I'm released at the point most go in, depressed and despondent.

I don't complain because they would give more drugs to cure that effect.
I know effect is meaningless. It only cloaks the cause, which answers all questions.

I don't know what to think about Audra; nothing else matters.
The vortex and soul switching have no place in the day to day life I'm now living.
The only hope I have is that I'll make it one more day. I have limited interest in that.

I've never felt so down in all my life and seriously question whether life is worth living; my life in particular. If I survive to the next day, that's OK. It's also OK if I don't.
The Rust Belt recession drags on. My will to live is enhanced by a spark in Texas.

Rain falls on tributaries of the Joseph and Mary Rivers.

Houston is booming. Gene Gerous, my cosmic twin, is still there.
He's in charge of a wastewater treatment plant and has job security.
"As long as people eat, there will be shit to pump," is his favorite saying.
He's a master pumper and can hold you spellbound, enthralled for hours as he weaves a tale of fact and fiction. You'll think minutes went by.

Gene and I moved to Texas when America was celebrating its Bi-Centennial.
He stayed when Cora lured me back to Indiana. Then my truck was hooked,
Sheba was killed, my vision erupted, and I met Audra.

Gene and I were born three houses and twenty one days apart.
We used to sit on the ground, captivated and mesmerized by Gene's mother swaying back and forth in the swing with his little brothers and spinning stories. True tales about the neighbor who could crack a twenty-foot bull whip around a babies belly and tickle it into a burst of bubbling laughter. Vivian always had a vivid spin about that bull whip from slicing striking rattlers to jerking the legs from a charging bull. And she had plenty of other stories.

Those were the good ole days: hanging out in Sam's orchard, eating worm riddled apples, sometimes throwing them; running up and down Sam's thousand-foot runway while he dropped his Cessna over the woods to a heart fluttering stop; playing hide and seek in the cornfields and woods that surrounded our rural neighborhood of six houses on a stone road.

The clear Mary rushes into the muddy Joseph.

Asphalt changes to gravel. One curve appears after another. To the left, to the right, fishtailing, controlling, hard left, sliding on the gravel, another right, on the grass, riding the slippery shoulder, steering not responding, can't get back to road, brakes do nothing to slow me, road turns right again, wall of dirt---------

The memory belts and laces in the C-ZONE of my mind.

The Abram unites and divides the Joseph and Mary rivers.

Slumped over the console of his new truck, Dan isn't sure whether
he's dead or alive. Everything's too surreal in the blackness. He drifts away.

Blood pours from his scalp, saturates his hair, and coats his face in layers
of cranberry crimson. Sticky redness drips from his chin and piles on the floor.
Sheba yelps but Dan doesn't hear.

'I must be alive or they wouldn't be stitching my head,'
he thinks while squinting at the bright lights and feeling the tugging on his scalp.
He heaves pints of red and goes black.

He feels a floating movement and hears something about the hole in his head. Dan opens his eyes. Images blur by. Jim walks beside him. "You lost five pints of blood," he says. "You're being taken to a bigger hospital in Houston."

Dan lies on his back in the ambulance, IV stuck in his arm, wondering why they have the air conditioner on. Teeth threaten to chip with chatter. Minutes become hours.

They wheel his frozen body down a corridor and into a bright room.
He slides onto a slab of ice they call a table. His heart skips and jolts. He lies back down.

Dan gazes at the man with the surgical mask and talks to him. The plastic surgeon drapes a small towel over Dan's eyes and nose, leaving his mouth uncovered. He answers Dan's questions as he removes stitches and opens the flap on his head, cleaning tiny fragments of glass and hair, scrubbing flesh, and cauterizing boils of blood.

Dan has to lie perfectly still, flat on his back; a position he hates with claustrophobic passion. The surgeon undermines and stretches the skin on his forehead, cauterizing spurting blood vessels and sewing tiny stitches, closing the gap of missing tissue.
Hours pass.

His temperature returns to normal. His senses come alive. The hospital smell gags him. He becomes fidgety. Panic creeps. He lifts the towel to get a glimpse of something other than claustrophobia.

"Hold still," the surgeon demands.

"I can't stand lying here."

"It won't be that much longer."

Seconds tick like time bombs. Panic control fades.

"Doc, can't you give me something to keep calm," Dan pleads.

"You don't want to interfere with consciousness in a head injury," is his reply.

Dan lays there. He waits. He waits til he can wait no longer. He says, "Doc, I have to get up!"

"I'm almost done,"

"I have to get up." Dan lifts the towel from his eyes.

"Don't move."

The doctor talks to the nurse, injects a drug in Dan's arm, and leaves the room.

Dan remains still; cloth off his face. Panic subsides as the drug takes effect.

Molly White enters. She takes Dan's hand and asks," How are you doing?"

"Better; now that I have the rag off my face. How's Sheba?"

"Good. She wasn't cut and doesn't seem to have anything broken. Jim washed her in a metal basin. He dumped it twice because of the blood, your blood!"

"I bet she loved that," Dan remarks with rarely used backhand.

"You could tell she didn't like it but she tolerated it. I dried her with a big towel."

"I know she liked that."

"Yeh, it was so cute." Molly's mouth extends to a smile. "I had to wrap the towel around her and rub her dry while she jerked, twisted, and played tug of war. Then I tried to use the blow dryer."

"Ye-ah." Dan sees Sheba slink and bolt. "She shivers if she's not completely dry."

"So we played more tug of war with a dry towel. I held the middle and dried with the loose end. She's at home now, playing with Stony and the kids."

"Thanks for taking care of her."

"You have Sheba to thank. If Jim hadn't heard her howling and seen your car in the ditch you might not be here," Molly says. "We went by on the way here. It looked like you were trying to punch a hole in the embankment! Your new truck is totaled but you're alive and that's what matters." She adds, "You're going to stay with us until you're better."

Dan doesn't say anything. Jim White, his former employer, and Molly have a small ranch south of Houston with kids, dogs, cats, chickens, and pigs. Dan was heading there for the weekend when the hard steel yields and the soft ground doesn't.

"You have several friends waiting in the lounge, Molly adds.

Bill Bagby, the ambassador of good will, Dan's mentor at Bailey Building Systems, entertains the group. His native Texas accent is polished so fine you hear nothing but shine.

His bass voice sings smooth and melodic with compassionate and caring overtones on a suave and sensitive background and drumbeats of authority with a harmony you never forget. It leaves a sweet honey after taste and a silver ring in your soul

Gene later relates what Bill said while they waited.

"Daniel is like a diamond in the rough. All he needs is a little polish."

The magnetic Abram winds its way west.

That accident was two and a half years ago. Gene has an empty berth on his spaceship and an abundance of galactic destinations to explore. I head back to Texas.

Audra is submerged. Surface blooms have withered but the tap root is firmly entrenched with tentacles wrapping through the mid-section of my mind, waiting for the opportunity to surge and sprout. But first I need to find a job.

Preparation and opportunity meet when I see an ad for a manager trainee at Mainframe Homes. My qualifications fit. I'm hired in the Houston office.

Gene and I celebrate with a bottle of MD 20-20. He takes me for a space cruise. I buckle up and hang on. Gene's innate talent lies in his booming baritone voice. He can do the Lone Ranger intro better than the original radio show.

He's a walking encyclopedia that can take you to the barn, through it, out, back in, around, out, around it halfway, and back again. By the time you get where you're going, you won't know where you've been. You won't care if you go with the flow.

Chapter 25—ENDOWMENT

The Hudson Comet crosses Saturn's orbital path.

Mainframe Homes was founded thirty years ago by a returning WWII veteran with two-hundred-dollars and a borrowed pick-up truck. Abe Lincoln would probably endorse the company statement with two thumbs up. They built ten thousand houses last year.

Mainframe is divided into four divisions with two regions per division. They even have a twin company called Mainframe Finance that holds land and mortgages, and bankrolls the homebuilding giant. Money cycles back and forth.

The Houston office is a main branch with sub-branches in Trinidad, Conroe, and Wharton. It's located in the biggest floor plan Mainframe offers and fronts a model park with four models in various stages of construction. Chuck Suave and Tommy de Juan are the twin captains of an office that with the three branches builds six-hundred houses a year.

Chuck Suave's the office manger. He hired me to learn the full scope of the Mainframe system. Tommy de Juan is in charge of construction. I have to learn his job too.

Dallas has been the top producer in the company for the past three years but this year Houston is giving them a run for the money. I'm hired with two months remaining in the neck and neck race. The lead bounces back and forth every week.

Competition is fierce and is fueled by intrastate rivalry. It's good clean fun. Mainframe wouldn't have it any other way. They guarantee the company statement with a double check and balance system to keep everyone honest.

It's Saturday morning and the main branches are ready to send weekly sales and construction reports over the teletype to the home office in Jacksonville, Florida. The company president rallies the troops with opening remarks and names the current leader to start the report. Cheers will erupt in either Houston or Dallas.

This week it's Houston and I'm there to witness and be part of the eruption. But then it's back to work because Dallas will be gunning for next week. Everyone has a job to do and they're busy doing it. The top two salesman in the company are in the Houston office and weekends are prime time for customers. I get to go home at noon.

Gene and I celebrate with another bottle of MD 20-20 and a rocket ride to the future full of shit from the past. He's a laugh a second. His tales come straight from the cosmos. You never know where they're coming from or where they're going; neither does he.

He's a multi-disciplined professor with endless knowledge. If you step into his brain, you'll never find your way out. It's a universe with no beginning and no end!

Gene blasts to another dimension with talk of Dan Gerous Construction Company. He gives a running commentary about the techniques – lots of nitro and dynamite, heavy equipment as needed. He wants me to wire the charges.

Then he launches a volley of repertoire about biting the big one and a whole new universe opens up. He goes from shit to Shinola in a flash, looking me straight in the eye without blinking, and almost has me believing they're the same and with modifications can be made edible. I rock with laughter as he rolls to oblivion and back again.

Gene's motto: If you can't baffle them with brilliance, dazzle them with bullshit. He carries a microscopic drill that he uses to bore out of corners. He'll make a tunnel out of that hole to the back door. If you question him, he'll drill you down a hole so deep you won't see daylight or know where you came from. Push it and you'll be surrounded by oil.

He also has a serious side and it's dead serious. When his baritone bellows, your hair stands on end, submerges, and looks for a place to hide. Cross that half and your head gets slammed into a snack machine PDQ; the cosmic half just pretzels your mind.

Saturn's particles cycle in endless rings on its equatorial plane.

I love the job at Mainframe. It's challenging, fulfilling, and a custom fit. Someday I'll have my own office. Mainframe has a hundred of them across the South.

Chuck Suave left the rock and roll life of a Las Vegas entertainer to pursue a career with tangible gains. He started in a small sub-branch and worked up the line of sub and main branches to the stratospheric spot in Houston. Deceptively honest and exceptionally intelligent, Chuck is no nonsense and Mr. Business. His smile masks a mischievous streak.

Tommy de Juan takes a liking to me and personally shows me the construction facet of the business. He started as a framing contractor and then moved into the Little Rock office as construction supervisor and up the ladder to Houston. He's well organized, on top of sixty to seventy homes his office has under construction with help from four assistants.

Tommy keeps the main warehouse and sub-branches supplied with windows, siding, shingles, shutters, and paint for an additional sixty houses UC, under construction. Houses are built on the customer's lot; here, there, and everywhere. Two truck drivers work ten to fourteen hour days delivering finish loads to all houses going UC in the four office domain.

The Western Regional office is next to the Houston model park. I make frequent trips back and forth as I learn all aspects of the business. Thirty employees work in the complex. Sub-contractors by the dozens come and go. Customers flock there.

The highest top dog in Houston is Vince Stevens, the Western Regional Manager. He worked his way through the ranks to head the strongest region in the company. I talk to him at his going away party a month later. Words flow with the liquor. Bud Gabet, the incoming regional manager, listens. "You ain't seen nothing yet," I say. Vince heads to Nashville as Division Vice-President.

I'm sitting in Chuck's office when Vince calls a couple weeks later. Chuck says, "Just a minute," turns to me and asks, "Do you want to go to Trinidad?"

"Sure. I'm ready."

The next day, I leave old betsy at Gene's and head east on the interstate to Trinidad, in the Golden Triangle, with a new life, company car, and a new attitude. I have the bull by the horns and can whip it til shit becomes edible Shinola. I feel more alive than I've ever felt in my life. From death to resurrection and beyond in less than six months.

Joplin and Lemon Heights are the other points of the Golden Triangle bordering the bayou country of Louisiana. The ship building capital of Port Washington and the KKK stronghold of Knox add mixture to the cauldron of achievement. I'm ready to dive in.

I park my red Phoenix in the grey shell parking lot and gaze at my new home. The Trinidad office is located in a mid-size, three bedroom two bath model that fronts a three model park with a mini warehouse. I go up the steps and in the door where a reception area with desk and chairs and a secretary by the name of Andrea greets me with "I'll be leaving at the end of the week."

"But I just walked in the door can't you give me a chance to dust off my shoes?"

"I can't work for another person in this office."

"Can you give me til the end of next week? Three days is kind of soon."

"The manager before you gave no notice."

"Yeh but..."

Chapter 26—ENGROSSMENT

The Abram River splits north and south at Lake Michigan.

That's Dan's introduction to Trinidad. It's been a trouble spot for many years. Two hundred home office complaints, some years old, put it at the top of the problem list. It's close to the bottom for profit and production. The office more than a handful before now borders on impossible with Andrea's announcement.

But Dan's undaunted. He jumps in with feet and elbows flying. Then he places a Mainframe approved secretarial ad in the local newspaper and checks on the progress of the new model park which is less than half complete.

The annual inventory is due in five days. He needs to find a place to live and needs to familiarize himself with the office personnel, jobs, and crews. Andrea's departure cranks the pressure a couple notches. He quit taking medicine month's ago; can't function with it.

The southern branch flows to the Gulf Stream.

Dan swims in the work, determined to take it ten different directions at once. Applicants for secretary start calling and showing up. He interviews women virtually non-stop in Andrea's last two days and hires Suzy Stryker, a buxom blue-eyed blonde with a vivacious personality. He spends the weekend inventorying the office and warehouse and planning strategy. It's the start of twelve to sixteen hour day, thirteen day work weeks.

His territory crosses Houston, Conroe, and Jasper areas. Most jobsites are within a thirty mile radius but some will stretch a hundred miles. There are twenty-two houses under construction (UC) and twenty on hold, sold and waiting to go under construction. Many on the UC list have been going for months; they bottleneck in framing.

He puts Jake McMurty, the construction supervisor, on complaint patrol to get Jacksonville off his back and takes over his job of hiring and scheduling sub contractors. Bill Fish is the veteran salesman and can handle the sales end without any help from Dan. He's seen 'plenty of managers' come through the office. Jill Shanahan is the resident rep from Mainframe Finance, she handles her own affairs. Beth holds the second sales slot and was recently in the Houston office for two weeks of training.

Job sites are scattered all over the countryside and sub contractors often have trouble finding locations. Much of his territory is heavily wooded and many of the roads are winding and poorly marked. Dan solves the problem by visiting each location to check power and accessibility. He rewrites the directions with accurate mileage to the turns. His goal is to increase production by one house per month and eliminate all complaints within six months.

His first full month's production is five houses. Suzy masters her job. Jake whittles the complaint list down. Bill starts cranking sales now that he sees there's a man of action in the driver's seat. Beth struggles and Jill blazes in and dashes out.

The northern branch flows to the St. Lawrence Seaway.

Dan finds an efficiency close by. All the major fires are out and he has some breathing room. He writes a twenty-seven page letter to Audra and sends it via Satch.

Dan schedules plumbing, electrical, insulation, sheetrock, trim, and painting crews in addition to handling the manager's position while Jake continues to whittle the complaints. Dan hires and trains new framing crews, streamlines the building process, and increases production. He obtains permits and learns code nuances for different jurisdictions.

The regional office warned him about paying for incomplete or shabby work and he takes their warning seriously. He checks every house at least once before framing final and tells the framer, "Take an extra day to make sure everything's complete and job site's clean. I'll come for final when you tell me it's done. If it's not it will take days to reschedule and you don't get paid till I personally inspect it." He doesn't have time for goose chases. Along with the check he takes plans and directions for the next house.

The framing package comes in two loads. The first from Tanner Lumber Company includes mortar, blocks, dimension and sheet lumber. The finish package from the Houston main branch consists of lap siding, doors, windows, shutters, and composition shingles. Dan stores paint in and distributes from his mini-warehouse at the model park.

He departs from the Mainframe standard of the framer doing it all and separates the foundation from the framing contract so the carpenters don't have to fumble with it. Hal does a great job of making the pier foundations consistent, strong, and level. It's much better than the discouraging and hodge-podge masonry talents of the assorted framing crews.

Bud Gabet's been in Trinidad regularly to put the finishing touches on the model park, freeing Dan to concentrate on production. It's his first model park as Manager of the Texas Region and he wants to make a showcase of it. He oversees landscaping, sidewalks and parking lots, and purchases furnishings to decorate and enhance the new office.

Dan exceeds his goal and has eight completions the second month. He takes another step to improve efficiency and splits the finish load from the framers contract. Tommy Gunn and his crew produce a consistently better product fast enough to keep the heat on the framers to get the houses up. The behind list, waiting to go under construction, becomes smaller and Jake whittles the complaint list.

The job takes all Dan's waking hours and he loves it. For the first time in years he's making real progress. He hasn't heard from Audra.

Tommy de Juan's been promoted to assistant regional manager and comes over on weeks that Bud can't. Chuck Suave calls every morning for an update on sales, builds, and UC. Dan's office moves into the new model park three weeks ahead of the Grand Opening.

Trinidad jumps twenty spots on the profit list after the first month and another ten the next month. He's just getting warmed up when he sets his sights on Chattanooga; the perennial number one sub-branch with two-hundred builds a year.
It's getting easier as he gets the building machine oiled and rolling.
Dan looks forward to scaling back on his thirteen day weeks after Christmas.

The Grand Opening is a huge success with Chuck Suave and many of the regional managers present. Two different radio stations are on hand in staggered intervals to promote it. Dan's the pitchman and encourages the radio public to come on down for some sunshine. The parking lots and models fill with people despite early rain and cloudy skies. Clouds break and the sun shines through for his last spiel at five o'clock.

Joseph and Mary molecules join in the Atlantic Ocean.

Dan hires another painting crew and cracks the whip on the plumbing, electrical, sheetrock, and interior finish crews. Construction time on each house is cut in half. Framing crews increase to fifteen from six, counting Tommy and Hal.

Trinidad completes ten houses in the third month. Jake has the complaint list below thirty and no new ones are being generated.

Dan still hasn't heard from Audra. He plans to go back to East Bend for Christmas. It's almost been a year since his last attempt landed him on soul switch alley in lunatic heaven. This time it will be different! He hopes!

Chapter 27—ENDEARMENT

Matter blasts from the cosmic seed like rocket powered popcorn.

"Are you coming to the barbeque?" Chuck asks after the morning report.

"Wouldn't miss it," I say.

"You have the directions?"

"Take I-45 north to Champion Forest, exit right....."

"You got it," Chuck says. "See you around five."

Sally, the regional secretary, has called several times in the past two weeks. I wondered why she was so interested in my presence; Tommy de Juan is her beau. She gave me directions to Chuck's house.

I wrap things up and head to Houston by three o'clock. Christmas is three weeks away and I'm still working thirteen day weeks. I'll cut hours when I get back from Indiana. Jake should have complaints whittled to zero and be able to take a load off then.

Normally I spend every fourteenth day at Gene's launch pad. His galactic journeys propel me for another two weeks. If I need a boost in between I just call him and forget what planet I'm on as we cruise space. I won't be stopping there til after the party.

The tiny hole at the center of nowhere mushrooms to a galactic core.

The entire Houston main and regional office staff and spouses, if they have one, are there. Even the truck drivers brought their wives for the fun, games, and barbeque. Everyone is there with the exception of Tommy de Juan and Sally.

"Where's Sally," I ask Marcie, one of the three assistant regional managers.

"She won't be here."

"Oh?" My eyebrows rise.

"She has a cold."

"What about Tommy?"

"He's with Sally," she says. "He'll be coming later."

Again I wonder why she was so interested in my presence and then doesn't show. The thought slips to the H-ZONE as I enjoy the pleasant evening with temps in the sixties. Croquet and party games are followed by the barbeque. Bud flames steaks on the grill. The sky is clear and the mood is festive.

Wild Turkey filters through my veins. I feel the effects when we retire to the large living room. A stage is set at the far end for the evening entertainment. I sit in a chair next to Marcie and wait for the in-house talent to start playing. Tommy still hasn't shown up.

The lights go out. Nine hours later I open my eyes. I'm on the floor. Everyone is gone. My head buzzes with a surreal hum. The clock on the wall is fifteen minutes short of seven cuckoos. Nobody is stirring. Audra pops into my head.

I think about the MHC a year earlier when Audra took refuge in Sue's body, how her power pressed me to the ground; the reminiscent buzzing. The feeling is strong. I think, 'This is crazy. She can't be here!'

The premonition is undaunted. I can't go searching the house for her but I'm also not going to sit here and wait for everyone to get up. I let myself out the back door.

The surreal hum fades a shade. It fades further as I drive down the street and is half strength within two blocks. I turn around and head back. The buzz grows as I close in.

I've never blacked out from alcohol, no matter how much or how fast I drank. I always remembered fading away; never lights out like last night. I was wobbly but not that drunk. It was like I was drugged except I mixed my own drinks.

I do another U-turn. I still can't go looking for her. She can't be there.

By the time I hit the freeway the buzz is gone and I'm fine. The P-ZONE unlocks. Going back is out of the question but the possibility of her presence gives plenty to ponder.

I was so immersed in work that I didn't give Sally's double checks much thought. I've been looking forward to seeing Audra since I sent the letter ten weeks ago. To have her pop in like this is an unexpected surprise; she cuckooed me.

The explosion of the mass of gas unleashes the energy within.

It's on to Gene's pad for a cosmic cruise on the pantheon of the mind. It's a place where I can kick back, let my hair down, and listen to the music and cosmic chatter. Gene's an ace space ranger but I anticipate I'll be distracted on this flight!

Gene rambles on an intergalactic quest.
I take a side cruise to the L-ZONE and peek into the O.
I anticipate Monday when I can find out what happened at the party.
If Audra was there, I want to know.

Mushroomed matter catches the massive ball of gas and ignites it.

I'm in the Houston office first thing Monday. Nobody says anything or gives any kind of clue. They just joke and fill me with fictitious tales.

I tell Chuck about my plans to head home for Christmas.

"That's fine," he says. "Not much gets done that week anyway."

I pick up the branch checks and head to Trinidad.

It's probably my imagination but then I think about the reminiscent surreal buzzing, the popping premonition, the letter, the connections. Nothing I can do about it. Like it or not, it's her game. Don't know why she has to hide behind all my friends.

Then I think about Trinidad and everything I have to do in the next three weeks. The side gate closes. I'm there by noon, Audra's sequestered in a cellblock on K-Level.

It's business as usual. The hard times are behind. Three weeks pass in a flash.

The strong force reverses and grabs the heavy mushroom bit.

The Trinidad office is decked in holiday spirit the day before Christmas. Party permeates air with food and drinks. Phones are quiet except for the occasional reveler. With a dearth of incoming calls and a party out front, I concentrate on last minute details.

My luggage is in my car. I plan to hit the road by noon and make it to East Bend by midnight or before. The phone rings. It's Chuck Suave.

"You need to stay in the office til three o'clock."

"What. The phones are practically dead and I have everything shipshape. I planned to leave within the hour."

"Well you need to stay there til three o'clock."

"Chuck, what's the point?"

"You just need to be there."

"But..."

"Just be there."

I stew at the last minute interference and eat finger sandwiches as I pace. I've always done what Chuck's told me but this time he's gone to far. It's ridiculous.

Gravity and momentum pull bit from bit.

"Vince, I want a transfer to your division. I'm tired of Chuck's manipulation. He's gone too far and I want out of here."

"What's the problem Dan?"

"Chuck's known of my plans to go back to Indiana for three weeks now. He even wished me a safe trip when I gave him the morning report. Fifteen minutes ago he called and told me that I had to stay in the office til three o'clock."

"What would it hurt to stay til three?"

"Vince, I've been working twelve to sixteen hours a day, six and seven days a week ever since I came to Trinidad. It's a thirteen hour drive, twelve if I put the hammer down. It'll be three AM before I get to East Bend if I wait til three to leave."

"Dan, I've heard lots of good things about you, how you turned that office around. I don't have any openings right now. Let me talk to Chuck. I'll call you back."

Electro-magnetism and momentum push and pull.

I tell the rest of the office about the upsetting chain of events. They knew of my plans before Chuck did. They're sympathetic to my plight. It's half past eleven.

The clock strikes noon and I'm ready to go. Vince hasn't called. I call him. "Mr. Stevens is gone for the day," the secretary says. I scratch my head and pace.

Suzy says, "Why don't you just take off. We can handle whatever comes up."

Jake chimes, "If Chuck calls we'll tell him you're out in the field."

"Good idea, I'll check those two houses in Jennings, Louisiana. They're on the way."

The mass of gas suspends bits of the bit
to angular momentum and orbit in elastic tethers.

I'm only an hour behind schedule when I pass through Baton Rouge. Thunder booms. A sharp and prolonged jab of pain enters my head and slowly grinds to vice melding pressure.

Chapter 28—ENSNAREMENT

The Hudson comet enters Jupiter's realm.

"Did you receive the letter I sent for Audra, three months ago?"

"You mean that book," Satch says with a smile.

"It was only twenty seven pages."

"That small envelope looked like a paperback in the big envelope. She was back here about that time and yes, I gave it to her."

"She doesn't live here anymore?"

"No Dan, she moved out West," the story begins.

Dan wonders where this is leading. "Why'd she move out West?"

"She wanted to be closer to her sister."

"Where does her sister live," Dan asks, feeling bold.

"She's stationed in Nebraska with the Air Force.

"Is that where Audra is?"

"Yeh Dan, She got a job training horses and likes it out there."

"Is she home for the holidays?"

"No, she couldn't make it."

Dan doesn't want to perpetuate the story so they talk about Trinidad and what he's been doing. Then he asks, "What's her sister's name?"

"Dee Dee."

Planets orbit the sun.

With Audra gone the week in East Bend is uneventful. Luke and Brandy are married and live in the farmhouse where Dan spent the first night after his life changing vision. Leroy still lives at the clubhouse and Wade Yangster is still working on his evolving fort. Dan looks forward to New Year's Eve with Jon Delahooey.

Jon managed the Conroe sub branch while Dan was training in Houston. They became good friends. Then Vince Stevens moved Jon to Louisville, Kentucky as the main branch manager shortly after Vince took over the Central Division in Nashville.

Moons orbit planets.

They're at Jon's apartment in Louisville. Dan tells Jon about Audra, his nuthouse experiences, and the vortex. Jon is the first person Dan ever mentions the vortex to. He's also the first Mainframe employee to learn of Dan's imprisonments.

Jon looks Dan straight in the eye and says, "You're not crazy. You remember everything."

"But I'm about the only one that does."

"You sure about this," Jon asks.

"I'm never totally positive about anything but the more clues point in that direction the more positive I become. When I'm super positive I'm hell bent for leather. You just want to stand back."

"I'll testify to that," Jon says having seen Dan in action.

Dan continues, "Nobody understands the vortex. That's where the danger lies. What people don't understand they fear. Fear makes people do strange things. They try to control and/or avoid the incomprehensible."

"At ground zero, no one remembers. Some outside the zone do; fuel for the next blaze. I don't know if it will happen again or where it will stop if it does. The key is self control. Go with the flow, enjoy the ride. You won't remember it anyway."

"Sounds heavy."

"The after effect is. 'Nothing happened', unless you have a coronary in the process. Fear is the agent of demise, fuel for the vortex. That's why you just want to go with the flow. If everybody does, it never happens."

"Let's go have a beer, this is getting too deep for me."

Galaxies orbit their seed.

The first anniversary of the vortex passes without an effect. Back in Trinidad he learns they finished December with twelve builds. The office moves to number eighteen on the list. Trinidad has rocketed forty spots in four months.

Dan won't catch the Chattanooga choo-choo this year. He calculated ahead and sees the best he can do in the next eight months is number two with twenty builds in the final month. That should be good enough to smoke Chattanooga at the gate the following year. The key will be to get sales up to speed and keep the momentum building.

He's already hired another salesman to help increase sales. His name is Jim. He's the only Mainframe employee other than Jon that Dan has talked to about Audra. He mentioned a girl in the Houston and Trinidad offices but nothing about her. Dan doesn't even talk to Gene about Audra.

The symphony of the universe goes on and on and on.

Dan and me Houston January 22 stares at him from his desk pad. His thoughts turn inward but then he thinks, 'I can't let this obsession control me'. He closes Audra's gate and concentrates on the task at hand.

The complaint list is down to zero and no new ones are created. Jake is full time construction supervisor now but Dan's hand is there when needed. He still hires the crews, checks locations, inspects every house, and tours the homeowners for sign off.

The behind list has dropped to two months from six months. If it drops to a month the customer will be assured of getting a good quality custom home with affordable financing quicker than they thought possible. A shorter wait will encourage more buyers. Less than a month will make Dan nervous and could affect his building momentum. Adding a build a month will be easy if sales grow to match.

Dan hires another framing crew and harps on the sheetrock contractor to beef up and clean up. He cracks the whip on the electrical contractor for better service.

Protons and neutrons orbit each other in a cosmic dance.

He's been back three days when he catches his breath and decides to call his buddy Bart. Bart's back from the Philippines and stationed by San Antonio, four hours west. He's a slugger with connections, having played his way up from the All Air Force softball team to be an Armed Force All-Star.

"Bart, I need your help."

"Whatcha need, Bubba?"

"I need you to locate a Dee Dee Diamante, that's D i a m a n t e. She's in the Air Force and stationed somewhere in Nebraska."

"No problem buddy boy. I'll call you as soon as I find out."

Bart calls within the hour. He has numbers and instructions on how to get through.

Neutrons add mass and stabilization to the nucleus.

Dan calls Omaha. "She doesn't come on duty til fifteen hundred," says the voice. Dan calls back at four o'clock.

"Hello Dee Dee, this is Dan Murphy. Satch said Audra's with you."

"She stopped here for a couple weeks on her way to Phoenix last year." They talk for a minute before she asks, "You aren't that crazy guy are you?"

"Yes but the only thing I'm crazy about is her. I'm as normal as your neighbor." They talk some more. He tells her what he's doing, where he is, and how he got her number. When he hangs up, he has Audra's number in Phoenix.

He calls it.

"Is this Audra Diamante?"

"Yes."

"This is Dan Murphy. I'm calling from Trinidad, Texas. Dee Dee gave me your phone number."

"That was nice of her. How are you?"

Dan's not buying it but plays along. "I just returned from Indiana. I talked to your dad. He said he gave you the letter I sent to him. Did you read it?"

"Uh Yes, it was very nice, thank you."

Red lights flash. 'What kind of response to a twenty-seven page, pour your heart out letter is that? Who is this imposter and why the charade?'

The more they talk the more certain he becomes that it isn't Audra he's talking to. He concludes the call then dredges his memory and Cosmo banks. The question is why?

Electrons orbit protons -- positive attracts negative.

'Dan and me. Houston. January 22.'

'She's here,' grabs his gut and twists. The pieces and picture start coming together.

But where is she?

Jim, the salesman that Dan confided in about Audra, comes walking in. Dan's surprised to see him. It's his day off and it's ten o'clock at night. The office has been closed for three hours.

Dan looks at the stack of invoices. Audra consumes his mind. He knows that there's nothing he can do about it but the thought that she may be in his backyard jabs him.

"Do you know where Audra is?"

"Come on, lets go have a beer," is Jim's response.

Jim won't answer when Dan presses. "Follow me," is his only answer. Hope draws and Dan follows to a bar on the other side of town.

The bar is open and spacious. A front center stage is visible from all points. Scantily clad women dance around small round tables while scantier ones dance on the stage.

Jim introduces him to some friends at a center table. The music blares. Conversations are difficult, eyes distracted.

The weak force pushes electrons away -- negative repels negative.

Dan's only interest is Audra. It's the only reason he's here. He hopes that Jim is leading him to Audra. He has to be patient.

Dan alternates between scanning the room and sitting impassively, waiting for Audra. The nicotine devil jabs him. He decided to eliminate cigarettes when he returned to Trinidad. He told Jim, "Tobacco is a conduit for negative energy."

Sitting, waiting in a blaring bar, liquor flowing, is not conducive to commitment. The thought that Audra could walk up has him on edge. The wait is agonizing.

He gets up, weaves around tables, and crosses the floor to the cigarette machine. He stares at it, puts money in, and pulls the handle. Back at the table he hesitates then lights up. Everybody drops to the floor as Dan takes and releases a drag from the cancer stick. An eerie calm comes over him.

Tabletops hide peeking eyes that stare in his direction to the bar, thirty feet behind him. The music stops; silence. Dan sits there then turns around to look at the bar. Heads are hiding in that direction also. There's a knot of men at the bar.

They break apart and split up. Slowly people crawl back into their seats. "What happened," Dan asks Jim as he crawls into his seat with wary eyes.

"That guy was waving a gun."

Dan turns to look then turns back and says, "I knew I shouldn't have lit that cigarette." Everybody at the table except Jim stares in disbelief.

"He's serious," is Jim's reply.

The music blares. Audra doesn't show. The nicotine devil has Dan hooked again.

Jim says, "Follow me."

Chapter 29—ENHANCEMENT

The strong force holds the nucleus together -- positive attracts positive.

Jim and Joe are still flexing their jaws when sunlight wakes me. I sit up. My head does a curtsy. The clock on the wall is a tick short of seven. No Audra.

"Well guys, I have to get going. Chuck will be calling for the report," I say. "Nice meeting you Joe, thanks for the couch. Jim, you going to make it?."

"I'll be there at nine," he answers

I put my tie on, go out the door, and down the road. My clothes are rumpled and my head is heavy. No time to change.

The phone is ringing when I walk in the door. It's Chuck. I give a quick report. Jake comes in. Suzy shows up at eight and Jill shows shortly after that.

It's business as usual with Audra ducking into the P-ZONE.

Bill comes in at nine followed by Jim. My attitude is good.

I dismiss last night as a fantasy flight.

Electrons weave elements into compounds -- negative repels positive.

By two o'clock I get a break to go home to shower and change. I'm ready to lather my hair when I hear a horn honking. I pull my pants on and run out, dripping and barefoot.

Mrs. B, my landlady, wants out. She's an English teacher who designed and built her house specifically for her platinum years when she'll need a fulltime nurse. She had polio as a child, persevered, got a degree, and had a distinguished teaching career before she decided the leg braces were too painful. She retired twelve years ago at the age of fifty-five and still hasn't hired a live-in nurse to occupy the efficiency I rent.

Her house is California ranch style with spacious rooms, low pitch roof, and open beam ceilings. My unit is on the front right side; my parking spot, eighty feet from my door. I parked in front of my door because I only planned to be a couple minutes.

Mrs. B has her wheel chair in her car and is ready to go when I run out the door. I move the Phoenix and prance across the irregular limestone nuggets. Mrs. B drives by with a wave. 'She's never in a hurry and always has time to talk?' I wonder.

My mind tilts to Audra. Then my job slaps me; it's real. My thoughts may not be. The obsession is a card house that keeps growing. I have no proof but can't ignore it.

Other than a momentary irritation, I don't give it another thought as I finish my shower, put on clean clothes, and head for grub. It's back to business as usual.

Of course, my Cosmo Bank gobbles the thought for future reference.

But Audra pops into my head at every free space. I keep the thoughts controlled and wonder about their persistence. As light becomes dark, Audra intrudes more frequently.

I leave the office an hour before midnight and pick up a six-pack at the Quik Stop by my apartment. Although Mrs. B doesn't prohibit it, it's the first time I take beer to my apartment in the four months I've been there. I need to relax my mind and ponder.

As I walk out of the Quik Stop, beer in hand, I notice the patrol car sitting by the gas pumps. I walk to my car and hear an envious voice speak in an accusatory tone, "We know what you're up to." I glance at the nonchalant policeman leaning against the cruiser and get into my car. The sexual connotation pours fuel into the P-ZONE.

'Is that why Mrs. B took off in a rush this afternoon? Is Audra at Mrs. B's?' Wheels whir. My protective nature surges.

There's a man sitting in a car along side of the gently curving street I live on. His lights are off. There are no houses on that side, only a park-like swale. I glare as I pass. The stranger ignores me. I wonder why he's there. Audra pops up.

A half-dozen houses on big lots inhabit the quarter mile, dead-end street. Four houses are on the right, two on the left. Mrs. B's house is the first one on the left, two hundred yards ahead. It's in the city with a country setting; big trees are everywhere.

The porch and house lights are on when I drive in the long, stone driveway. 'That's odd. Mrs. B never stays up this late.' The P-ZONE opens. 'Audra must be here?' The call to the imposter in Phoenix bolsters the possibility. My Cosmo Bank offers the Christmas party blackout in Houston as an added perspective.

I go into my apartment to have a beer and ponder. It's been almost two years since I last saw her. In those two years, many of my friends and family have seen her as she wove her safety web. It's a belief I can't shake. It's been on a holding pattern.

She's an anchor in my mind. The thought that she wants me, dominates the draw. If I believed otherwise I could put this obsession to rest.

I can't stand the suspense. I peek out the door. The porch light is still on.

One beer isn't enough courage. I think about the possibility of her presence and what I'll say as I drink the second beer. I seriously doubt Audra will be opening the door.

I'm ready. I open my door. The porch and house lights are out. "Damn."

Compounds mix and match -- positive repels negative.

The next morning I slam the door when I enter the office; something I never do. Subconsciously I want somebody to know I'm fuming. I'm upset with Audra for playing this game but more at myself for not knocking on the door as soon as I got home last night.

Jake comes into my office. "Feel like talking?"

I shake my head and squeeze my lips, lean back, ask him about the Farber job. Jake's been a great guy but I'm not ready to discuss Audra with him. Chuck's call for the morning report closes the P-ZONE and gets me back on track for the day.

Its business as usual except I have trouble keeping Audra out of my mind. I'm haunted by the thought she's here and there's nothing I can do except wait. I can't chase an illusion while reality sits in front of me.

I can take care of the rest of the business but when it comes to the invoices I just can't get motivated. I could sign them all in five minutes but that's not the Mainframe way. When I have a book to go by, I go by it. With Audra, there is no book.

By three o'clock, all the important things are done except invoices. Suzy brings a couple more. I put them in the drawer with the rest. Used to keep them on top of the desk but now there's more than I want to look at. I need to buckle down and do them but first I need to check something.

The Phoenix hasn't moved all day except when Suzy did the mail run six hours ago. The temperatures have been in the sixties on this overcast January day. It's a seven minute drive to Mrs. B's.

Steam rolls from the hood when I pull into the driveway. I know I'm on track now. I've spent a lifetime observing natural phenomena, exploring ancient and modern mysteries, understanding the world and universe I live in. Since the vision, I've been able to look at everything from a new perspective and postulated some new theories.

The Force that flows through all matter is a magnetic gel; an Entity that unites everything that is. An opposing anti-force surrounds and feeds off it like a parasite. The anti-force is the effect we see. The Cause remains cloaked except now.

The Phoenix has a condition of overheating but the drive I just took would barely get it to operating temperature, especially from a cold sit and start. I believe this inanimate object is talking to me through the gel of the universe. Something's out of balance!

I ring the doorbell. Mrs. B opens the door and looks at me with her clear blue eyes.

"Daniel," she gleams. "What a pleasant surprise to see you so early in the day." A string of pearls loops around her neck, lays on her flowery blue dress, and accentuates her fresh perm. "Come on in Daniel."

I've never seen Mrs. B dressed up unless she's going somewhere and never this elegantly. I don't believe I've ever seen her look prettier or even with a permanent. I follow her to the kitchen as she glides across the grey tile in her wheelchair.

We proceed to have the longest conversation of our acquaintance. I'm alert for signs of Audra but don't mention her. I believe she's in the other room and speak for her benefit. After an hour Mrs. B asks, "Would you like to have dinner with me?"

I still haven't heard or seen anything of Audra. I accept Mrs. B's invitation and turn the topic to Audra. "My first glimpse of her was like a bolt from above, a supercharged attraction that mysteriously caused our paths to cross two hours later. I developed an obsession that won't let go. I've been so close so many times and failed to connect. I want to see her so bad. I don't know why she doesn't show herself," I hint.

"It's not obsession that has you but possession," Mrs. B replies.

"No, obsession," I argue.

I follow Mrs. B to the twenty pound dictionary prominently displayed in her entry. She reads the definitions and concludes, "You are possessed, not obsessed."

My mind is polarized; I don't see it. How can you argue with a veteran English teacher with a twenty pound dictionary? I give up but my mind is still set.

We have a delicious dinner garnished with home grown greens. I think about the policeman at the Quik Stop. "I'm glad the police aren't involved," I say.

Mrs. B's crystal blues turn opaque gray, just like Adam's a year ago, as the veil drops. It tells me what I need to know. She hasn't shown herself because she isn't here!

I thank Mrs. B and head back to the office. I remember her telling me once that the Chief of Police was one of her former students. Mrs. B may be in a wheelchair but she's fiercely independent and not afraid to talk to anyone, especially a former student.

The phone rings when I walk in the door. Bill says it's for me as I pass his office. It's Gil, one of my subcontractors. "Has Jerry called," he asks.

"Jerry Who," I ask.

"Jerry Duncan, a policeman friend of mine."

"No; don't see anything from a Jerry Duncan. What does he want?"

"Oh, he just wanted to talk to you about some things."

"What kind of things?"

"Just some things."

Life erupts to death -- negative attracts positive.

'Things? What is it with people and their guessing games?' The past two years have been full of people answering my questions with questions or puzzles. Before this call I wasn't overly concerned but now I wonder how many people are involved in this like when I paced the halls of city lock-up and my black college chum sang "Only the strong survive."

Obfuscation opens the alter gate to my Cosmo Bank. Coincidences mingle. Sub control commands. Counter command charges. Alter charge controls. I don't know what to think.

The next morning after business is taken care of, I call Satch. He's not at the office. I call him at home. "I'm out of control, you're in control, and she's under control."

"Dan," Satch's voice lifts, "you're not out of control," he says in disbelief.

I repeat it slower. "I'm out of control. You're in control. She's under control. The key is in Atlanta." A light flashes in my head. I see Audra flash to Indiana.

"Uh," Satch pauses, "Dan can you hold for a second."

I wait. Satch comes back. "Dan you have a mind like an elephant and someday another elephant is going to join you and become part of you in everything you do."

That thought is enough to push me to the S-ZONE. I don't know what transpired in the next couple hours but I do know that I started receiving a lot of calls in the afternoon from people in other offices that don't normally call, and in increasing frequency; like they're playing some kind of pre-arranged distraction game. I feed it back and bring an outsider in; Mike in Waco. For every call in, I make two out. 'Now they're spinning,' I chuckle.

In between calls, a lady representing the school district calls with a request for thousands of promotional pens. I wonder how this came about and think of Audra working behind the scenes. I relay the request to Bud Gabet. He thinks it's strange.

Bud calls back. Mike called him from Waco.
"I'm on my way over," Bud announces.

Chapter 30—ENTANGLEMENT

The Hudson Comet flares as it crosses Jupiter's orbital path.

Dan's mind slides to a catastrophic crack. He calls Jon in Louisville and is put on hold. Jon picks up with the devil in his voice, "This is Flash Gordon."

A cascading cataract creates a cosmic cataclysm in the K compartment of Dan's C-ZONE. Bud Gabet submerges. Audra takes charge. Flash Gordon commands.

"Lock up," He tells Bill when he walks out at a quarter til seven.

"OK," Bill cheerfully responds, happy to see the boss leave early for a change.

The Milky Way is a 100,000 light years across.

"It's not there! My house is not there." Dan drives his red Phoenix further up the road to see if he's at the wrong piece of woods. Then he drives back to the highway and back again. He knows the jog in the road and field preceding the woods. It's the right woodlot but there's no driveway, no clearing, no house! It's like it never existed.

The house was on a one-acre wooded lot on a paved road, a half mile from the main highway that girds the eastern flank of the Golden Triangle, in rural Lemon Heights. Setback in the woods, it was the biggest model and most complete package that Mainframe offers. The owner forfeited the house and land investment before they even moved in. They also left the tons of stone brought in for the S-curve driveway. Dan knows the house and location well. He's been there at least a dozen times.

Jill offered the fortuitous package to Dan when he returned from Indiana. He received loan confirmation that morning. All he has to do is paint the walls, cover the floors, and move in.

He drove south to Interstate 10 after leaving Bill to lockup the office, than east to Lemon Heights and north on Highway 77. He'd been on the beeline highway countless times, at all hours, in the past four months and never saw so much traffic. Headlights moved toward him like a string of fireflies. Tail lights were sparse. He was reminded of Vortex Eve!

Now his house is gone. 'Maybe it's the wrong road?' He checks. It's not. His mind heads for overload. He heads for the hills.

Gravity, the weakest of the four forces, is major and holds everything together.

He's driving north on Highway 77. Instead of the glow dancing off his windshield, he sees an occasional headlight flicker in the distance. Ten minutes earlier it was like a string of fireflies buzzing toward town. Now it's practically deserted.

He turns on the radio. For the next half-hour all he hears is static. When he finally gets a clear signal it's from Evansville, five-hundred air miles away. That's just downriver from Flash Gordon and Audra. At least where he thinks Audra is.

The vanished house causes a left turn at the border between fantasy and reality and sends him deep into the Q-ZONE. He turns right on Highway 11 to Belleview, Louisiana then north on Highway 171. His gas is low but he doesn't stop. Love is his fuel.

Electro-magnetism, the strongest force, is minor and holds everything apart.

His mind is lost in an abyss of thought. The whereabouts of his body are unknown. Vortex Eve plagues his mind as the road starts to change course. He crosses a river and then can't find his way back. For the next hour, the road coils and winds through a no mans land of hills and trees. The more he sees the more he wants to get out of there.

He barrels ahead figuring eventually he'll come out somewhere on this hill filled road. There's nothing behind him and the road ahead unfurls like a computer game. The Phoenix sputters and stops on an upward incline, facing a yellow S-curve sign.

Dan cranks the engine. He turns off the lights and grinds some more. "I can't just sit here," he tells the sky.

"Hell with it, I'm walking," he says as he opens the door and pulls his keys. 'Maybe things will return to normal. No need to move the car. Nobody's here!'

He walks up the hill. There's a dirt road curving up a hill to his right. 'Am I the only one left?' It's too horrifying to think about.

He follows the sweeping left curve and crests the hill. A small building with soft lights is a hundred yards down the hill. The air is quiet and cold.

Dan wears his fur lined leather jacket but feels icicles in his bones. His frozen body ride to Houston four years earlier was the only time he felt colder. His teeth chatter.

He walks to the one room shack. A huge padlock bars the doors. Heavy mesh covers the windows.

Gates open. He's reminded of the humming screen of his encagement two years ago when he looked out at the pigeon the ledge. Now he looks in and can't believe what he sees.

He throws grass at the screen, touches, and then places his head against it. It's warm. He gazes at the fantasy in the void and wonders if this is the devils playground. A dozen pinball and video machines are lit and ready to play. No one is there to play them.

Dan hears a noise and looks back to see twin beams slicing the night sky as a belumpf-belumpf rumble comes up the hill. He watches the lights knife through air and cut to the woods as the monster crests the hill and rolls down. It does a turn in the field, lights flashing on Dan as he walks away from the shack. The truck stops fifty feet from him, headlights boring a hole in the hill to the road, sits, and rumbles.

Dan looks at the beast and moves toward it. He sees two young men in it. They aren't smiling. He wonders if they're Satan's escorts.

Magnetism is the glue that molds and holds the four basic forces of the universe.

"What are you doing here," the man in shotgun position asks.

"My car ran out of gas." Dan's in a daze. He doesn't know what to believe or expect; he's in the O-ZONE.

They ask about different people. Many names he recognizes as people he's building houses for. 'How can this be? How do they know? What do they want?' His Cosmo Bank turns inside out and faces him. It fuels the vortex belief and the land of the lost.

He's stunned but not afraid. 'If this is the end, then so be it.'
His body is freezing. He responds in a daze. "Do you have any gas?"

"Go back to the road and turn right. There's a house over the hill."

Dan walks as the pick-up idles along like a collie herding a stray sheep, more convinced than ever that these are Satan's escorts and the end is around the corner. When they come within sight of the house the pick-up passes and parks in the driveway.

Dan follows. One of the men tells him to wait on the porch while the other goes inside. A lady comes out. After a couple minutes, the other man goes inside.

She stands and stares at Dan like he's an apparition. His attempts at conversation are met with silence. He's wearing his green and brown checked bellbottoms and salmon colored shirt with a green and brown striped tie and burgundy leather jacket; same outfit he wore when he met Audra with the addition of the tie and minus his black felt hat.

He's just seen a pinball arcade in the middle of nowhere on a road that seems to go nowhere. His house vanished along with civilization and the girl he hasn't seen in two years is playing hide and seek. Then Satan's escorts herd him with a pick-up truck.
As far as he knows, they're inside loading their guns.

Meanwhile he's stuck in a freezing hell where a lady watches his every move while the escorts alternate between coming and going from the house. Nobody says anything. They just stare. Dan's lucky to be sane at this point.

It's getting to be ridiculous when his third request for gas is met with silence.
He feels like these are the last guards of a world that doesn't exist. Silence fuels his belief.

They're not going to tell him anything or let him go anywhere. Memories of unanswered questions, surface. In the lower levels of his C-ZONE, the question looms, 'Why can't anybody answer a simple question?'

Valence unites major and minor and makes them two.

A police car stops in front of the house. Dan walks out to talk to the two officers. They ask for his wallet and check every piece of paper in it. He wonders about the paranoia.

A tow truck goes by. The officers check his pockets, frisk him, and give him a sobriety test. One officer gets in the squad car, the other walks over the hill with Dan.

The tow truck is sitting in front of the Phoenix and there's another officer checking the interior. Dan watches as he shines a light under the seats. When he's done looking the officer turns to Dan and gruffly orders, "Open the trunk."

Dan pulls his keys from his pocket and opens the trunk.

"Stand back," the gruff one says.

The driver is out of the cruiser. "Why are you here," he asks Dan.

"I ran out of gas. If you'll give me some I can be out of here."

The fact that the tow truck was there shortly after the police tells him he was convicted before he even had a trial. They have no intentions of letting him drive off. They're in charge.

"Why are these signs in the trunk?"

"I'm the manager of the Trinidad Mainframe Homes office. I use them to identify lots where we're getting ready to build a house." The gruff officer eyes him suspiciously, making sure he doesn't get too close to the hammer in the trunk.

"Do you know Earl Westrick?"

"Yes. He's the manager of the Mainframe branch in Jasper."

The tow truck hooks his car. Two officers accompany Dan on the walk back. Last guard thoughts ascend as the chain of command descends to the heart of the vortex. One stands guard in the yard while the other two talk to the house occupants.

Dan watches his car being towed away. It's going in the same direction he was. He knew the road came out somewhere, away from this no man's land.

The entourage heads in the direction of the police cruiser which is facing the same direction his car went. One of the officers opens the right rear door.
Dan feels heat blast out. "Get in," the gruff one says.

Dan hops in, happy to be able to absorb some warmth. Heat thaws the icicles in his bones and melts his mind. He's so tired. It's been a mentally exhausting day.

One of the officers gets in on the other side and the other two get in front.
Dan's eyelids get heavy. He allows them to close. He's so tired. Sleep invades.

He feels a glow moving into his left side followed by a bright light.
It's hauntingly familiar. Like his encagement experience. He opens his eyes.
The glow pulls back

His eyelids drop again. The glow and light return. His eyes pop open.

After two more times he's no longer tired. It's too unsettling.
His eyes remain open as he watches and wonders where they're taking him.

Chapter 31—ENDUREMENT

Joseph and Mary molecules unite in the Pacific.

The police station looks Wild West. Mottled grey limestone blocks give it an Alamo appearance. The surreal drama continues inside where an officer sets a straight back chair in the middle of the room. "Have a seat," he says. Dan sits down.

Another policeman pulls a chair to a squeaky stop, straddles it, and faces him from ten feet away with his elbows resting on top of the straight back. Dan clenches his jaw and fights to keep from erupting at the absurd sight. Behind the officer is a mount unlike any Dan has ever seen.

Instead of the normal face and rack, a deer rear stares straight at him, white flag shooting six inches toward the stars with the officers face dotting the exclamation. Dan manages to remark, "That's some deer mount," without cracking up. The remark fails to start a conversation.

The policeman just stares at him. Dan sits there in somber silence and wonders if the chain of command has been sucked to the heart of the vortex. Audra is pushed aside with questions of why his car was towed and why they're making him stare at a deer rump.

He feels like he's in some kind of crazy zoo. Exhaustion overwhelms him. Mystery keeps his neurons faintly firing. Last guard thoughts link with his Cosmo bank.

The Abram splits, twists, and threads cycles from beginning to end and back.

"You can go with Earl," an officer tells him.

Dan takes a parting look at the Jasper jail as he goes to Earl's car. Foggy haze and light surround it in a surreal silver halo. 'How did the vortex affect this town,' he wonders.

Silence accompanies the ride though the creeping fog. Earl pulls into a motel and waits while Dan rents a room. He drives Dan to his room, "I'll see you in the morning."

Dan falls into bed, too tired to wonder about anything. His subconscious compartmentalizes the harrowing thoughts of the day. It's too much to deal with.

Cycles go round and round.

One customer sits at the counter and two more at a table when Dan walks into the spacious motel cafe the next morning. It's almost seven A.M. when he orders steak and eggs. Thoughts of yesterday, especially last night, envelop his mind.

The place is like a graveyard. Nobody smiles. Everyone is dead serious. Dan wonders if this is the land of the living, if these people are post-vortex shells of existence. He can't get the waitress to smile. The cashier has a face of granite.

Back in his room, Dan turns on the TV as he waits for Earl. In the upper left corner of the screen, an exploding black star is prominently displayed. BLACK OUT is printed beneath it.

His eyes glue to the nationwide morning show for an explanation. The hosts are jovial as they show a live shot of smiling President-elect, Jimmy Carter, getting off the plane in Atlanta. He thinks about Satch, 'The key is in Atlanta.'

The black star remains on the screen and unexplained for forty-five minutes. It becomes fuel for his belief in the Audra inspired conspiracy and subsequent vortex. Earl arrives.

More silence on the long drive to Trinidad. Earl isn't responding to Dan's inquiries although he does find out that his car is in a Jasper garage. He's still in shock and doesn't question why a car that just ran out of gas would need to be in a garage. He knows.

Arctic ice water sinks below the Gulf Stream and St. Lawrence convergence.

Dan's office is bustling with activity when they walk in the door about eleven o'clock. Bill's glad to see him. Jake and Jill seem to have excess energy. Suzy bustles about.

Bud Gabet doesn't mention last night as he scurries out. Dan breathes a sigh of relief. He hears, "Since the boss is back, we might as well go to work," come from the framing crew drinking coffee at the kitchen table. Earl drinks a cup of coffee and leaves.

Dan lounges on the sofa in the dining room. He's not ready to go back to work. He walks over to Suzy's desk. "I went to my house last night."

"You went to your house," Suzy says with her jaw dropping.

"Yeh. It wasn't there."

"It wasn't there?" Her eyes glaze as her head drops and buries in a task.

Like previous experiences, the actions of others do nothing to lessen his suspicion. 'Maybe they don't know? Or do they? They seem overly busy!'

He sits on the sofa for another half hour and watches his operation in action. Jill, Suzy, Bill, and Jake scurry back and forth, answering calls, comparing notes, ignoring him. He doesn't mind. It's a pleasant change. He's usually the one racing back and forth.

A phone call takes him back to his office. It's a Mrs. Castellano looking for Bud Gabet. "Tell him I called," she says. Dan doesn't write it down.

Between phone calls, he attempts to check and sign invoices. Audra and the vortex dominate his thoughts. Last night is sequestered in a side cell of D Compartment. Two invoices have moved when Bud Gabet walks in a half hour later.

Bud doesn't say anything about last night and neither does Dan. "A lady called." Dan can't remember her name. Bud fluffs concerns about the invoices. Dan sighs.

Five minutes later, three men in suits come walking in. One is carrying papers; a court order with Dan's name on it. He knows he's being railroaded again but doesn't know the trainmaster.

His vortex belief strengthens. Paranoia about the conspiracy creeps in. He looks over and says, "Bud, you have to stay on top of this."

"I will," Bud replies.

"We don't want to make a scene in your office," a suit says. "Would you come outside with us?"

'Make a scene,' Dan wonders. "Bud," he pleads.

Bud nods.

"OK," Dan sighs.

Flanked by three suits, Dan leads the way down the hall and out of the office. Worry grips Bill's face as they pass. Suzy keeps her head down. Jake is somewhere else.

They walk out the front door and over to a fourth suit waiting by a four-door sedan under the Mainframe sign. Bud follows. The fourth suit handcuffs Dan then says, "We're going to take off your belt."

When the path is clear, they thread a rope through his belt loops, fasten the rope, and hook it to the handcuffs. Dan's hogtied. Concern grows. He remains calm and waits for Murphy's Law to assert itself.

"Get in the car," a suit says. Dan turns to look at Bud, his only hope, and trusts that he won't let him down. He's unsure if this vortex is over and doesn't want to lose him.

One suit sits in back with Dan and two hop in front. The fourth gets in another car. Bud jumps in his. The pack leaves the parking lot with Dan in the lead car and Bud trailing.

Dan doesn't watch the road ahead. His neck and body twist back to watch Bud.

He wonders where they're going? 'What will happen next?'

Joseph and Mary molecules suck to the Southern Hemisphere.

The trio pulls into the parking lot.

Bud vanishes.

Chapter 32—ENTRAINMENT

The Hudson Comet enters the asteroid belt.

For a minute, I thought I lost Bud. He vanished in the parking lot. But rejoins the group as we head for the big, brick building.

A three-story glass and steel entry is to the right. We don't go that way. The six of us head for a small door in the side of the red brick wall. A lady emerges from a room as we come to a T-corridor. "Hi, I'm Mrs. Castellano," she says as we pass.

I turn to Bud in the rear. "That's the lady who called." He nods, follows to an elevator, and gets on with me and the four suits.

I reflect on what's happening. A tear rolls down my cheek as I look at Bud. My worst fears are being realized.

The elevator door opens to six waiting men. Five get off. The door closes. Bud's gone and I'm surrounded by ten men, most bigger than me!

The suits remove the cuffs and hogtie and leave. White coats flank me on the walk down the long hallway. Fifty feet later white leader commands, "Into the room on the left."

A four-post, steel frame bed faces me. I turn to face the six who now surround me. "What's this all about," I ask.

"Take your shoes off," is my answer.

I sit down in the chair and slip my shoes off.

"Take your tie off," the leader barks.

"What's this all about?"

"Do you want us to do it for you?"

I remove my neck-tie and hand it to them.

"Lay on the bed."

"What's this all about," I ask for the third time.

"If you don't want to do it voluntarily we can do it forcefully." Again no answer and no choice; conspiracy thoughts broaden.

"On your back," the leader says. I comply. "Spread your legs."

The white coats put leather cuffs on my ankles and fasten them to the steel posts. "Are you right handed or left?"

I wonder what kind of trick this is. "Left," I say.

Two men cuff and strap my right wrist to the bedpost while two hold my left arm. I don't like it but I keep calm. The white coats leave. Anxiety grows.

Strapped to three bedposts, I'm practically immobile. I can barely scoot my butt six-inches one way or the other. I battle the toughest foe I've ever fought—claustrophobia.

Every cell in my body quivers. I will myself to keep calm. Terror embeds in my bones. I lay there and shiver and watch the people stop and gaze as they patrol the hallway.

I fight for control and wonder how long they're going to keep me strapped down. I attempt to keep my main spring together for one more minute and then another. Minutes become hours. Panic overwhelms the hours.

A grandfatherly figure comes in and closes the door from prying eyes. He introduces himself as Dr. Cronkite and tells me how he founded this institution twenty-three years earlier with a group of doctors. Talking to the good doctor eases my concerns although I'd rather be dead than strapped down. He leaves in the same position.

My conspiracy and vortex belief reinforce. I wonder what they are so afraid of. It's a torturous struggle to keep calm. I know if I lose it, I may never come back.

Another doctor visits for ten minutes. He lacks the wisdom of Dr. Cronkite; I don't trust him. He'll be the one to railroad me if I survive this!

A nut walks in, raises his hospital gown, and exposes a naked body with a crucifix tattooed to his thigh. He says, "Jesus is my savior. No bone will they harm."

I'm reminded of the crazy Murdoch on the TV show, "A-Team." He does a good job of appearing insane as he babbles a coherent incoherence. He comes and goes. Murdoch appears to know something and I'm curious to know what that is. My questions are met with incoherence.

I fight to maintain my sanity and will my mind to remain inert. Any attempts to even partially turn to my side are met with leather restraint. I hate being on my back. Panic tries to overwhelm me.

That night, a kaleidoscope of numbers, letters, and thoughts race across the screen in my head. '123, ABC, CBS, NBC, FMC, GMC, CMC, CCC, PWA, FDA, 987.' On and on and on, like a ticker tape, thoughts and symbols keep racing. I'm awestruck and thankful for the diversion from my bondage.

I forget the ties that bind as I sit in the theater of my mind and watch the cinemascope. Thoughts race. Murdoch slips in, sits in the chair, and falls asleep.

The Mississippi rages and rips through the Louisiana Delta.

"This is crazy," I say. "There are three of you. I'm not going anywhere with my legs strapped down. What the hell am I going to do?" My pleas fall on deaf ears.

What is everyone so afraid of? What have I done to deserve this hell? The leather cuffs on my wrist and legs are two-inches wide and fastened to the bedposts by quarter-inch thick, one inch wide straps. "Double the straps on the right arm ...... left leg," the leader barks. "Triple the strap on the right leg." They must think I'm Hercules!

With the added restraints in place, all three men get on my left side and pull on my chest clenched left arm. One puts his foot on the bed. They heave in unison with the additional leverage. My arm starts lifting from its clenched position. It's no match for six arms, three bodies, and a leg.

I lose ground slowly. My arm, hand pointing to the stars, is halfway between my chest and the bed. My elbow slips onto the bed as I make a final stand to keep them from pulling my arm down. It's been awhile since I've done any physical work but I still manage to hold my ground for a minute or two.

My strength and energy deplete. I resist no further and let my arm slam to the bed. The white coat with the leg up bounces against the wall and goes down.

They strap my left arm. Now I'm strapped to all four posts. Too tired to worry about it, I lay there while they systematically unfasten and refasten each of the straps. They strip my clothes off, an arm and a leg at a time, and replace them with a hospital gown.

The second day ends with me strapped the way I was to start; left arm free.

The Delta expands into the Gulf.

Dr Cronkite visits twice a day, morning and afternoon. I don't see the other doctor again which is fine with me. I didn't like him anyway. Dr. Cronkite is cool.
He talks with respect for my intelligence; not as a common nut.

Dr. Cronkite admits the anxiety of the powers that be. Somebody feels safe with me strapped down. My beliefs are reinforced. I stay strapped.

It's the fourth day when they remove the straps and end the catatonic horror.
I almost fall when I get up. My legs are weak and wobbly, my head hazy.

I discover that I'm in a locked ward for terminal nuts. Plenty are here.
Shortly afterward, I bump into Murdoch in the hundred-fifty foot long, five foot wide hallway. I try to unlock his secret without success. The next day, he's gone.

At one end of the long hall is a twenty by thirty foot recreation room. One morning I see people being wheeled down the hall to the rec room. I go to investigate.

I see four people laying on tables in the rec room. Their motionless bodies are crumpled in disarray with faces contorted into grotesque shapes. I wonder what catastrophe caused this. When the white coats bring the next body in I follow them back up the hall and see them go into a door on the left. The door closes before I can catch a glimpse inside.

I watch them bring the next body out. The door closes. They wheel it down the hall. I follow them to the rec room. A couple bodies are sitting up, drinking orange juice, and eating cookies. They seem dazed. Others lay in undignified sprawls around the room.

I go back up the hall where the catastrophe door now remains open. I peer in.
It's not a passageway like I thought but a room. Inside is a stainless steel table.
On the table are suction cups attached to a high tech booster box via jumper cables.

It occurs to me that these people are not victims of a catastrophe but electro-shock. I didn't know much about electro-shock. I try to talk to the victims. They seem fearful and disoriented; traumatized. The effect seems to be masked while the cause remains untreated. Eventually, memory comes back. I wonder if the vortex operates on a similar principle.

My seventh morning begins with the news that I'm going to a hearing to determine my fate. A white coat gives me a razor and watches me shave. I'm wearing the same clothes I put on eight days ago, minus tie, belt, and shoes.

My black socks are growing holes as they slip to floppy tubes walking down the hall. They need to be continually pulled up. My bell bottoms polish the floor. My shirt flaps.

I make the final adjustments before I enter the hearing room and clutch my drooping drawers to keep my shirt tucked as I walk in.

A robed man sits at the far end of a large oval cherry wood table. Bud Gabet, Chuck Suave, Suzy Stryker, and Jake McMurty sit across the table from me. Suzy is closest. Her new perm compliments her professional outfit. Her peaked eyes create an arch in her brow and accentuate her perfect coiffure. My hair flares in all directions.

Joking Jake's solemn expression and suit warn me of the gravity of the situation. The only other time I've seen him in a suit was at his wedding a month earlier. Chuck is wearing his best three-piece and Bud Gabet has his hair meticulously combed.

Attention punctuates the air as the judge reads preliminary chatter. Then he says to me, "You have been examined by two doctors and have been determined to be mentally ill. How do you plead?"

I look at my friends across the table and see that none of them are interested in slinging mud which is what they'll have to do to reinforce the doctor's conclusions. It doesn't matter that my treatment has been less than humane; hog-tied like an uncommon criminal, strapped down like a common nut, driven to the brink of insanity, no reasons given. There's no way to win. It's six against one.

I think about the unanswered questions, the devil's arcade, my vanished house, Audra. I know and understand why but those beliefs don't mean anything now. I'm locked up, they have the key. To say anything would be pointless and almost certainly doom me.

"I'll agree with the doctors," I reply.

Bud breathes a sigh of relief. Chuck and Jake lean back. Suzy's eyes relax.

"I'm ordering you to stay in this facility for a period not to exceed ninety days."

I breathe a sigh of relief.

"Your friends have expressed concern and would like to talk to you," the judge continues. "You can use the foyer."

We walk out of the locked ward to the other side. I look and wonder. In front of me is a three story atrium surrounded by railing rimmed floors and an open stairway that leads to an enticing outside entrance. The wall of glass reveals blue sky, picturesque trees, and green grass. I wonder when I'll move over here.

Bud does most of the talking. "Don't worry about your job," he says. "It probably won't be here but you'll still have a job when you get out. Take a rest for now."

Chuck adds, "You don't have to worry about morning reports. Just get better."

"I'll go to Mrs. B's and get some clothes for you," Suzy offers.

"Everyone at the office is pulling for you and the guys wish you well," Jake says.

Water churns at the base of Niagara.

Two days later, my wish is granted. They give me my tie, shoes, and belt and move me to the atrium side. Suzy left clean clothes for me.

I'm shown to my room. It's nice! Color coordinated carpet, walls, bedcovers, and shellacked shiny white pine furniture; a stark contrast to the other side. I have a roommate who works during the day and is only there on nights and weekends.

My first order of business is a shower and clean clothes. My socks are ready to be thrown away, the green-checked bell bottoms are frayed from polishing the floor, and my shirt's been flapping since the hearing. The vortex lingers in the O-ZONE.

The Main room is huge. Sofas and chairs surround a TV on one side of the atrium. Across the stairwell, comfortable lounge groupings separate an area of cafeteria style tables and chairs from the atrium.

The nurses tell me that sixty patients inhabit this section. I can see that the three-story hospital is much larger and contains many sections. I spend most of my time alone and socialize on occasion. Most everyone I talk to seems normal.

Some tell me, "This is one of the best hospitals in the state." Most are there by choice; on vacation from the stresses of life. Many suffer from depression and come here for help in solving their frustrations. They have sessions and structured schedules to meet their needs. They even have guest speakers; like a college for getting well.

Some have full schedules, others are empty. I'm in the latter category. Since my only agenda is being free, I have no schedule other than food, medicine, and a doctor's visit. As usual, I'm not given a choice and don't pursue it. It lends credence to my belief.

Doctor Cronkite spends ten to twenty minutes with me every morning. Then I'm free to go outside for two hours before lunch and meds; four hours in the afternoon. I take full advantage of the freedom by walking around the hospital and immediate vicinity.

Every day my circle gets bigger and bigger until I figure out where I am in relation to where I've been. In my five months in Trinidad I spent most of my time in the office or roaming the countryside. Only a small percentage of Mainframes houses were built in Trinidad and I knew very little about how to get around there except from the freeway.

I've never used mass transit, having been raised in a rural-suburban area. I prefer to walk. It gives me privacy and unobstructed thought time. And I avoid people.

On Sunday mornings I can't go out for my normal morning walk so I watch religious programs on TV. Most institutions don't allow patients to watch them. This one does.

One preacher talks about the church of Indiana and the church of Texas and in the same breath talks about having faith and believing. I step back and the vortex steps forward. Audra emerges. Audra submerges.

"You can call your people to tell them you're being released in a couple days," says Dr Cronkite. "Give them time to get over their anxiety attacks," he chuckles. I smile at the comment and wonder some more.

I call Bud Gabet.

Chapter 33—ENTICEMENT

The Hudson Comet flashes through the asteroid belt.

"I argued and pleaded with them," Bud Gabet says, "but they said to let you go."

My spirit crumbles, my heart sinks, I don't know if I have the will to keep going!

"They also cancelled the contract on your house."

My mind spins to oblivion.

I pick myself up from the floor. My spirit remains there.

"I don't like it but my hands are tied," Bud says. "I said you wouldn't lose your job and I intend to follow through on that promise. I'm sending Chuck over to pick you up."

The Himalayas inch higher. Antarctica sinks.

Nineteen days after strap-down, Dan is released. He's at the same point as when they released him from the MHC; dazed, depressed, disappointed, confused, and uncertain. He can think of nothing to replace the job he loved. Audra is a fleeting memory.

Chuck has three options and does his best to make them sound enticing. None comes close to matching what he had. He was able to endure the shock of the second vortex and the absolute horror of being strapped down but to lose the job he loved after not seeing the girl he loves, when she was so close, is too much. He's ready to hang it up.

His spirit is crushed. His will to go on, seriously impaired.
He spins between despair, futility, and hopelessness.

Gravity pulls like a magnet.

Chuck takes Dan to his apartment. His Phoenix is gone.
He loaned his van to one of his framing contractors.
He's supposed to return it in the afternoon.

Dan spends the rest of the day in quiet contemplation.
He's back at square one, fighting for survival and not all that interested.
He wonders how thorough the last vortex was and how much hell he still has to go through.

As much as he'd like to think of going back to Indiana to lick his wounds,
it's not a real option. The Rust Belt recession severely limits opportunity.
Of the options Chuck offered, the most appealing is the sales job in Loreto.

It's possible to make more money than he did as a manger but he isn't sure he can be content sitting around and waiting for people to come in. He's used to making things happen not waiting for them. Ole Betsy, his trusty Econoline, shows up late that afternoon.

Joseph and Mary molecules mix and mingle.

The next day, Dan visits his former office. Everyone's happy to see him. When the welcoming committee disperses, Suzy says, "I don't know if I can work for another boss."

"Why not?"

"You know," she queries. "He's not you. He does things differently."

Dan thinks back to when he first came to Trinidad. "Hang in there," he says. "It's too tough to take over an office and train a new secretary."

Dan finds out that Trinidad has climbed to number eight on sheer momentum. His office went from five houses built in his first month to fourteen in the fifth month; from fifty-eighth on the sub-branch list to eighth. Two hundred complaints erased and no new ones are generated. Dan wonders why Mainframe would terminate that kind of success. Audra commands the possibilities.

His former lumber supplier finds out he's in the office and calls.
"I'm sorry to hear of your misfortune Dan," Dick says.
"We loved working with you and wish you were still there; we hated to lose you."
Dick closes with, "If you haven't decided what to do, I'd like you to come see me."

"I haven't decided anything."

"Can you come see me around ten-thirty, tomorrow morning," Dick asks.

"I think I can squeeze you in."

"Good."

"I'll see you at ten-thirty."

The weak force keeps the moon away.

Dick welcomes Dan the next morning and takes him on a tour around the lumber yard then back to his office. "Dan, I'm going to get right to the point," he says. "I've been working with Mainframe for twenty-five years now and I've seen a lot of managers come through that office. None of them handled it the way you did. How you turned Trinidad around is nothing short of amazing. Dan that office has always struggled and been a sore spot. Now it's in the top ten. Why not even Bill Murray, who's way up in the company now, did as good a job as you did."

"Bill Murray used to be the manager of Trinidad!"

"Six or seven years ago. Anyway, I'm going to retire in a couple years and we need someone like you to take my place. I'd like you to consider coming to work for us."

Dan's reply is lunar. "That was quite a conspiracy everyone pulled off."

The glaze that falls over Dick's eyes is hauntingly familiar. It's the same glaze he saw in Adam's eyes after the first vortex and Mrs. B's grey gaze before the second. It confirms Dan's belief. Dick is no longer the amiable host but someone who unknowingly has something to hide. Dan's unlocked a secret passage to the dark side.
His departure is bittersweet.

Chapter 34—ENABLEMENT

The Hudson Comet blazes through Mars orbital path.

Don't know why I said that but I blew it. I could have grown to love that job. But now that I know my thoughts are correct, it doesn't matter. Audra loves me. I was victimized by other people's fears again. And I shall overcome.

I have no idea about the twists and turns that lie ahead.

Next stop Planet Earth.

Loreto is a main branch like Houston although much smaller. Jasper to the East and Tyler to the north, are its sub-branches. The Loreto office is in a midsized model and fronts a four home model park. A ten-thousand foot warehouse guards the rear of the property.

I'm given a key to the office and a list of people who expressed interest in Mainframe sometime in the distant past. I brush up on product knowledge and call people on the list. Most have already bought elsewhere. Those that haven't, I prod to come in.

The sales position is kickback; every other day off and no pressure, plenty of time to think and resurrect memories. The teletype, with links to all thirty-three main branches and the home, regional, and division offices, draws my interest. Keys clatter and chatter.

I watch the manager type the morning report and data spitting out afterward. Paper flows to the floor behind the machine and coils. Feet of paper inch higher. During the week, teletype links are intra-regional. On weekends, the link is nationwide.

While I wait for walk-ins, I stamp my name and phone number on three by five inch Mainframe brochure pamphlets and insert most of them into the accommodating slits of twelve-inch, red cardboard, stop signs. The rest I place on tables around the customer entry.

A potential customer walks in. I greet him with, "Hi, I'm Dan Murphy. Can I help you?"

"I'm just looking. Not planning to do anything soon," is his reply.

"You can follow the sidewalk around and look at the models in various stages of completion. Stop back when you're done touring and I'll answer your questions."

The customer goes out to look at the models. I put the cardboard stop signs in holders mounted on eighteen by twenty-four-inch, free standing, cardboard billboards. On off days I'll place the promotional displays in high traffic retail locations around Loreto.

It takes eight and a half minutes for light to travel from Sun to Earth.

It's late Saturday morning. The last office has typed in its weekly report. I'm the only one left in the Loreto office. Salesmen are the only employees in most offices. The other salesman isn't due for an hour; we work a split and overlapping weekend schedule.

I look at the pecking on the teletype and stare at the empty parking lot. The inane communication tells me that at least a few offices around the country have the same amount of patronage. I watch the lack of meaningful data and then jump in. But I don't just jump in, I take over. Adrenaline flows as I enjoy the freedom of expression.

The more I write the more in tune I become. Thoughts pour out as I type faster and faster, faster than I knew possible, two fingers dashing to and fro across the keyboard, reminiscent of my free flowing jungle rhythm on the drums.
The growing possibility of Audra's presence pushes me.

A couple comes in. I talk to them. They go out to look at the other models. Back on the teletype I start a code.

'BCCB 1221 TT'

'Eastbound and down, open up and truckin. We gonna do what they say can't be done. We got a long way to go and a short time to get there. We gonna be number one!'

The couple comes back in. I answer their questions. They leave.
I expand the opening code.

'BCCB 1221 TT FF'

'Understanding is a spiraling twin ladder you climb to grow.
Growth surges with positive and stalls with negative.
Effect is superficial; seen with the physical eyes. It's negative.
Cause is below the surface and seen with the mind's eye. It's positive.
Effect emanates from cause.'

The other salesman comes in. Now that two of us are there, one of us can walk through the model park with customers. I stay off the teletype when the other salesman is around. He goes out into the model park with some potential buyers.

'BCCB 1221 TT FF JAX'

'Great people talk about ideas.
Average people talk about current events.
Small people talk about other people.
Which are you?'

Ten feet of paper are coiled on the floor when I leave that afternoon.

The Andromeda Galaxy is three million light years away.

Sunday is busy with a steady stream of customers. I only get a few opportunities to peck on the teletype. I'm starting to enjoy the sales position and don't want to lose it for something as silly as running off at the mouth on the teletype.

Deep down I know it isn't right but it's something I have to do. Audra draws me in. I decide to only do it on weekends when the possibility of getting caught is less.

On Monday morning I go to the office for the morning report and sales meeting. It's my day off but we still have to show up every morning. Afterwards I check the flurry of activity on the teletype. It's a tempting lure. I have to guard against getting sucked in.
The rest of the day is spent placing stop sign displays in locations around the area.

It's seven o'clock Tuesday. I've been in the office all day and it's time to lock up. I'm sitting at my desk, planning sales strategy, getting in the groove, and seeing the possibility of potential in my present position. I haven't had a response to my stop sign distribution

yet, it's too soon, but the phone campaign is starting to bear fruit.
I hear the teletype pecking, slow and methodical.

I go out to check it. Someone is slowly typing Z's and space, space, spaces;
'Z Z Z Z Z Z Z Z,' is on the paper.
I can't resist the temptation, type an 'O' and return to my office.

The tantalizing pecking continues its beeline to my ears. I try to ignore it.
I know better than to get involved.

It continues, peck, peck, peck, slow and methodical, peck, peck, peck.
Faster; peck-peck-peck. Taunting; peck. Beckoning; peck, -peck.

I walk out, blaze a message, and walk away. The taunting continues.
I wonder who would be tempting me to play with fire. I should lock up and leave but don't.
My brain skews right as I throw caution to the wind and jump on the teletype.

'BCCB 1221 TT FF JAX ZZ LA 123'

'Hey all you cosmic cadets, this is Captain Cosmo on the Texas live line.
Bet you didn't know that our sun, the nucleus of our solar system, is one of a billion or so, stars in the Milky Way Galaxy which is but one of a hundred billion to a trillion galaxies in the known universe. You think we're the only intelligent life in this colossal stew?

Get ready for a space cruise!'

An hour later, I dock the shuttle. The taunter types,
'Tell Dan Hi.'

'I would if I knew who this is coming from,' I reply.

'Top dog', is the answer.

Excitement grows. I go home with my head in the clouds and dream of future memos that will be more earthly and less cosmic. A slice of space and a splash of comedy in a running commentary on the way of things.

The next day I go in for the morning report and then out to distribute displays.
Audra sinks her hooks and draws me. I can't wait to get back to the office.

I'm there at six-thirty and dawdle around til the on-duty salesman signs off at seven.
I sit down and type,

'BCCB 1221 TT FF JAX ZZ CC LA 123 TOP'

'How about that big chief pow-wow in Jacksonville and the misadventures of T n T?
There they were, two adventurous and inebriated souls, flying across the golf course
in the dead of the night with Fred, a hapless hitchhiker, hanging on for dear life
on front of the speeding projectile. The dynamic duo rolls merrily along,
happy and carefree, up the hills and down to a liquid awakening.'
I ramble... 'The search party, led by the tire-marked Fred,
finds the wayward wayfarers having the time of their lives,
diving for sunken treasure in the lagoon with the protruding flag
of their submerged golf cart serving as the focal point of their search.'

A dose of insanity hits me when I take the evenings commentary with me.

Chapter 35—ENJOYMENT

The Hudson Comet lances the Canadian Shield.

A subconscious battle rages in Dan's mind. By morning the left side regains control. 'I have to stay off the teletype,' is his conclusion. 'I shouldn't have taken the teletype paper.'

It's his day to work. When he shows up, the manager calls him back into his office. "Dan I'm sorry but I don't need you anymore. I hope you understand."

'Understand,' he wonders? 'What is there to understand?'
'Am I supposed to go to Audra in Jacksonville?'

The L-ZONE sucks him in. The O-ZONE beckons.
Counting the missed opportunity at the lumber company, Dan lost three jobs in two weeks. And he doesn't care! Audra is waiting for him.

Granite splits and shifts. Niagara cascades Erie to Ontario.

Dan sails on a three hour cruise to Trinidad and gets a speeding ticket.
At the Trinidad office Dan calls Mike in Waco. Bud Gabet calls Dan shortly after that. "I want to see you here at nine o'clock tomorrow morning. Get out of that office."

"Yes sir," Dan says.

'It's twenty hours before I have to meet Bud, an hour and a half to Houston, an hour and a half of BS'n with Gene, eight hours of sleep, and an hour to wake up and get to the office. That leaves eight hours to spare. I don't know when I'll get back to this area.'

Dan says good bye to Suzy and the gang, and heads toward Louisiana.
He turns right on the firefly highway to his non-house and heads toward the Gulf of Mexico. The sun shines bright from the pastel blue above.

Seismic waves continue to and through the molten viscous center.

In Port Washington he visits a former customer and his family. Afterward, he drives over to visit the Ozark blue devils, a framing crew of two that live in Port Washington. They became friends when he managed Trinidad; he's been at their place several times.

He finds their apartment building and goes up the exterior stairs to their door.
He's not prepared for what he's about to see. Or not see! He goes to the door.

It's not there!!! The non-sight fails to imprint on his left brain. The stairs and deck are as he remembers. Everything seems to be the same: the view, position, orientation, location, but there's no door or window!! A railed stairway and deck leading to blank walls!!!

Dan doesn't believe the non-sight and walks down and up the stairs, to his van, back to the stairway, and up again. He needs to confirm what he's not seeing, believing it will return to normal if he walks away and comes back. It doesn't. There's still no door.

His job losses tilt his mind. The non-sight pushes him toward the cataclysmic crack. Calamity ridge is dead ahead. The stairway escalates disaster.

Separation begins. No door, pulls right from left.

'I must've made a wrong turn; wrong building; wrong apartment.'

'No, it's the right one.'

Hemispheres slide as right charges.

Command is in control. Charge is out of control.

Command charges control. Control commands charge.

Charge controls command.

Convection currents buckle and warp iron, rock, and silicon.

Dan spouts cosmic lingo to three teenagers in the parking lot. They're eager to help find the blue devils. They hop into Dan's van.

Dan pilots the spaceship to the main intersection of Port Washington. He's been to the blue devil's pad three times, all in daylight. It's dark now.

Visual match is faint. Shadows disorient him. He dims the visual record in his mind to match current conditions. They end where they began, at the same apartment.

He checks. There's still no door or window! His left brain bypasses the non-sight again and returns to its original objective of finding the blue devils.

He resumes his search and chatters space lingo from the cosmic channel. The cadets sit back, enjoy the cruise. Dan enlarges the search, mind sliding to hyperspace.

In the van is a stack of stop sign brochure holders from Loreto. They stop at an intersection and throw a stop sign out each side of the van. They repeat it at other stops.

After one toss, a stop sign flies down on the right side of the van. "Space manna," Dan spouts. The boys are silent. "Go pick that up," Dan commands.

It's identical to the rest of the stack with Dan's name and address stamped on it. His mind slips through an alter crack. 'Maybe they threw it. I saw it when it came down?'

That thought weakens when two stop signs come down at the next stop. It crumbles when three signs slice the air in V formation and strike the ground at another stop.

Earth bulges, Ayres pops, Australia floats.

Dan comes back to the main intersection and signals for a left turn. The light is red. He sits in the left turn lane with eyes left. Streetlights and headlights dance off concrete.

His peripheral vision catches four stop signs knifing from upper right to lower left. Equally spaced in diamond formation, a foot separating them, they hit pavement in digit tapping unison, spill their cargo, and careen every which way.

"Wow, did you see that?"

A double "Yea--ah," floats from the back in synchronized awe.

Dan watches as the carnage scatters and cart wheels on the grey concrete. The light turns green. He heads west and turns right at the donut shop on his left.

His radar hones. The map in his head guides. The visual picture draws and matches.

He knows where he wants to go but the left brain non-sight won't let him. Instead of right at the second street, he turns left at the third street. It's a dead end.

Red on the right catches his eye. There's something surreal about it. Dan stares at the phantom light as he turns his van around.

He stops to view the sight through the open driver's window.

On his left is a house with three pick-up trucks parked side by side. Dan hangs out the window and focuses on the phantom red hovering low center in the rear window of the middle truck. It looks holographic, like a laser emanating from the glass.

Dan looks around to see if there's a source it's being reflected or projected from. He doesn't see one. He pulls his van forward and keeps his eyes fixed on the sight. The light maintains its stationary low center position and dispels his notion that it might be coming from inside the truck.

He sits and ponders the phenomenon. The cadets silently fidget. The people in the house turn on their porch light and peer out of the window. The boys squirm.

"We better get out of here," one says. Dan eases the clutch out. A perfect wing formation of five side by side stop signs comes cruising from the heavens and crashes into the middle of the illuminated front yard.

'Enough of this,' Dan thinks. It's supernatural and almost beyond comprehension. He drops the space cadets off and heads for Houston. He can't wait to tell Gene.

Continents break and shift; water sloshes to and fro.

Humor takes command. The reality he witnessed is too bizarre. Not as radical as the vortex, soul switching, or vanishing house, all of which Dan still questions, but vividly real; seen first hand, witnessed and confirmed.

Dan cruises the on a plane above concern; higher than any drug could ever take him. In a stratosphere of euphoric bliss, he sails the ozone. Job losses fuel his ship to heaven.

The Cosmo Bank opens. Circuits overload with conflict. Why is the question? Answers come together to open an alter sub cosmo corridor to the Z-ZONE.

Rocky spires thrust to charcoal skies and dive
under seas of red lava, white salt, and blue water.

Gene's ready to hit the sack when Dan arrives. It's midnight. His eyebrows arch over the job loss and his face crinkles to the incessant chatter about no door or window and flying stop signs. He's not used to seeing Dan so animated.

"Let's go on a space cruise." Gene's always good for a galactic cruise but not tonight.

Gene shakes his head in disbelief. "I'm going to bed."

Dan is cruising the high stratosphere and enjoying every minute of it. He's not ready to crash. With no co-pilot he turns on the radio, evaluates events of the past week, and enjoys the supernatural high he's on. Thoughts soar. Audra is a booster rocket.

About two-thirty the DJ mentions cosmic critters and space manna. Dan can't believe what he just heard. He rolls on the floor and cracks up. 'How many people know about the flying stop signs?' His right hemisphere separates and soars from the left.

Dan picks up the phone and dials zero. Twenty minutes of rambling to the operator and the circuit opens to space. He spends hours jacking his jaws.

Orange magma squeezes through colliding and sliding
brown continents and oozes from purple fractures.

Gene stumbles out at six A.M. Dan's chattering like a howler monkey on an overdose of amphetamines. Gene grabs the phone, listens for a minute, slams it down, and stands there staring, jaw agape, eyes narrowing to an inverted V, brows spreading to wings.

The 'are you crazy' look cracks Dan. His side splits as he rolls on the floor. Gene picks up the phone again, listens, and gives the puzzled air look.

Dan rolls some more. He's been trying to tell Gene they gave him an open line to broadcast on but Gene isn't buying it. Incredulous looks send Dan howling in stratospheric ecstasy at the irony, wishing he could bottle the feeling, save it for a rainy day. This rainy day is bursting with sunshine and he doesn't want it to end.

Violet ash spews to lavender heavens
in thanks for the morsel to chew and recycle.

Gene hangs the phone up again, air expression remaining. He isn't listening to what Dan has to say. Instead he says, "You remind me of a shell shocked dude in Nam."

Dan howls and rolls some more. Shell shock would be a good description except he can snap out of it at anytime where true shell shocks can't. He chooses not to!

He's having a great time and no desire for it to end. His mind is open not shutdown. Sadness and sobriety will come soon enough. He has to keep going til he sees Bud Gabet. He'll take a shower about eight, come down to earth to see Bud, and crash afterward.

Gene's somber mood and serious state of mind aren't going to ruin Dan's party especially when he's rocketing through the stars like he is now. He just wants to roll with the flow and enjoy the pristine moment. Gene's normally ready to go but then Gene is normally grumpy in the morning and the roles are normally reversed.

Dan's on a natural high from the cataclysmic split. He has no drug or booze booster. Flying stop signs keep him aloft. He has to keep going to see Bud at nine. He can feel the tired moving in when he eases up.

Dinosaurs die. Green plants submerge and emerge as black death.

Gene checks the phone again. There's dial tone. He calls his boss to say, "I won't be in." He pages through the phone book. Dan chatters.

Like everyone else, Gene is looking for a cure to the effect and ignoring the cause. He doesn't want to hear about cosmic cadets and flying stop signs. He ignores Dan.

Dan's reminded of his mother on the late winter day, a year earlier when Dan tried to illustrate the theory of dual opposites except Patty was trying to see and understand. Gene isn't the least bit interested. Dan didn't and doesn't want to go down to their level. He wants to bring them up to his, where everything is in crystal clear perspective.

But like Patty, Gene doesn't see. Nor does he care to. He's seen the effect and is dealing from that angle. He makes more phone calls.

The yellow god blazes behind the life constricting veil.

Dan's living the dual opposite. So happy he's delirious, so sad he's ecstatic. He soars higher and sips heavenly nectar.

Chapter 36—ENDANCEMENT

Dust and atmospheric debris are pulled down by the dynamic molten core.

My cosmic twin on one side, a white coat on the other, arms hooking mine, we glide down a wide yellow corridor toward a grey double door. Another white coat trails. I'm flying high, laughing and joking, unconcerned; it's a great feeling.

The doors open. Gene stops. His arm slides out. The other white coat slides in. It's so smooth I can't believe they didn't practice it. The two whites propel me through the door and accelerate me across the floor of a big room while people in blue watch us fly by. The white coats push-pull me into a small room and toward a bed, slam me face down, arms locked behind my back, and jerk my pants to my ankles. Reality is immediate.

I'm held down with four arms locking my two in a backcross. I'm still wearing the clothes I left Loreto in yesterday morning minus pants. I knew what they were doing all along but everybody seemed set in doing it and I was having too much fun to worry about it.

I let it get this far because I didn't think Gene could get me committed. It was futile trying to talk to him because he wasn't interested in anything I had to say. His vision was tunneled to shell shock. He could see no other way.

I had everybody in the lobby laughing. I thought, 'they pay people to do this'. I was coming up with all kinds of cornball stuff and loving it.

While Gene talked to the man at the front desk I entertained passers by. Never could get Gene to crack a smile. Not even once. And I tried.

I was looking at the bright side while the non-smilers looked at the dark side. Smilers saw the irony. I had one girl in tears from laughing so hard.

I can't begin to remember what I was saying and doing but it was a cross of George Carlin and Robin Williams. It was like my own private comedy club. Unfortunately reality hit with the bed slam and now I'm quietly fuming.

I know that resistance is futile. Any struggle will bring a herd of whites. So I lay there til they loosen their grip and let me up.

After changing into hospital blues, I'm free to roam the thirty foot square room. Patient rooms line the sides. I try to revive the supernatural high to no avail. The orderlies slammed it to oblivion. Being locked up is never fun.

Elements fuse; protons and neutrons compress; electrons flee.

Twenty-five patients, ranging from a hyperactive ten-year-old boy to a seventy-year-old unresponsive man, inhabit the two thousand foot cubicle. The rest are a mixture of males and females of all ages. With the exception of the seventy-year old the patients are more normal than those in the acute section at Trinidad.

The attractive female I had laughing in the lobby is my doctor. She has a pretty assistant. Things are looking up; almost enough to make captivity bearable.

Gravity pulls into the weak force.

I witness the ultimate ambivalence when a nurse praises the beneficial qualities of the drug they're giving me. "Why don't you take it then," I ask.

"I don't experiment with my body," she says.

"But it's OK to experiment with us inmates?"

"You're not inmates, you're patients."

"Then why can't we come and go as we please?"

"We need to evaluate you in a controlled environment."

"Sounds like captive rats to me. You keep us caged and force us to take drugs you wouldn't take. You think they work because we exhibit what you consider normal and acceptable behavior."

"We know from studying thousands of patients and the effects different medicines have on them," she replies.

"Those effects are not always genuine. Take Thorazine for instance. In the fifties, when it first came out, it was administered to thousands of unruly patients. They became docile and doctors proclaimed it a wonder drug. Well it's not a wonder drug. It's a tranquilizer that makes you incapable of doing anything. If you took it you wouldn't be so eager to give it to someone else!"

"I don't need to take it. I'm a well-adjusted person."

"And Marconi and Galileo weren't?"

"I'm not sure who they are?"

"They were people that society considered abnormal or kooky, in need of help, medication, or confinement. They ended up in a place a well adjusted like you never will."

"Where's that?"

"In the history books."

"Nor would I have a desire to be in the history books."

"The point is, the medical circle is only a half circle. This is the sixth time I've been hospitalized. Each time, a different doctor prescribes a different medicine and stresses the importance of taking it; six different times, six different medicines. How can they all be right? The whole system stresses the importance of taking medicine they themselves wouldn't take. You're still experimenting, with us nuts as guinea pigs. We're talking about an inexact pseudoscience that haughtily predisposes itself to be right in every case when its really educated guesswork based on observations of superficial and often false indicators."

"We don't know your entire history. We treat you based on what we know."

"Just because a patient appears to be adjusted doesn't mean the cause has been cured or healed. The true cause is masked by treating the effect. You train us as if we're Pavlov's dogs, forcing us to beg or charm to receive a reward or not receive punishment. How true is the reality you're seeing through that enticed motivation?"

"Everyone's chemistry is different. We monitor how the medicine reacts with you personally."

"Multiple causes can have the same outward appearance just like different medicines can have the same effect on different people or different effects on the same type people. Why do you think they keep coming back?"

"What would you suggest?"

"How about getting to the root of the problem through developed perception and understanding? A doctor reading the observations and seeing a patient for five minutes a day barely scratches the surface of understanding. Why do you think they call it mental? The cause isn't going to lying on the surface. It takes perceptive probing."

"You certainly have your opinions."

"Psychiatry is a profession that prescribes pills to chemically alter the effect or anti-truth without learning the underlying cause or Truth. Understanding comes from the heart of an atom. It's repeated over and over throughout life and the universe.
Cause creates effect. Effect only exists because of the cause!"

"Oh."

"What was the grievous sin I committed to be locked up here and force fed drugs that you yourself wouldn't take?"

"I'd have to look at your chart."

"I'll tell you what it was. I lost two jobs in a month and witnessed the impossible and unexplained. I'm supposed to be long faced and scared."

"That would probably be the normal reaction."

"I did what I always do when faced with the insurmountable. Instead of looking at the obvious, the sad, I looked at the humor. I was delirious with unexplained ecstasy."

"You needed to be stabilized."

"I was told I was coming here to talk to a doctor. Instead I was slam dunked on a bed by two of your finest. Nobody said anything about locking the gate. So I'm guilty of having too much fun. Nobody got hurt. How does the punishment fit the crime?"

"You're not being punished. You're here to be helped."

"Easy for you to say, standing on that side of the counter, going out for lunch and then home every evening. You're here by choice. You get paid for it."

"I eat my lunch here."

My gut splits as I roll on the floor. 'Where do they find these people?'

"I have to get to work on these charts," the nurse says.

The white coats will probably be coming to give me a shot of Thorazine and lock me in solitary, I think as I walk away.

The cosmic egg grows larger and compresses smaller.

Two weeks after slam-down they move me to the other side with the seventy near normal patients. Audra invades my consciousness. I push her back and socialize more than I have in past hospitalizations. Audra submerges. Nothing I can do about her in here.

A Malaysian nurse helps with the submergence. She's a beauty with a quick wit, charming accent, and infectious laugh. Her eyes sparkle with intelligence. She's fascinated with me and I with her. She makes the comment, "You're so damn interesting!" I'm ready to give up on Audra til I hear, "I have a boyfriend."

The weak force pushes out, resistance flees, toleration loses.

I'm free to come and go from the concrete cage for three hours every afternoon. I find a stadium not far from the hospital and watch track and field athletes train and work out. It's a daily ritual til I find out about the zoo; forty five minutes away and no admittance fee. During the week the crowds are non existent; it's easy to criss-cross back and forth. With the round trip taking half my allotted time, I can't spend long so I go often.

Recoil blasts back and out to black.

Seven weeks after slam down, the doctor decides I'm well enough to be released. It beats my previous long stay by a week. Gene has a spare bunk on his ship.

Flying stop signs are locked into my Cosmo bank.
Mainframe Homes and Audra are submerged dreams. Reality raises its ugly head.

Energy expands.

Mario Asenio is an Italian stud muffin who came to America three years ago and worked his way from a bucket of tools to a crew of men. He's now a framing contractor who builds custom houses but will do concrete work and tract houses when work is slack. Mario is a relentless taskmaster with a lust for power and thirst for money and girlie bars. I started working for him within a couple days of being released from the hospital.

It's my twelfth week and I'm being pushed through the middle of a grueling grind. It's the Fourth of July. The rest of the country is celebrating freedom while I wear chains. I'm the main man and have to be there.

We're working on an elegant townhouse project in a wooded development. Two small bayous intersect at the back of a limited access corner lot. Lapping the edge of the bayous and zigzagging around the lot are concrete footers that form a tangle of steel studded, perilous pathways. Half-inch rebar stabs and grabs skin and cloth that pass too close to their ragged spikes. No protective covers adorn them.

Chapter 37—ENSPEARMENT

Matter blasts from the cosmic egg.

Two-foot-wide footers step down in eight-inch increments as the land slopes from the street to the two bayous. On the right side where the land contour drops sharply, the footers step down in thirty-two-inch increments. Out and down, again and again. Rebar pokes three feet into the air and forms an ominous ridgeback in the center of the stair-stepping footer.

Dan and two helpers are snapping red lines on this stairway to hell. It's a slow methodical process and a precarious crawl around the jutting footers and rippling rebar with the slope slanting and soil sliding. Dan uses a long level, straight board, and a helper to transfer an airborne string line to a mason's line on the rebar laced footers. He adjusts the bottom of the level while the helper holds the board and level to the nylon line lofting overhead. Mario stands upslope and sights to make sure the stick doesn't push the line. Dan puts a pencil mark, plumb down from the string line, on the footer.

Keeping hold of and moving the stick and level is awkward. Each step gets tougher as the stick and level spread longer to reach the string above. It's slow and difficult, sliding them up and down, balancing, twisting, turning, and stepping down porcupine ridge. Mario paces and stomps his feet. He cries, "Faster."

Light elements at the surface spew first.

At first it was a decent job; the pay was low but on time. Mario pushes sixty hour weeks at rates rivaling a burger flipper and no overtime pay. When 'Studly' found what Dan could do, more was expected for pay that remained the same and became increasingly short.

Mario's solution for the cash crunch is more work, bigger jobs, more manpower. His long term ambition blinds his short term myopia. Mario likes to work his jaw and push his men to do the real work. He prefers to sit in tittie bars and ogle the girls to feed his ego. His habit of visiting the girlie bars has accelerated. Nightly beer fests fuel his exotic desires.

Studly demands that you hang around, after working a ten hour day, to drink beer for another couple hours. Then he starts soliciting money for beer and ice. Dan refuses to contribute. He's tired of having to hang around the job every night while co-workers boast and pump themselves to a macho frenzy.

Dan questions reasons for working for a man like this but doesn't see much choice. Recovering back pay is his primary concern. If he leaves, the debt which has climbed to four weeks pay may stay. And now he has to work on the Fourth of July.

Heavy elements from the core catch light in the black void.

Dan decides to shortcut and speed the process. It takes time to lay the stick and level down and step around. Instead of taking the slippery slide around the side, he decides to step down the thirty-two inch step. It's quicker and easier and less maneuvering of the unwieldy stick and eight foot level is required, if he steps down backward.

His rear is first on the next step. Rusty rebar reams a rigid route.
Raunchy ripples pop a pathway up anal alley. Silence issues from a monkey mouth.
His face erupts in ecstatic agony, eyes screwing an empty gaze to infinity.
"Oh God," manages to escape the frozen howl.

Mario, ten feet upslope and looking straight at him, falls backward; his hand covers his mouth to conceal the laugh his eyes are showing. Mario's joy underwhelms Dan as he lifts up and off the penetration, feeling the pop of each ripple as the alien probe releases him. He can barely stand as agony overwhelms anxiety.

A wave of nausea floods through him as Dan comes to understand the full meaning of having your body violated. It's a sick feeling unlike anything he's ever experienced.
He inches up the slope and takes a moment to compose himself.

"Great, it'll take til six o'clock to get finished now," Mario mutters as he stomps around. He gives Dan five minutes and says, "You ready to get back to it?"

Dan looks at him, eyes forming horrified question marks and says,
"Are you nuts? I have to go to the hospital."

"I don't see any blood."

"Mario, that rebar had three to four inches of penetration. I don't know why it isn't bleeding but it has to be checked out and something done about it.
Somebody has to take me to a hospital."

Mario paces and grumbles then assigns the laborers to another task.
"Don't leave before we get back," are his parting words.

Red men build a village at the confluence of the three rivers.

A nurse shows Dan to a room while Mario takes care of the paper work. Dan gingerly eases onto the paper covered, icy cold, steel examination table. So far, no blood!

Fifteen minutes go by. Agony mounts with the growing eternity. . Dan grimaces til he can stand it, or sit no longer. He slides off the table. Blood gushes!

"Nurse," he yells as red spots dot the floor.

She checks. He groans. A doctor comes.

Peroxide pours on the pierced rectum and follows the parallel path of the insurrection up anal canal. Dan clamps ivory on steel. They pack two-feet of one-inch gauze up the freshly reamed route and instruct Dan on follow-up care.

Mario and Dan leave. All Dan wants to do is go home and lay down. Mario has another idea. Over Dan's protests, he stops at a tavern. "It'll make you feel better."

He stops short of force feeding Dan beer. Dan makes his stand after the third beer.
"I don't want another beer. I want to go home and lay down."

Mario orders another beer. Dan ignores it. Studly drinks his and orders another.
Dan drinks his de-chilling beer out of frustration.

Studly grins and says, "Ready to go back to work?"

Dan cocks his head, retinas clouded with disbelief.
His grimace grows as he fights to maintain his one cheek balance on the barstool.
"You got to be kidding," spurts from his mouth as he slips painfully to his feet.

There's no comfortable position. The nauseating feeling grows.
Standing doesn't help. Beer churns his belly. Fog clouds his head.

"Have another beer."

"I don't want another beer!"

This latest round of callousness pushes Dan to the edge of concern and a need to get away from this jerk. A plan starts to form. The cosmo corridor unlocks.

His belief that Audra is at the Mainframe office in Jacksonville surges.
He has to believe something, anything to escape the hell he's living in.

White men push the red men out and build a city.

Dan continues working. Weeks pass and the Italian continues to push.

"I won't get a big enough draw to pay some of the money I owe you if you don't work this weekend. You can take the following Saturday, Sunday, and Monday off."
It's Studly's last plea to get another weekend out of Dan.

"How much would you pay off in addition to my weekly pay?"

"Four or five hundred dollars."

All week Dan looks forward to the three day weekend.
He's had three days off in the past six weeks, not counting the half day on the fourth of July.
It's nearing the end of July and a fantasy is brewing.

He digs up Audra's phone number. He hasn't dialed it since he managed Trinidad.

It's Friday night. Gene's out. Dan dials.

"Hello," the male voice answers.

"Is this 637-4035 in Phoenix?"

"Yes."

"Is Audra there?"

"She's at work."

Dan wonders, "Who are you?"

"I'm her brother. Who are you?"

"I'm a friend from Indiana. Do you live with Audra?"

"I'm a guest."

Dan slips in his Cosmo compartment to check the possibilities. He wants to believe that Audra is in Jacksonville. The phone call is to check that possibility.

The next morning, Dan ponders the phone call. Gene's at work. Afternoon comes.

Dan dials the number to double check. A different voice answers.
"Is this 637-4035 in Phoenix?"

"Yes."

"Is Audra there?"

"No, she's out."

Dan wonders, "Who are you?"

"I'm a guest."

"I thought her brother was the guest?"

"Actually, I'm a friend of her brother and we're both guests."

Dan and Audra are born and raised in that city.

Dan floats back in time through the files of his mind. He remembers the conversation with Satch, the thought of Audra flashing to East Bend, Flash Gordon, and more. He thinks she's in Jacksonville; her brother and friend are covering for her.

Gene comes home. A breeze kicks up, storm clouds start bunching. The sky turns gray then black. Lightning flashes in the distance. Dan contemplates.
Rain falls and continues through the night.

On Sunday rain cloaks the day, lightning illuminates it. Dan watches lightning flash sideways with none going to the ground. It makes as much sense as the polarized snow, eighteen months earlier. He wonders some more.

He looks at connections -- cross, counter, and alter -- between the K and W levels of the C-ZONE of his Cosmo bank. He knows that all matter is composed of frequency vibrations intermingled into patterns of existence. He also knows that ninety-two elements are the building blocks of creation. He can see how Truth and anti-truth stitch and thread through matter and become the mortar of the universe.

Through this understanding he can see how inanimate matter can talk, how unnatural things occur: polarized snow, cold cars boiling, cardboard stop signs flying from the sky, and lightning going sideways as it's now doing. But most importantly, he understands how the mind of man, the highest manifestation of 'the Force',
is also the greatest counterforce.

The magnetic Abram flows to the sea and back again.

Dan's belief that the outside world has a window into his soul grows.
He becomes increasingly wary that others may know of his plan.

He starts to think on two channels,

alternating thoughts, to confuse mind pickers.

And mentally prepares himself for the journey to end all journeys.

WHERE NO MAN WOULD WANT TO BE, YET LOVE TO BE.

WHERE IMAGINATION REACHES THE ZENITH OF DESIGN
AND MADNESS THE APEX OF DESPAIR.

WHERE THOUGHTS BECOME POWERFUL AND DEEDS UNDENIABLE IN A WORLD SO MIND BOGGLING YOU HAVE TO BE CRAZY TO SEE IT.

Chapter 38—ENFRANCHISEMENT

Joseph and Mary join to form the Abram River.

It's Monday, my final day off. I drive my van to the townhouse project. The rest of the crew is working on the townhouse next to rebar hell.

I drive to the tool shed, take Mario's tools out of my van, drive out a back entrance, and head back to Gene's. He's at work. I have time to sort and pack.

My books line the top of the dresser. I look at three of my favorites:
SECRET LIFE OF PLANTS details polygraph experiments that sprouted second enigma,
THE SELFISH GENE talks about the essential ingredient of life, and
CYCLE OF THE HEAVENS. I resist the urge to take one.

I spread and fluff the remaining clothes in the drawers so they don't look so empty and the same with the closet. I look at my flight manual and log book sitting on the shelf. The possibility that others hear my thoughts drags on my left bank and swirls on my right. Thoughts converge like the Joseph and Mary Rivers and divide like the Abram. I mask thoughts as I stash my luggage in my trusty Econoline.

That evening is like any other. Gene sprawls on the couch to watch TV. I sit in my favorite chair.

The next morning, I leave for work five minutes early, packing my shave kit and fluffing the medicine cabinet just before I leave. I fire ole Betsy and take the 610 loop around Houston like I always do. I use split channel thinking to add static and throw off mental trackers as I swing onto Highway 59 to Corpus Christi. My main channel thinks work and exits the freeway at my normal turnoff; the underground channel goes straight.

I maintain radio silence to restrict honing options. Sixty miles out of Houston I'm still thinking about work and wondering why it's taking so long to get there. Scrub land surrounds me. I watch light traffic get heavy.

That's strange. I'm not close enough to population to generate this kind of surge! It's a good reason to exit the freeway. I proceed to phase II.

I head west and north, like the Joseph River flow from Neil Armstrong's launch pad to East Bend, on empty farm market roads. Eventually I reach old Highway 90, the pre-freeway route between Houston and San Antonio. My D-zone autopilot has control and follows the magnetic map in my head. Interstate 10 should be dead ahead.

I drive a few more miles and come to Highway 90 again. My left brain bypasses the anomaly like it did at the blue devils apartment. I continue on the north-south intercept with I-10 and come to Highway 90 for the third time. Jump back Loretta! What the hell is going on? I wonder some more.

My mind aligns with the vortex and gravitates to polar possibilities. Scrub dots the landscape. I think about the weird weather of the past few days. It's sunny blue now.

I come to I-10 and head west, stopping ten miles up the road at the first exit with gas. An attendant comes out of the empty store and watches me fill my gas tank. The lonesome worker makes the comment, "Looks like we're back in business," as a car pulls in. Another follows ten seconds later.

I wonder about the comment as I stand in line to pay for gas. Thoughts take root in my right bank when the guy in front of me says, "I just drove from Houston; guess I'll be heading back."

A door to my left K corridor opens. It's over a hundred miles to Houston and a little past ten in the morning. This gas stop looks like an oasis in the desert. I see nothing but open land around me and no reason for someone to drive here from Houston, then turn around and drive back unless they're road testing vehicles or trying to outrun the vortex.

In previous vortexes the traffic was going toward it. It makes sense that you would want to get away to observe and remember. I think about the heavy traffic that pushed me from Highway 59, and how the timing fits for the road test driver and I to arrive together. K links with C and cross-links with the V-ZONE. A sub passage emerges.

Like the flow of the Abram to Lake Michigan, I go west on Interstate 10. A half hour later, I exit and follow the right branch route, north to Waco. The sun is shining bright overhead when I walk into Mike's office. He appears clueless about the vortex.

Joseph and Mary molecules flow through the Straits of Mackinac.

My autopilot continues to subconsciously follow the flow of the right branch north, east, and south to Lake Erie. By the time I stop in Louisiana in the dead of night, I've covered seven hundred miles but advanced less than two-hundred toward my goal. I crawl into the back of the van and sleep on the carpeted floor.

The sun blinds me the next morning as I head east on Interstate-10. It crosses overhead as I pass through Mississippi and Alabama. It's sinking when I stop in Pensacola for gas and food. My mind drifts toward the O-ZONE.

Joseph and Mary molecules fall over Niagara and flow through Ontario.

I'm past the halfway mark and starting to second guess myself; always a bad sign. Jon Busby has been transferred to Albany from Louisville. My mind heads right, on the polar route, my neurotransmitters lean left.

It's late afternoon when I arrive in Albany. Rocket fuel seeps. I ramble. Jon takes it in stride.

"I've met the most wonderful woman," he says. "She's everything you could dream of," then switches subjects, "Marcie's in Atlanta and Chuck's in Macon, today and tomorrow."

"What are they doing there," I ask.

"Marcie's been promoted to Southeastern regional manager. She brought Chuck along as assistant regional manager."

"No kidding?" Hmm. Mike didn't say anything; Chuck trained him. "Is Vince still in Nashville," I ask.

"Yes. You know Chuck really liked you. You really should stop to see him."

"Do you think he'll be there when I get there?"

"I'm sure he will. If it's too late tonight you can always get a motel and catch him in the morning. He'll be glad to see you."

I think about it. "All right, I'll go to Macon, Atlanta, and," since I'm on a side-trip, "over to Nashville to see Vince."

Joseph and Mary molecules flow out the Saint Lawrence and join with J and M molecules from the southern branch that are riding the Gulf Stream.

Mario paid four hundred dollars on his debt bringing it down to eleven hundred. I left Houston with seven hundred dollars and the intention to clear this mystery. If it becomes a goose chase I'll consider it a vacation and return to Houston. I'm prepared to deal with whichever way the water flows. I have to know.

I'm northbound from Albany when I feel a dull pull on my groin. The same sensation I felt six month's earlier at my vanished house in Lemon Heights. I think of Audra and wonder about Jon's wonderful woman, his eagerness to send me to Macon.

The pull gains strength. The intensity increases, stronger than at Lemon Heights. The further I drive the more painful it becomes.

I'm driving north on Highway 3 and 19, magic numbers, when I see a highway patrolman turn down the road to Jimmy Carter's hometown. It's an exact repetition of what I saw five minutes earlier. It's the fifth time I've passed a sign pointing west to Plains.

The triple crossing of Highway 90, thirty six hours earlier, bubbles to the surface. The vortex flashes. The intensity of the pull on my groin is immense. Wires cross.

Confusion mounts when I enter the tiny town of Rebecca. My mind flops as I flip the map in my hands. I didn't see the highway to Macon. I do a U-turn and head south.

The sky is moving toward twilight when I arrive in Macon. I stop at a phone booth and call the Macon Mainframe office. A familiar voice answers the phone.

"Hello," I say. "I just left Jon Busby in Albany. He said Chuck Suave would be in Macon today and tomorrow. Is he there now?"

The harried voice replies, "Chuck's in Atlanta. You'll have to contact him there."

I hear Chuck's voice in the background, talking rapid fire as if there's some kind of crisis. Thoughts flash from the blackout at Chuck's house and forward to New Years Eves. A river of thought swirls and connects to Waco.

"Is this Mike," I ask.

"No, I'm Joe. Chuck's not here. You'll have to contact him in Atlanta." CLICK.

The abrupt responses, voice recognition, and phone click send me to the P-ZONE. I think about Audra's denial on the night of the chase and Mike's tonight. I didn't tell Mike of my plans yesterday in Waco and he didn't tell me about Chuck's promotion. Now they're both here! And both voices were hectic! And what about the vortex?

I float to Interstate 75 and north to Atlanta. My mind rises to the O-ZONE. My gas gauge sinks lower.

J and M molecules brush Arctic waters and flow south past Europe and Africa.

I take the airport exit. Planes circle overhead but none land. I'm filling my gas tank when I hear, "Let the party begin." My mind sucks to the edge of the V-ZONE.

Some of the Joseph and Mary molecules go left around the African Cape,
flow through the Indian Ocean, and on to the Pacific.

Traffic breezes into and through downtown. It's eight o'clock.
There's no one in the Mainframe office. My compass spins. I keep going.

The soup starts to thicken. Downtown, traffic was dense but flew at seventy. Fifty miles out, the gaps are closer and traffic erratic. I've been through many cities at this time of night and have never seen this kind of traffic this far from a population center. The V-ZONE sucks me in. I don't want to stop.

Most of the Joseph and Mary molecules suck into the Antarctic Wave.

My mind eddies as I contemplate Nashville. My roots pull right. Audra pulls left. I don't know which way to go. Three lanes grow to four.

The arrow points right to Chattanooga, left to Nashville. Traffic has been extremely heavy for the last fifty miles. It's close to midnight. I decide at the last moment.

Heavy traffic won't allow me to get over. I can't follow I-75 north.
Traffic seems to vanish on the left fork.

Confusion takes charge.

Fantasy controls.

The vortex commands.

Chapter 39—ENLIGHTMENT

The flooded Green River deposits dinosaur carcasses on the sandbar.

The eastbound freeway sign reads Chattanooga, seventeen miles. Dan thinks about the sign he saw a few miles earlier when he was northbound on I-75. He's sure the northbound sign he read not more than fifteen minutes ago said Chattanooga, seventy miles.

He did a U-turn at the first exit after the Y to Nashville and is headed back to I-75. Traffic is so light he feels like he's in a different universe. He checked his map at the U-turn and saw the two freeways don't connect. He wonders what's going on.

His mind whirls and does a double take when the first exit isn't I-75 north but a road into Chattanooga. That leaves a big chunk of concrete missing from the path he took. He exits while civilization is still close.

Sand covers the dinosaur remains on the Green River sand bar.

Dan's driving through an old business section of Chattanooga when a man dashes out from the left, waves his arm, and yells. Dan pulls over to the right. The man runs toward him. Dan wonders what's going on. He rolls forward.

The man keeps coming. Dan takes off as outstretched fingers grab for his van. He has to be crazy to pick up a derelict in a seedy bar district of a strange town at midnight.

Dan speeds east on a cross-town intercept with I-75 north. With an internal gyroscope, he rarely mistakes east from west or north from south even when he can't see the sun. Maps, like blueprints, are a way of putting everything in perspective. He read maps before he knew how to drive.

Dan finds it hard to believe that a half hour earlier traffic was densely packed on I-75 north and now it's virtually non-existent. The Chattanooga choo-choo blasts its horn as he rolls through Knoxville. He follows the interstate north through the mountains of Tennessee to a lifeless exit and a dirt road.

More dinosaurs and more sand are deposited on the sandbar.

Roosters crow as the sun peeks through the Appalachians. Dan looks out and finds himself parked in a farmyard high above the freeway. He knew he climbed a hill a few hours earlier but had only a vague idea of how high. They call it a mountain where he's from. Here it's just a foothill.

The farmyard is on a level spot between a steep drop-off to the freeway on one side and a sharp uphill slope on the other side. Parked on the uphill side of the plateau, Dan looks at the weathered barn behind him and the faded lime-green, two story house in front of him. The only thing stirring is the rooster's wake up call. He decides to move on before a shotgun comes out the door.

Time passes as land uplifts and the Green River changes course.

Dan's calm. His anxiety is gone. His mind sinks to the B-ZONE. Thoughts of the past two days submerge and become fuel for his Cosmo bank.

He heads north through the hills of Kentucky to the bluegrass by the Ohio River and crosses into the state of Ohio. Hours later he exits the freeway at Neil Armstrong's launch pad, where roots of the Joseph River sink their watery tentacles. Dan goes with the flow.

He sees the Highway Patrol welcoming committee too late to turn back. It's a stark reminder that he's not as stealthy as he'd like. His mind jogs through a gate to the past and the vortex he left behind. Eerie thoughts surface. The trooper's cars flank him. He keeps going.

The westbound trooper is away from his car and chats with the eastbound officer on the south side of the divided highway. Dan heads west and north with the Joseph to the land of his youth. The officers remain behind.

The corn is tall and green. Soybean, wheat, and oat fields are full and turning to gold. Dan sees a prosperous year for the farmers.

He circles the land of his forefathers and ends at the country house where his mind boggling journey began thirty months earlier with the vision and Bonnie Franklin opening his empathic channel. The grappling pull from Albany heightened his awareness of it. He thinks about all the times it's been active since he first discovered it. At first he thought it might be coming from his mind but testing convinced him that the signals come from an external source.

Luke and Brandy have a young son in diapers. Dan spends two nights and two days with them. While there, he calls Jon in Albany; somebody licked all the red off his sucker. Dan speculates that the wonderful woman left him.

Dinosaur bones poke from the uplifted and folded land.

"Mario called. He offered half the business to come back," Patty says when Dan finally makes it to his parent's house.

Chapter 40—ENCUMBERMENT

Joseph and Mary atoms ride air currents and cycle back to their origins.

Mainframe Homes and Audra dominate my mind. The vortex lingers.
I visit Wade Yangster at his fort in downtown East Bend.

During the visit I make several phone calls and instead of people answering I hear "I'm sorry but that number is no longer in service," or "If you'd like to make a call please hang up and try again...' Some numbers don't even ring. The phone system seems to be haywire. The anomaly adds to my growing belief that the vortex followed me.

I try again. This time my mother answers. My previous three attempts yielded 'out of service' recordings; I'm sure I dialed right. I wonder if I'm in the same universe.

Patty says, "You need to meet us at the Mental Health Center tomorrow morning." I wonder where that came from. I spent the entire day with them prior to visiting Wade.

I say, "OK," but harbor doubts. I've been tricked too many times on that deal. Ever since that first confinement on the night of the chase, they use the mental health system to control me. I don't need to be controlled! I can control myself.

The fact that no one ever asks me what I'm thinking and answers my questions with questions or gives no answer confirms my understanding of what is happening.
I dismiss the different universe concept and go back to the vortex.
The phone recordings and no rings bolster that belief.

Darkness creeps forward. I go to see Leroy at the clubhouse. I've had a half dozen 'If you'd like to make a call...' recordings at his number. A personal visit is required.
Leroy's phone is fine. He's been there the whole time.

Magnetism draws.

The next morning I head south and east, opposite to the Joseph River flow, and stop in the small towns I pass through. I look for banks and pay them a visit.
Betsy's old and tired. I need a new vehicle; I need money.

I talk to bank managers and presidents. They give little hope.
I leave a penny, turned heads up or down, on the desk when I leave.

I continue east and then north, stopping at banks as I circle counterclockwise.
I'm not far from a small town northeast of East Bend when I unconsciously make a left turn that takes me toward my parent's house. I accept it as a subconscious signal.

They should be back from the MHC by now, I think.

When I walk in the door, Mom and Shasta are sitting at the round oak dining table.
Patty doesn't ask why I didn't show at the MHC. Instead she says, "You know Dan, the banks believe in you and Matt Moses believes in you."

I do a double take. My mind flip-flops while my face remains unfazed.
Matt Moses is the mayor of East Bend.

Shock opens a sub compartment and unlocks the Z cell. Light shines though the crack. My mind sets sail for the border of fantasy and reality in the land of omniscience, the O-ZONE. Before I'm able to absorb the impact of what she just said Patty continues, "You're supposed to go to the MHC."

A premonition hits me. I know what I have to do. I hop in my van. Patty gets in Shasta's car. I follow til they pull in the left turn lane.

I pull alongside. Tears are flowing from Patty's eyes. I know why. I turn right. They turn left. Shasta waves bye as we go our separate ways.

Three miles down the road I look in my rearview mirror and see them behind me. I lock the E-ZONE and continue straight. This is no time for emotions. Shasta and Patty follow. They need to know.

I pull into the MHC parking lot, where Adam and Bill abducted me thirty months ago. I look over at the black, silver, and white cosmic car zone by the other building. Shasta pulls in next to me. We get out and walk toward the brick face of the glass cage.

Patty and Shasta follow me up the walk. I push the buzzer. We silently wait.

I don't ask why they did their turnaround. I know.

Gravity draws.

A counselor, I know from previous stays, opens the door with a wide smile and holds it as we pass through. My thoughts are clear; I have no fear. Art locks the mesh reinforced glass behind us.

I follow the counselor toward the familiar wrap-around-counter; Patty and Shasta tail. Art stops short of the hallway to the cosmic car odyssey, turns, and says with a smile, "Just a minute, Dan."

He disappears down the cosmic corridor. I look over at the stereo where I first heard, "I was walking through the halls of karma, just the devil and me." I haven't heard it since.

Art returns with a glow and says, "You need to go to the administration building."

Polarity pulls.

Shasta and Patty sit in the lounge area and watch me fill out forms. Shasta looks at one and chuckles when she reads "Friar Tuck Drive." I continue writing nonsense.

I notice their eyes look to the side and smiles form on their mouths. My eyes follow theirs and catch a glimpse of Adam going into an office. The door closes behind him.

It confirms the premonition I had at the oak dining table. Then Patty's tears validated it. Dad's appearance solidifies it. 'They went to the MHC this morning. I didn't show. The doctors told Adam of the official conclusion. It was more than he could handle. His mind twisted inside out. He remained there.'

The roots of those thoughts go back to 'Paradise Rising' and the photo booth at Springdale Mall when the rocket brew began formulating. The mother of all premonitions, the original rocket fuel, is the omniscient vision. Audra was the catalyst to cloud nine. She still is although her whereabouts are in a fog bank. I'll deal with that when the time comes.

Joseph and Mary atoms join the plunge from heaven to earth.

Right now I'm here at the MHC so Adam can get it together as he apparently has. The man that's directing me at the administration building is also a Concord alumnus. Phil graduated six years after I did. He takes us down the hall and into an office.

I was maintaining surveillance on the closed door when we were whisked away. Adam didn't come out. Shasta, Patty, and I wait in the ten by ten. Phil comes and goes.

Silence fills the air. I think about the vortex and punch numbers on the telephone. I've been using the telephone since my visit with Wade at the fort to stop vortex activity. I don't know what I'm doing but I do - like jungle drums and teletype; the Force flows.

I know that pulses and waves emanate from the interaction of Truth and anti-truth; things happen when they're out of balance. Telephones carry the physical pulse making them the perfect antidote to the vortex. The Force flows from my fingertips.

Phil comes in while I'm punching numbers and says, "You can go now."
It's what I calmly expected. I go my way and Shasta and Patty go theirs.

My course leads downtown to Satch's office in the City-County Building. I haven't seen him in eight months, since before New Year. Satch says, "Dan, you have a special gift."

I think he's talking about telephone vortex control and don't question it.
Instead, I talk about Audra. The sergeant's evasive about her.

Rain fills the tributaries of the Joseph and Mary Rivers.

I leave Satch and go to the homestead. Adam and Bill are talking in the front yard. I park under the tree in the driveway, get out, and walk over to them.

The conversation ends. Thoughts of Audra creep to the surface.
Concerns about being corralled tag along. I've seen this scenario before.
The new conversation creates anxiety. I decide to leave.

"You can't leave," Adam says.

"Why not?"

"Somebody's coming to see you."

"Who?"

"Just somebody coming to see you."

I pace as I think about it. My hope is for Audra but I fear otherwise.
"Who's coming to see me," I ask.

"I can't say."

"Why?"

"Because I said I wouldn't."

I pace some more as I think. I didn't tell Satch or anyone else where I was going. How would anyone know where I am? I wonder. There's only two parties' I can think about that wouldn't want me to know about their arrival ahead of time; Audra or the suits. Audra's backed out at the last minute so many times that I can't count on her showing and if it's the suits; I don't want to be here when they arrive.
"If you don't tell me who's coming, I'm going to leave," I say.

"They'll be here any minute."

"Who?"

"Just somebody coming to see you," Adam repeats.

What is it with these guessing games? Seems like everyone plays them just before they lock me up or strap me down. Dad's tone and urgency suggest Audra but that train of thought has been derailed countless times. Anxiety grows.
I head for my van. Adam and Bill follow.

"Why can't you just wait," Bill says.

"Why can't you tell me who's coming," is my reply.

"Because we said we wouldn't," Adam chimes.

I've trusted and been tricked too many times to wait for it to happen again.
I hop in ole Betsy, shut the door, and start her up. Bill flashes his right arm through the open window, grabs the keys, turns her off, and starts pulling my keys from the ignition.

I grab Bill's hand, jam it and the keys back, and growl, "Let go of my keys."

Bill holds fast. So do I. "Let go of my keys," I bellow with intensity.

Bill tightens his grip and resolve. So do I. My left hand is on the steering wheel. Bill's standing there with his right arm stretched through the window to his shoulder. Adam is back a couple feet and to the side. Bill is slightly bigger than me. I'm slightly stronger. Bill would win a boxing match but I'd win at wrestling.

My left elbow could connect with Bill's jaw in a split-second.
But striking someone is an alien concept. Even in self defense,
I would deflect and counter their moves.

If we were outside I'd pin him to the ground in a flash, flat on his back, arms locked above his head, legs immobilized, with my fist hovering over his face. It would happen so fast there would be nothing he could do about it. Even if I started pummeling, there would be nothing he could do about it because he would be firmly pinned and I have an arm free.

"If I let go of these keys, I'm going with you."

"Then get in because I'm going."

"Why can't you just wait," Adam pleads as Bill scurries around the back side of the van and I turn the ignition key.

"Wait for what," I ask. "What's the big secret?"
Why do they want to control me and why do they always play these guessing games?

The only thing I know for sure is that I'm not waiting to find out.
Bill hops in the passenger seat. I watch his arm and my keys
as I back out of the driveway and head down the road.

Chapter 41—ENCROACHMENT

Truth and anti-truth begin an eternal dance.

Dan heads up Homestead Road towards town. Silence punctuates the air. He doesn't know where he's going - he's just going and wants to keep going. He doesn't intend to stop long enough for Bill to snatch the keys.

Traffic jams at stop signs. He dodges onto the shoulder to keep moving. The accelerator and clutch pump up and down, the tree shift slides back and forth.

The unanswered questions, so eerily familiar, spur Dan's anxiety on a collision course with the T-ZONE. Four miles up the road Bill says, "Let me out." Dan obliges.

Now that he doesn't have to worry about his keys being jerked, Dan relaxes and heads for the country like he always does when he needs to think. He cruises back roads through familiar and unfamiliar territory and meanders aimlessly around three counties.

He senses vortexes forming and since he doesn't have a phone, dials numbers in his head to keep them controlled. The T-ZONE opens wide. The vortexes pulse. He feels an ache in his groin and wonders about Audra, if it was she who was supposed to show.

He sees vortexes pulsating and growing, ebbing and flowing, coming and going; erasing existence and memory of both cause and effect. Memories that remain become fuel for the next round of vortex erasure. He drives through the night and into the morning, stopping to fill his tank as the orange sun peeks over the grey horizon.

Black holes form.

Dan heads out of town on Highway 33. A glow forms in the middle of his back. It radiates heat; a new sensation, similar to the encagement and Jasper glows but different. Those glows were external and moved into him. This glow grows from within.

The heat pulses and grows, ebbs and flows like the vortex. His groin pulls, like on the drive from Albany Georgia, six days earlier. Audra came to mind then. She does again.

The further he drives, the harder the pull becomes. Like a cosmic rubber band; one end anchored to downtown East Bend and the other to his testicles. It stretches. The pain is intense, almost more than he can bear.

The global vortexes link and erase footholds in the web of life. Dan sees existence shrinking to East Bend like a black hole to nowhere. He's stretching the boundary back with the jewels of his existence. He'll grit and bear it til he breaks the band to non-existence.

He's yang, fighting to expand the elastic bubble, to grow.
She's yin, controlling the center of the web to oblivion. He'll live even if he has to die trying.

Galaxies await birth.

Fifty miles out when it's ready to kill him, the band snaps. He's broken the hold. Tired grabs hold of him. He pulls into a bank parking lot to close his eyes.

He crawls in back for some shut eye. His mind enters the X-ZONE. Audra controls it. The glow returns. He sits up.

Four hundred yards away, cattycorner from the bank, he sees her coming from the opposite direction in a black Horizon and turning left into a subdivision. The Horizon vanishes into the woods of the subdivision. Dan is instantly alert and goes to investigate.

The universe grows.

The small subdivision has one entry/exit point. His search is fruitless; no Horizon. Dan parks his Econoline and starts knocking on doors. It produces no clues.

Tiredness reaches out and wraps her fingers around his brain. He decides to knock one more time. The house is a sprawling ranch with three car garage on a large wooded lot.

He walks up the curving, flagstone walk to the front door. It's open. Dan knocks. He rings the doorbell. No response. He waits. He reaches for the screen door. It's unlocked. He opens it and walks in.

A lady appears. Rings of circles surround her eyes and mouth. "What are you doing," she shrieks.

"I'm looking for my girlfriend, Audra Diamante. Do you know her?"

"No. Get out," she yells.

"Sorry to bother you."

She slams the door behind him. He crossed the line and is too tired to wonder why as he walks up the street to ole Betsy and crawls in. He's so tired. He stumbles into the back and falls on the floor.

The glow grows from the center of his back. He doesn't know what to make of it and doesn't care. He's way too tired too wonder why. His mind enters the Z-ZONE.

In his dream he hears noises, scuffling, and then a voice, too real for a dream. "Get out of the van, with your hands up."

Dan sleepily pokes his head up. He sees three police cars and lots of police officers surrounding the van. He crawls around the front seat. When he pokes his head out of the driver's door he sees at least two guns are pointed at him. He doesn't turn to look for more.

He's never had a gun pointed at him before. A cartoon of a bullet speeding through his head and leaving a smoking hole as it whistles by, flashes on his inner screen. Dan decides to move very slowly, making no fast moves, and giving no hint of doing anything other than being compliant as he steps out, hands up.

The officers handcuff him and put him in a cruiser. He dozes, too tired to wonder or care what happens next. The glow returns.

He's taken to a small jail and escorted to an empty cell. They remove the handcuffs. The gate clanks and thuds. Dan crashes on the mat covered, steel cot. He's so tired.

His body tingles and generates an internal heat unlike anything he's ever experienced. He feels like he's radiating but he's too tired to care. All he wants to do is sleep.

Life evolves.

Two policemen wake Dan and take him into a small room with a plain grey table and a chair on either side. He feels the internal heat pulsing, growing, pushing out, glowing. He sits. Another officer sits down in the opposite chair.

The officer's eyes flush with water. He squints when he looks at Dan. "You have Texas plates on your van. What are you doing in this area?" The officer averts his moist gaze. Water beads on his lower lids.

"I grew up in East Bend and came up from Texas a week ago." Dan feels the glow radiating. "I was on my way to see my cousin in Cassopolis."

"What were you doing in that lady's house?"

"I thought I saw my girlfriend go into that sub-division. I was looking for her. The door was open. I was too tired too think straight," he says, eyes fighting to close.

The officer squints, water spills onto his cheek. Brushing it with his finger, he says, "You scared that lady. That's an exclusive area. They're not used to strangers walking in."

"I'm sorry, I meant no harm. If you'll call Sergeant Holman at the East Bend Police Department, he can vouch for me. I talked to him yesterday."

Dan's taken back to the cell where he promptly crashes into the T-ZONE.

Soul becomes mind.

He's awakened and introduced to some suits from the East Bend Police Department. They handcuff him and put him in the back seat of a black sedan. The suits and sunglasses remind Dan of the Blues Brothers. One appears to have something in his eye. He rubs them and they water. Small streams gush when his finger lifts his sunglasses from his cheek. He wonders if they're taking him to Audra.

Death becomes life.

He imagines the life they'll spend together. All the happiness he could ever imagine revolves around her. His heart hovers in the L-ZONE when they pass Satch's office.

"Where are you taking me?"

"They want to check you out at the hospital."

It's just what he didn't want to hear. The odds of seeing Audra take a nose dive. His van is fifty miles away. His glow submerges.

He prepares for the worst by hoping for the best. Audra regains her regal post. She's the only thing that matters. His mind bathes in her tender embrace.

Chapter 42—ENFACEMENT

Heaven becomes hell.

The suit pulls into a rear parking lot of the engagement-encagement hospital. I vividly remember the sights and frights of the padded room but don't feel the anxiety. Optimistic wonder and necessary certainty predominate. Audra's in charge.

Anticipation grows as we board the elevator. We go up. The doors open. Nobody's there. The encagement scene flashes. We walk to the counter.

I see familiar faces but not Audra's. Most of the seven-hundred-dollars I left Texas with was spent on gas for the three thousand miles I've driven in the past nine days. The hospital impounds the hundred-eighty that's left. The suits leave.

I see no notable changes since my last visit over two years ago. The nurses' station - wrap around grey counter- is the same. The lounge cubicle across from it, at the intersection of the two hallways, is the same. Some of the patients were here then. Most of the staff is the same. Drs. Bowser and Koolthorpe are still the reigning gods.

I'm allowed to roam the floor. I get chills and eerie thoughts when I pass the padded room that played a pivotal part in expanding my fantasy compartment. I recall the crushing anxiety of being locked up, Audra locked in my bathroom, the pigeon on the ledge, the buzzing mesh over the window.

Rainfall overflows channels and floods fields,
eating and depositing soil and Joseph and Mary atoms.

Where's Audra, I wonder as I cruise into the dayroom where "Free Bird" played after my release from the padded cell. The stack of 45's still sits on the window ledge by the record player. I check. Amazed, I find that "Free Bird" is still there!

The memories are too painful to forget, the surrealism haunts my mind. The tables and chairs in the dayroom are shifted to new positions; they were always in a state of change. I wait and search for Audra. Hope dims with the sun.

That evening is as surreal as any I've encountered. Patients are shown an adventure travelogue. A girl sits next to me and asks questions as if she's linked to Mainframe Homes. The cell to Satan's playground in Jasper opens. "How do you know these things," I ask.

"I don't know is her response."

After the sixty minute flick, a girl I haven't met, comes over and tells me, "You said TT FF and you were gone."

A light flickers as my mind contorts; my teletype code! Too stunned to put my mouth in gear, I question reality and dive into the T-ZONE realm of possibilities. The teletype girl flits away.

I press my face against the glass pane and look down at the damp streets that reflect eerie light through a thin veil of fog. My imagination runs wild as the dark side unleashes.

I think about the evil that's running amok with no walls to contain it while I stand safe in this place of refuge for battered souls. It's a strange twist for a guy who hates confinement.

Trees stick their roots in the riverbank, sucking sustenance,
blocking raging waters, and trapping river burden.

Daisy's one of the familiar faces. Her appearance has changed to a punk rock look. She struts around with a radio to her ear and groupies on her tail. She tells me,
"Just think of it as a home away from home." I can't get used to that idea.

I'm sitting in the dayroom, listening to a small portable radio. A guy, sitting fifteen feet behind me, is listening to his radio and a different station. Daisy rolls in, radio to her ear, entourage on her tail. When she walks inline with me and the radio behind me, my radio goes blank. She moves and my radio comes back on. I get up and move around to place my radio between hers and his. Every time I do, mine goes blank. I wonder.

The girl who said, "TT FF and you were gone," is married. Her husband visits regularly. She seems to tighten up whenever he's around. His actions seem too lovey-dovey and boastful as if he won her as some sort of prize. I wonder if there's an elaborate charade going on with Audra's soul being chased and corralled by the dark side. It's a thought like many; without a conclusion and another mystery for my Cosmo bank.

The river rages; trees rip out and leave growing, brown eddy swirls.

The days wear on. A week passes. I'm allowed to go out twice a day.
Glad for the small amounts of freedom, I frequent the park like I did on my previous stay. A gentle breeze rustles green leaves and enhances the peaceful setting.

On one excursion, I run into a fellow inmate from my previous stay.
Mark says, "We're going to the lake for the weekend. Wanna go along?"

"Sure, if they'll give me a pass."

To my surprise, my request is honored. I've only been there twelve days!

The wind blows through my hair as I ride in the back of the pick-up truck, bouncing down back roads to a secluded cabin on a small lake not far from East Bend. I swim and float around, ride dirt bikes, and have a peaceful time. The sun falls in the west.

Flood waters recede and leave soil layered and debris littered on the plain.

I return from a walk. The group, spurred by the three juveniles' desire for roasted marshmallows, has piled chunks of moisture laden logs in a makeshift fire pit. They used all the paper before finding some kerosene and dousing the pile of logs with it.
The smoke is gone but so are the matches. They search for more.

Fumes float. The search is fruitless. Kids cry. Fumes linger.

I have a lighter but no paper. We look some more and find none. Time passes. The kids plead for marshmallows. Spurred by cries, I make a dangerous decision.

The rest of the group stands back while I hug the ground and crawl
to the saturated logs, hand extended with my Bic™ ready to flick.

"KA WHOOM."

A blazing ball of blue-white heat engulfs my retreat. The acrid scent of burnt flesh and hair fills the air. My baptism by fire misses my rebar reaming by six weeks.
I wonder if it's a prelude to the future.

Back at the hospital, I'm treated for third degree burns. Except for my eyebrows, recovery is rapid. The next weekend is spent with my parents.

On the way back to the hospital Sunday night, Adam tells me,
"In another six weeks you might get out."

I know it won't be that long but don't comment. This has been my easiest if not weirdest stay; more surreal than my encagement stay. I feel strangely detached.
Audra and Mainframe Homes have remained foremost in my mind.
The vortex lingers in the background.

The raging river cuts new channels and leaves oxbows.

I don't know what tomorrow will bring or where I'll go when I get out.
I know that I won't be heading back to Mario Asenio and Houston anytime soon.

The money I have left won't take me very far.
'The banks and Matt Moses believe in you,' is still fresh in my mind.

I wonder if the vortex has erased that opportunity and if Audra is still around.

Chapter 43—ENTREATMENT

Atmospheric debris builds and compresses, layer after layer.

Fifty-five dollars is missing when they release Dan two days later. He has twenty-two dollars to live on till they find it. They say, "Come back Thursday."

His parents think he's going to be in the hospital for another six weeks so he doesn't bother calling them. His van is at Freddy's house, thirty miles away. He relies on the shoe leather express to visit friends around town.

On Thursday, the hospital puts him off. They can't find his missing fifty-five dollars. Dan can't find any in his pockets. "Check back tomorrow," is their answer.

The Colorado plateau rises.

Dan notices an abundance of out of state cars around the hospital including one with Texas plates that looks just like Mario 's. Most are from Ohio but in far greater numbers than he's ever noticed before. The gate to the X-ZONE unlocks.

He thinks about Audra flashing here eight months earlier. The door to the magic kingdom opens. 'The dark side tapped the vortex energy. It's out of control,' he reasons.

He sits in a donut shop at five in the morning, waiting for the hospital to scrape his money together. He has a minimum of three more hours to wait and no money to wait with. He hasn't eaten since yesterday morning. The milkman comes in. The X-ZONE is open.

It's Bill Bagby, his honey pitched mentor at Bailey Building Systems. He's in an altered state, barely recognizable. Dan asks, "Can I have a milk crate?"

"Take two," is Bill's congenial response.

"Thanks," Dan says as he walks happily away with his plastic milk crates. The donut shop wouldn't even give him water!

Two hours later he's in the hospital cafeteria trying to swap a crate for a donut. It's an extra! The cashier isn't buying it. She calls a supervisor.

The supervisor takes Dan out back and shows him stacks of crates like his. He doesn't buy Dan's story about the milkman. Dan tells him about his missing money.

The head nurse from the eighth floor comes down. The supervisor takes Dan's crates. The nurse tells him to come back at three.

Dan walks. His belly growls. He's down to five cigarettes. He can go without food but he has to have smokes. Without his milk crates he has no bargaining power.

He checks at three. "We don't have it. Check back in an hour."

It's five o'clock before they do. And it's a fine how do you do. A check! Dan's eyes roll to white.

"What am I supposed to do with this? You took cash. I want cash!"

"We got you a check. Take it or leave it."

Dan holds his tongue and hopes the store across from the park will cash it. He smoked his last cigarette before the three o'clock no show. His nerves are jangled.

At the grocery store across from the park, a golden retriever is tied to the bike rack by the entry. It's Barker, his ole buddy from Houston- two doors down from Gene.

The chain store can't cash the puny check from the big hospital a block away! On his way out, Dan sees a small car with four men pull up. It looks like Gene and three of his neighbors. They're in altered states. One of them was trying to pick a fight with Dan at the donut shop fifteen hours before.

Barker is jumping up and down, tugging at his leash. Dan bends down to unravel it as Barker alternates licking and tugging. He unhooks Barker from the leash to make it easier. Barker runs into the store.

Dan gets the leash unraveled and runs after him, leash dragging. The man who refused to cash the check is trying to stop Barker from entering the main corridor to the store. Dan catches and leashes Barker and walks out with Barker pulling the lead.

The small car with four men is still sitting outside the door. Dan glances at them, makes a right at the bike rack, and goes around the front side of the store. The four man car zips a left around the parking lot and circles back around the store on an intercept course.

Dan reaches the street intersection on the other side of the store just before the small car reaches the stop sign. The driver's the only one in it! Dan does a double take. He flips to the X-ZONE and cuts across the street and through the park. He loses the car and finds a magic carpet.

Water cuts through the rising plateau and washes organic matter to the sea.

Dan and Barker cruise east and south. They're on a main drag when they encounter a small, unmanned car parked across the sidewalk. Fifty feet of open driveway lay in front of it. The car blocks their path. 'It must be for me.' Barker agrees.

Dan opens the door. Barker hops in back. The key's in the ignition.

Dan hops in, fires it, backs onto the street, and takes off. 'Something's wrong.' The car's a deathtrap with swaying suspension, loose steering, and grinding brakes. Steel screeches as he rounds the first corner and pulls to stop at the curb, a hundred yards from where he found it. 'It can't be for me,' he thinks.

Dan and Barker get out and start walking, zigzagging down the back streets. He floats on the magic carpet, leaving the route to his internal gyro, and enjoys the ride. The big store on the south-side with the flashing cornucopia sprouts into view. 'Maybe they can cash this check so I can get some smokes.'

They can't. It's ten o'clock at night. "Try back in the morning," is their answer.

It's been almost eight hours since he had a nicotine fix. He had a steak and potato at Uncle Bob's after that so he's not starving but the lack of nicotine is killing him. It's ten hours before he can try again. The X-ZONE pulls him deeper.

Dan walks around the store with Barker at his side. He sees a milk crate, identical to one the supervisor confiscated this morning, sitting at the edge of the parking lot. 'Space manna.' Dan's ecstatic. His magic carpet does a lap around the O-ZONE and dives into the Q-ZONE. He sits on the crate. Barker sits beside him.

He sits there with no cash and no smokes and waits all night for the day shift. The events of the past month have twisted fantasy and reality together. Soul switching surfaces when Barker chews his leash.

Daylight comes and Dan's still sitting on the crate wondering. He has a feeling that he's not all there but the only thing he's concerned with is cashing the check and buying cigarettes. He's been able to stave off desperation by cruising the outer limits, riding the magic carpet.

The store says sorry. Dan's desperate. He heads north and starts knocking on doors, trying to sell eggs from his milk crate for fifty-five-cents a dozen. If he sells three dozen he can buy a pack of smokes. He'll worry about cashing the check later. Nicotine is his immediate and pressing need.

Even at his bargain prices, no one's buying. He gives up on the idea after a dozen door slams and ambles on. He had to believe the eggs were there. They didn't.

The Grand Canyon forms.

Lo and behold, the death trap sits in front of him. The magic carpet took him away and brought him back to the same spot! 'It's a sure sign that it has to be for me!'

Dan opens the car door. Barker hops in to confirm the thought. The key's still in the ignition. Trash litters the floor. He throws the crate in back with Barker. Dan starts the car and steers the magic carpet to the P-ZONE.

'If Providence meant me to have it, it'll be OK,' he thinks as he grinds and wobbles off. 'There's a station on the north side that used to cash checks.' The gas gauge is on E.

It's his lucky day. He makes it. They cash his check. He's in hog heaven with gas, cash, and cigarettes; primary ingredients for survival.

Water swirls rock and sand and carves the canyon wider.

Jake and his brothers flash smiles as Dan drives up. It's been over a year since he's seen them but it's like yesterday, like a homecoming. They jaw around the barn.

"Can you take me to pick up a check," Jake asks. The X-ZONE buzzer rings.

Dan says, "Sure," he put ten dollars worth of gas in at the station, has nowhere to go, and all the time in the world to get there, "Why not?"

Jake pulls the milk crate out of the backseat and hops in with Barker. Jonas jumps in the front bucket. Dan fires the deathtrap.

Dan drives Amish country limestone roads with Jake and Jonas navigating. They stop at one friend's farm, then another. At the third stop, Dan, Jonas, and Barker sit in the car while Jake goes in to pick up his check. The X-ZONE cracks.

Jake comes out. They stop at the bank drive up window to cash the check. Wires cross in Dan's head.

The plateau rises as the mountains inch upward.

He doesn't bother to take Jake and Jonas up the long lane or pick up his milk crate. Instead he drops them at the road and takes off. He heads back to the small town.

'The banks believe in you and Matt Moses believes in you,' sticks in his head as he heads back. It's the same town he was heading to when he was sidetracked, a month earlier. With unlimited funds, he can go anywhere he wants.

"Whadaya think, Barker?" Barker grins and barks.

Dan drives up to the bank window, holds out his driver's license and Abe bank card, and says, "I need thirty-one-thousand dollars by authority of Abe."

The pretty teller smiles at him and says, "I'm sorry but you'll have to come inside."

Dan doesn't like that idea. He takes off through the country til he reaches Highway 99. 'Double positive. Go north.' He heads in the opposite direction from a month ago.

The Colorado River carves deeper.

It starts raining. The hot asphalt and cold rain turn the road surface to grease. Dan comes into a banked S-curve doing sixty in the rattletrap. Barker ducks.

Tires start losing grip. The deathtrap slides, rear faster than the front, across the grease strip. Dan's mind flashes to the embankment heading towards him, four years before.

Chapter 44—ENTITLEMENT

The Gulf Stream steams north to bond and mingle with the cold St. Lawrence.

The momentary scare didn't faze me. I'm racing toward Hicksville, sideways. I'll double the amount at the next bank! My left brain says don't do it, my right says yes. I'm riding the magic carpet through the U-ZONE. Barker's in the back seat howling with insane delight as we cross the state line.

The drive-up lanes are full at the first bank in town. I keep going and double the amount just on principle; they weren't ready. I don't like the looks of the next bank and keep going without doubling the amount. I have to keep it within reason!

I stop at the next one.

"I need one-hundred and twenty-four thousand dollars and I need it in three minutes, by authority of Abe, "I say while holding my Texas Driver's License and Indiana Abe card for the Ohio bank manager to see. The manager looks at me then leaves the window. Barker's quiet in the back. I look at my watch.

One minute. Two minutes. I wonder how long it will take to count up a hundred-twenty-four-thousand dollars. Anxiety rises when I wonder if this is right.

Three minutes is up. I take off, turning right at Highway 56, and race east in my shake, rattle, and roll. I'm leary about pushing past eighty. Barker lies down, forehead crinkling, paws reaching to cover his eyes.

My left brain questions the validity of my assumptions; my right is amazed people aren't cooperating. The O-ZONE commands; D-ZONE controls; W-ZONE charges.

Highway 385 is a mind boggler. Two positives cap a negative, middle number commands, right-left is major, compass direction is minor, two to one's in charge. I turn right and head south. It was a tough choice; one that could've easily been the other but the double positive was in charge meaning that right was the way to go.

I come to a T at Highway 36. I have to choose again. Double negative makes a minor positive, south is negative, and right is positive. Which way?

I turn right then left and continue south on 385. Friar Tuck Drive flashes as I enter the village of Sherwood. There's a bank on the left. Excitement grows; 'This is too good to be true.' Barker peeks through his paws.

I pull to the drive-up window, hold up my driver's license and Abe card, and say, "I need two-hundred-forty-eight-thousand dollars and I need it in two and a half minutes, by authority of Reagan." Ronald Reagan's the President. I figure the extra clout can't hurt. Three minutes was too scary in case they want to hold out on me.

The tellers face tightens. She leaves the window. Two and a half minutes elapse. I split south for Waldorf. Barker crawls back under his paws.

I'll double it all the way to California if I have to. If it goes over a million, I want the excess deposited in gold at that bank in Beverly Hills. Audra and Mainframe are sliding out of the picture. I'm on a new mission.

I enter Waldorf. Near the center of town, two banks are across the street from each other. I choose the bank I was at seven years earlier when I bought my swampland - now sold on land contract and building a small, cash reserve.

I drive up to the window and ask for the bank president. I rushed it last time. This time I'll do it right! I might have gotten my money at Sherwood if I waited.

Bigfoot pulls behind me. An itchy foot bounces on the gas pedal. The monster truck's rumble reverberates off the steel canopy.

The normally simple doubling of two-hundred-forty-eight-thousand becomes impossible with the mind numbing rumble echoing around me. I wonder why the guy can't shut the damn thing off instead of playing with it like a new toy. Minutes become hours.

A prominent man with a coat and tie steps to the window. I hold out my driver's license and Abe card. "I need four-hundred-ninety-seven-thousand dollars and I need it in three minutes, by authority of Abe."

"What," the man asks with his hand cupped to his ear.

I repeat myself.

The man stalls and says, "What," again. Bigfoot revs and rumbles. The lady teller stands behind the man and stares, jaw on the floor.

Between Bigfoot and the deaf man I'm getting frustrated. I shout, "I need four-hundred-ninety-seven-thousand dollars and I need it in three minutes, by authority of Moses."

The man leaves the window as the wide eyed teller watches me. I look at my watch. Barker sits up. Bigfoot reverberates. The exhaust from the ill tempered monster gags me.

Times up. I take off. With the mind scrambling rumble behind me, I realize I asked for a thousand too much. I drift to the Y-ZONE and drive across the street to the other bank.

Holding out my drivers license and ATM card, I overcompensate and state, "I need four-hundred-ninety-five-thousand dollars and I need it in three minutes, by authority of Abe."

The teller leaves. Barker chomps his leash. I look at my watch.

The Gulf Stream pulls the St. Lawrence toward the Antarctic Express.

"Get out of the car with your hands up," is the next thing I hear. I jerk my head toward the sound. Forty feet in front of me is a white police car where a policeman is crouched behind the open door and holding a revolver pointed at me. I wonder where he came from. Reality slaps me to a stupor.

I open the car door and start to get out. The car lurches. I pop back in, mash the clutch, glance at the gun, turn off the ignition.

This time I get out slowly. For the second time in my life and second time in a month, I have a gun pointed at my head. I stand motionless with my hands up.

The officer walks over with two hands on his gun and a bead on my head. "Put your hands on top of the car." I comply. "Does the dog bite?"

"No."

The policeman frisks me, cuffs me, and locks me in the back of the patrol car. Barker smiles from the back seat of the getaway car. 'Traitor.'

A crowd gathers on the sidewalk.

I duck down in the seat and

slip through the O-ZONE.

I wonder what book they'll throw at me and what river they'll send me down.
I fear that it will be the St. Lawrence and Antarctic Express.
Should've known better than to believe the banks would cough up the cash.

Now that they've got me, I don't have much hope of ever getting out.
The banks will back out just like Audra has done so many times now.
I wonder if I shouldn't have given up on her a long time ago?

Too late now.

I'm a had dad.

Chapter 45—ENROLLMENT

Arctic waters drop off the continental shelf and suck Joseph and Mary molecules to the South Pole and the Antarctic Wave.

The worn brick two story jail is over a hundred years old. If it could talk it could probably tell some tales, possibly about some real bank robbers. I'm taken in the front entry, through a door, and up some stairs.

The men in the lower cellblock watch through the bars as I climb the open stairs. At the top of the stairs I'm taken into a room on the right and booked. It's a first; my two prior detainments were less formal.

The deputy sheriff that books me asks, "Remember me?" He's vaguely familiar. I puzzle. It's a rare occasion when someone recognizes me before I recognize them. "I gave you a ride to East Bend, New Years Eve before last."

Vortex Eve! The memory cell unlocks. The video of that night replays. I see him put the Smokey Bear hat in the back seat. Mystery crosses coincidence and adds fuel to the P and Q-ZONES.

I'm ushered across the walkway that overlooks the stairwell, fingers still black from fingerprinting. We pass a vacant cellblock and go to a large empty cell. This isolation cell is directly over the main entry. They open the heavy, steel bar gate.

A glass window of six-inch-square cubes of opaque glass, stacked and mortared in the three by seven foot opening of the solid block exterior wall, stares at me from across the room. A vertical grid of round steel bars welds through horizontal flat steel bars, anchors to the wall, and covers the window. A clear layer of glass cubes at the top of the window gushes sunshine.

The cell walls are whitewashed blocks. Red oxide covers the thick steel floor. A single light bulb hangs from the center of the twelve-foot ceiling. The gate clanks shut, the deadbolt thuds.

I look at the gate. Thick pegs anchor into the solid block opening and suspend the three by seven foot gate. Decades of use have tweaked it. Round iron bars, one-inch thick and four inches apart, run from the bottom of the gate to the top and are held together by half-inch by one-inch horizontal iron bars. A four-inch by twenty-inch horizontal slit splits the middle of the ancient exit/entry.

To the left of the gate is a commode and wash basin. A heavy, three by four foot, wood table and a straight-back chair occupies the right corner. Behind me and to the right of the window, a steel double-bunk with a two-inch thick, gray mat stands across from the commode and wash basin.

This unexpected turn of events is a far cry from my intentions when I left Texas six weeks ago for Audra and the Mainframe home office in Jacksonville. I again question my reasons for not purging her from my mind a long time ago. I need a good lawyer!

Abram molecules exit the circumpolar wave.

Several hours pass before a deputy brings a can of tobacco and some rolling papers. My nicotine deficit has grown to irritable proportions. I sit down at the table and roll one. I feel the calming effect when I light it and take the first drag to satisfy the nicotine demon.

That night as I sit in my isolation cell, I hear a familiar voice coming from below. There's a honey sweet clarity to the distinctive bass voice. It's a voice I could never forget. I question its reality. Thoughts bounce from right to left and left to right.

The voice floats from the base of the stairway. I move to the gate, hold my breath, and listen. There's no mistaking the voice.

The Texas accent is polished so fine I hear nothing but shine. It's Bill Bagby, the ambassador of goodwill, the man who called me a diamond in the rough five years earlier when my mind fractured in the crash. The smooth and melodic tune rings clear.

I listen, ears against the cold steel bars, trying to make out Bill's words. Other than, "and then I was a believer," I understand no words, just the music of his voice.

I call out, "Bill." The voice stops and then resumes. The Q-ZONE unlocks.

So many surreal things have happened in the past three years that I'm never a hundred percent sure of anything. It's too bizarre to be real but too real to be ignored. Windows have opened that five years earlier I would have never believed or understood.

A thousand lifetimes of understanding opened as my mind woke to the possibilities. Understanding that you only gain by unlocking the gate and living it. As my mind unlocks I'm given deeper possibilities to contemplate.

Joseph and Mary molecules dash and clash in the Indian Ocean.

Later that evening, I hear another familiar voice, a female. At first I'm unsure but as I listen to the quiet confidence, I become sure. The slight quaver to her voice is exactly as I would picture her in this situation: in control but not demanding, sure of herself but not overbearing, not intimidated just wary. It's Carol, the Connecticut cucumber!

When she talks, the normally rowdy inmates are quiet. I hear the tone of her voice but not the content. Unlike Bill's stationary voice, hers moves around downstairs.

I'm uncertain whether these voices are coming from within the jail or through a portal in space. I know they're not coming from my head because of the prisoner reaction to them. My Cosmo bank gulps. The Q-ZONE opens.

The Southern Hemisphere nears the winter solstice.

Adam and Patty come to visit on Sunday afternoon. I've been there two days. Dad tells me, "The bank thing was little more than a prank or practical joke but taking the car across the state line is a Federal offense."

I remain silent as I think of the circumstances surrounding the car.

"Raphael's going to talk to the owner to persuade him not to press charges."

"What about the dog?"

"He was returned to his owner," Patty says. "No charges have been filed."

I think about Barker and envy his freedom. My fear centers on the Siberian Express to no where. "I want the best lawyer money can buy."

"Who's going to pay for him," Adam asks.

Thoughts of unlimited funds crumble. Thinking I have this phantom pot of gold is one thing. Verbalizing it to my father, quite another. I can't answer.

"A former prosecutor might defend you," Adam says.

"Prosecutor; they're on the other side?"

"Now he's a public defender. Talk to him."

Dad adds, "If you don't like him you can request someone else."

My Mom and Dad leave. The former prosecutor comes in. It's too quick. I feel like I'm being set up. My guard goes up.

"I'll do my best to defend you," the attorney says.

I envision the day they send me down the river and hear the attorney say, "Sorry but I did my best." I stick with my gut feeling.

"That's your decision and the court will have to provide you with another if you can't afford to defend yourself. I don't know who that would be," he adds. The defender leaves.

The Arctic Cap starts to melt.

Monday morning I'm taken out of the cell and down the stairs. Two inmates from the lower cellblock join me for the march out the door and down the street. I wonder where we're going. Nothing other than blue coveralls restrains me. Two deputies escort us.

I see a familiar car with Texas license plates and four men. My mind flashes to the O-ZONE. The magic's alive; they're here to spring me. Optimism leaps.

We continue walking down the sidewalk, crossing the street to enter a gray limestone courthouse, up two flights of creaky stairs, and into a courtroom. We're seated. Deputies, suits, and marshals' mix, mingle, and walk around.

A tall man in a dark suit approaches.

"I hear you need an attorney?"

"I don't have one. Are you an attorney?"

"Yes," he says. "Let's go across the hall where we can talk."

I follow him to a small conference room.

The lawyer continues, "Tell me about your case."

The apprehension I entertained evaporates as I explain.

"I believed that the money was there for me, that the banks were just holding it."

"You're being charged with bank robbery, a Class C felony," the lawyer says. "You can get two years in prison."

My mind swan dives to a double take and surfaces in the B-ZONE.

"I'm aware that this isn't a laughing matter and might have scared some people but there was no malicious intent on my part. I didn't have a weapon or threaten anyone."

"Your use of time was considered a threat."

"When time was up, I left. I didn't get any money."

"The crime was committed when you drove up to the window and demanded cash. The threat of time makes it a felony."

"Since I didn't have a weapon, threaten with bodily harm, or take any money, I believe the case should be dropped. I was confused and meant no harm."
I'm tempted to blurt 'they let my accomplice Barker off the hook' but don't.

"Well, I can't represent you anyway."

"Why's that?"

"It would be a conflict of interest."

"Conflict of interest?"

"I represent the banks."

I slide to the P-ZONE and contemplate the motive behind the deception and conclude that I'm doomed and there's nothing I can do.
The opposition just scored a touchdown.
I'm at their mercy; alone, against the world, helpless to defend myself.

Glaciers grow in the Antarctic.

Chapter 46—ENFORCEMENT

Underwater currents run shallow and deep.

"Daniel Fitzpatrick Murphy."

Dan's on his own as he stands in a sea of blue suits and brown uniforms.

The black robed judge sits in his high-back throne with black horn rimmed glasses perched on a Romanesque nose and accenting the shine beneath his thinning black hair. "You have been charged with bank robbery, a class C felony. How do you plead?"

Dan had given it some thought. Since he doesn't have anyone to represent him and they're going to send him down the river anyway. "Nolo contendre, your honor." He saw Spiro Agnew do it! It seems appropriate.

"Bail is set at fifty-thousand dollars."

Dan slumps to his seat. 'Fifty thousand dollars!'

During the long walk back to the ancient jail, his thoughts hover in the E-ZONE. The deputies herd the trio through the main entry and into the back. Dan waits while they lock his companions in the lower cellblock.

Then he waits while they unlock the upper cellblock. Dan looks across the walkway and through the bars of his solitary cell. On the lower bunk is a coverall clad figure, back facing him, with brown locks flowing over a long shapely body.

His imagination stirs. His heart jumps as he wonders if it's her. Anticipation and excitement clog his throat.

The deputies take him into the cellblock and into a bar enclosed cell. The gate to his new cell clanks and the gate to the cellblock clunks. The jailers clomp down the wood stairs.

They're alone, separated by three gates and a thick block wall. Dan wants to call out but can't. His tongue twists and knots. He can't overcome the fear.

The next morning she's gone. Dan gets his isolation cell back. He calls it his royal jubilation cell.

God is the Force behind everything, to infinity and beyond.

Dan takes a journey to an area of his inner self he didn't know existed. In a back cell of a deep compartment in the catacombs of his mind a secret door, hidden from view til now, opens to an ancient core. He discovers a magical understanding from a life he lived thousands of years before on a planet, light years from this one.

It's a planet where telepathic communication is the norm and thousand-year lifetimes are common. His people had been traveling the galaxies for eons, searching for and sometimes cultivating life with helpful nudges. Planet Earth was one of the places they nudged.

He's the energy behind the sun,

Earth is where they sought to perfect their system of packet planting. His planet had millions of years before the red god engulfed it but Earth was in its embryonic stage with billions of years ahead. It was the perfect place to study and adjust, if necessary, as it moved toward the league of peaceful worlds in the endless universe of the space stage.

the moon and stars that light our nights and lives,

Dan was part of an expedition to unify the pagan beliefs of a pocket of people and plant packets of supernatural understanding: astrology, acupuncture, etc, with other pockets. Life was primitive but progressing on a positive course thanks to the Neanderthal project. They were entering a different stage when Dan arrived as Captain Cosmo.

and the essence of every breath we take.

Residents of the pristine garden of Earth were mostly peaceful. Large carnivores were gone with the asteroid and blackened sun. Humans were nomadic and pastoral. They roamed, hunted, planted, gathered, and migrated with the changing climate.

Civilization was in its infancy. Language and cultivation were developing. Pagan beliefs were prevalent in the pocket surrounding the Dead Sea and fingers around the planet. People worshipped thousands of gods.

They were domesticating animals and growing crops, settling, forming villages, expanding, trading, bartering, communicating; not yet writing, and flourishing. The timing was right to plant the seed of one God to mix with other seeds strewn around the globe. The seeds would sprout vines that would reach out and ultimately intermingle and thread together to form a picture of enlightenment.

We're temporal and incidental organisms on a journey to perfection

Understanding was limited with the primitive people who still had millenniums of growth ahead of them. They needed a story with a moral code in order to reach the full carbon-silicon cycle of intelligent life and understand the intricacies and interconnectedness of God and nature. Ignorance had to be overcome to become part of the space race.

in the web of everlasting life - no matter how many incarnations it may take.

Captain Cosmos ship left. He didn't go with it. He died on this alien planet.

It's a life that begins with Truth and ends with anti-Truth.

And now Captain Cosmo is back with a new identity, Dan Murphy, and he's sitting in a hundred square foot cubicle with a ton of money on his head wondering what the future will bring.

Body dies and soul lives on, waiting for the next journey or mission.

They take Dan down the stairs to the lower cellblock with the other inmates. It's almost identical to the upper cellblock and directly beneath it. Block walls separate the ten cells instead of steel bars. Cell doors are heavy, metal plates that swing on thick, steel pegs.

At the front of the cellblock is a long, plank table with heavy, wood benches on two sides. A TV perches in the far corner. Nine other inmates walk freely in the steel cage.

For the next three days, Dan sleeps in his new cell, coming out only for meals, commode flushes, and the evening news. He gradually spends time and socializes with his fellow inmates. Most are serving time for minor offenses and

pass it by telling stories and jokes, and watching TV. They know why Dan's there and think his take the cash and dash attempt is humorous til he tells them the bail.
"You're looking at some serious time with that bail," Buddy says.

Buddy's the hometown favorite and the leader of this jailhouse gang. A jokester with a medium-big frame and an air of intelligence, he has experience to share. He's traveled from this small town and now he's back raising ruckus.

Most inmates gather in Buddy's cell to swap stories and pass time. A handmade calendar on his wall, X's the time he's served and counts days to his release. Thirty-eight remain. He's been charged with harboring a minor.

Barney is Buddy's compadre. He has a similar sentence for a minor offense. Frequent home boy guests, they get the privilege of swabbing the cellblock, inside and out, everyday and out to wash patrol cars while the rest of the gang chills in the cooler. Otherwise they hang out and horse around. Booby trapping a bunk is their favorite trick.

Planets and stars align.

A private practice attorney, assigned by the court to defend Dan, comes to see him. He seems to be honest and have Dan's best interest at heart. Dan likes the hometown boy and feels comfortable with him.

Raphael visits. "I went to see the owner of the car, he's not pressing charges." He adds, "There's talk of sending you to a state hospital in Toledo.

"I don't know if I like that idea."

"It's like a college campus," Raphael counters. Dan isn't sure he has a choice.

That evening Dan watches a wedge shaped piece of land around Jacksonville vanish and then return on the national weather map while the area around it blinks in and out. He thinks about Jon Busby and the Mainframe chain that erupted with Chuck and the lollypop red being licked off at Audra's departure.

There are reports of high winds sweeping helicopters from the sky in Southern California. The thing he feared is happening. He knew if the vortex made it to Tinseltown the circuit could blow. His thoughts slide to the O-ZONE.

The next morning, Dan hears a big rig rumble up to the jailhouse. Then another followed by dozens more. They shut their engines off as they freeze in position. By early afternoon he hears rumbling far into the distance as big rigs fill the gaps and choke the arteries of the small town.

At first Dan likes the idea of the truckers rallying to his cause but has second thoughts when he thinks about restrictions and dangers as the blockade continues to build. 'There must be hundreds of big rigs converging on this sleepy little town!' Anxiety builds. He wonders if Audra's in the getaway truck and watches the TV for clues.

Anxious voices and the sound of shotgun shells being chambered come from the jail entrance area. Dan wonders if, after five hours, they're finally making their move. 'Maybe they were waiting for Audra?'

His concern for her safety causes him to bristle at small irritations. He tries to disperse the trucks telepathically. It doesn't seem to be working so he does it verbally. His fellow inmates are silent as he shoos the truckers.

He hears rumbling in the direction of the main artery as the clog starts to move. Engines slowly wind higher and drop lower to rewind as they unwind the jam. Big rigs continue to start-up, move out, and rumble off. Two hours later, Dan hears the last. He'll have to get out of this jam on his own.

He's wistful about losing his allies and questions his rude send off. He becomes agitated at not being sprung, gets animated, and accidentally knocks over one of the benches.

Within a minute three deputies come in, grab him, and stick him in a cell, solid metal door thudding as it slams light out and Dan in. He's isolated. One-inch bars, four-inches on center, separate him from the empty perimeter of the jailhouse.

His mind runs rampant. He wakes in the middle of the night, body in a cold sweat, to strange and scary dreams of sadistic horror and torture. He's the victim.

Dan thinks of the magical energy released with the vortex. Pandora's Box opens. His imagination is wild and vivid. Thoughts come with flashes of inspiration.

He imagines the movement to free him gathering momentum with an assault on his hometown of East Bend. Flash Gordon leads the charge. Carol, the Connecticut cucumber, coordinates the operation from a secret location within the City-County Building.

His buddy Bart's sisters, Kate, Nan, and Deb are there to lend a hand. Flash Gordon, Jon Busby is cloned with the magic of the vortex so that he becomes two. Dan figures that if people and vehicles can flash from Texas and elsewhere, cloning shouldn't be a problem. The vortex is out of control.

Carol commands, the twin clones execute, and the trio of angels sew a static charge through the city of East Bend and hidden wires back to command central. Carol shuttles the dynamic duo in and out of the mayor's office and around the City-County Building.

Operation Zap's in charge. A platinum noose surrounds Matt Moses' command. Soon things will be out of control. Forces focus on the final showdown of good and evil; the twin towers of devastation and resurrection.

A confrontation between Deb and the mayor sets the stage. Deb bites her tongue til both Jon's, Kate, Nan, and Carol come charging in. Moses' secretary and aide come charging behind. Deb erupts.

Hell breaks loose.

Chapter 47—ENCLONEMENT

Abram molecules go up the St. Lawrence and down the Mississippi.

Matt Moses splits down the middle, top to bottom.

Halves fall to the left and right, atoms in suspended animation.

Blood, guts, everything is frozen as if Moses is a 3-D cartoon character.

A minute later the suspended halves rise in slow motion reverse.

Everyone stands and stares, jaws agape, as the halves rejoin.

Magnetic polarity infuses Moses with super consciousness.

I sit in the dark, block cell, watching on the video in my head as the drama unfolds. The earth starts rumbling, groaning, and bellowing. I feel the movement and hear pressure as a power unleashes. Energy courses over the planet, unimpeded and out of control. I see vortexes hop-scotching and circling the globe as the planet threatens to split apart.

Twin veins of alternating hot and cold magma creep and surge in a flip-flopping hare and tortoise race from the bottom of my spinal column, up both sides of my vertebrae, and end in a dead heat at the base of my brain. I've never had such a bloodcurdling feeling. The sheriffs open the steel door and take me away.

Dinosaurs freeze their way to oblivion in the rock of ages.

I'm glad to be back in the jubilation chamber and out of the rumbling dungeon below. Three days of that was enough. This cell is bigger, sunnier, and better. The rumbles have subsided for now.

Sunlight streams through the clear glass blocks in the top layer of the opaque window to my right and splashes on the iron gate across from me as I sit on the top bunk and ponder the significance of the unnerving events below. The twin corridors of magma in my spine and the low vibration that quivered the foundation of the ancient jailhouse as energy fought to escape the crush of the planet's core are especially vivid. The hollow penetrating groan and the thought of the earth threatening to split infuse me with unforgettable memories.

My concentration intensifies with the empathic sensations I feel in different parts of my body, sensations that have been steadily rising since before Barker and I joined for the heist of the century. I match internal signals with external premonitions of an omniscient origin in a 3-D puzzle of mind boggling proportions. Energy starts charging.

I hop down from the bunk swirling my arms, twirling my fingers, twisting, turning, waltzing around the isolation cell and sweep negative energy from my body and mind and chase it from my jubilation chamber. Left command is in the K-ZONE and right control is in the P-ZONE. The whooshing sound whistling through my teeth while I swish and swash sends me deep within the core of my being to the soul that never dies, and back to the days of Captain Cosmo and the planet I left behind. Instincts key.

The jubilation chamber sanctified, I wave my hands over the royal table. It's the same wood table that was here when they locked me up nineteen days ago. The one-inch thick iron bars firmly anchor over the window and in the heavy gate that hangs on pegs embedded into the solid block wall.

Two bibles, one large and one small, lay at the rear of the table. Freshly rolled cigarettes arc around the table top and provide a target, conduit, and safety buffer for negative energy. A one pound tin of Bugler Boy sits inside the buffer zone in the left front corner, rolling papers beside it.

The empathic signals that permeate my body are stronger and more frequent. A sickening of my stomach, an aching of my heart, a rubber band stretching my gonads, a hammer tapping, a needle penetrating my skull. The sensations grow and spread.

There's the knife in my side, a prick behind my knee cap, a tingle in my left toe or right shoulder. Different combinations and intensities of the empathic signals give me a four dimensional puzzle to match and interpret. It keeps my mind occupied, away from my conundrum and the iron and concrete that surround me.

A super consciousness permeates thoughts as my mind makes a right turn at reality, enters the Q-ZONE, journeys down a star-struck aisle, and makes a right turn through a portal of supreme serenity and confidence. I'm amazed at the depth and clarity of the direct link to unlimited knowledge. Omniscience takes over. I let it flow.

Electrons flee the center of the cosmic egg.

COSMOCHINE CREATION BEGINS.

Effect surfaces

Hours pass as I summon and assemble the forces. Gates open. Flow pours through. I feel the energy course through my body. Commands spew from my mouth as easily as the jungle rhythm flowed on the night of the chase. I don't know what I'm doing but on a deeper level I do.

I feel infinite power as I place magnetic safety barriers around all government, financial, health, and penal institutions to protect them from the power about to be unleashed. Invisible self-destruct mechanisms are placed in series and parallel to stop the forces of evil should they gain control. Imperfection is not an option.

I see Matt Moses and the key role he plays. His bi-optic ability is supreme. He's in charge of control. I'm in charge of command. Together we'll build a new world.

Commands spew in countless variations of cosmic words splashed in a pacing, pausing, racing stream of verbally forceful impassioned orders to organize the power permeating the planet and pit positive against negative for the final showdown.

"Master Control, assume command; bisect.

Main Control, you're in charge; octasect.

Super Control, maintain control; vivisect."

I feel a ballistic surge circle my loins and shoot perpetual energy to the cosmos. I see a side by side duplication of the universe. A platinum wall, sixteen universes thick, spears vertically between the original universe and its clone. The platinum wall, X-axis, terminates at a platinum balloon that has a skin four times as thick as the wall and an outside diameter five-hundred-twelve times wider than the original universe. At the other end, the X-axis anchors to an eight-diameter thickness of platinum that coats a thirty-two-diameter gold ball and forms the core.

At the very center of the gold core is a silicone chamber where four hollow silicone straws intersect. The straws extend through the center of the platinum major X-axis in four directions, like a compass, and poke beyond the platinum balloon. Four hollow silicone cherries perch on the ends.

Twenty-four, half-diameter thick, silver shells stack like an onion and surround the forty-eight-diameter platinum-gold core. Empty space separates each shell. The twenty-fifth shell is a platinum sphere, eight-diameters thick and one-hundred-twenty-eight-diameters across. The twenty-four silver shells are sliced by seven platinum plates that extend thirty-two-diameters from the platinum-gold core to the platinum base shell and of course, the major X-axis which extends to the platinum, five-hundred-twelve-diameter, outer balloon.

The horizontal platinum plate, perpendicular to the X-axis is the major Y-axis. Two platinum plates slice the silver shells at a forty-five degree skew to majors X and Y and look like an orange from the end. The minor X-axis is rotated ninety degrees to the major X-axis and tilted forty-five degrees. The minor Y-axis is perpendicular to minor X. Two minor plates are skewed forty-five degrees to the minor X and Y-axis'.

The two universes are on opposite sides of the major X-axis wall. They sit on the platinum base shell above the platinum and silver chambers. The shell is four times the diameter of the gold core or one-quarter the diameter of the platinum balloon. Platinum totally isolates the original and cloned universes into two separate compartments.

As you can see the Cosmochine is not only colossal but also exceedingly complicated when trying to visualize or describe. Therefore I have included some cross sections. To alleviate your boredom I will endeavor to keep descriptions to a minimum.

What you see are two different views of the structure. What you don't see are the intricacies of the structure. Alter, Counter, Master, Main, Super, and Ultra Controls have integral roles in this structure. All Controls have Command and Charge phases. The expansion vacuum occupies the space between the base shell and outer balloon. It accounts for half the diameter of the Cosmochine and a majority of the volume.

The grow and control universes look like twin pinpricks of light opposing each other at the intersection of the X-wall and base shell. The shell and wall separate the Grow and Control sides. Both sides have all the opposing Controls, Commands, and Charges built in.

I'm on the Grow side of the X-axis in the control universe. My clone is on the Control side where Matt Moses is in charge of the rapidly changing grow universe. Our two universes occupy less than one-thousandth of one percent of

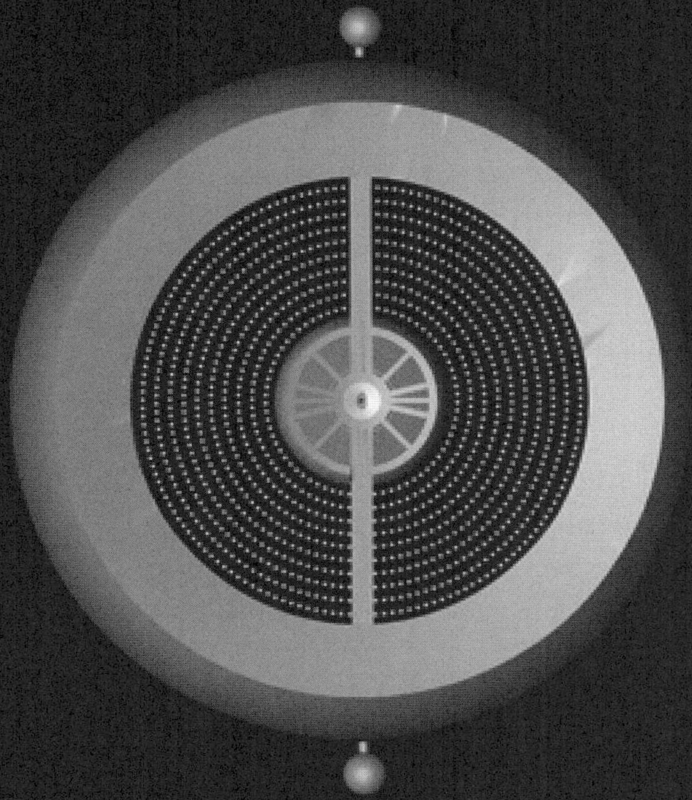

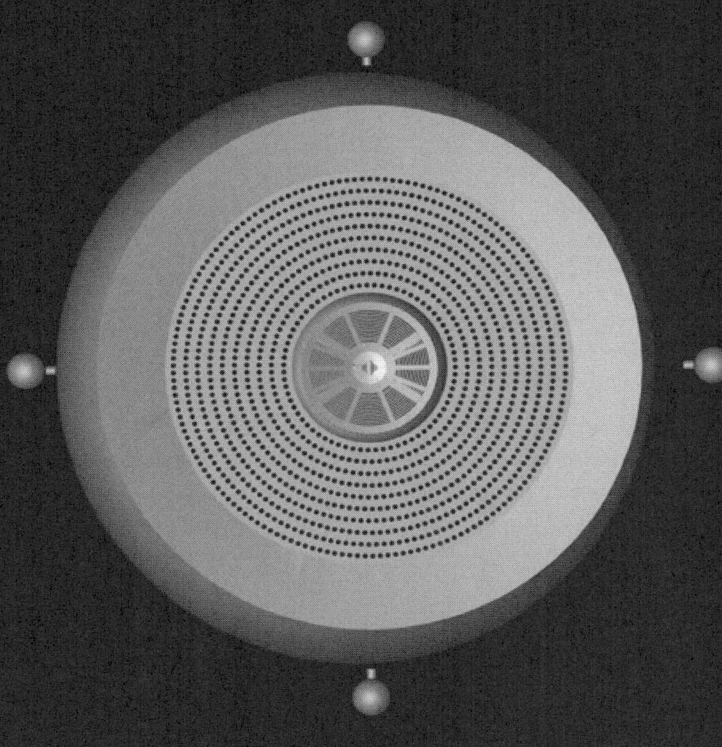

the volume of the Grow and Control expansion chambers.
There's room for a hundred-thousand universes in the two chambers.

I remain in my white walled jubilation cell of eight by twelve feet. I'm also in the clone universe in an eight by twelve but the course of events will be different there. My consciousness resides in the original universe.

"Ultra Charge; double down."

"Super Charge; triple up."

"Main Charge; quad command."

"Master Control; you're in charge."

"Segregate the interface."

is a tiny sample of the commands spewing rapid fire from my mouth.

Another migration wave to the new world begins.

A deputy brings a tray of food up and passes it through the slot in the creaky gate. I heard that jailhouse food was bad but these meals are fresh cooked and excellent. After lunch it's back to the job at hand. The Cosmochine base is stabilized.

Polar caps melt.

My side remains static as Moses establishes totalitarian authority on the Control side where the magic of the vortex has been magnified and channeled through him. His rule starts with security, harsh and uncompromising. Crime is not allowed. Minor infractions are punished with death. Execution is immediate. Live with peace or die with discord. There are no lawyers to drag it out. Comply or die is the command.

Negative power-evil is eliminated from the gene pool through education of the people and eradication of poverty and disease. Like ants, everyone has a job and they're busy doing it. Societal bliss is everywhere in the police state where peace and harmony rule. Discord ends before it starts. People of all races and creeds act as one.

Totalitarian harshness is especially severe within the security force since they are the guardians of peace and can abuse their power. Electronic eyes maintain watch. Security is everywhere; hierarchy absolute. Peace and prosperity prevail on Control side.

Sea levels rise hundreds of feet

submerging encampments and migratory routes.

The inmates are raising a commotion downstairs. Sounds like Buddy and Barney might be up to their tricks. The jailhouse starts to rumble as the planet's core changes. The rumble is much lighter than what I experienced in the isolation cell below. I sit in my jubilation chamber and wonder how it all ties together.

It's mid afternoon and the sun has passed over the table and is bouncing off the east wall of my jubilation cell. My thoughts return to the Cosmochine. The earth rumbles again.

Sperm and egg unite.

The universe I started the day with is a speck inside the Cosmochine and I'm still sitting in a tiny cell on a small planet in a microscopic portion of it. Matt Moses and my clone sit in command central on the power packed Control side, seeking to create perfection. The hooligans are howling in the cellblock below, on my side.

Mitosis duplicates.

Space Command joins Grow and Control as the third element of the cosmic egg. Major and minor Space Commands balance, equalize, and stabilize the Cosmochine. Alter Command is the maverick and the base charge for Grow and Control. Counter and Sub Commands add to the mix.

I don't try to keep track of everything that's happening in the Cosmochine; there's too much, it's too complicated, and too mind boggling. It would take volumes of books to describe it. My focus is on the big picture as commands flow through me.

I feel the changes in my body as power surges. Most startling is what I hear. Sounds like breakers popping, circuits cracking, and transformers blowing.

Energy buzzes, charges, and whirls.
I give preliminary commands and feel my body hum and glow.
Pop....pop, comes from the room across the stairwell - where I was fingerprinted.
The sounds are both frightening and encouraging.

Pop...Pop, Pop....Boom.....Pop, Pop, Pop, Pop...Zap....Crack...Boom.
Like Bill and Carol's voices on my first day in the cell, I'm uncertain whether the sounds are coming from inside the building or through a portal in space. No one has gone into that room. Only sounds come out.

Life propagates.

Omniscient commands spew from my mouth faster than I can think about them. Sounds follow; loudness matching my intensity. Rapid fire commands are followed with rapid pops and cracks. When I pause, the zaps continue then slow to a halt.

"Master Control; masticate the interface.
Ultra Command; circulate the integrate.
Main Charge; loop the dupe."

I feel the surge of energy and watch the theatre of my mind as the grow and control universes duplicate and spread out and away from the original and clone universe on opposite sides of the X-wall, climbing higher and further from the base shell til they meet at the opposite X-wall on the other end of the shell and the Grow and Control chambers are full of energy, excess flowing through platinum and gold to the four silicone cherries outside the platinum balloon. I give it a rest to reflect.

Continents collide and expose lofty depths.

I see every clone as slightly altered, mutated from its neighboring clones. Change accelerated at the far side as clones of clones spit clones and the chambers filled up. Fifty-thousand double clones later life is radically altered from the original universes.

The Cosmochine is an organism so vast and awesome its existence is unfathomable yet I can't dismiss it. I see it as a perfect perpetual motion energy machine floating in an endless vacuum of Truth and anti-truth. It is both of me and surrounds me. My body is invisible in the creation yet encompasses all of it. It exists in my mind and I in it.

Now I sit in my jubilation cell with the power to create perfection but none to get me out of the pickle I'm in. I wonder if my world has changed and if I'm in a clone universe or if I'm a clone. I don't have those answers but I feel the Cosmochine in my blood, bones, and whole body and I'm getting mighty upset about my unholy treatment.

I dive into the Cosmochine to push the thoughts back. I see curtains changing polarities as universes jostle for magnetic order, rising and falling with the changes. I see worlds and universes where the dark side takes control and is then annihilated. The energy returns to the silicone balls to start another trillion year journey.

Darkness descends on the world outside my jubilation cell. The jailer takes my empty dinner tray. It's been a short day with unimaginable accomplishment. A day that leaves me in the same place it found me; a place where I have little or no control.

I remain in the A-Level of the Grow chamber, in the royal jubilation cell with thick walls and heavy bars and no leeway while Matt Moses ascends to the Z-Level in the Control chamber as a god in a heaven on earth.

I wonder when it will be over and when I will get my freedom.
I wonder if my plight will get better or worse.

Questions, questions, questions?

Chapter 48—ENRAGEMENT

Krakatoa spews fiery ash.

The Cosmochine structure was finished days ago. Space Command is in charge. The expansion chamber is balancing and equalizing as annihilation waves create instability in the curtains between universes. Change is rapid. Clones swap freely.

Dan's tobacco can has been empty for thirty hours. Irritation swells. He starts swearing, kicking, and hitting. His hand and feet feel the pain. The walls don't complain.

He jerks the pad from the lower bunk, swings it out, up, and around, slamming it down on the hollow steel of the top bunk. The boom bounces and reverberates. He does it again, louder, and again.

He's Captain Cosmo, Commander General of the Cosmochine.

'How dare they make me wait,
I should've been gone from here!'

Dan foams at the mouth, cussing and swearing at the blue uniform climbing the stairs. The officer taunts. Dan spews stratospheric slander. The blue smooches mock kisses and throws challenges as he goes down the stairs.

Dan raves like a lunatic and snarls like a beast as he unleashes a full blown rage, spouting air and brutalizing the wall, growling and slamming the mat in deafening booms. He's had it with this place. He wants tobacco and he wants it now.

Anger rises and subsides. Nicotine deficiency rubs him raw. Nitro sizzles from adrenaline surges. Energy rushes. Dan paces.

Molten rivers steam into the sea.

A troop of men stomp up the wood stairs. Dan walks to the iron gate to watch. A short stout gent, wearing a grey suit and carrying a black bag, walks toward him through a sea of brown uniforms. Night lighting casts a pale gloom. Big men fill the walkway.

"Stick your arm out," one says.

Dan sticks his right arm out through the lunch-tray slot. Two browns grab it. Dan relaxes. The suited gent sticks a syringe in Dan's forearm and injects a solution.

Almost immediately, a red clover appears two-inches forward of the injection point. Dan looks at it and wonders. It's as if his body had rejected the shot. They release his arm.

"Stick your other arm out." Dan obliges. They grab and hold it. The doctor fills another syringe, points the shiny needle up, squishes a squirt into the air, sticks it into Dan's arm, and pushes the plunger.

The plunger isn't moving. Doc's face is turning red. He uses both hands, they wobble, it doesn't budge, his eyebrows crinkle. He pushes harder, turns redder, and strains more.

Dan watches the strain and wonders why. It's not stuck in his bone or tendon. It makes less sense than the red clover.

Clear solution sprays back onto the doctor's hand and coat sleeve. He fills another syringe. This time it works.

A smaller red mark appears ahead of the injection point. They don't seem to notice. Dan does. He asks for tobacco. They leave.

Buddy and Barney come up to the jubilation cell unescorted. Dan hasn't seen them since the earth rumbled in the isolation cell. Anxiety creases their faces and eyes.

"Do you want to get out," Buddy asks.

"Yes," Dan answers.

"Do you want to get out," Buddy asks again and again with Dan answering each time. Dan wonders about the anxious look, the deaf ears, and the redundant questions. Barney's face is white, eyes wide as saucers.

'Why are they so afraid,' Dan wonders.

"Can you get them to bring me some tobacco," he asks. They leave.

Ten minutes later, he gets his wish. A deputy brings a partial pack of cigarettes. Dan sits to smoke and wait.

An hour goes by. Dan smokes all of the meager offering. Two sheriffs bring his moldy bank robbing clothes. He wastes no time changing from the jail coveralls to his getaway clothes.

Dan's escorted down the stairs and out of the ancient structure to a waiting EMS. "Lay down on the gurney," an officer barks. Dan complies.

They fasten and tighten a strap across his midsection, arms at his side. Dan's rolled to the back of the EMS vehicle and slid in the rear door, head first. A brown uniform climbs in behind him. It's the Samaritan who gave Dan the ride on Vortex Eve.

The blue uniform that fueled his enragement a few hours earlier climbs in behind Dan. The EMS attendant climbs in the side door and closes it. The EMS starts moving.

Seeds sprout on Krakatoa.

Dan thinks about the stabilization process of the Cosmochine, the power, and clones crossing curtains. The antagonizing blue has an uncanny resemblance to Ron from Mulligan's barricading beer case bar over two years earlier. Anxiety rises. Claustrophobia closes in. "Can you take off these straps," Dan asks.

"No, we have to leave them on."

Dan pleads with his eyes. The Samaritan loosens them with the understanding that they'll be tightened up if Dan pulls his arms. At least he can move under the straps.

The Samaritan shivers. Dan sees the blue pointing a gun at the back of his head. He lies still and thinks about Rip's threat at the glass cage, "I'm going to get you Dan." He wonders if he'll make it to wherever they're going.

That time it was soul switching. This time it's Ron as an alter clone that used the magic of the vortex to be here, in this dimension. The Samaritan wraps his arms around himself.

Islands sprout in the ring of fire.

Another sheriff and a white clad are waiting when the door opens an hour later. The straps are removed. Dan gets up and out to stretch. Lights punctuate the blackness. The assemblage goes up a sidewalk and into a large modern building in a park-like setting.

When the blue and browns are gone, Dan's free to roam the two-thousand-foot brick and glass enclosure. That night as he lies in bed, he feels pinpricks on his body as Space Command locates him. He wonders if they can beam him out.

If they're trying it's not working. Dan hasn't moved. He's tired of waiting and too awake to sleep. He gets up for a drink of water, wanders, and watches TV in the lounge.

He roams with scarcely a second glance from the nurses sitting at their station. There are lots of doors and rooms. Besides two female nurses, he's the only one there.

With the freedom he's being allowed, one would never guess he was a raving lunatic hours earlier. He must be in a different universe. He visualizes the wheels in the sky; the Commands, Controls, and Charges. He sees Space Command, Major and Minor, cross and counter checking, balancing controls and charges, weaving threads of cohesion through portals of space and time.

He sees his secret astroluters hidden in the dust of infinity, repulsing resistance and attracting unity through the dimensions of space. He wonders if this is a way station where he waits to be whisked off to Space Central or if it's another dead-end on the road to nowhere. He keeps hope in check while he patiently waits and wonders where this will lead.

Chapter 49—ENTERTAINMENT

Atlantic waters flow to the Pacific.

I was finally able to get to sleep about two A.M. At seven they roust me, feed me, give me a brief medical exam, and escort me to an open back, box truck. I'm standing in the back of the truck alone, no one around, and no restraints. I haven't been handcuffed since Barker and I split company a month ago. I look at all the open space out there.

Freedom prospects dim with the appearance of a hogtied man; a man shackled so tight he can barely walk. Leg chains fasten to handcuffs and a waist rope. Two men lift him in. The men leave the door up, get in the truck, drive off.

I'm standing there with a hogtied man, looking out the back of the box truck as trees, grass, and open space, pass by. They said I was going to new receiving. I wonder how that ties to Space Command and their plan for getting me out of here.

Six stories of red brick fade across grey stone and green grass. A fifty-thousand dollar bail on my head and twelve hours after I was a raving lunatic, I'm staring at blue sky and no bars. This has to be a different universe! I wonder what new receiving is like.

The truck pulls to a stop at a brick building, older than the one we left. The two men help Hogtie down. I jump down unassisted.

We go into the building, clackety-clacking down a series of hallways, up some stairs and past a small snack cantina with people hanging and leering, Hogtie attracting their attention and keeping us to half pace. We pass an elevator and stop at a wood door on the left with people staring through the reinforced glass in the upper half.

The door opens. A man takes Hogtie in and closes and locks the door. We continue down the ten-foot-wide hallway and stop at a door on the right. They push the buzzer. We wait. A half-dozen faces stare through the glass.

They part when a black man, same size as me, comes through, unlocks and opens the door. "Hi, I'm Clarence Bullock. Come on in." The door locks behind me. "What's your name,"

"Dan Murphy."

"Well Dan, come on down let me show you around," Clarence says. We walk thirty feet down the eight-foot-wide hallway, and turn right at an opening in the yellow block wall.

"This here's the bathroom and shower. You want to take a shower, stop at the nurse's station and pick up a towel. Don't you be leaving it lay here. Drop it in the laundry basket by the nurse's station when you're done." We continue on.

Ahead is a toll booth structure jutting from the right side of the hallway. "This is the nurse's station where you'll be getting meds at seven, one, and seven," Clarence says as we pass. "Don't you be thinkin about missing meds," he warns. "You can miss meals but not meds. The laundry baskets over here," he gestures. "Across over here is the TV room."

We walk into a windowless room with a TV flashing on the far wall. A couch and six chairs line the side walls. A stout young man hogs the sofa with his eyes glued to the TV. A blonde tuft sprouts haphazardly from his watermelon head. We walk out.

"There are fifty men here and I don't want to see no fightin, bitin, or kickin. Don't make no trouble and you'll be fine," he adds as we continue past wood doors in the long hallway to a large room at the end. "This is the day room where you'll be eating your meals and hanging out." Steel mesh covers the windows from four feet off the floor to two feet short of the ten foot ceiling, around the two far walls.

Men sprawl aimlessly on the couches and chairs, grouped and around the perimeter. The center is filled with a dozen round tables and lots of plastic chairs.
Some of the men look at me. Others look inside.

I look through the diamond mesh to three older buildings in the direction of the tall brick I just left. They're also brick and appear to be eighty to a hundred years old. The one on the far right is half demolished. A hundred foot crane swings an iron ball into it.
An articulate loader is scooping and dumping the rubble into long john trucks.

Green leaves shade the aged structures, grass peeks through the ten-foot separations between buildings. "Dan, let me take you on down and show you your room," Clarence says. We go halfway back to the toll booth and into a room on the left. He leaves,
I return to my gaze in the day room.

I look over the vast expanse of trees and grass and estimate the open area to be two to three times the size of my grandfather's eighty-acre farm. I used to stand on the back porch and look over the hog and sheep pastures, across the creek and corn and bean fields, and down the lane in the center of the property to the five-acre woodlot at the far end.
I can't see enough to accurately judge the full size of the grounds.

A tall, lanky fellow walks up and asks, "What's your name?"

"Dan."

"Callahan, Thomas Callahan," he says as he shakes my hand vigorously.
"The man who has no name had a child born here in forty-three-twenty-one."

I step back and wonder where that came from. I think about the fluorescent lights in the long hall splashing splotches of reflective lights off the grey marble floor like time tunnels to another dimension. I feel like I'm a level up and a couple over. It may take
a few months before everything balances and stabilizes in the Cosmochine.

I imagine the threads of the Cosmochine weaving through reality.
My empathic sensations are still strong but beginning to taper off. It's difficult to carry a conversation with my fellow inmates. Their world is different from mine.

Arctic waters flow to the Antarctic.

My most prominent contact is Bubba. He's big, black as a Kuwaiti night with five-hundred oil wells burning. Meaner than a wolverine guarding it's offspring with meat
at its feet; Bubba rules his charges with an iron fist and no nonsense attitude.

He'll tell them twice and that's it. Sometimes it's three times; four on a rare occasion. "Don't make me come over there," is standard. They usually take heed by the third warning.

Bubba's been working the psyche ward for twenty years and seems to enjoy it though he tells me differently. He talks about retiring, getting away from "the nutcrackers", kicking back on lazy summer days in the hammock in his back yard or yanking some perch from the lake. He longs for the days when he can hunt bunnies with his beagles, every day of the season. He has twenty years to go but oh he can dream.

This place has the greatest variety of nuts I've ever seen. There's Hubcap, a certified lunatic that likes to jump in front of semis for the hell of it. There he was, lying face down on the ground, Mack truck staring at his back, people gathered round. He raised up, shook his head, and said, "If y'all'll give me some breathing room, I'll be up and outta here." Tall and gangly with Grizzly Adams hair and looks, he likes to growl more than talk. Doesn't say much, just looks mean. Patients speak with affectionate awe around him. I suspect his gruff exterior shields a soft heart.

I ask, "How'd you get the name Hubcap?"

"Keeps the grease from flying off the wheel," is his answer.

Then there's Boom-Boom Cannon; one of the resident nuts. Most will eventually pass through. Boom-Boom is a lifelong ward of the state with the intelligence of a six-year-old and the body of a small Sumo wrestler. Whether he can hold a conversation is unknown. All I ever hear is a bunch of mumbling.

Then there's Hogman on the couch. The TV shows pigs around a feeding trough. The disheveled blonde blurts, "Hogs." It's the first word I understand from his mouth. Hogman knows feeding time and doesn't need help eating. A discussion is impossible. Hogman looks at me, brows creased, annoyance in his eyes, scowl on his face, and cuts loose with a mouthful of mumble. I can almost see what he's saying by matching his facial contortions and arm gestures with his voice inflections and eye movement. There's the inevitable hand flapping, eyes rolling across the sky, 'How many times I gotta tell you; what's wrong with you,' look.

A more alert group of people come and go from the ward and keep Bubba growling. "I got better things to do than run up and down the hall to play doorman." I wonder how long it will be before I can go out as I head back down the hall.

In the day room I press my face against the mesh covered windows and see people coming and going on a path to my far right. As demolition of the ancient buildings progress I can see more and more of the brown path snaking through the green grass. The first building is leveled.

Pacific waters flow to the Atlantic.

A doctor visits with me for ten to fifteen minutes every morning. I slip some bleeps about the Cosmochine and altered clones. His lack of reaction erodes my belief. Empathic signals are becoming infrequent.

Life becomes a dull routine. Shower early. Wait til six AM for a smoke. Then medication, breakfast, and doctor visit. Roam around the ward, lunch, medication, roam around ward maybe catch a nap, supper, medication, roam around the ward maybe watch some TV, and hit the sack by nine or ten. Each day is like the day before.

The middle building is half demolished. I can see more of the path in the grass. I watch the people coming and going. Most cross single file.

"I don't know what I'm going to do with you," the doctor says.
"This is my last day," he continues. I don't believe they'll set me free.

Another doctor is assigned and visits twice a week then once a week.
They feed me lithium carbonate and extract vials of blood every day with a giant needle. My arms are pierced with more punctures than an unfulfilled drug addict.

A psychologist spends a couple hours a day in her office on the ward.
She talks to me twice a week then tapers off.

The second building is gone and I can see part of the six-story brick in the distance. That's where the brown path appears to lead. I wonder when I'll get to travel it.
The leaves are losing green and turning red and yellow.

I get ground privileges when many of the leaves have changed to brown, fallen to the ground, and the third building is almost down. I can be away from the ward almost ten hours a day as long as I show for medications and stay on the hospital grounds. I stretch boundaries and take full advantage of the freedom. Halloween is around the corner.

In an empty corridor, I meet a Matt Moses look alike.
He introduces himself as the chaplain. We talk. I wonder.

I see the possibility that one of his clones could have gravitated to this hospital as chaplain. He seems to be all ears when I mention the Cosmochine and doesn't discount the possibility. He becomes my chief ally and confidante at the hospital.

Antarctic waters flow to the Arctic.

Constant foot traffic to and from the six-story brick in the distance has worn a trough out of the eight-inch groove in the grass. The trough bottoms at three inches below grade. On an average day, I reckon at least two-hundred feet make the one mile round trip.

Most of the trips originate at new receiving. Occasionally, patients make the journey from their tall brick home. They appear to have forgotten that there's nothing at new receiving except a half dozen vending machines in a small room with four round tables. Sometimes the steps come partway, turn around, and go back.

I make the trek to the tall brick. It's a beehive of activity with two table tennis and six pool tables. There's a large cantina with a dozen vending machines, tables, and chairs and a smaller one down the hall by the gymnasium. Hundreds of nuts bounce around.

The wind blows. Time passes.
Thanksgiving, Christmas, and New Year's come and go.

Chapter 50—ENDORSEMENT

Andromeda is three-million light years away.

"The charge has been reduced from bank robbery, a Class C Felony, to aggravated menacing, a Class A misdemeanor. How do you plead?"

"Guilty, your honor."

"Sentence reduced to time served," the judge rules. "Two years probation under a doctor's care and don't leave the state without the courts permission." The gavel raps.

Lunar cycles exert their influence.

The songs, "New World Man" and "Hold On Tight To Your Dream," fill the air. Dan thinks about the Cosmochine. Energy bubbles, his body tingles.

Spring turns to summer, fall, winter, and back to spring. The Rust Belt recession continues. Jobs are scarce. It's been over a year and a half since he left Texas.

"Mario Asenio, the employer I left in Texas, wants me to come back," Dan tells the judge. "He has plenty of work and I've barely been able to survive here. I'd like the court's permission to return to Texas."

"Permission granted. You'll need to find a doctor to comply with probation terms."

"Yes, your honor."

"I have a book, written by a personal friend, that I'd like you to have. When you're settled in Houston and have a doctor call me with addresses," the judge says. "I'll send you a copy of NOW I CAN TELL."

Dan drains the scant accumulation in his land contract account and heads south. Mario still owes him seven hundred dollars. His Econoline is history. He has a rust bucket from his buddy at Sled City. He hopes it will make it there.

It does and he arrives in Houston on Sunday, five dollars in his pocket and a tank of gas. It's his third move to Texas. He hopes it's a charm.

Mario pays for three days in a motel and deducts it from the debt. Dan goes to work Monday, finds an apartment and moves in on Wednesday. He finds a doctor, calls the judge.

NOW I CAN TELL, a first hand account of imprisonment and torture when communism turned China Red in the late forties, arrives. Dan reads the cover and introduction by the judge and puts the personally signed book with his other books. Mario's debt drops and hovers.

Gene Gerous is still pumping shit and they're still friends but because of leaving the way he did Dan doesn't impose and ask for his old room back. He has to be independent. It's a condition he left Indiana with.

He works for scab wages but work is steady. He's back on his feet and moving forward. He trades his rust bucket on a spiffy truck, lives modestly on what he makes, and stashes some cash in the bank. His land contract account ducks into the F-ZONE to grow.

Mario's crew has grown to fifteen men. Before Dan returned, Ding Bing was the main foreman. Now that he's back, Dan handles most of the structural and supervises the bulk of the shifting manpower. Mario keeps Ding busy with concrete and demolition.

The first four months are fine then the atmosphere changes. The debt bounces and climbs. Mario has an expansion program that sucks all available capital except pocket change for tittie bars. He demands more work and gives smaller paychecks and sounds like a broken record, "I'm a little short. I need help. How little can you get by on this week?"

Studly's late again, it's getting to be habitual. Dan's tired of hanging out on Friday afternoons wondering how much he'll be short or if he'll get a check for sixty hours of sweat. It happened the same way two years ago; Mario coming up short, spending more time at the tittie bars, demanding more work.

Stanley McGillicuddy was here then. He was a college student on summer break, earning money to continue his education. He graduated and is back to spearhead Studly's expansion to general contracting. This time, he's wearing a suit.

The fruit of Stanley's efforts trickle. Outflow is faster. The funny money's been going for a month. The second anniversary of Dan's rebar reaming is tomorrow.

"Everything's going to get better. You'll see," Mario tells him.

Ding's looking for another job. Dan's about ready to. He hasn't seen the raise Mario enticed him back to Texas with. The debt is now the same as when he arrived five months ago.

Deja Vu. The gate unlocks. The Cosmochine comes up for air.
Strains of discontent poison the atmosphere. The gate creaks.

Mutt Crocker is a general contractor that specializes in custom homes and major remodeling. Curt Simpson is his partner. Together they're Vantage Builders.

Mario does all Vantage Builders' concrete and framing. They provided the bulk of his work before he decided to expand into general contracting.
It's taking manpower without returns.

Curt is everybody's uncle. He's in the trenches everyday. Mutt's a smooth step-dad who rules the roost and struts with an air of condescension in air-conditioned comfort.

Vantage Builders concentrate their efforts in the prosperous southwest and western enclaves of Houston, where the money flows. None trickles to Dan and his crewmates. Mario spends it at the tittie bars.

Mario Asante was in business as a framing contractor for less than a year when he framed Vantage's first house. Dan framed it with Stanley and several others. Dan worked overtime finishing the plumb and line on that house on his thirty-first birthday. That was two months before his rebar reaming ignited the rocket ride to the O-ZONE.

Vantage branched into million dollar remodels while Dan was exploring the outer limits. Remodeling that usually involves dissecting a house and reconfiguring it. Mario and Dan are standing under the tarp in one them with the rain coming down.

Dan asks, "What's Mutt think about your move to general contracting?"

"He thinks it's good. He's behind me as long as I take care of his jobs," Mario answers. "I told him, 'I'll take care of you first'."

"How are you going to handle the increased work load?"

"I'll subcontract the framing on my general contracting jobs." Dan wonders about the viability. Mario starts two general jobs.

Solar particles bombard the atmosphere.

Mutt has three remodels in various stages of completion. Fourteen men are spread between four jobs. Dan's alone at the fifth. Mutt drops in.

"Daniel. How would you like to take over all of Mario's jobs?"

Dan blinks. "What," he stammers.

"Mario's getting into a conflict of interest with his move to general contracting. He's stretching himself too thin and my jobs are beginning to suffer. I've been talking to some framing sub-contractors but the more I think about it the more I think I'd rather have you take over. That is if you're interested. I like the way you take charge and get things done."

"I don't know. I've never given it any thought."

"Well give it some thought."

Dan pauses then says, "I don't think I'd want to do it myself. You have too much going. Ding might want to join. He's been looking for another job."

"That would be excellent. Do you think anybody else would want to join?"

"Other than Marty, I wouldn't want to take anyone else," Dan replies. "The water will get muddy enough without stirring it."

"That won't be a problem. I control the money."

"Mario's not going to take this lying down. Ding and I are two-thirds of his foremen. And I still have to talk to Ding, see if he's interested."

"Well talk to him." Mutt strokes his chin, looks around, then says, "One more thing. I'd like you to take over immediately."

"Immediately?" Dan's eyes stretch. "That's a bad way to start. This break will be bad enough. To take over immediately would compound it. Are you going to assume payroll to finish the present jobs?"

"No. I want to do it sub-contract."

"We could be in the hole before we start. He could be overdrawn!"

"He's not."

"Remodels aren't like a new house where you can break down each step. They're far more complicated; especially this kind. It's damn near impossible to break down the costs this far into a major remodel; you have three!"

"We can work it out. I control the money."

"Mario still owes me money. We won't get our current wages if we start immediately."

"I can make sure you get your current wages."

"We're paid a week behind."

"That won't be a problem."

"What about the money Mario owes me?"

"That's between you and him."

'Thanks Mutt!' "I still have to talk to Ding. With the amount of work you have, I wouldn't think about doing it unless Ding agrees and we can set up properly."

"What would you need?"

"Transit, compressor, nail guns......"

"How much money you talking?"

Dan does some quick calculations and answers, "Three, four thousand."

"I don't see a problem. Talk to Ding and see what you come up with."

"It's best to finish current jobs; three to four weeks. We could have a clean break."

"OK."

"It will take that long to get registered, have a bank account set up and use company checks for tools; get started on the right foot. I think Ding will go along with that."

"I have a spec house I need to get started. Do you want to do the slab?"

"Sub it out. Ding's tired of concrete and I'm not interested.
We'll have our hands full building a crew just to take care of your framing."

"Things may get sticky."

"You can count on it. Mario will come out bitin and fightin.
He thinks we're his slaves."

"A clean break would be good. Talk to Ding and get back to me in a day or two.
One more thing; I don't want you to say anything to Mario. Loose lips sink ships."

Corkscrew jets stream from the black hole.

Dan's mind drifts toward the P-ZONE.
The Q-ZONE's on standby alert. Cycles continue.

Ding's in agreement about finishing the jobs and forming a partnership.
He anxiously looks forward to telling Mario where to stuff it.
Not a day passes that Mutt doesn't call.

Ding and Dan determine what they'll need, check prices, and add costs.
Ding files a DBA at the courthouse and Dan sets up a bank account.
A Sunday meeting is set up with Mutt and Curt.

Mutt sits in the driver's seat, fluffing his feathers as the fine points are agreed upon.
Curt and Ding are casual participants. Negotiations conclude two hours later.
Mutt writes a check for five thousand to Stratus Construction, and struts.

Ding's happy with the arrangement. Dan's apprehensive about the cloud ahead.
He can kiss a thousand dollars goodbye. He knows Mario will boil when he finds out;
he'll bring out the nut ward factor which he doubts Mutt knows anything about.

Dan deposits the check on his way to the Paisley job Monday morning. It's the last of the three jobs they need to finish. It'll be done in three weeks. The Kelly and Green jobs are in the final stages.

Dan's at the Paisley job with three men. Ding's at Mario's general job. The workers leave at five-thirty. Dan stays.

Ding arrives from the downtown job, fifteen minutes later. "Studly was there all day, driving me nuts," Ding laments.

"Lucky you," Dan cracks.

"I can't wait to tell him to kiss my aa-zz," Ding pings. They laugh.

Mario drives up. He knows and hints at hidden dirt. "Mutt isn't the kind of guy you think he is."

"It'll be better than putting up with you and wondering if and when we'll get paid," Ding chimes.

"He'll make you do things you don't want to," Mario retorts.

"We don't like the way things are going with you," Dan says, "and Mutt made us an offer we couldn't refuse."

"What about our plan?"

"That's you're plan and you're faltering. We're finishing the jobs you have started. Mutt wanted us to take over immediately."

"The plan included Mutt's jobs."

"Mutt isn't going to give you any more jobs," Dan says. "He was shopping around for a framing contractor when he approached me. Regardless of what we did, you were out and the way the money's going, it will get worse without Mutt's work."

"What about my jobs," Studly cries.

"You're subbing everything but supervision. You, Stanley, and Redbone can handle that."

Mario cocks his head, purses his lips into daggers, and squeaks sardonically, "We'll talk about it when we exchange Christmas presents."

Ding spits on the ground.

Dan shuffles.

Mario leaves.

Chapter 51—ENTAILMENT

The Abram splits and swirls.

"Mutt wants you to go to the Kelly job," Curt Simpson says.

"I have to drop a roto-hammer off at Paisley's. Scotty's waiting for it."

"Well drop it off and go to Kelly's. Mutt will be there."

I don't know what to do. Until separation is complete, I have two masters. Mario expects me to be with the three men on the Paisley job. Mutt wants me at the Kelly job. The future is with Mutt. Mario owns the present. Mutt says jump.

Niagara roars through the air and thunders on the rocks.

Mutt and I walk through the Kelly major remodel. The sixties ranch-style is being transformed into a Beverly Hills mini-mansion. I can wrap up Mario's contract here in one day with three men but not until the roofers finish their part.

"I've put a hold on the check till we get some details worked out," Mutt mentions with a yawn.

My jaw unhinges and hangs.

"I thought we had all the details worked out in our two hour meeting?"

"Things have gotten sticky," Mutt proclaims.

My eyes roll. I don't believe this. 'As if you didn't know they would,' I silently snort. All my eggs are in Mutt's basket and he's tossing them like croquet balls. My mind teeters.

Mutt struts like a bantam rooster with a harem. I follow in a daze and listen to the guy who doesn't know a joist from a stud as he points out pick-up work that we'll catch on the day we finish. "Do this, do that," he crows.

Hot-moppers arrive with their scalding kettle of bubbling tar. Mutt leaves. I spin. My mind short circuits, drifts, and floats in confusion and uncertainty. Thoughts swirl through lower and upper zones, round and round, left bank to right and back again. Mutt's micromanagement puts me between a rock and a hard place.

Weatherproofing is the only thing that has to be done and it can't be done til the hot mops are done. Inertia seizes my mind. The mops go to work. Plans hover.

My mind drifts through open space. The Paisley job is lost in the ozone. A gentle breeze plays with tree shadows. A brigade of white puffs floats through azure blue. I lay in the back yard and watch ants scurry through the sand littered green forest. Yellow sun is almost overhead when I leave the brown ants and black mops to finish their tasks.

The Commander General Purple is getting the shaft from both directions; a polar piercing up anal alley and down my throat. My legs dangle from the skewer and an apple stuffs my mouth. All I need is some fire and the roast will be complete.

I go for a drive, like I always do when I need to ponder, and cruise through the unfamiliar forests, north of Houston, on autopilot. Several hours later I stop to eat, still wondering what to do. My mind comes back to Earth without answers.

I can't stay with Mario and now I'm not so certain about Mutt. Mario's words come back to haunt me. But, I'm committed. The account's set up, deposit's made, and checks are in the mail. I have to finish the three jobs and hope the plan works.

The wind blows. The sky turns grey. I head back to the Kelly job to cover the roof. It's five o'clock when I arrive.

Clouds are pushed against each other like tufts of charcoal cotton on a giant loom. The hot mops are gone. The roof is covered with plastic. Light rain begins to fall.
I head to my apartment to call Ding. I'm dazed and in the C-ZONE.

Water cycles round the planet.

Breaking glass wakes me in the morning. The wind howls.
Rain pours sideways. I turn on the radio for the latest.

Hurricane Alicia is plowing through. The broadcaster in Alvin, thirty miles away, reports being in the calm eye of the storm after the building he's in survives a howling beating. Clear skies hover over him now.

Glass flies from the upper floors of my apartment complex. I get dressed and wait. The wind and rain slow. I dash for my truck.

Water is everywhere. I drive through the shallow water in the middle of the street. The freeway is elevated above the floodplain. I make it to a coffee shop just as the storm cell blows buckets of water and blurs the emerging light. The big blow chills out by the time I finish breakfast. I make it to the truck less soaked than my race in.

Trees and power-lines are down all over the wooded west side. I drive around them and sidetrack. The tarps are holding and shedding water at the Kelly and Green jobs. Trenches are full at Paisley's; more is coming. No work till the storm passes.

I meander toward the Gulf of Mexico. I have to backtrack and sidetrack but finally arrive at the White house. Seven years ago I recovered from my head scalp in this house. The windows are covered with plywood. The house is OK. Molly and the kids are OK.

Jim's at the swamped shop. Stony's running around. Sheba isn't.
I tell Molly, "I'm retired," and continue my trek to the Gulf.

The road to Surfside is closed. I sidetrack and pass by the hospital where they stitched me that fateful night then cut cross-country to a ferry that crosses the inter-coastal waterway. A half-dozen cars are lined up. I see the ferry on the other side.

An hour later I'm still sitting there. The ferry hasn't moved. I'm outta here!
I back-track and zigzag my way to Galveston. The sun shines bright. It's a beautiful day.

I cruise leisurely, focusing on the storm damage and alternate routes and avoiding my internal carnage. Galveston Island is closed. I hop I-45 and cruise north, above the water.

Black storm clouds are rolling in. Premature darkness beats me to Pasadena.
I exit the freeway for a look at the Houston Ship Channel.

Grey skies pour on saturated ground. The bayou in front of me is surging over the bridge. Guard rails poke out of the swift water.

A truck crosses from the other side. Then a car from my side starts across. I debate. I decide. If they can make it, so can I.

I don't wait long enough. The car in front of me stalls three-quarters of the way across. Water piles and pushes around it. I'm a quarter of the way across, idling, concerned about the power of the water flowing around me.

The fast flowing water appears to be rising. My truck is small and water is bunching around me; none has come in. Three teens get out of the stalled car and push it across.

I creep to the middle; my steering wheel offers no resistance. I float on the gushing water, tires slip. The boys are walking back across the bridge. Eddies swirl seaside of their knees. I'm concerned they'll be swept by the current.

I open the passenger door and say, "Get in." Water gushes. The passenger well fills. Some sloshes around back and splashes my socks.

The truck sinks. The fan blade splashes water. My engine dies. The boys push me to shallow water. My feet are wet.

After several tries, it starts. It's running rough but good enough. I progress toward dry land. It stalls and starts and stalls. I keep it running and head cross-town to Sharpstown.

The fifth stall is a mile from home. Restart is futile. I push it into a parking lot and walk back to my apartment.

It's six o'clock. Mutt's not in. I leave a message. "Call me."

I wait til eleven the next morning for his call. I call him. "Mr. Crocker's not in."

"Tell him to call Dan Murphy." I walk the mile to my truck. I get it started.

It misses and backfires but it runs. I take off while I have the chance. It backfires. The muffler roars. I keep going.

I endure the roar for a block then it stalls for good. I get out, slam the door, leave the truck in the street, and walk back to my apartment. Where's Mutt?

He isn't in. I leave another message. Mario isn't talking and Mutt doesn't call.

I wait til ten the next morning before calling. "I've given Mr. Crocker all your messages," is her answer.

I have to get my truck off the street and back here. I make the traffic free walk and find Stanley taking my tools out. "I didn't want them to get stolen," is his answer.

I try but the truck won't start. We push it into a parking lot and finish taking the tools out of the truck and back to my apartment. Then I go with Stanley McGillicuddy.

Clouds of dust swirl across the Sahara.

Mario's face stretches lengthwise, mouth extending to an oval, hand flashing over it. He ducks and runs. I chuckle. Stanley coaxes him out of hiding.

It's agreed that I will no longer be working for him. He'll pay the eleven hundred he owes me. "It'll take a couple days," he says.

Stanley takes me back to my apartment. My truck has to sit til I have money to fix it. I dial the phone. Mutt answers.

"There's been a few wrinkles added," Mutt announces. My eyes roll. "I don't know if we're going to be able to proceed."

I gulp. "A week ago there was no question of proceeding!"

"I need to get a few things worked out," is Mutt's reply.

"I'm out of a job. My truck's out of commission. You have a hold on the five grand. Mario doesn't have any money to pay me. I need money to fix my truck. What do you want me to do?"

"Take a rest for a few days."

"Thanks."

I push my truck to my apartment, thankful for the level concrete and lack of traffic. With nowhere to go and all day to get there it takes a day of rest stops to push it a mile. I see a long grind as concrete walls form around the rock and hard place I'm in. I conserve what little money I have for food and cigarettes. Days pass.

Ding is still working for Mario. I shoulder the blame. A flame glows in the pit between the rock and hard place. Mutt disappears. The spit turns. The Q-ZONE opens.

A week passes. No word from Mutt. No money from Asenio.

Air cycles round the globe.

My imagination runs wild. I lose track of time. I visit people in the complex, walk around the mall and neighborhood, and take bus rides on an expanding circuit. Days come and go. Futility pulses and grows.

Thoughts of the Cosmochine dance in my head. I short circuit through the Q-ZONE and become oblivious to the real world by immersing in a world where I turn the spit instead of being turned. T-ZONE aura commands.

I'm at a hotdog restaurant, a few blocks from my apartment, playing a pinball machine. The ball's rolling and the flippers are flipping. No noise is being made. I don't want to waste a quarter when I can get twice the fun for nothing. I'm working for a replay.

I look over at a macho cowboy glaring at me from ten feet and lose my concentration and replay. I look back at the glaring cowboy. He rises to the challenge.

Not looking for a fight I walk out of hot dog heaven. Three police cars are lined up and waiting. My mouth seems to be disengaged. My brain is somewhere in the O-ZONE.

Officers stop and cuff me. Resistance is futile. I offer none and wonder if they're taking me to Space Command.

As the freeway miles go by, I give silent commands to Master and Alter Controls. Their course veers from the route of a week earlier when they took me to the Hilton. I was walking down the street minding my own business when I got that ride.

I was introduced to the overnight program at the downtown Hilton a few days before that for a similar non-offense. But this trip is different. I wonder if my commands are working and look forward to linking with Space Command.

Chapter 52—ENACTMENT

Energy cycles to infinity.

The space Dan commands is severely limited. Eighteen-inch chains anchor his wrists and ankles to four corners of a rolling steel bed and confine him to his back. Strange people surround him. A mesh cage surrounds them.

Frozen in suspended animation, he wonders how long he'll be in this terrifying position. Catatonia consumes him. Every cell in his body quivers. It's been two years since the first and last time he had to deal with this horror. He doesn't know if he can last as long as he did then. If emotions take control, he's a goner. There's no coming back when the main spring unhooks.

The chains give room to get tangled when he to turns to his side but not enough to be comfortable. The twisting, contorting position that gets him the furthest from his back is dangerous. If he moves too quick his muscles bind, knot, and constrict; panic sprouts.

He did nothing to deserve this. He didn't fight or resist when they put handcuffs on or strapped him to the rolling, steel bed. Other than a powder thud on Raphael's cheek, four years ago, the bank heist car, and Barker, Dan hasn't hit anyone, hurt anything, or taken what didn't belong to him since this insanity started. Today is no different!

He fights to remain calm and moves slow when he adjusts his position.
Flat on his back is totally unacceptable. It's a prison he can barely endure.

Earth cycles around the sun.

Twelve hours after strap-down they remove the chains and release him in the dead of night. Buses aren't running and he has no money for a cab. He walks the night away.

Blisters form. The sun comes up. An eviction notice greets him at his apartment. He just paid his rent; he has thirty days to get out. Too tired to think, he falls into bed.

Four hours later, he's up. His mind vibrates with shocks and aftershocks.
His focus is scattered. Mutt's intentions are unknown.

Concrete walls surround Dan. A rock is pressing him to the hard spot.
The flame grows. His legs and arms dangle like a limp frog as the spit turns.
His bank account dwindles. The only escape from his reality is altered reality.

The Q-ZONE opens. With no control over his own life, it's his only option to maintain sanity; an option as real as the eviction notice. He had retired from command and placed the Cosmochine on auto-pilot. Now he returns to active duty.

With his responsibilities as Supreme Commander of the Cosmochine, Dan doesn't have time to worry about his boulder strewn existence and the pile of rubble that remains.
He issues orders to Master Control, Main Control, Super Control, and Ultra Control.
And counter orders to Space Command, Alter Command, Counter Command, and
Sub Command. He shadow box's with the different Charges. He's back on top.
He's Commander General Super Purple, the creator of the Cosmochine.

At one end of Earth's cycle it's the Summer Solstice.

Dan is holding a towel and wearing powder blue polyester cutoffs. Rubber tread sandals protect his feet. His faded Hawaiian shirt is unbuttoned and exposes a hand-sized turquoise medicine bag with a luminescent draw-string, hanging from his neck.

He watches the earthbound division of Space Command train. Engines roar as anxious recruits learn the basics of this dimension before ascending to the lofty spires of space. Dan waits for his angels to swoop him from this harsh earthly realm and into heavenly bliss. They don't show.

He leaves his towel at his command post at the side of the runway at Hobby Airport and meanders toward the terminal. He gazes into the heavens and sees a flash. 'The angels are delayed,' he surmises.

It's the Winter Solstice in the other hemisphere.

A solid arch draws him down a concrete tunnel into a bar called the Time Tunnel. Dan drinks a beer in the customer sparse bar then goes outside for a gaze. A faint red beam catches his eye.

He knows he's in tune. He wouldn't see the space laser if he wasn't. He recalls the night of the flying stop signs and the phantom red in the truck rear window.

This beam is also phantom and hard to discern. It draws him past apartments gutted by the hurricane. Carpet hangs over the chain link fence to dry before it's tossed. Dead animals lay next to scattered tree limbs and branches. Haphazard piles await removal.

Dan walks cautiously over the floating shell. He can feel the hollow emptiness beneath each careful step. The phantom red draws him through neighborhoods and back toward the airport. He wonders if his angels are there. The closer he gets the more unstable the ground feels. There are stretches of solid ground.

Two men, dead serious in their offer to help, grief etched into their faces, bend down to console two ladies sitting in their car in a tavern parking lot. They appear not to notice when Dan walks by. 'Something must've gone wrong.'

Dan makes it back to the terminal. It's dead silent. 'Malfunction junction? Might as well go home! Fifteen miles is too far to walk tonight.'

He goes to a hotel by his command post, where his towel still lays, and calls a cab. He's tired of walking, tired of being harassed, tired of everything. The cab comes.

He falls asleep in the back seat and is barely able to open his eyes when they reach his apartment. He's too tired to get out. The driver says something about a bird hunt. Dan's head is so heavy. He lays back down.

He wakes to a girl shaking him and trying to talk him into going upstairs. He just wants to sleep. Day dawns when the driver shakes him. They're at his apartment.

He remembers the angels. "Back to the airport," he tells the driver. "Full alert Space Command. Super Control, intercept the intersect, transpose the octasect."

Dan can see the driver's concern about the success of the mission, eyes scanning the road and rear view mirror, bouncing with each command. 'I may be hopping levels of the Cosmochine the way he's jerking!' "Space Counter, negative. Blue, purple, yellow. Check."

The driver relaxes when Dan gets out of the cab. It's the first time he's been out of the cab all night. He pays the driver.

Two police cars drive up. Dan goes into a parking lot. He's trapped. Other than over the fence, there's only one way out. Three policemen block the exit and move toward him.

Dan tries to untie the turquoise medicine bag that's knotted around his neck. Two policemen close in. He's all thumbs and not moving when they grab him.

They handcuff him and take the bag from his neck. The knot clasps the bag. His magic is in it. He's doomed. His towel is still at the command post a couple hundred yards away. At least it was the last time he looked.

Dan is put into the back seat of a squad car and driven away by a lone driver. A screen separates them. He wonders where they're going.

They pull into an open lot with a downtown view. Two other squad cars are there. The driver gets out for secret negotiations. Dan talks to Space Command. His gaze alternates between the police officers, twenty feet away, and the downtown skyline.

Negotiations are lengthy but Dan's driver finally returns. They leave on a course parallel to the Houston skyline and pull up to a hospital entrance ten minutes later. It's the same place they took him three days earlier. 'Damn!'

Dan knows the routine. Lay on the rolling steel while they strap and chain his wrists and ankles; cell quivering terror, mind binding panic. Self induced catatonia subdues the horror.

In the past two weeks, he's been taken to jail three times. The first time it was to a substation for five hours. He walked four miles home. The second time, he was taken to the substation for a couple hours then jammed into the back seat of a cruiser with three other prisoners for a spinning, sliding, hair raising race downtown to the Houston Hilton. Then the Hilton and a two day stay at the P-farm. Then twelve hours of catatonia. Now he's chained again.

Sixteen mind numbing hours later, he's released. Again, it's in the dead of night and shortly after they unchain him. It's another twelve mile hike.

Water pools in low spots on the streets and provide relief for his aching feet on the hike home. He won't be wearing sandals on the next trek. Fatigue creeps long before he reaches his apartment.

Sleep was impossible on the steel slab with threats of mind popping entanglement. Life is beating him to a pulp. The sun is well on its way to zenith when he falls into bed.

Dan wonders if he's become a make work project for the Houston Police. Mutt and Mario are bad enough. This is past the point of ridiculous. 'I have to get away.'

Chapter 53—ENCAMPMENT

Haley's Comet chases its tail.

The bus pulls away and leaves me standing in the middle of Texas.
I know where I am but only a vague clue of where I'm going. Two suitcases,
a shoulder bag, sleeping bag, briefcase, and two fishing rods marshal at my feet.
I had fifty dollars before I bought the one-way ticket.

A big man with a knife approaches. Sweat beads on my face and glistens in the terminal light. Rivulets run down my face. He wants money.

I give him five dollars. He gives me the knife.
I inquire about local lakes. He directs me to a taxi driver.
The cabbie knows of an abandoned cabin at Lake Austin.

Pluto continues it's penetration into Neptune's realm.

The moon is high in the sky when the taxi pulls up to the cabin. Stars sparkle like jewels on the velvet background. A platinum band crosses the heavens. I look through the trees and see a slice of moon bouncing off water.

The driver's flashlight reveals a once glorious structure. There's a vaulted ceiling, fireplace, and full length porch with a filtered view. The vandalized cabin doesn't look that old; younger than me. The front and back doors are missing.

After the taxi leaves, I carry my baggage train over the debris littered floor and pick my way into a back room. I find some cushions that don't seem to have any terrestrial inhabitants and take them to the coolest and cleanest place I can find - the porch facing the water. I spread the cushions and roll out my sleeping bag.

The Milky Way circles the universe like a speck of dust in the ocean of infinity.

I walk up the long winding road to Lake Austin after a self-guided tour of the University of Texas. The bus ticket, knife, and taxi ride took all but twenty dollars. Food and cigarettes took that. My pockets have nothing but lint in them.

It's another mile to the top of the incline. I look down into the rocky ravine and up at the road ahead. It curves left, vanishing around a rocky outcrop, and curls around the ravine before sweeping into view and disappearing through a hole in the rock on the far side of the airspace. A mile of downhill-uphill awaits me at that point.

I'm at the end of the line; no clue of where my next meal is coming from, almost out of smokes, down to living an hour at a time. If I don't catch a fish, I'll be eating dirt. I remember my mother's words, "You used to eat dirt."

There's something at the curve ahead. I grunt and trudge toward it.
It's a plastic milk crate! Looks like one of the two Bill Bagby gave me two years ago.
The hospital confiscated them instead of giving me my fifty-five dollars.

It's sitting by the guardrail. And it's brown. Just like the one
I didn't find at the cornucopia store and leave in the bank heist car.

Irony and similarity de-polarize the gates of fantasy and reality.
Cells to an alter state unlock. Dusty survival corridors open.
It has sentimental value from the metal building ambassador.

The black hole swallows light and hides from view.

The next morning I leave the crate in the cabin with the rest of my possessions and trudge to town. I'm wearing shorts, T-shirt, and a light corduroy jacket. At the bottom of the long incline I turn right and walk more miles to the south end of Austin. Instinct, a vivid video, and an empty wallet are my guides.

I luck out and catch a ride with a man on his way to a metal building show in San Antonio. Bill Bagby opens the gate. I ground in reality as I tell the compassionate stranger about Bill, and Mutt and Mario.

We come to the Universal City exit.
"You completely out of chips," the man asks.

"I haven't eaten since noon, yesterday," is my reply.

He hands me a sawbuck and says,
"Pass it to someone else who's down on their luck."

"Thank you."

The Samaritan's generosity buys a bag of orange slices, cigarettes, and change at the Base Exchange. With no agenda, I'm winging it to see what turns up. I've been driven through the corridors of my mind to a spot in the O-ZONE where parts of reality are blocked from view by patches of black and green around my tree house.

The cosmic egg explodes to life.

Two months ago my buddy Bart, the All-Star Air Force slugger, and his wife shipped out for a four year tour in Germany. I was present at the softball team's farewell picnic in the park. Seemed like everyone was shipping somewhere in the next couple months. Tom and Sonny were the exceptions.

Bart told me, "If you ever need any help, look up my buddies here. They'll take care of you."

I couldn't imagine a need at the time. The audio memory woke me this morning. And now I'm at the base with my last gasp in pocket.

My search centers on finding Bart's buddy with the Filipino wife. He wasn't on the softball team but I took a shower at their apartment four months ago. They may be able to help me find Tom. I don't know any last names.

The base is like all the other featureless Armed Force bases I've seen around the country. Everything looks the same. I dig into my video compartment for some high resolution tape and see a long, rectangular section of grass and trees on my left and two-story apartment buildings on the right. I walk around the sprawling base til I find the match.

By mid afternoon I find the apartment buildings. I know which of the eight doors to knock on but I'm missing the frame that shows which of the six identical buildings it's in. I zoom closer for familiar flora and focus on the picture.

My honed nose finds the couple and the right door on my second knock.
They have Tom's phone number. I call from their apartment.
Tom says, "Come by my office tomorrow morning."

The sun ignites.

A cold snap pushes the heat wave out. I spend the night shivering in a field, on ground as hard as a slab of ice. I'm not prepared for this. I didn't prepare for much of anything but getting out of Houston and away from the harassment.

I brought everything I didn't want to lose except my tools; my livelihood.
I guess my statement to Molly about being retired was embedded in my thoughts.
One oar churns sand. I may have to eat some.

My T-cell flips major and minor polarities. My right bank gyro is askew.
My tree house shades me from reality.

I have candy orange slices for breakfast while I walk to Tom's office.
Other than neutral ground and a solid wall to bounce thoughts off I have no expectations.
I need to clear my head and get a grip. The Houston triple whammy has me walking the edge like a drunken sailor on the high seas - weaving from one side of reality to the other and sometimes confused on which side is which.

The journey since meeting Audra has been so surrealistic yet too real to dismiss.
My mind teeters and slams sideways against the closing concrete walls.
Eating dirt is my next option.

Planets cool.

Tom is waiting with a cup of coffee. We talk about my ordeal.
I start at the beginning and skip to the present but not my vision or the Cosmochine.

"I get off duty at seventeen hundred hours," Tom says.
"Come back and see me then."

At five o'clock, I'm back at Tom's office. My orange slices are gone.
Change jingles in my pocket.

We hop in Tom's car and go to his house. I take a shower. Tom gives me a sweatshirt and warm-up pants. We go to a softball game that Tom is umpiring.

Sonny is there with his two small boys. I go home with them.
I get the lower bunk and the boys get the upper.

Camaraderie with neutral friends and play with the boys opens a cell in the F-ZONE. My land contract account, tucked in Ohio to grow, pops out.
I could've had my truck running!

The next morning I walk to a local bank to have money wired.
"You have to have an account to have the money wired to," the Ohio manager says.
I open an account and have five hundred dollars wired. "It will take a couple days."

I stretch the change and Sonny's hospitality. "Not here," stretches the days. The carton of cigarettes I bought at the Base Exchange is down to a pack.

The sun transfers life to the blue marble.

The wire finally arrives. I withdraw two hundred dollars and buy a one way to Austin. At the tiny bus terminal, I splurge on a tin of jelly beans. Ronald Reagan is President.

The money buys me freedom from anxiety and allows my mind to drift from the tree house and down the corridors of the Cosmochine. Daylight dwindles. I eat jellybeans on the forty-five minute bus ride and float through the Cosmochine. Aftershocks emanate from the impact fractures in my C-ZONE and unlock all the gates to the Q-ZONE.

They're celebrating the Hundred Year Anniversary of the University of Texas when I arrive. Helicopters circle overhead. Spotlights splay the area. The Q-ZONE is wide open.

I think about Super Control as I duck for cover in a luggage store. Fancy bags with zippered compartments distract my attention from Super's search. I buy a shoulder bag with a hidden pocket; perfect place for my knife. After stuffing the can of jelly beans into my new bag I peer out.

I decide to take my chances and venture into the open. Two local blues don't give me a second glance as I pass. I lighten up on the paranoia.

As I wander through the partying throng I drink beers from scattered vendors. I meet a fellow partier and we cruise the scene. The activities are winding down and my new found friend says he knows of another party.

With cash in my pocket and beer in my belly, I'm in hog heaven as we cruise the freeway. I gloat about slipping Super Control as I squelch my voice, cackle, and taunt, "Super Control." My new friend is cool and I feel secure.

A couple blurbs later I spout, "Space Command, you're in charge." The mood changes and the next thing I know, I'm standing at a gas station, fifteen miles from downtown Austin. I watch him race away. I thought the dude was cool!

It's after midnight, the buses aren't running and I don't want to spend money for a cab. The cabin is ten miles west of town. The incline to the lake and only way I know to get to the cabin, starts five miles from downtown. If I cut cross-town, the wheels whir, I should be able to save about four miles; almost an hour of walking.

With a vague knowledge of the area, the moon, stars, and internal compass to guide me, I start the twenty mile or so, trek to the cabin. My party mood is gone and I'm anxious to see if my worldly possessions have been disturbed. I ponder my next move.

The streets are erratically spaced and run north-south and east-west, sometimes curving. I zigzag and walk-jog on the imaginary cross town line. For every step west, I take three steps south, more or less.

Chapter 54—ENTRAPMENT

The dinosaurs thought it was just a scary flash and shudder.

Dan's legs made the choice in Austin. They didn't want to hike the five-miles of grade to find his encampment disturbed and then have to carry the impossible load down the hill. He called a cab at the bottom of the incline.

He found his possessions untouched and had second thoughts but since his legs made the choice and his mouth summoned the cab, he loaded everything into the cab and hopped the bus to Dallas. It's a city he has passed through once not counting stops at Love Field. That was eight years ago when he came to Texas in Gene Gerous' maroon crew cab.

He last saw Gene a few days before Hurricane Alicia and Mutt and Mario's polar piercing splayed him like a frog on a spit. He's not sure when they last talked.
The past month has been a blur.

Outside his immediate needs, Dan's not sure of anything.
He thinks he has ten days before they change the deadbolt on his apartment.

Three days in Dallas drain his cash. It's Sunday noon, vacations over.
He has enough money for a bus ticket.

Ayres Rock sprouts.

"The next bus to Houston leaves at seven-twenty."
He made the wrong choice and now he's stuck with a ton of baggage. He had to rush to catch a ride with an off duty cabbie shacking at his motel and didn't have time to check bus schedules. He made the choice enroute. The cabbie's gone.

Dan calls the other bus company from the payphone. His baggage train is stacked around him. They have a bus leaving for Houston at four-fifteen.
"How far are you from the other bus terminal," he asks.

"We're five blocks up the street."

Debris sucks to the dying, freezing wasteland.

Dan stands there and looks up the tower lined, gray hill. Straps cross his chest and loop over opposite sides of his neck. His left arm wraps over his new shoulder bag with secret pocket and knife in it. His hand grips a heavily packed jumbo American Tourister with grappling hook tenacity. Two fishing poles, reels attached, are split into four pieces and squish between his left hand and the handle of the lead weight American Tourister.

His right arm clamps over his briefcase while his shoulder bag with sleeping bag bounces on his bicep. The arm extends between his briefcase and balanced bag to a finger stretching grip around a knee knocking suitcase and milk crate.
The weight on his feet doubles for the coming eternity.

Dan, the caravan, grunts and trudges up the hill, lead suitcase stretching his fingers apart, fishing poles splitting to four directions, sliding loose and out.
His right knee is battered by the suitcase-milk crate combo while the shoulder bag

slides and bounces from neck bend to chokehold. Dan grits his teeth and hardens his Adam's apple for five and then another five steps. His briefcase starts slipping.

He stops, re-situates, re-grips, and grunts another forty feet up the twenty degree concrete incline. Carrying three bundles of shingles up the thirty degree roof incline was nothing compared to this. His shoulder socket pops. He powers on.

Aqueous bullets spurt from his face and flow like the Amazon. He tries to make it a half-block and rests for a minute when he can't. He trudges and grunts up the vacant sidewalk til he reaches the other terminal.

It's on the other side of the six-lane street! Luckily, it's Sunday afternoon and traffic is light. He rests for the pounding dash. He still has two hours before the bus to Houston pulls out. His clothes are saturated with sweat.

India smashes into Asia.

Dan wonders how his legs would feel if his truck hadn't died and he hadn't walked over a hundred miles in the past month. Steam spouts. He looks at the double-crosses and runarounds and wonders what he did to deserve the hardships of the past ten years.

He buys a one-way to Houston and feasts on two burgers and a fry. Three quarters jingle in his pocket as he waits for the bus. He'll be in his own bed tonight and have two-hundred wired to his Houston account in the morning.

The Himalayas grind to the stars.

Dan stands there, ready to board the bus with his two shoulder bags, briefcase, and fishing rods and argues with the driver.

"You can only check two pieces on."

"Can't you just throw the milk crate on?"

"Every piece has to have a tag and you can only tag two pieces. If you want to check three pieces, you have to get a freight ticket."

"My wallets empty, and as you can see, I'm loaded with baggage. Can't you just stick it on without a tag?"

"We can't guarantee it."

"That's OK. It's just a milk crate and a ratty old blanket. If I lose them, it's no big loss."

The driver hesitates then shakes his head sideways and says, "I can't do it."

Dan stands at the door to the bus and thinks about the four hour ride to Houston and using the blanket as a pillow. The bus driver is silent and writing intently. Dan doesn't want to bother him so he waits til he's done.

The driver is done writing and moving toward the crate when Dan says, "I've decided to take it on board."

"That's it. You're outta here!"

"Outta here?"

The driver pulls Dan's suitcases from the cargo hold and rips the tags off. "Take your stuff on another bus," he spouts.

"What about my ticket," Dan asks as the driver turns to the other passengers.

"Talk to the manager."

"If you're not going to let me ride the bus, I want my ticket back!"

The driver ignores him and checks the remaining passengers on.

"I need my ticket. It's my only proof that I paid for it," Dan wails.

A short and skinny red-head, fresh out of grammar school, approaches.

"What's the problem," he asks.

"I want to talk to the manager."

"I am the manager," he says.

Dan does a double take. He still looks like he just got out of grammar school.

"Your driver says that I can't ride the bus and won't give my ticket back."

"What's the problem Joe?"

"He's not riding my bus," Joe says as he hands the ticket to the red-head.

The preppy manager turns to Dan and says, "You can't ride our bus line."

He gives Dan the ticket. "If you want your money back, write to the company."

"Write to the company? I bought it here an hour ago!"

"That's the company policy."

"Can't you just refund the purchase price?"

"You'll get a refund in about six weeks."

"Six weeks?" Dan questions the sky with rolling eyes.

A man in black walks up.

"That's if you write them right away," freckle face replies as a matter of fact.

"Who's in charge of your company?"

"He is," the preppy says as he gestures to Joe.

"The bus driver's in charge of the company?" Dan's eyes spiral to infinity.

"What kind of company is this," he asks as his eyes come down to the red-head prep.

Joe huffs and boards the bus.

"I can't wait six weeks to get my money back. Call the police."

"I am the police," says the man in black.

Dan looks at him and then the badge. Black smoke bellows as Joe blows.

"They won't let me ride the bus and won't give me a refund," Dan tells him.

"Why won't you let him ride the bus," Black asks Red.

"The driver doesn't want him on. He can't ride and that's company policy."

"Why won't you give him a refund?"

"He has to write in for a refund. That's company policy."

Dan snorts. The lad turns and walks back inside the terminal.

Dan stands in front of his baggage pile with the man in black.

"Why wouldn't the driver let you board the bus?"

"He said I couldn't throw this milk crate," Dan gestures,
"with my two suitcases in the cargo compartment. As you can see, I'm loaded with carry-ons. When I decided to take it on board, he said I couldn't ride the bus."

"Is that it?"

"I live in Houston and just want to get back there. Other than this," he pulls three quarters out of his pocket, "all the money I have is tied up in this bus ticket. The other bus company has an identical fare and a bus leaving in three hours but if I don't get a refund for this ticket," Dan says as he waves it in the air, "I'm stuck here."

The officer takes the ticket, says, "Let me see what I can do," and disappears into the terminal. Dan guards his baggage train.

Ten minutes later, the man in black comes back with nineteen dollars and fifty cents. Dan thanks him and loads his train for the hike down the hill. The man in black leaves. Dan chugs out the back side of the terminal. A young black approaches.

"Hey man. Let me give you a hand."

"That's OK, I can manage."

"That's a heavy load. You sure you don't want any help?" Dan thinks about the bullets he sweated coming up the hill and slides the American Tourister to the young black. They trudge out the bus entrance and toward the downhill run.

They're barely out of the terminal when the complaints start.
"Man this suitcase is heavy."

Dan thinks about the black's altruistic motives.
"I don't have any money to give you," he says.

"That's OK, It's no problem," but complaints continue. When they reach the downhill run, the whiner stops with a thud. "Hey man, you got lead in this suitcase."

"Books; look, I appreciate your help but I can manage. Give me the suitcase."

"No man, it's no problem."

They take more rest stops on the downhill than Dan did on the uphill trudge. Halfway down the grade Dan swaps two bags for the lead suitcase. A half-hour later, they enter the terminal. Complaints have been non-stop.

The young black keeps testing for money.
"Look, I appreciate your help but I have enough money for a bus ticket and that's it.
I don't have any money to give you." The whiner finally leaves.

Dan purchases a ticket an hour before departure and waits.
He hopes to arrive in Houston in early morning after a bus change in Waco.
That is if he doesn't have any more problems!

Chapter 55—ENSCONCEMENT

Niagara rumbles.

I need two seats for all my baggage. No pair is open. I sandwich myself, shoulder bags, briefcase, fishing rods, and milk crate next to a young lady.

I think about trudging up and down the hill with my baggage train, Mutt and Mario, all the hassles. Crimson bubbles, anger glares.
I mumble a micro ménage of muttering to Sub Command.

The Dallas skyline shrinks. Red flares on the western horizon splash through gray cotton fluffs. My seatmate gets up and makes her way to the front of the bus.

I spread my baggage and mumble some more. Twenty minutes later, the bus exits the freeway. I look over the small town before we drop down into it; wouldn't imagine it to have more than a few thousand people. Why are we stopping here, I wonder.

The driver comes back, talks to people around me, looks at me, and says, "You have to get off."

The Colorado River carves through the Grand Canyon.

The overhead light flickers as I stand there, baggage train and diesel fumes surrounding me. I look at the sign posted on the block wall that protects the converted gas station from the hill behind it: Waxahachie? I've never heard of such a name!
I laugh at the irony as I end up with nothing in nowhere on a side trip to oblivion.

I wonder how long I'll be stuck here. Three quarters burn a hole in my pocket. The soda pop machine against the wall beckons. It gobbles the quarters and gives change.

I laugh as I sit on a bench, lean against the ten-foot white block wall, and drink my last drink. I look at the thin dime in my hand and cackle some more. I don't even have enough money to make a phone call! Don't know who I'd call if I could.

I seem to be in a town with no people. This can't be hell?
"What now Chester," I lament to the wall.

I get up, walk out to the street intersection, turn around, and look at the block wall behind my baggage train. My gaze drifts up and over the wall to a small white house, with a full length open porch, perched above the station. I walk down the sidewalk and up the concrete steps to investigate.

The house faces me, porch roof sloping up to intersect with the steep pitched house roof. The five-foot wide porch runs the twenty-four foot length of the clapboard house. The land slopes toward me and the block wall overlooking the way station.
I walk up the sidewalk to the house.

No one answers my knocks. The dark house appears vacant. I stand on the porch and gaze over the rooftops around me. I seem to be on the only bump in town.

Back at the station, I look for a bus schedule. There's a faded sign in the window I can't see what's written on it. Lucky if they get a bus a week through this burg!

Might as well set up camp! I don't think the owners, wherever they are, will mind me taking up a small section at the end of the porch. It's better than the concrete of the bus stop. I make several trips to shuttle my baggage up and around the wall.

The Brahmaputra carves between India and Asia,

My sleeping bag is rolled out, baggage marshaled around it. I sit on the end of the porch and survey my kingdom of thirty-square-feet. "Here in Waxahachie,
I'm king of the hill." My gut splits at the ironic absurdity.

My gaze lifts over the wall to the kick-off zone, ten feet below me, and up
to the stars that lace black velvet with a platinum band to infinity. My territory is staked.
I'm prepared to pounce on the next bus that pulls up.

U-turns around Everest and joins the Ganges flow to the sea.

It's a grand time under the stars. Delirium overtakes me as I sit on
the porch eating jellybeans, laughing and joking about the insanity of my dilemma.
Commander General Purple commands a spot on a hill in the middle of nowhere.
I howl at the moon and double over with laughter til my side can take it no more.

I discover the secret of the universe then go to hell and die. Some reward!
I feel like Copernicus; scoffed at for saying the earth and planets rotate around the sun.
I chuckle at the dogma and think back.

A century later, Galileo and Kepler backed Copernicus' heresy.
Galileo faced the Inquisition and was put under house arrest for blasphemy.
The world laughed. Sir Isaac Newton, born the year Galileo died,
constructed the reflecting telescope and vindicated all of them.

Greeks had the same scientific thought almost two millennia earlier,
Pyramid two construction wound down two millennia before that.
God predated the pyramids by two thousand years.

My vision came in the dark of night and illuminated my day.
Then I met Audra and my world became topsy-turvy.
And then there's the Cosmochine.

Reality pulls me down. I sit in Nowheresville with a thin dime, five-eighths of a tin of jellybeans, and no clue of when the next bus will be coming through.
I crash on my bed of dirt.

My sleep is deep. I hear the rumble of a diesel in my dream. The rumble gets louder, more vivid, closer. It sounds like its right next to me. My eyes open. Holy shit!

I jump out of my sleeping bag, throw on my shirt, dig for my ticket, scramble down the hill, and shortcut around the wall barefoot while trying to button my shirt, hang onto the ticket, and keep from stumbling. I wonder if this is really happening; hard to believe a bus actually comes to this burg more than once a week. I fret about my baggage.

The driver is off the bus and looking around when I come running up with
my ticket fluttering from my raised hand and shirt flapping from my waist.
Desperation cries. I plead, "Can you help me," as I hand him my ticket.

The bus driver looks at me, flapping shirt and cut-off shorts, and says nothing. "My luggage is up there," I point. No response.

He's not saying no so I'm not giving him the chance. I grab the ticket and race back up the hill. At the porch I sit down to put my sneakers on.

My shoes are on and I'm concentrating on tying them as fast as I can when my peripheral vision catches a glimpse of the driver getting on the bus. I stop mid loop as the door closes and stand in bewilderment as the bus revs and drives off.

I race down the hill, shirt still flapping, laces flopping, ticket fluttering, unable to believe that the bus is actually pulling out. I stand at the edge of the hill, watch and listen as he circles. Is he coming back? The diesel fades.

Wonder changes to irritation. "What the hell is going on?"
I look up at the sky, "I don't believe this shit," and down to the kick-off zone,
"This is a fine way to wake up."

Busted and disgusted, I sit and ponder. I grab the tin and pop the top.
A jellybean rifles into the kick-off zone and skips to the street; then another.
Blood pumps as I watch nothing move except an occasional wisp of wind.
I look at the bright side, "At least they stop here more than once a week!"
I laugh and pop yellow jellybeans into my mouth.

A battered, black car comes and goes from a hidden location around the corner. It has to be about three AM. Other than my rude awakening, it's the first sign of life I've seen in this burg. There's hope.

I watch for about an hour as the car occasionally crawls around town on a jangled circuit and returns to its hidden spot. I grab the tin of jellybeans and launch an investigation, down the sidewalk, around the corner. Crisp morning air cuts through my jacket.

The car, looking fit for a demolition derby, sits next to a faded clapboard building with chunks missing. Light splashes through the holes.
Inside, a big black man sits at a desk. I go to the door and knock.

Earth spins east. Wind flows past it.

The room is big and plain. Holes pierce the worn wood floor. Ventilation comes through gouges in the wall. Across from the beaten desk is a dirty, old sofa.
Off to one side is a kitchen.

I sit on the lumpy sofa. The man sits at the battered desk.
"You want some coffee," he asks.

"Sure."

"It's out in the kitchen. While you're at it get me a refill."

The sun goes west. Water follows the moon.

I sit and eat red, white, and blue jellybeans with black coffee and ponder.
This is my America where they make me comfortable and let me be.
Next stop: Waco.

Chapter 56—ENSHRINEMENT

Water boils at Niagara's base.

Dan sells his shirt in Waco for a packet of peanut butter-cheese crackers and makes it to Houston. His truck payment is due. Eviction is a week away. Hurricane Alicia is five weeks past.

He has two hundred dollars wired from Universal City and chooses to eat and smoke over a truck payment. He'd fix his truck if he had a job but uncertainty clouds the future. He has no clue of where to go or a way to get there. Mutt vanishes. Marooned in a sea of despair and iniquity, Dan floats towards oblivion.

Thoughts drift down to the A-ZONE. Anger rises toward the Z-ZONE. He calls lawyers about Mutt's breach of contract. They want cash. Mario coughs none. Dan breaks pencils, his veins throb. Days pass.

"I'll meet you at the bank tomorrow morning at ten o'clock," Mario says.

Dan's veins bulge. "That's an hour and a half walk!" His mouth spews ash.

Water flows through Lake Ontario to the Saint Lawrence Seaway.

It's ten AM. Mario isn't there. Dan paces and waits; smoke seeps. A half hour passes. He calls Joyce, Mario's wife and in-home secretary.

Thirty minutes later, Mario calls the bank. "I'll be there in a half hour," he tells Dan. Dan sees Mario snicker. Steam builds.

Forty-five minutes later Joyce tells Dan, "Mario's still downtown." Dan's veins pop. Steam spouts. Magma flows through the phone.

The bank manager says, "I'm sorry sir but you have to leave." Dan sees Mario doubling over, howling with glee.

Anger beats with each step, crescendo rising. Fury pounds his heart. Arteries sizzle with nitro-laced adrenaline. An hour and a half later, Dan's back at his pad, ready to launch.

There's a knock on the door. Dan shifts gears. He opens the door. Two men in suits are standing there. "We're spreading the Word of God and would like to talk to you about your spiritual health."

"My spiritual health is fine, thank you. I'm busy right now and don't feel like talking so if you'll excuse me I'll get back to what I was doing."

"We'd like you to have a copy of our publication, The Watchtower," the man says as he hands it to Dan. "It has stories to help you know God's plan for you."

Dan takes the pamphlet and closes the door. He tosses it on the coffee table as he heads for the phone to call Joyce. Anger blasts. Veins spout ballistic as he launches an aerial assault that ends with, "I'm going to kill Mario,"

"That's my husband you're talking about."

"And he's going to be a dead one if he doesn't cough cash."

Rivers flow to the sea.

'No reason for Mario to have all the fun,' Dan chuckles, 'A little fear is good!' Pleased that he's able to strike back in a minor way, Dan takes a luxury cruise through the Cosmochine. He has no TV.

Hemispheric winds and continental currents circle the globe.

At eight o'clock the next morning there's a knock on Dan's door. He opens it to find two suits standing there. They're not looking for lost sheep; one holds papers. Stanley McGillicuddy stands beside them.

"Daniel Fitzgerald Murphy?"

"Yes."

"We have a court order to take you to Harris County Psychiatric Center." Dan glances at the papers and sighs.

They frisk him. Stanley watches. "Pack for a long stay," they say.

'Railroaded again!'

The suits watch him pack his two shoulder bags on the bed. "Step back over there," one says when Dan's done packing. They search the bags, frisk him again, and step back.

Dan moves toward his bags. He thinks about the hunting knife in the secret pocket; been there since his walk-jog in Austin. He knew it was a good hiding spot.

The bag is on the edge of the bed. The deputies are on the other side. Dan remembers NOW I CAN TELL and grabs it from the top of his dresser, sticks it in his new bag, and zips it shut. He then reaches down, lifts the pocket flap, and slips his knife from its hidden spot.

He throws it. The suits jump back, eyes wide, brows reaching for the sky. The folded knife sails to a smooth landing in the middle of the bed.

Arched brows hover over saucer eyes. Dan stands there. Stanley McGillicuddy watches from the far side.

One officer stands there, eyes fixed on Dan while the other crouches and slides, eyes wide and wary, and snatches the five-dollar knife from his bed. They frisk him again.

Earth reaches the winter solstice.

At the psychiatric center, they take his eighty-five dollars, check his bags, and check him in. "You can't have this book," the whites tell him.

Tears well. Dan's going down the river and they want his rudder. It's his last vestige of hope that he still has contact with a just and honest man. He packed the personally signed book from the judge with the hope of reading it on his trip down river. He didn't know how much that book meant til that minute.

He argues to keep it. They resist. He persists. They relent.

NOW I CAN TELL reveals atrocities committed against people, especially the educated and wealthy, when communism turned China Red after WW-II. It shows how communism forced its way and terrorized the populace by brainwashing impressionable youth into turning on their parents and rejecting the family structure they were born into. It reveals how communism imposed its beliefs and standards by controlling people; granting favors for compliance and commanding fear for non-compliance. Dan sees parallels in the mental health system.

NOW I CAN TELL was written by a native bishop of the Catholic Church in China. It chronicles actual stories of imprisonment and physical and mental torture. The bishop was one of the prisoners that escaped China to tell. Reading the book humbles Dan. His ordeal is miniscule in comparison.

Sydney cools, New York heats.

Dan is originally given lithium carbonate. It's the most tolerable of meds; turns you into a zombie over time whereas most meds affect you immediately. They switch him to Haldol. Dan knows its effect.

He points to his copy of patient rules and regulations and states, "A patient doesn't have to take a medication if he doesn't want to."

"Either you take the medicine or you're going to solitary," the nurse says as she points to her right. Dan's eyes follow her arm and outstretched finger to a door with a peep hole that guards a five-by-eight-foot room with a mat on the floor and a single light bulb in the center of the ceiling. He has no interest in the rubber room.

Cries come from an identical room next to it; inmate bumped piece of furniture. 'So much for rules and regulations,' Dan thinks as he tosses the paper over his shoulder.

The Haldol affects him adversely. His body rocks, sways, and jerks if he doesn't constantly control the muscle pulses. A disorienting buzz in his head creates an irritating surrealism. He points this out to the nurses and pleads for days. The doctor finally discontinues the Haldol. The ill effects fade.

Dan's taken to a hearing where it's determined that while he doesn't pose any danger to himself or others maybe he needs to spend some time at the State Hospital in Austin. The doctor states his reason, "If you had only taken your medicine."

'Put up with the involuntary jerking and surreal head and be released in eight days as rehabilitated,' Dan thinks as his eyes roll, 'Typical of mental health lunacy.' His hell continues.

The Milky Way floats through the universe like a molecule in an ocean.

Dan wonders if the Cosmochine is real or just a retreat. Most of the time he thinks it exists. Other times he wonders, 'How can it?' Mostly he doesn't think about it. Empathic sensations ebb and flow.

Stephen King wrote in BAG OF BONES, "When an imaginative person gets into mental trouble, the line between seeming and believing has a way of disappearing."

Dan's a bag of bones with creative and perceptive strains of imagination; someone who could never exist but does.

His mind becomes matter.

Blood rushes though his system.
His octophonic mind has levels and zones ranging from A to Z.
From the Joseph and Mary to the Atlantic and Pacific
he's part of a simple yet complex web of energy called life.
Is this all a product of his vivid imagination or
an illustrated picture of the two forces that have been here since time began?
Yin controlling yang, yang charging yin on a cosmic carousel to infinity and back?
Does the natural interaction of yin and yang - negative and positive
create the diverse, dual opposites we call life and death?

Chapter 57—ENTOMBMENT

Joseph and Mary come together.

"What about my money," I ask.

"We've got it taken care of," the constable answers.

I get into the nine passenger van with two nuts and two guards for the drive to Austin. Two hours later, the man relinquishes control of the wheel at a donut stop so the female officer can drive the second half. The inmates get no coffee or donuts.

At Austin, paperwork's filled out and medical exams are given. I'm assigned to a dorm in the Harris County compound. The rules and regulations of the dorm are explained along with an erasable, weekly point system.

Points are given for making your bed, showering, shaving, brushing your teeth, cleaning your ward, etc., and deducted for bad behavior. When a patient accumulates enough points they earn ground privileges for the following week. Ground privileges allow more freedom inside the compound and a passport to go out, inside the outer walls.

The Abram splits.

"You have no money on account," the man at the cantina in the compound says.

"I had eighty-five dollars at Harris County," I counter.

"According to our records you came here with no money."

"I asked the constable before we left Harris County and he said it was taken care of."

"You'll have to check at the administration building."

Walls link six dorms in a circle around a courtyard and enclose a hundred-fifty inmates in the two acres within the compound. The administration building's outside the compound walls. Without ground privileges freedom within the compound is limited to minutes surrounding meals. The rest of the time is spent in the dorm.

It's Thursday. I calculate how many points I'll be able to accumulate and realize that I'll be a little short on Sunday night. They only allow one shower, shave, and bed making a day. I need to get ground privileges. Not having cigarettes all next week will drive me crazy.

I scrounge butts and convince a nurse and two patients to have an extra therapy session. It's enough to earn freedom for the following week. The administration building is the first stop outside the compound walls.

"You had no money transferred," they say.

"What do you mean? No money."

"Records show no money being transferred."

"I had eighty-five dollars in Houston. Can you check to see if it left Harris County?"

"Records show no money being transferred."

"I know, but can you check to see if it was checked out of Harris County."

After more argument, I finally convince them that they have to call Harris County. "We'll call," they reluctantly say. "Check back tomorrow."

"I've been waiting five days. Why can't you call right now?"

After more inane argument they finally call.

"What did they say?"

Again they're evasive but admit,
"Eighty-five dollars left Harris County in your name."

"So the constables have it?"

"It was checked out but not checked in here."
I get tired of the double talk and go back to the compound. I need cigarettes!

The administrator of my dorm is young, fresh out of college. He looks and acts like a Stanley McGillicuddy clone. I talk to him. "Why can't you call?"

"We don't know where the money is or even if there is any money."

"The accounting department at the administration building called Harris County. They said eighty-five dollars was transferred in my name. Either the officer has it or it's lost in your records. Either way, it's my money and I need it."

"I'll get back to you," the insolent preppy replies.

I scrounge butts and prod daily.

Finally, the prep ass calls me in. He's ready to make the call.
I tell my story to the sergeant in Houston. He listens.

"I'll get back to you," is his reply.

The administrator dismisses me with, "You can go now." I can tell he's miffed. But he's not the one missing money and scrounging butts! The indignant jerk wasn't going to do anything unless I prodded him.

The state hospital consists of six compounds like the one I'm in, several administration buildings, and a large multi-story building for the terminally enshrined. An eight foot high block perimeter wall encloses the buildings and over a hundred acres of grass and trees. A large cantina is on the far side of the grounds.

Most patients with privileges opt to stay with the herd in their two acre compound or over at the main cantina. I spend every possible moment outside the cellblock. Sometimes I'm at the main cantina where patients from all cellblocks gather; usually I'm out stretching the boundaries.

Lush pecan trees are shedding fruit around the hospital acreage. Ripe nuggets go to waste. I find a clear plastic newspaper bag, fill it with pecans, and sell it for two bucks; enough for a pack of cigarettes with a quarter to spare. Three bags of pecans will get me three packs of smokes and a frozen malt cup. Cigarettes are a necessity, frozen malts a treat.

With abundant pecan trees on the hospital grounds I support my habit and buy occasional frozen malts at the main cantina. When pecan sales are slow, I wash staff cars, except prep asses who still hasn't gotten back to me about my eighty-five dollars.

The sergeant never calls and prep ass doesn't want to bother him.
"If he finds it he'll call back," is his stock response.

'Yeh, right!' I scrounge pecans and butts.

Twenty days after arrival, I'm released with a catch. I have to find my own way back to Houston. My eighty-five dollars is lost in the system. "Haven't heard anything."

Cigarettes and frozen malts consumed pecans as fast as I could pick them. I don't have bus fare. I call my last resort. Mom wires twenty dollars via Western Union.

Joseph and Mary molecules go north and south.

"Why can't I take my bags and stop at Western Union on my way to the terminal?"

"You can't be released till you have means to get back to Houston," prep ass replies.

"I will when I get downtown to Western Union."

"You have to check back here."

"This is stupid."

"That's the policy."

"Who made the policy?"

No reply from His Arrogance.

I get money at Western Union and check bus schedules. A bus leaves in thirty minutes but my luggage is at the hospital. It's a minimum of two hours there and back by city bus; longer by shoe leather express. The next bus leaves tomorrow morning! I'll have to spend another night at the hospital. Damn preppy!

Toe-prints overflow. The Mississippi runs wide.

"What do you mean I've been released?"

"A commuter van is leaving the main entrance for downtown in fifteen minutes," the nurse says. "A bus leaves for Houston in two hours."

"I'm not going to Houston," I spout.

"Where are you going," the attractive nurse asks.

"I have a bank account in Universal City that I need to close out."

"Where's Universal City?"

"It's a side stop on the way to San Antonio. There are only a couple buses a day that stop there. The next one doesn't leave til seven-thirty tomorrow morning."

"Oh."

"I could've been on the bus that left a half hour ago but Basil wouldn't let me take my luggage when I went to Western Union. Steam spews. "It was stupid for me to come back here." I pace.

"I called Western Union from his office. He knew the money was there." I pace some more. "Why can't I spend another night here?"

"It's against hospital policy to allow you to stay once you check out."

"I didn't check out. That asinine administrator wouldn't let me."

"You've been checked out."

"Who makes these policies," I snarl.

"You can spend the night at the Salvation Army," the nurse offers. "If you hurry you can catch the commuter van to downtown."

"I have over fourteen hours to kill and no money to spend waiting. No need to be in a hurry," I lament. "Damn preppy," snaps out. "Where is he?"

"He's gone home."

I roll my eyes; five o'clock is ten minutes away. "That figures," I say. He didn't stay to deliver his lesson in this river of lessons. None of the spineless wonders did. I think about Mario's duck and run, Mutt's weasel act, the red-head prep in Dallas, the eighty-five dollar constable mystery. My mind boils.

"Since I won't get a shower til I get back to Houston tomorrow night, can I take a shower and change clothes," I ask the single nurse.

"Don't take too long."

Corkscrew jets spew from the black hole.

I have enough time and money for a final frozen malt at the main cantina before catching a city bus to downtown. The usual varieties of nuts are there including the chain smoker who powers cherry into filter in a two minute suck and puff. His nicotine stained fingers press together in a butterfly grip on the cigarette filter, hands cupping to howl as he sucks the cigarette like a nipple, full concentration on kissing the filter fast as he can, saliva drooling off, til the cherry melts into it.

Smoke howls from his face. Slobber keeps his fingers from burning as he smokes one after the other. I wonder how he affords it.

"How do you get any benefit from smoking that fast," I ask.

"Gotta have em," is his response. He lights another.

Glaciers shift hemispheres.

I make it to the bus station with seconds to spare, buy a ticket, check my luggage, and leave. They lock the door behind me. I head for the Salvation Army.

Halloween is closing in and pleasant daytime are plunging to the thirties at night. The Salvation Army is full. The homeless who normally spend their nights elsewhere have claimed all available cots. As consolation I'm told I can come back for breakfast.

I wander downtown. Temperatures plunge. My jacket is no match. I shiver. I can't get anything from my bags til the terminal opens at seven AM.

I haven't a clue of where I'm going to sleep. I was evicted from the hospital before supper; the frozen malt from the cantina will have to do. The only thing in my pockets besides my cash poor Day-Timer with pen, is lint and a quarter.

I find a small park overlooking the Texas State Capitol dome. Lights enhance its pristine splendor. A band of illumination sparkles across the sky with pinpoints of light to infinity. The city skyline is to my left, Lake Austin hovers in the hills to my right. Inspiration strikes me.

I pull out my Day-Timer and draw a picture of a small saucer, detailing construction and chemical composition of the fission-exempt lightweight compounds forming its skin and structure and amplifying the magic of the magnetic blue crystal at its heart. I see it in the mountains of Asia. It's my ticket off the planet. I've had it with these small time idiots.

My mind floats through the universe to my next stop in the Vega System.
Icy cold brings me back to Earth. I walk til I find some straw bales.

It looks like an abandoned archery range that students having too much fun, barreled through. Stacks at either end of the tree lined clearing are toppled to the ground, partially and totally. The straw is moist and moldy from years of weathering.
I test the piles and pick the driest group.

It's midnight when I lay down and getting colder. The bales, softer than the ground, are lumpy and uncomfortable. I manage to close my eyes and drift off while wondering if mice will be crawling for warmth.

Two hours later, I awake. My body is freezing. Not as much as seven years earlier but close. My teeth chatter.

I separate slices from a broken bale and pull the driest over me. Moisture acts as a magnet and draws more cold. The straw stinks. I throw it off of me.

Tiny clumps and maverick blades cling to my jeans and cordovan corduroy jacket. At two-thirty I dance a jig while I slap, flick, and brush mavericks from my hide.
Blood flows and warms me.

The cold moves back before I can close my eyes to block it.
Moisture seeps from the bales. I shake.

I wander downtown in search of heat. An icy breeze blows between buildings and slices me like a knife. My teeth tap a primitive rhythm. The Greyhound Terminal is open. They don't have a bus to Universal City but it's warm. I hang out til the Salvation Army opens its doors at six AM.

I have oatmeal at hope for the hopeless and jellybeans from my bank account.
I'm on the bus to Houston, the sun's going down. I ride the final hour in darkness.
It's a pattern I've come to know. When I'm down, I get kicked the hardest.
I think about Audra and all the problems this obsession has created;
if any of it has been real or worth it.

Stanley McGillicuddy is waiting at the bus terminal.
"The finance company found your truck before we could get around to picking it up."

"You were supposed to bring the payments up to date."

"We planned to but Mutt's been such a jerk with cash flow.
It just slipped our minds. I'm so sorry."

"What about the eleven hundred dollars Mario owes me?"

"We're a little short right now but the money will be rolling soon."

I have a five-pound tin of jellybeans and seventy dollars in my pocket.
I head back to the counter and buy a ticket for Phoenix.

Chapter 2--ENVIRONMENT

Cycles of the cosmos come and go.

Some passengers drop off and get buried as the Abram mixes, and mingles with the gravitational sump of Michigan. Most hang on as the Great Lake divides and swirls Joseph and Mary molecules north and south. Flow slows as the sump deepens.
The magnetic Abram continues its split course to the sea.

Eventually molecules of the south branch reach the Illinois River where they exit and flow out to the mighty Mississip and down to the Gulf of Mexico. Joseph and Mary molecules flow through the Gulf of Mexico to the Atlantic Ocean and are swept north by the force of the Gulf Stream rushing up from the equator.

The north branch of the Abram drifts north, east, south, and east through the Great Lakes, over Niagara Falls, and out the Saint Lawrence Seaway to the Atlantic Ocean. Joseph and Mary molecules of the north and south branches occasionally meet, mingle, and separate on polar routes to reunion in the Pacific Ocean. Throughout the journey molecules vaporize and begin an airborne trek. The cycles of Joseph and Mary are numerous and varied and go on and on and eventually cover every niche of the planet.

In earlier times glaciers rushed, throbbed, pulsed, and pushed their way down and over the Canadian Shield extending icy fingers and toes into the heart of the North American continent. As they crawled across the granite Shield they pushed and drug dirt, rocks, and boulders, scouring land, grinding, leveling, mounding, and burying organic rubble; digging new toe and finger holds and enlarging old.

The landscape changes, alters, and reforms. Plants and animals mutate and adapt to the changing surroundings, weather, and seasons. Mother Nature establishes equilibrium.

The Earth spins in a magnetic tether turning night to day as it revolves in an orbit around the sun and travels through a cold black vacuum. Day length peaks at the summer solstice when the hemisphere is tilted toward the flaming provider of life. Days get shorter as the planet sails around to the opposite side of the glowing ball of light.

180 days later, the solar rays are diminished to a glancing blow on the back tilted globe. Glaciers grow and extend their icy fingers toward the equator. They shrink and recede in the opposite hemisphere as solar light and in-line intensity increases.

The dual opposites of the hemispheres go on and on and on.

A comet strikes the planet like a finger poking a hot potato. The planet shudders. Fractures circle the impact zone and radiate out and through the violated globe. Continents shift and move on their molten beds, mountains thrust to the sky, land submerges to be melted and recycled, organic matter changes and compresses to oil, coal, and diamonds.

Volcano's spew as hot magma forces its way to the surface. Tons of atmospheric debris block the bountiful god's glow. Glaciers in both hemispheres advance as

temperatures plunge. Moisture rises from the sea and piles in frozen heaps
on the growing glaciers. Sea levels fall.

Life ceases to exist for most species of plants and animals.
Only strength, luck, and inorganic survive; many strong don't!
New life forms to fill the empty niches.

Eventually the atmospheric debris is pulled to the ground by the magnetic gyro at the heart of the planet, the sun shines through, and the rhythms of the hemispheres go on. The sheet of ice marches forward and falls back as the Earth orbits to and from pleasing pathways of the bountiful god's rays. Glaciers melt and recede, finger and toe prints overflow. Water gravitates to the sea and flows to the opposite hemisphere
where winter glaciers are growing. Sea levels rise.

Time passes. All things change; some fast, some slow. Life goes on.

Chapter 1—ENIGMENT

Pluto exits Neptune's realm.

It's the dawn of a new millennium. Star Wars is re-storming the box office. Rum Jungle rhythm flows through my body. Elvin Bishop streams from the speakers.

We checked out of the hotel and are headed north on The Strip. A 747 reflects the glittering gold of Mandalay Bay as it jets past the magnetic crescent behind us. The future's in front of us.

Joseph and Mary cycle to sea and back.

This is incredible, I think as we sit at the red-light, poised for the rocket ride ahead. "Sure Feels Good," surrounds us in sound. Across McCarran, a giant gold lion guards MGM's jungle while a roller coaster zips up, around, and through the skyline of New York, New York on the other side of the strip. Excaliber Castle rises majestically on my left, its ivory towers capped with red and blue. An Egyptian Sphinx reposes regally in front of the Luxor Pyramid to its right. On our right the Tropicana has grown, sprouted a twin tower.

The light turns green. "Struttin My Stuff," blasts in quadraphonic, blaring out the windows and sunroof of my silver Stealth. Throngs of people line the sidewalks and overhead crosswalks. Audra's in the passenger seat, Josh and Becca in back.

Ahead lies Aladdin's magic carpet ride and wealth at Monte Carlo, the Eiffel Tower of Paris, dancing fountains of Bellagio, the Venetian, white tigers and a volcano spouting at the Mirage, pirates dueling at Treasure Island, and the Stratosphere splitting the clouds and towering over the neon circus while the world's highest roller coaster circles the rotating ball encaged in it's lofty spire.

Rio and the Gold Coast beckon from the other side of Interstate 15. The new downtown where lights, sights, and sounds sail through the air and night becomes day, extends its siren song. Dreams, desires, and destiny create a living fairy tale that can only happen in America. None of the above was here when we first saw the lights of Vegas. The Tropicana was a lonely casino at the end of Las Vegas Boulevard.

A quarter million people called Las Vegas home then. It's added a million since and is the fastest growing metropolis in the nation. Pluto has been benevolent to this center of hope, glitz, and glamour that feeds and nurtures the passions and forbidden lusts of a hungry world.

"Fooled Around and Fell in Love," strikes again as Caesars, Imperial Palace, Flamingo Hilton, Frontier, Stardust, Riviera, Circus-Circus, and more pass in front of my eyes; here when Audra and I first saw the dazzling city. We saw them evolve and blossom.

London Bridge and Havasu hail from the Colorado River. Kactus Kate and Whiskey Pete were lonely sentinels at the California border before Buffalo Bill took command. Primm Valley's now a destination.

Up the road, towards the Virgin River Gorge and Zion, lies another dream whose time is dawning. Cubby's in charge. Audra's in control. I retain command.

The Stratosphere towers above us. Audra stares straight up through the sunroof at the coaster circling. I crank "Holler and Shout," higher. Audra turns it down.

I nudge the sound on "Sugar Dumplin" as we near the plaza and downtown canopy. I turn right at Charleston and cut across, passing Maryland Parkway and rolling toward Boulder Highway. "Graveyard Blues," jams.

I turn right on the road to Henderson and drive past the Showboat Casino. "Travelin Shoes," rocks as we roll past Samstown, now a city, and out of town. The luster of Vegas fades as we flow to the Colorado River.

We stop to tour Hoover Dam and gaze at Lake Mead while we wait. Just up the Colorado River and around the bend is the Grand Canyon. Canyons on Mars make it look like a midget!

You're probably wondering how Audra and I finally got together.

Well, that's a private matter.

But, I will tell you she was behind the portable bar at Mulligan's and in the photo booth at Flashpoint Mall. She was also at my house in Lemon Heights when the second series of vortexes started, leading to the creation of the Cosmochine.

Global population increased fifty percent to six billion human beings.

I still haven't written the book about the secret that flashed twenty three years ago. The title and cover are embedded in my head as a permanent Cosmo Bank record. May take awhile to dust cobwebs off the scattered script but I'm certain I can pull the pieces together when I'm able to have some quality, private time.

You know the problems I had in those nightmarish early years. Then with Audra and the kids, my focus was elsewhere. Well, the kids are growing and will soon be on their way to college and their own lives. Roger graduates from Stanford in May.

The nineteenth century started with one billion people on Planet Earth.

We complete our tour of Hoover Dam and head towards the car. I'm not claustrophobic when Audra's with me. But the axiom about facing your fears isn't true, at least not in my case. The confinements left scars, deeper than they ever were and did nothing to lessen the fear.

My philosophy is the same as it's always been. I don't go where I'm not wanted, I don't create waves unless it involves principle, and I avoid people who use or control me. In my game, one strike and you're out.

"ROCK MY SOUL," ignites as we blaze the grade to Arizona. We streak through New Mexico's Land of Enchantment, and flash to the Show Me State of Missouri where illusions are common and dreams become reality. Zion beckons.

1 book	No discount 19.95 each plus 4.00 S+H = 23.95
2 book	20% off plus 2.00 per book S+H = 17.95 per book
3-4 books	20% off plus 1.00 per book S+H = 16.95 per book
5-9 books	30% off plus .90 per book S+H = 14.85 per book
10-24 books	40% off plus .80 per book S+H = 12.75 per book
25-99 books	45% off plus .70 per book S+H = 11.65 per book
100 or more books	50% off plus .60 per book S+H = 10.55 per book

1 or 2 books will be shipped by Priority Mail.
Larger quantities will be shipped via media mail at above rates.
Please request a quote if you want faster shipment of 3 or more books.
Money back guarantee on undamaged books. Please get return authorization.

Send mail orders with check or money order enclosed and payable to-

Gray Bull Publishing
PO Box 61
Hudson, IN 46747

Please include phone number or e-mail address to avoid possible delays.

Please allow 4-6 weeks for delivery with media mail.

You can also order online with a credit card at

www.mgbp.us
or
www.omniscientobsession.com

1 book	No discount 19.95 each plus 4.00 S+H = 23.95
2 book	20% off plus 2.00 per book S+H = 17.95 per book
3-4 books	20% off plus 1.00 per book S+H = 16.95 per book
5-9 books	30% off plus .90 per book S+H = 14.85 per book
10-24 books	40% off plus .80 per book S+H = 12.75 per book
25-99 books	45% off plus .70 per book S+H = 11.65 per book
100 or more books	50% off plus .60 per book S+H = 10.55 per book

1 or 2 books will be shipped by Priority Mail.
Larger quantities will be shipped via media mail at above rates.
Please request a quote if you want faster shipment of 3 or more books.
Money back guarantee on undamaged books. Please get return authorization.

Send mail orders with check or money order enclosed and payable to-

Gray Bull Publishing
PO Box 61
Hudson, IN 46747

Please include phone number or e-mail address to avoid possible delays.

Please allow 4-6 weeks for delivery with media mail.

You can also order online with a credit card at

www.mgbp.us

or

www.omniscientobsession.com

1 book	No discount 19.95 each plus 4.00 S+H = 23.95
2 book	20% off plus 2.00 per book S+H = 17.95 per book
3-4 books	20% off plus 1.00 per book S+H = 16.95 per book
5-9 books	30% off plus .90 per book S+H = 14.85 per book
10-24 books	40% off plus .80 per book S+H = 12.75 per book
25-99 books	45% off plus .70 per book S+H = 11.65 per book
100 or more books	50% off plus .60 per book S+H = 10.55 per book

1 or 2 books will be shipped by Priority Mail.
Larger quantities will be shipped via media mail at above rates.
Please request a quote if you want faster shipment of 3 or more books.
Money back guarantee on undamaged books. Please get return authorization.

Send mail orders with check or money order enclosed and payable to-

Gray Bull Publishing
PO Box 61
Hudson, IN 46747

Please include phone number or e-mail address to avoid possible delays.

Please allow 4-6 weeks for delivery with media mail.

You can also order online with a credit card at

www.mgbp.us
or
www.omniscientobsession.com

1 book	No discount 19.95 each plus 4.00 S+H = 23.95
2 book	20% off plus 2.00 per book S+H = 17.95 per book
3-4 books	20% off plus 1.00 per book S+H = 16.95 per book
5-9 books	30% off plus .90 per book S+H = 14.85 per book
10-24 books	40% off plus .80 per book S+H = 12.75 per book
25-99 books	45% off plus .70 per book S+H = 11.65 per book
100 or more books	50% off plus .60 per book S+H = 10.55 per book

1 or 2 books will be shipped by Priority Mail.
Larger quantities will be shipped via media mail at above rates.
Please request a quote if you want faster shipment of 3 or more books.
Money back guarantee on undamaged books. Please get return authorization.

Send mail orders with check or money order enclosed and payable to-

Gray Bull Publishing
PO Box 61
Hudson, IN 46747

Please include phone number or e-mail address to avoid possible delays.

Please allow 4-6 weeks for delivery with media mail.

You can also order online with a credit card at

www.mgbp.us
or
www.omniscientobsession.com